THE THIRTEENTH KEY

THE THIRTEENTH KEY

SERAPHINE'S CHOSEN
BOOK ONE

CARA NOX

STELLA CHARTA PRESS

THE THIRTEENTH KEY

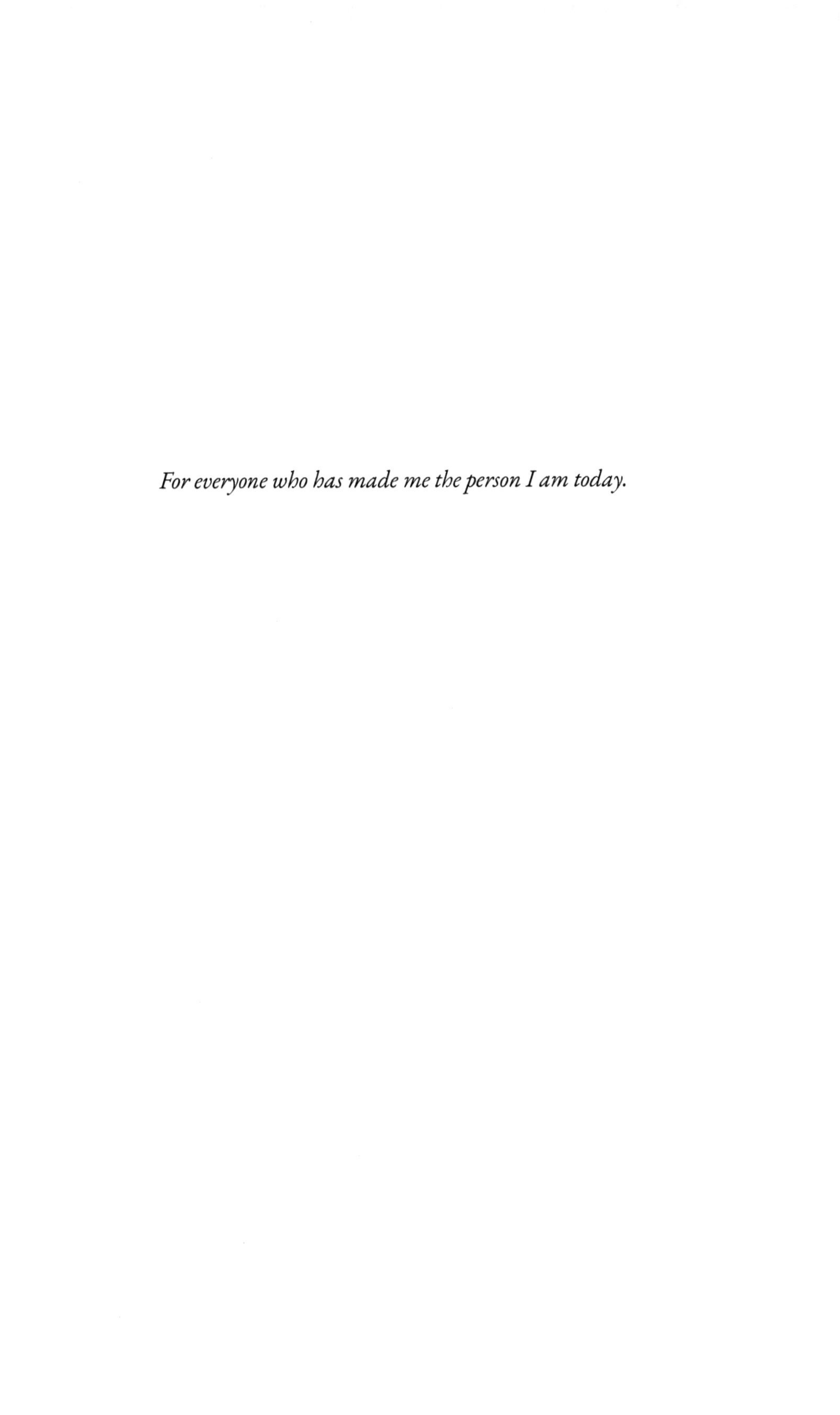

For everyone who has made me the person I am today.

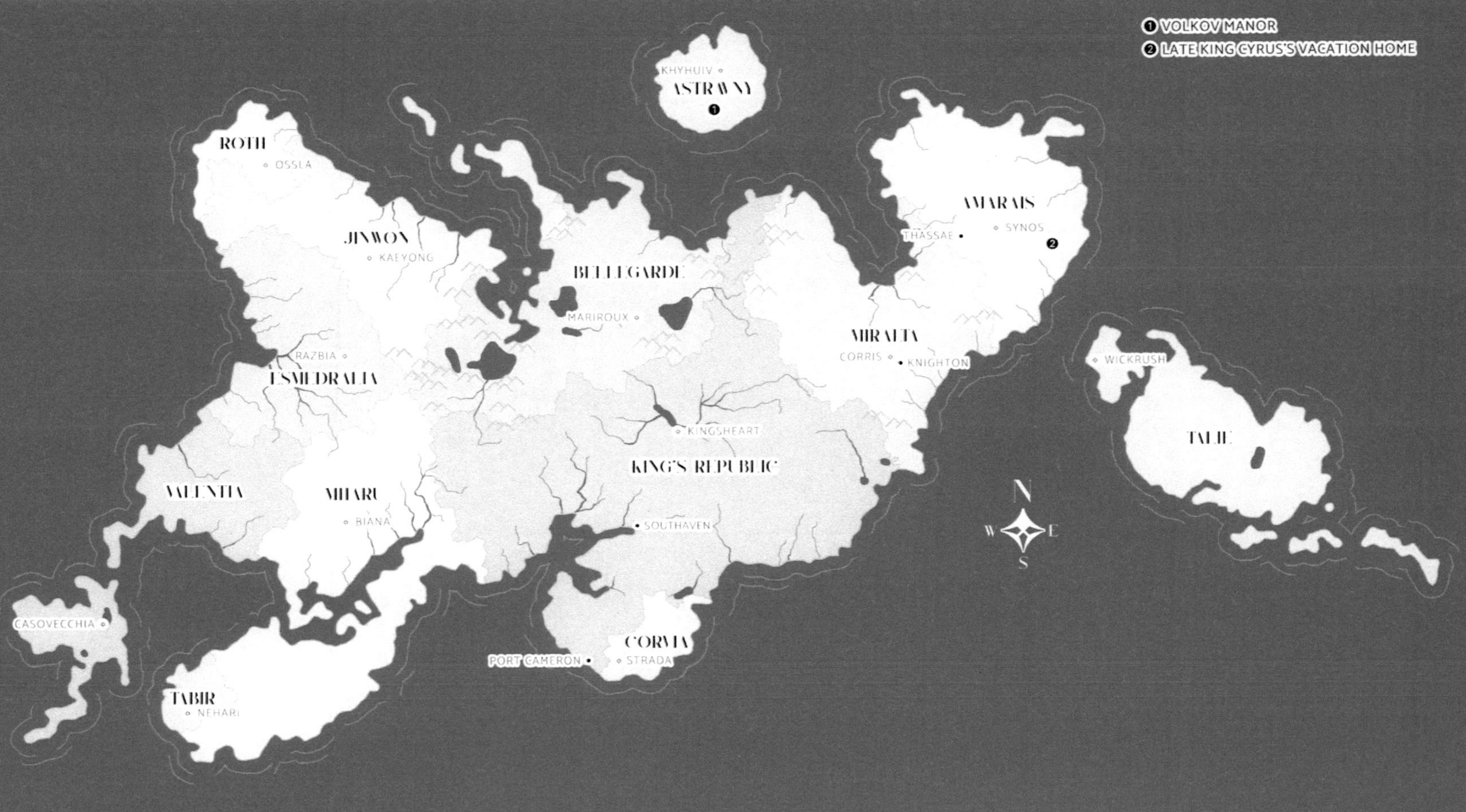

① VOLKOV MANOR
② LATE KING CYRUS'S VACATION HOME
ROTH
OSSLA
ASTRAWY
KHYHUIV
①
JINWON
KAEYONG
BELLEGARDE
MARIROUX
AMARAIS
THASSAE
SYNOS
②
MIRALTA
CORRIS
KNIGHTON
WICKRUSH
ESMEDRALIA
RAZBIA
KINGSHEART
KING'S REPUBLIC
TALIE
VALENTIA
MIHARU
BIANA
SOUTHAVEN
N
W
E
S
CASOVECCHIA
CORVIA
PORT CAMERON
STRADA
TABIR
NEHARI

CONTENT WARNINGS

I've attempted to compile a list of prominent warning keywords to the best of my ability. However, since I'm only human, it's very possible I've glossed over something that could be sensitive to you. Please use your own discretion when reading and only continue if you feel safe to do so.

This story contains: alcohol, anxiety, blood, childhood trauma, death, depression, discrimination, mention of drug use, emotional abuse, gore, grief, loss, manipulation, murder, parental neglect, physical abuse, suicidal thoughts, violence, and mention of vomiting.

THE THIRTEENTH KEY

1

AMARAIS ✧ 2704-11-12

NOA

When Noa had first arrived in Amarais, she hadn't imagined it would've struck her with such familiarity. The breathlessness that ripped through her as she stood mere meters away from the Amaraian palace wasn't so much due to its size or pristine exterior that gleamed a glittering white from the glow of the streetlamps, but rather how it loomed over its dominion. The gated courtyard-garden fanned out behind it, littered with fir trees woven with dazzling lights that carried through the tall privacy hedges. All of it danced as an embellished image in her mind of a place much further from here where snow had also once crunched beneath her boots and forced the air from her lungs through puffs of cold smoke.

She rubbed her hands together, feeling the friction of her gloves and ignoring that annoying ache that began to form in her legs. She'd been crouching for too long in the bushes on the perimeter of what was legally palace grounds. Then again, everything within Synos's palace sector was considered palace grounds. Some would say that what she was about to do was the most foolish thing she'd ever done, but she was almost certain she could remember something far stupider, given enough time.

A figure crouched down beside her, his black hair obscuring his face until he brushed it away with his own gloved hand. Calm, dark eyes peered forward from the corner of her vision, surveying the same structure she'd been taking in. "Gluttony's counting guards," he said. "They're about to change posts."

"About to hit the five-minute mark," she breathed.

"What happens if it's not here?" he asked, sliding his attention back to her.

"Then we bust ass to that other house, case it, and get the hell out." She shrugged, her fingers running along the edge of the flat, black mask resting on top of her head, tucked just inside her hood.

"Five minutes until guard change," came the voice in her ear. A monotoned, collected woman's voice that made Noa's core tighten at the sound— Sloth, the final member of their party doing overwatch.

Greed put a finger to his own comm piece. "Greed and Pride in position. Gluttony, status?"

"On my way back," came a man's voice that didn't sound all that different than Greed's. But the soft, velvety tones were traded for something a little rougher around the edges and a lot more irritable through a grumble. "Two guards are already calling it quits."

Noa narrowed her sights on the ridge of the upper windows barely visible through the garden, catching the heads of people roaming the upper ring of the ballroom. "I bet you're wishing the two of us were in there right now, aren't you, Greed?" she asked with a teasing smirk. "Taking in the night sky through that observatory-esque window, arm in arm with glasses of champagne."

He rolled his eyes. "You mean thrown into a car and hauled off to a high-security prison for party-crashing whatever the hell *this* is?" He made a circular motion toward it. "I think I'll pass."

"We can dye our hair blond and get some contacts."

"You going to ask Gluttony to dye his hair blond too just in case?"

"I *could*…"

"Could what?"

Noa whipped her head around to find Gluttony crouched down

behind them, his gold-flecked eyes watching her with suspicion. Her lips formed a line, humming. That was the one visible difference between him and his twin brother that allowed her to tell them apart at a quick glance. A characteristic that she decided didn't go all that well with blond.

"Forget about it," she said, tapping her comm. "Sloth?"

"Forty seconds."

"What was she saying?" Gluttony asked, furrowing his brows as he nudged his brother's elbow.

"That you'd make a good blond," he replied, lips twitching while he pulled down his mask.

Horrified, Gluttony's head swung toward her. "Why the hell would I ruin perfection?"

"Twenty."

Noa gagged and tugged her own mask over her face, shielding her lack-luster brown eyes and plain pale face from view like her mousy brunette mess of pulled-back hair tucked into her hood. "Everyone know where you're going?"

"Straight for a drink on the ride out of here," Gluttony said as he snapped his mask back into place.

"Ten."

Noa eyed the last guard begin his final lap down the street, clad in navy blue and silvery—sorry, *platinum*-white trim with a short sword at his side. Once he was out of view, and Noa heard that magic word of "go," she sprinted across the street. Moonlight poured over cleared pavement and decorative stone walkways as the three of them kept to the shadows that spanned along the fence line. It made a sharp turn toward a door with a small pad beside it that flickered green right before she grabbed the handle.

"Unlocked," Sloth said. "All clear and cameras are locally looped."

"Thank you," Noa said in a sing-song voice back to her, throwing her shoulder into the hard metal.

It flew open to a white hallway turned gray with the overhead lights shut off. A thrill worked through her as the dark closed in behind them. She kept to the wall, stalking down the hall on silent footsteps until it gave way to a trickling of light from around a corner. She motioned for Gluttony to move to her side, which he did before he stopped to check that the route was clear.

"*Go*," Noa hissed, hurrying him forward.

"Sorry for checking my damn corners—"

"Consider this a trust exercise. Now *move*."

Grumbling, he jogged down the hall ahead of them, glancing back before he vanished down another corridor. It could've been a glare, but Noa shrugged it off in favor of the double doors to her right, framed by frosted wall sconces and ornate end tables. Weird little twisting porcelain sculptures sat on either side, which she guessed probably cost more than a night in their hotel room. She slipped a square key from her pocket and pressed it to the sensor under the handle, watching it pulse yellow a couple of times until it flashed green. A satisfying *click* granted her entry.

It was a tidy space, holding a minimalistic desk in its center, framed by decorative built-in shelves that were cluttered with digital picture frames, more weird sculptures, and... books? She started over to one of the horizontal stacks, gentle in her removal of the thick tomes until the whole thing came free, held together in her hand. She frowned.

"Why?" She held it up to Greed in his search along another wall, turning the fake, glued-together books around. "Why the hell would someone do this?"

"Would you stop fooling around and help me look for the safe?" he asked, standing up from one of the floor cabinets.

With a huff, she put it back down and dropped to the cabinet portion of the shelving unit. It opened to a bunch of cables, old devices, and dusty hard drives. She closed it, biting down on her tongue as she crawled toward the middle cabinet. A quick tug on the handles, and her eyes went wide.

"Well, shit."

Greed's muffled footfalls against the carpet greeted her, and he pulled open the cabinet a little further. He pushed up his mask, confusion consuming his features. "A *manual* safe?"

"Should I call Gluttony?" she asked.

"No, move."

She stood, worrying her lip as he took her place, put his ear to the small metal door, and began to turn the dial.

"Have you ever cracked a safe like this before?" she asked.

"Once..." The far-off look in his eye didn't instill much confidence in her.

Noa gripped one of the shelves, pressing her thumb into it a little harder with each passing second. Her jaw began to clench in the wake of the silence. Well, at least, until that was broken by the sudden, distant pounding against the tile in the hallway.

Greed froze, locking eyes with her. That horrible, clawing sensation started working its way up her throat as she grabbed one of the small statues and rushed to the side of the doors. He threw his mask back on, standing with his hands gripping the desk, poised to overturn it. They waited. Noa's pulse pounded in her ears as the footsteps grew louder, echoing with every nervous readjustment of the ugly little thing in her hand.

A shadow passed over the crack under the door, fading in and out, taking the running with it. Noa turned her face toward Greed again, the two of them stock-still for another moment before he dropped back down to his knees.

"Keep an eye on the door," he whispered.

"Then hurry it the hell up." She pressed a thumb to her earpiece. "Gluttony, is there anyone down there by you?"

His pause slipped into an eternity that tightened her grip on her makeshift weapon.

"No, why?"

Noa let out a breath. "Someone was running over here. Keep an eye out." She kept her eyes on the door, taking a couple steps back while she strained to listen for some sort of indication of Greed's progress. The only one she got was the final pop of its small door coming free, followed by his alleviated sigh. She fell to her knees next to him.

He pulled it open to reveal documents. Paper documents but documents, nonetheless. Noa's stomach dropped just before she gritted her teeth and reached inside, shuffling through it all in hopes that there might be something sitting underneath.

"First fake books, and now *real* paper with—"

"Art receipts," Greed finished, tapping the top of one in her hands.

"You got to be kidding me."

"Let's hope Gluttony found something."

"Yes, let's, or I'm going to be pissed that we're spending another gods-damned night in this frozen hell."

He tensed, clamping a hand over her wrist to stop her manic paper shuffling, filling the void with the sound of jogging. She scrambled to stand, reclaiming her statuette just in time to watch the shadow pass by the doors again.

"What the hell is going on?" she hissed down to him.

Greed tucked the documents back into the safe and pushed himself up. "I don't know, but let's wrap this up." With a click of the small door and a spin of the dial, Noa relinquished her toy to its former home on their way out.

"Did we lock the doors?" came Gluttony's voice in her ear.

"Um... no..." Sloth answered. "Why are you asking?"

Greed checked their own door, pulling it open for Noa to go first. When there was no follow-up from Gluttony, she decided to hop in with a question of her own.

"Sloth," she said, "who the hell was running up and down the hall?"

"What? What are you talking about?"

Noa felt her features twist in confusion. Was she that distracted she completely missed all of that? Her pace quickened at the sight of Gluttony taking a stroll down the main hall at the end of the intersection. Something was wrong here—she just couldn't place *what* quite yet. But once she rounded the corner, she found their next major problem of the night.

A boy and a girl were pressed up against the double doors leading to the center of the palace, neither of them all that much younger than her—maybe twenty or twenty-one. Both were dressed in black party attire: a suit and a simple long-sleeved, knee-length dress with dark leggings that registered in Noa's mind as an unadorned staff uniform. The girl's wide blue eyes stayed pinned on them in terror while she gripped the boy's arm. However, *he* was the one that gave Noa pause. He had those tell-tale blue

Amaraian eyes like his companion, but his hair wasn't blond like hers. It was *black.*

"The doors shouldn't be locked," she said, unable to really compute anything else in her automatic advance on their two witnesses. This was something she needed to deal with, simple as that, even if she wasn't sure *how* to deal with said problem just yet. The main problem was that voice cutting through her sluggish thoughts.

"I don't see any of you on the camera feeds," came Sloth's reply, her voice climbing. "Hold on—"

That was when Noa saw it: the red, blinking light barely visible under the balcony past the half-glass doors. A small *cluster* of them stuck to the entrance to what had to be the ballroom. And they were blinking *faster* with each passing second. In an instant, she lurched forward, a motion that Greed mimicked.

"Get down!" she shouted, throwing herself over one of them as they flinched down.

The five of them hit the floor just as the world erupted in a loud chorus of shouts and booms and the tinkling of shattering glass.

2

AMARAIS ✦ 2704-11-12

Noa gritted her teeth at the static shrieking coming from her comm piece. She ripped it out and threw it to the floor, cursing at the echo of shifting glass before she tore off her mask and tossed it to the side. The subterfuge portion of the evening was now over, and now the chaotic finale was about to begin.

"What the hell just happened?" came a voice from behind her. Gluttony.

"I don't think we have time for that now," the voice to her right responded. Greed.

He stood, pulled off his mask, and pushed back his hood—looking as calm and collected as ever while towering over the girl he'd shielded. Her wide, blue eyes looked between them, terrified and confused.

Welcome to the club, Noa thought just as her eyes darted over to the boy she was still hunched over. He seemed just as stunned as her with his dazed expression and lack of movement, but at least he appeared uninjured. The doors themselves seemed to have taken the brunt of the damage, despite their now-buckled and shattered state. *If only they didn't skimp on the damn glass.*

"The garage. Which way to get to the garage?" Noa asked, shoving herself to her feet as her mind finally kicked back into crisis mode.

"There's a stairwell back where we came from," Greed said, pointing back toward the hall. "That should take us all the way down to the garage. Let's pray it isn't blocked off like the doors to the main hall here."

"And them?" Gluttony asked.

"They're coming with us." She jerked her chin in the direction of the corridor. "Gluttony, scout the way to the stairs, make sure whoever might've locked this place down isn't lurking around any corners while we get the hell out of here. Greed and I will follow with these two." She grabbed the boy's arm, pulling him to his feet as Greed did the same with the girl.

At first, Gluttony didn't move, like he was about to argue. His lips pressed into a thin line, and then he spun on his heel to carry out his orders. This left Noa to her own trust exercise of letting him guide them to safety while she mulled over the fact that she was dragging along some half-Amaraian through the palace, which is the last place she'd expect to find one. Sure, there'd been a few far-flung foreigners on their way into the country, most claiming some sort of business on their documentation just like she had—not technically a lie, though one could argue it. But here? In the midst of an Amaraian council party filled with territory leaders? Then again, he could possibly be staff, a ward, an illegitimate child, or—

Noa shook the list from her thoughts, trying not to scrunch up her face as they navigated the turns. Though, the weirdest part was that neither of them were calling for help or struggling to escape when they started down the stairs and encountered movement behind one of the doors.

Well, they were sneaking around the palace while everyone else was enjoying the party.

She held onto that sentiment as Greed started past her with a shaky, almost-inaudible whimper from the girl, pushing through the exit at the bottom of the stairs into the garage. Noa's jaw nearly dropped at the sight of so many white cars. The overhead lights revealed the metallic sheen of some and sparkling glossy coat of others. Sleek town cars, sports cars, muscle cars, and SUVs...

Gluttony grabbed a square key from the rack by the door and jogged toward one of the SUVs—the practical choice. Her heart sank as she walked past a muscle car, letting her gloved fingertips trail along the hood. It must've been a year since the last time she'd actually driven a car, seeing how most vehicles were typically out of the average person's price range. The feeling of the wind whipping through her hair and the warm sun tickling her skin wouldn't be an easily recreated memory here either, considering how she was far more likely to be inhaling snowflakes at any given second.

The soft purr of the engine brought her back to the present, where Gluttony sat in the driver's seat.

"You drive," Noa said with a motion to Greed.

"Fine by me." He pulled open one of the back-passenger doors, nudging his captive forward. "Get in."

She hesitated, glancing back at her companion still in Noa's grasp.

"*Go,*" Noa barked.

She jumped and scrambled inside as the boy pulled free of Noa's grip to help her. With Gluttony taking the other front seat, Noa got in behind their abductees, cueing a chorus of slamming doors.

As the car nudged forward, the garage doors began to part at the top of the exit ramp, allowing Noa to lean back with a sigh. That is, until the stairwell door burst open. The resounding clang of the heavy, reinforced metal thrown back so hard against its hinges sent Noa twisting in her seat to take in the mix of wait-staff attire, guard uniforms, and street clothing. Shouts rang out with orders to apprehend them. Some shot toward the control panels to try to close the doors again while a few bolted for the key rack. However, the most alarming part wasn't the fact that they were trying to stop them, but rather the sight of some of the *wait-staff* pulling daggers from hidden folds in their clothes.

"This night just keeps getting better," she grumbled, yanking a disc from her pocket and shoving the door open again. "Floor it!" she yelled to Greed, hurling it behind the vehicle. It erupted into a wall of smoke the second metal scraped against sleek tile—a satisfying sound to hear right before she pulled the door shut. They jolted up the ramp, peeling out onto the street.

The boy turned to take in the scene unfolding out the back window, his eyes wide as the doors began to collapse shut in their wake. Noa expected panic or mumbling, likely accompanied by him shrinking into his seat with the realization that he'd just been kidnapped. So, when his eyes hardened and his jaw set as he faced her, she stiffened in surprise.

"What do you want with us?" he demanded.

Ah, a spoiled brat.

"Oh, I'm sorry," she said, leaning a little closer with her eyes narrowed on his. "Did you *not* want me to stop you from getting a head full of glass? I'll try to remember that next time—Or would you rather me have Greed here turn the car around and drop you off with those very nice individuals back there? Because I can arrange that."

He opened his mouth to reply, but it was cut off by the Amaraian girl's gasp that coincided with the SUV's deceleration. They both followed her wide-eyed stare out the windshield where dozens of cars lined the streets, blue lights flashing through each vehicle's dashboard. Barriers and makeshift checkpoints were being set up at the chokepoints of the main intersections, corralling gawkers and those hurling obscenities at the officers.

"There's no way we make it past all of this," Greed mumbled, craning for a better view before he spun the wheel to take them down an alley. Another set of lights flashed off the windows of a storefront up ahead, and he cursed under his breath. "We might have to get out and walk."

"Are you insane?" Gluttony hissed. "Just floor it past them! We can't just blend into the crowd here. They'll take one look at us, and we'll be detained—"

"*Quiet!*" Noa shouted, bringing a wave of tense silence through the SUV. The girl fumbled with the small handhold in the door, taking in a shaky breath, as if she was considering saying something. "Spit it out."

Greed's seat complained as he shifted, but Noa's focus kept on the girl while her hand rose to the window. Her eyes closed right as her fingertips grazed the glass, and the car dimmed—the windows darkening at her touch. Noa sat up straight, repositioning herself to peer in the driver's side mirror. On the side of the car, a logo matching the other officer-driven vehicles emerged from the plain white surface.

No. Way. Chills ran down her arms at the display of power—of *magic*. When she turned back to the girl, she was struggling to maintain slow, even breaths. The clock was ticking.

"Drive," Noa commanded. "Hurry up and get us the hell out of here."

By the time they reached the hotel on the other side of the city, the girl—*the Mage*—was pale. She'd held the illusion for about ten minutes, long enough for them to get all of thirty seconds outside the palace sector. After that, the rest of the twenty-minute ride was endured in complete silence.

A Mage. In Amarais.

Noa's head spun at the mere implication that she'd managed to step foot inside the palace in the first place. She'd heard stories of Mages declared as traitors to the throne on the front steps of the palace before they were dragged away and executed. Anything to do with magic here became a muttered curse under one's breath. It was a threat of rivaling power—or whatever the hell else that gave them the reason to hate it and everyone who supported it. And yet she'd somehow *lived*, further adding to Noa's growing bafflement.

The SUV rolled to a stop in the parking garage, and she yanked on the handle, stepping out onto the concrete with both Amaraians on her heels. They followed her without a word to the back of the car, where Noa waited for the twins to join them. It was enough time for the girl to shiver, running her hands up and down her arms while the boy slid off his suit jacket and draped it over her shoulders. She kept her eyes on the pavement, angling away from him, despite how his face fell.

There was shame there. But was it shame because she was an Amaraian with magic, or shame because she helped their abductors escape? That also brought Noa to her next question: why not let the authorities catch your abductors? And: how could she use them to salvage at least part of this mess?

They piled into the elevator and then their hotel room, where Greed sat the two Amaraians at the foot of the bed. Noa ripped open the nightstand drawer and grabbed out her phone. She put it to her ear, squeezing it during the single ring it took to hear a voice on the other end.

"Where are you?" Sloth asked.

"Excuse me? Instead of asking where I am, maybe you should explain what the living hell just happened back there?"

An eerie quiet fell into a sigh.

"*Nyx.*" Noa gritted her teeth.

"That's what I'm in the middle of figuring out. Nothing should've happened, but everything went black. So I tried to restore communications and force my way back into the system, but when that wasn't getting me anywhere, I went back to the forums we discussed—Noa, everything's shut down."

"What's that supposed to mean to me, Nyx?"

"I can't tell you what happened because I was locked out. Not even the rebels' network is online. Something went sideways, and I don't know what it was. None of this was supposed to happen yet, so believe me, I'm just as pissed and confused as you are."

Noa tilted her head back, angling the receiver away from her face. "Pack. Now."

Greed and Gluttony began shoving everything into their bags as Noa rolled her head forward again to stare down her two new problems.

"All right," she said. "So what's the damage, then?"

Something jostled at the other end of the line. "It's... not great. The most important thing is that you need to be leaving right now. You'll have to cross the border to the southwest since they've already started shutting down all major traffic to and from Miralta, starting from the east."

"What?" Noa asked, huffing out a disbelieving breath. "Why? There weren't any Miraltans anywhere."

"Turn on the news or look at a feed, Noa."

Noa tapped the side of the TV, waking the screen to reveal red ticker tape scrolling along the bottom.

"The regent's dead..." Noa's voice was barely above a whisper.

Of course, he is. She clenched and relaxed her fist, tamping down her frustration as she faced two slack-jawed survivors.

"I'm going to need two new IDs when we get to Miralta."

"Names?" Nyx asked. "Assuming you didn't pick up a couple of ID-scrubbing criminals within the last hour."

Noa pointed to the girl. "Name."

She glanced over at her companion, hesitating as she choked out, "C-Cecilia Angelis."

"Cecilia Angelis," Noa repeated. "I'm assuming her record doesn't have her marked as a Mage." She paled at Noa's comment, clutching a hand to her chest now while the boy looked between them with a renewed, fighting spark.

"You can't just—"

"*Name.*" She pointed a finger at him, watching his vision catch on the TV again. His shoulders fell, and that fight fizzled out. Annoyed, Noa stepped in front of him, but he might as well have been looking straight through her.

"Glacier Caelius," he finally said, lifting his head for her to take in those sapphire-blue eyes again. The phone almost slipped out of her hand.

"*What?!*" Gluttony dropped his bag with a light thud.

"TV, mute."

All the movement in the room came to a halt as Noa pulled the phone away from her face to put it on speaker. She leaned against the TV stand and set it down, steepling her hands in front of her face with closed eyes. So, maybe breaking into the Amaraian palace *had* been the stupidest thing she'd ever done, but perhaps she'd managed to hit a stroke of luck after that unexpected mess.

"All right," she said, folding her arms over her chest. "Let me paint you a picture of what just happened. I saved both of your lives. I took a gamble that both of you were worth something I could cash in on later. So, I find it a little strange that you two were not only wandering around the palace so freely, but you were also cooperative with us because one of you is a *Mage* and the other is the *Prince* of Amarais—a prince who's been kept out of the public eye because of rampant rumors that he's half-Amaraian. A rumor that's clearly not a rumor, and I'm thinking that there's also a fairly damning reason for why there's an Illusionist Mage attached to his side... Much like me, you two decided to take a gamble in assisting in our escape because you didn't want to get caught, and you've just discovered that your last line of defense is dead, right?"

Glacier let out a bitter laugh. "What? Do you actually think *that man* wanted to keep me alive? That was all—" His eyes lit up with sudden realization. "I'll give you whatever you were looking for if you take us to Miralta."

Noa hesitated, faltering with that sudden push-back. "And what, exactly, is waiting for you in Miralta?"

"Katerina Caelius. My cousin and the new regent of Amarais."

3

AMARAIS ✦ 2704-11-12

RUNE

Gluttony's head fell back against the headrest of the passenger's seat. "This isn't how things were supposed to go, Rune," he said, his voice climbing with irritation. "We're supposed to get in, get the thing, and get out. Not walk out with a couple of useless rich brats. I don't know what's worse—the fact that we almost got caught, or the fact that I let you talk me into all this."

"Shut up, Crow," Rune mumbled, rubbing his forehead. "You're giving me a headache."

"Oh, *I'm* giving *you* a headache?" Crow scoffed. "I got blinded by that godsdamned Mage back there. I thought I was having a seizure. We should've just ditched them in the chaos to find what we were looking for rather than dragging them along."

"That's not your call. Noa calls the shots. That's what we agreed to."

"*We* didn't agree to it. *You* did."

"And what would you have done then? If you had a better idea before all this, you could have spoken up, you know."

Crow huffed, bumping his head against the window, his gaze set on the elevator. "Maybe we should've stayed in King's…"

Rune sat up straight again, biting back frustration. "You know if we'd stayed in King's Republic that things could be far worse for us. Don't even try to tell yourself otherwise."

Crow chewed on his lip before he opened his mouth to speak. Rune shook his head, knowing that he'd throw down the same argument he used a couple months ago.

"They wouldn't bargain with you then, Crow, and they sure as hell won't do it now. Don't be stupid. Even if you'd manage to cut any sort of deal, it'd be in their favor, not yours. You'd regret it."

His mouth clamped shut again right as the elevator doors slid open, and Noa led the charge toward the car with their two new passengers on her heels. Rune got out, earning a dejected noise from his brother as he followed suit.

"Miss anything?" Rune asked.

"Nope. Room's clear. Key?"

He dropped it into her open palm, and Crow rolled his eyes, thrusting his hands into his coat pockets.

"Nyx said she'll have the IDs ready at a drop point," Noa said. "But she won't be joining us until later."

"Why?" Rune asked with a frown.

"Something about backups and resources." She waved a hand. "I don't know exactly. Purposely vague for security or whatever." She spun to point a finger at Glacier. "However, *you* need to have Cecilia drop whatever magic is on you. If your photo ID doesn't match what you actually look like, you're not getting into Miralta. They'll be able to detect magic at any major checkpoint, unlike here, where you've somehow been able to get away with it."

Cecilia started to object until Glacier cut her off. "It's fine," he said, not breaking eye contact with Noa. "You can drop it."

She shifted, wearily stepping in front of him to brush a thumb over his right eyelid and quickly danced away. Pity washed over Rune at the sight of that eye. He'd heard rumors mingled with any sort of mention of Amarais's war threats with Miralta over the years, which is why he'd thought if their hidden prince truly had mixed blood, it'd be anything but their Mage-praising enemies. But sure enough, that eye was that emerald green—*Miraltan* green, offsetting the other's Amaraian blue.

"Better?" Glacier asked, tucking his hands into the pockets of Rune's spare coat that was at least a couple sizes too big on his smaller frame.

"Better." Noa turned on her heel, heading to the driver-side door with Crow climbing into the seat behind her.

Rune popped open the opposite door for them and peered through Glacier's brave façade as he coaxed his Mage friend to follow.

GLACIER

"So where are the rest of the deadly sins?" Glacier asked, glancing between Gluttony and Greed. He thought he'd heard the latter twin murmur 'Pride' in reference to the woman on the way to the hotel, but he couldn't be sure. "Are they waiting for you back in Miralta?"

She adjusted the rearview mirror with a smirk. "Unfortunately, there's only four of us, so just one is waiting in Miralta. But since you mentioned it, I'm Noa. This is Rune, and that's Crow."

He wasn't sure about the name 'Noa,' but the other two sounded a lot like aliases. "Funny," he said flatly.

Rune adjusted his seatbelt. "We've never gone by our real names outside of our last profession."

"And Nyx doesn't use her real name either," Noa said as she finished up typing something into her phone and dropping it into the cup holder. The car shifted into reverse and Crow tensed next to him in its slow roll back-ward. "But it's what everyone goes by, so it's better than nothing."

"So Noa isn't even your real name?"

"It is as far as you're concerned."

"Route is still clear," Rune said, tilting the phone toward her.

A devilish grin tugged on her lips, and the car shot forward. The force of it threw Glacier back into his seat, Cecilia yelped, and Crow cursed in his reach for the handhold. Glacier's palms went for the roof of the car since he didn't have many options crammed between his sole ally and one of his captors.

"We're going to die," Cecilia gasped, triggering a sadistic laugh from Crow.

"Make a left out of the garage," Rune said, seemingly unfazed as she jerked the car onto the street, sending the rest of them sliding. "Follow this road until you hit the local station line intersection. It'll run parallel to the national station hub from there."

"Got it," Noa said, flicking her gaze to the rearview mirror again. "So, the rumors are true. You're half-Miraltan? Considering all the bad blood, that's probably a bit of a problem for you, isn't it?"

Crow scoffed. "That's pretty obvious..."

"Watch it," Noa said, her voice dropping to a near-growl. His attention turned to the window to sulk while she continued with, "Well?"

"Yes..." Glacier said cautiously. "To be fair, it is pretty obvious."

"So did people just assume you're half-Bellegardian or something with the black hair?" she asked with a motion to her own, though he didn't miss her glance at Rune.

The twins fit the bill of what he'd assume a Bellegardian would look like between the dark hair and eyes with paler skin, not all that different from his own coloring.

"What do you plan to do with the information I give you? Use it to blackmail me?"

Noa barked out a laugh. "Oh, please. You caught me breaking into a high-security Amaraian building, which I'm pretty sure is an offense punishable by death or life in a snowy wasteland prison. I think you have enough over me already. Just consider it curiosity."

"Left at the intersection," Rune said, calling for another sharp turn. "Follow the tracks on the right."

"Anyway," she said. "I think someone's avoiding the question."

"Does it matter?" Crow grumbled, receiving a hard, warning glare from Rune this time.

"Well," Glacier started, "people typically *assume* I'm something other than Miraltan because they couldn't imagine Louis Caelius allowing anyone with Miraltan blood to be considered for the crown, let alone *live*. The council approved of my uncle as regent because of his stance against Miralta and anything to do with magic. That doesn't mean I outright lie to them—I just don't correct them because I don't claim any nationality outside of Amaraian."

"Considering what I've heard about your father and how he wanted to make peace with Miralta before he died, I'm surprised no one has declared you as an enemy of the country yet."

"I probably have my cousin to thank for that."

"And what about your friend there?" she asked. "Cecilia?"

Glacier looked down to where Cecilia was disappearing into her seat, death-gripping the door handle and his coat. She froze when she noticed, and shoved herself back up, smoothing out her dress. She was still self-conscious about appearances, despite entertaining thieves.

"She's my former tutor's daughter. Louis discovered she was a Mage, and we managed to use it to our advantage. It worked since he couldn't get rid of either of us without some sort of repercussion."

Noa shook her head with a chuckle. "So, rather than being caught by Amaraian authorities to face whatever's left of the council, you two were willing to take a chance with the three of us? Even I have to admit that's a bold move. But I can't say I'd do any different."

"If you didn't even know who we were, why bother saving us, anyway?"

Noa paused. "I... tend to find that desperate people are often more than willing to do whatever it takes to repay me for pulling them out of the fire."

"You make it sound like you're not a criminal."

Rune's soft voice cut in like a knife, "I'd like to argue that the real criminal is the man who wanted to kill his own nephew and an innocent girl just for being different."

Glacier's hands pulled away from the roof of the car, falling into his lap.

"You're right," Cecilia said in a near-whisper, her face tilting down to her clasped hands. "He would've liked nothing more than to get rid of us both if it meant he could continue living in his perfect bubble, completely isolated from the rest of the world. But I still can't believe he's just... gone..."

"Good riddance," Crow grumbled, transitioning the car into an uneasy silence.

Glacier sank into his seat as the minutes ticked by, watching the snowflakes dance past. Crow's head dipped after an hour, pressing against the car door. A few minutes after that, there was a weight on his shoulder, accompanied by the sound of Cecilia's light, rhythmic breathing. Noa and Rune whispered back and forth about directions or something else on occasion. Unable to make any sense of it out, he leaned back, listening to the blades against the windshield in their never-ending task of brushing away the snow.

That sharp, stinging sensation against his eyelids forced Glacier's eyes open to the cold. But instead of wind whipping up snow at his feet, there was darkness. It was a deep, blue-tinted void wherever he looked, preventing him from telling up from down. Every movement was sluggish, like pushing through water. When he found the source of the light, he propelled himself upward, pushing his hands against that top barrier—smooth and biting cold. Ice.

A strange, disturbing sense of curiosity worked through him as he automatically pulled his hand back and slammed his palm against it. His stomach began to knot with dread. All calm replaced by the sudden, choking sensation that hadn't been there moments prior.

Again.

It creaked, starting to give as a shadow fell over him. A blurry figure dressed in white stood at the edge of his watery grave. Glacier drew in a sharp breath to call out, his lungs filling with icy water.

Kat.

Her features were too distorted through the hazy, glassy patches to see if she reacted, but she didn't budge. His protector wasn't rushing to his aid like she had every time before, finally letting him drown.

The world twisted then, warping the scene into something a little more vivid—a replica in which a young woman didn't stand over him, but a *man*. He donned a white winter tactical suit that matched the gloves on Glacier's own hands now, which he swore had been black moments prior. His vision began to blur as the man began to walk away, and an inaudible scream tore from Glacier's throat. Fists pounded against the ice over and over and over again against his will, the ice barely giving each time.

✧

"Glacier."

He jolted awake to Cecilia's hand on his shoulder, her brows knitting together in concern. "Are you okay?"

Glacier nodded, trying to swallow in spite of his dry throat so he could answer. A rush of cold air followed a door being thrown open, pulling the breath from his lungs.

"I suggest everyone gets out now before it gets really warm in here," Noa announced. "Don't leave anything you want behind unless you expect to never see it again." She shoved a few items into her coat pockets as the twins hopped out into the snow.

Even though Crow vanished from view, Cecilia's door opened to Rune, who motioned for them to get out. "Come on."

"Wait, why here?" Cecilia asked. "I didn't think we were in Miralta yet..."

"We have to walk across the border from here," Noa replied. "Anything with any sort of non-Miraltan tracking code will get immediately flagged and tracked." She slipped out of the driver's seat, her boots hitting the snow. "Which means we have to ditch this sweet ride."

Rune offered his hand to help Cecilia out of the car.

"Thanks," she said under her breath, taking it with a small leap into ankle-deep white. After that, Rune backed up to give Glacier space, which he managed to fumble anyway. He winced as his half-asleep leg buckled slightly, pinpricks shooting through it on impact.

"You good?" Rune asked, moving to help him.

"Fine, thanks," Glacier replied with a shake of his head. It was enough for him to step away again, but a frown lingered. He dusted himself off, trying to ignore it, and made his way around to the trunk, where Noa was pulling out their bags. "How far of a walk across are we talking about?"

"About fifteen minutes," she said, tossing a bag to Crow. "Anything longer than that and we might freeze to death out here. Take this—" She held out a bag toward Glacier before she passed another to Rune, who stepped up next to him. "Have the coordinates memorized?"

"Of course." Rune handed her a small chip in return.

"Crow!" she called, holding the chip between gloved fingers. He cursed, dropped his bag in the snow, and fished out his phone to toss over to her. In one quick motion, she popped the SIM card free and pocketed the phone, repeating the process with her own before she dumped the cards in the now-empty trunk. "You weren't attached to this car, were you?"

Glacier hesitated. "Why do I feel like that doesn't matter right now?"

She shrugged. "Just thought I would ask before I turn it into a smoldering heap of unusable evidence."

"I-I'm sorry, what?" Cecilia asked, her expression horrified.

"She's blowing up the car so we can't be tracked," Crow snapped, which earned him another disapproving look from Rune.

"Everyone got their belongings?" Noa asked with a too-bright smile. "Good, now follow Rune safely away from the vehicle while I destroy the love of my life and mourn her untimely death." She pulled a small gray brick from the bag Glacier held and motioned for him to follow Rune.

Glacier reached him just in time to see Noa sliding out from under the SUV, wiping away the snow once she was back on her feet. She jogged back over, and Rune started to lead the way with Crow on his heels.

"Explosion's on a timer, so let's get a move-on, shall we?" She retrieved the bag from Glacier's arms, giving a mock bow to follow. "After you."

Cecilia started forward, glancing back after a few steps. He was rooted to the spot for a moment, unable to comprehend that they were fifteen minutes away from stepping outside of the only world he'd ever known. He pushed down that anxiety and turned his back on the last familiar remnant of his life about to melt away.

He'd be back in a week's time, at most. Kat would return with him, and they'd set everything right again—maybe even to something even better than what her father would've ever allowed as regent. A radical upheaval into peace that no one believed could ever be accomplished, but one that she'd promised to negotiate in a secret deal with the Miraltan Prime Minister while she was away. One that he could now potentially be a part of like Kat had wanted: a symbol of unity.

And yet, with every step he took, he shivered at the image of her standing there. Watching him drown. "There... um..." he began over his shoulder to Noa. "There aren't any lakes or ponds around here, are there?"

Noa slowed, all signs of satisfaction slipping from her face. "Not that I'm aware of... Why?"

"I'd just... rather not have to cross ice right now," he said, rubbing his arms as he dropped the rest of his comment to a mutter. "Especially after everything else that has gone wrong today."

The crunching of their footfalls carried on for about ten minutes until Rune paused up ahead, fumbling with something before a screen cut through the dark.

"How are we looking?" Noa called out.

"Just slightly off, but we're close," Rune called back.

"Does that mean we're in Miralta?" Cecilia asked.

"Yep," Noa said, rubbing her gloved hands together. "Welcome to the land of magic and Mages. I'm assuming this is your first time out of the country?"

"Yes," Cecilia said, shivering as she bumped shoulders with Glacier.

Noa broke into a chuckle. "You're in for a wild ride. Now let's hurry before we start losing fingers. I'd very much like to keep mine."

Two lights flicked on up again, interrupting Cecilia's next breath of a question. "Which one of you is Amelia?" came a heavily accented voice.

Glacier almost didn't understand what the man was saying, but Noa pushed her way forward, moving past Crow and Rune, who kept their distance from the road up ahead. It sounded almost... Bellegardian from the intonation and lilt, though Glacier's only reference point was various educational recordings that referenced their native language.

"I am," Noa spoke up as her voice slid into a similar accent. "*Et ton nom?*"

Rune held up his arm as Glacier and Cecilia caught up, holding them back as Noa continued her conversation in fluid Bellegardian. His mind made every effort to decipher it, but it was rare to hear another language outside of the common, international language that Amarais had adopted as a baseline centuries ago. Glacier eyed Rune again, frowning with a brief glance back at Noa. Why wasn't someone like Rune doing the talking when he looked far better suited for the part?

"Je m'appelle Étienne. J'ai ta voiture," he replied with a quick motion to the vehicle tucked behind the one with its lights on and the windshield wipers flicking back and forth in agitation. It matched the driver's expression, who huffed out wispy, white breaths and drummed his fingers on the steering wheel.

Noa bowed her head in thanks. *"Merci, Étienne.* A million thank-yous."

"Mon plaisir, Amelia," he called back as he slid into his car, and it lurched forward. The vehicle emitted a low, deep hum on its way past, causing Glacier to cringe. Those two would be lucky to make it to their destination if it was anywhere further than a couple kilometers away with something in that bad of shape. But he supposed they were fortunate to have any sort of self-transportation at all, this far out in the middle of nowhere.

Rune hurried them up the slope to the road, where they piled into the car behind Noa. She'd already cranked up the heat, letting out a sigh as all the doors slammed shut. "Well..." she said, picking at the worn cloth seats with a grimace. "This isn't exactly the luxury ride I would've asked for, but I guess as long as it still runs, we'll make it the thirty kilometers to the station."

Rune toyed with his phone again. "You're not going to question why Nyx sent a Bellegardian native all the way out here to deliver a car?"

"There are certain things I've learned to let go with her, specifically ones involving resources. I'm just going to call this a win since there's heat in this trash heap." She spun the wheel to guide them back onto the road, much gentler than back in Amarais, and Glacier settled in for the remainder of the ride.

4
MIRALTA ✦ 2704-11-13

The soft light of the train station became a distant beacon somewhere past midnight. And while Noa was sad to ditch the car, it wasn't practical to keep it—not with where they were headed. A rush of warm air greeted their entrance from the overhead heaters in the breezeway, and a trickle of relief spread through her at the sight of a bare station platform up ahead, decked in black and green. Gold pendant lights descended from the ceiling, illuminating the cozy sitting nooks tucked away on the far reaches of the archway's view.

The only obstacles between them and the small checkpoint were two late-night station attendants, chatting while they manned the ticket kiosks. Both wore dark gray uniforms with embroidered Miraltan green badges on the breast. The one closer to Glacier's lighter complexion bore eyes a few shades darker to his emerald, dipping into a leafy, forest color, while his companion had piercing eyes of peridot that blended with his darker toned skin and rich, brown hair.

Noa pretended not to notice Glacier's unease as she pushed into the locker room, wandering past label after label until she found the one Nyx had texted her. She punched in the code, it chirped, and she was rewarded a small cloth bag. Individually bagged fake ID cards—complete with stamped passport seals, train ticket cards, and two sets of new SIM cards to make up for the spares they'd ended up burning through. Noa leaned back against the lockers, taking a moment to thank Nyx—wherever she was camping out right now.

After her little break, she re-emerged into the small cluster of people in the far nook of the entry, nodding past the chokepoint to the pre-security-check lobby. "Let's get a little further in before I hand out the tickets." Leading the way, she flipped one of the ticket cards over to find it registered for a 1:15AM departure time to Knighton. She elbowed Rune. "How far's Knighton from the capital?"

He hummed, pulling up the map on his phone again. "Looks like... fifteen minutes via commuter train to Corris."

"I can work with that," she mumbled. It was far enough out of the way to let them lay low, catch up on some rest, and then arrange a meeting with the new ruler of Amarais during her stay in enemy territory to deliver her cousin safely back into her care.

Fortunately, Nyx would be around to handle the delicate matter of delivering the finer terms of the deal. She'd intervened the first time Noa had given someone an ultimatum—because that's what it was—and had later reprimanded her, instructing her to not outright *threaten* the 'client.' Noa scoffed at the term until she'd been pinned by Nyx's icy glare and opted to roll with it, rather than argue. Clients they were then, forcing her to conclude that her little ultimatums were amicable deals, rather than the obvious: life-debts.

They stopped around a booth, their final stop before testing out how accurate Nyx had managed to detail their new identities. Noa tossed the twins their respective bags and slid Cecilia's ID out for examination. 'King's Republic' was stamped on the front, hovering above the name 'Elodie Andreas.' Some of the text fell under the small, holographic stamped circle with a diamond in the corner, and Noa couldn't suppresses a bemused smirk when she tilted it in the light. A Mage stamp. Something that Miralta would consider a badge of honor.

"Elodie," she said, holding it out to her.

Cecilia was gentle in tugging it from her fingers, hunching as she flipped it over a couple of times while Noa moved onto Glacier's. His read, 'Miralta' in bold, blocky letters along the side, and the pulled database image had been altered so the green matched the shade Noa had described to Nyx hours before. Next to it said, 'Morgan Hawthorn,' along with a neat list of the rest of his cursory details.

"And Morgan."

He gripped its sides, analyzing every letter with a deepening frown.

"Something wrong?"

"I'm not twenty yet."

Noa choked back a laugh, turning it into a snort. "Oh, I'm quite aware, seeing how we're going to see the defaulting *regent*. However, even though you're over eighteen, you'd still need a guardian's approval to travel, which we don't exactly have. So, congrats. Happy birthday."

He narrowed his eyes at her, unamused.

Crow rolled his eyes, grumbling, "Go get a drink or something."

Rune's head snapped in his direction, shooting him a glare.

Noa cleared her throat. "Let's just get through security, and then we'll unwind a little before we board. I doubt you'll have much of an opportunity once we get you to Corris. You'll probably get bombarded by the media once you reunite with your cousin and announce world peace or whatever." She shoved the rest of the bag into her travel pack, waving a hand. "Let's move, people."

She dumped her luggage on the table, allowing one of the guards to run it through a machine while she tapped her new ID to the scanner. The other guard on duty nodded when it pulsed green, and she collected her belongings to wait for the others.

Rune started toward her in the midst of putting away his ID when the speakers chimed. Grinning, she pointed up at the ceiling. "Train's here."

"You have no idea how much I want to lock the door to our cabin and pass out," he said, rubbing a hand against his forehead right as Cecilia wandered over.

"As sexy as that sounds for us to finally be alone again," Noa purred,

"I'm sticking you with your brother and the prettier young lady. I still have business to discuss with *that one*." She nodded toward Glacier.

"Wait..." Cecilia said, glancing between them. "We're going to be in separate cabins?"

Rune, ever the picture of patience, put on a gentle smile. "There's a limit of four to a cabin, with the occasional exception for small children. So, it seems you'll be with me and my moody brother."

"I'm sorry, did you say something?" Crow asked as he came to a stop next to them, and Glacier took a side-step a little further away, brushing against Cecilia.

"Nothing you need to worry about," Rune replied, starting toward the platform.

Crow and Cecilia followed, the latter looking back with dismay as Noa stopped her new cabinmate.

"You're with me. It's time we finish the conversation we started back in Amarais."

She led the way up the ramp, making her way down the narrow hall to their compartment. The door slid free with a tap of her ticket to a plush cabin with inky black benches across from each other, spilling onto dark green carpet that mimicked the tear-drop shape of leaves in an orderly pattern. She dropped her bag onto one of the benches and half-heartedly motioned to the other, an invitation for Glacier to move out of the doorway.

He flinched at the door snapping shut behind him once the sensor recognized he was inside. Noa folded her arms over her chest as they took their seats, examining every little tick he corrected. His hands started in his lap, fidgeting before mimicking her own posture with his chin up like he was ready to hold his ground.

"Well, what do you want?" he asked.

She ran her tongue over her teeth to hold back that snap of irritation, reminding herself that he wasn't in danger around her. He'd grown up in a palace, so it was reasonable to assume he'd be nervous in doing something on his own because he'd almost certainly had someone hold his hand his whole life.

Don't pity him.

Noa leaned back in her seat. "The Soul of Amarais."

A dumbfounded look took over his features before he broke into a short, sporadic laugh. "Y-you're kidding, right? You won't be able to sell it. There's nothing you can do with that," he said, shaking his head. "If you're after money, you can just ask for it. I'd gladly hand some of it over, seeing how it's been going to waste for years anyway."

Noa had to tamp down her surprise. Usually, when she was offered money in exchange for saving someone's life, it was because they weren't willing to part with something more valuable, not because they thought it wasn't worth *enough*.

She shook her head. "No, I'm—I'm not after money, Glacier. I broke into the palace to steal the Soul of Amarais, not the entire treasury."

"But... why? It's just an old relic that's been locked up in a vault for years. It's useless, outside of maybe being put on display at the museum, which no one wants to do."

"Despite that," Noa said. "Would you be willing to promise me the Soul of Amarais in exchange for delivering you safely to your cousin?"

He bit his lip, staring down at the carpet. "Well... Since it's technically *mine* to give away..." His tone dropped to something more authoritative as he looked her in the eyes again. "You can have it under the condition that you take *both* Cecilia and I to Kat, unharmed, and causing as little trouble as humanly possible."

Noa raised an eyebrow, a small smile tugging at the corner of her lips. "I've gotten you this far with minimal incidents, haven't I?"

CECILIA

Cecilia watched out the window as the train left the station behind. She swallowed down the discomfort of being stuck in a cabin with twin strangers while Glacier remained trapped elsewhere with their ringleader.

"I need a drink," Crow grumbled, stopping in front of his brother. "Want anything?"

"Just sleep," Rune said from his spot beside her on the bench. His eyes closed in the reflection of the windowpane since she didn't dare glance their way just yet.

Crow huffed. "Suit yourself." And left.

When the door shut, she braved a look, finding him stretched out with his arms folded loosely over his chest.

"Um, Rune?" she asked, sounding too quiet to her own ears.

"Hm?

"What's... Miralta like?"

He cracked an eye open. "That's a bit of a loaded question."

"I-I'm sorry—" she said, fumbling with her sleeves.

"It's fine." He shifted to sit up in his seat. "I'm assuming you want to know more about Knighton and Corris since that's where we'll be going, right? I've only been to Corris, but if Knighton is anything close, then... it's a picture best viewed. I doubt my description would do it justice, but it's a nice place. Certainly, better than where we came from."

Her straw-colored hair fell past her ear, giving her pause. "I... have a feeling anyone there won't like seeing me though," she said, biting her lip as she tucked it back into place.

The corner of his mouth dipped down. "From what I've seen and heard, most Miraltans don't care too much about appearances—Not to say that there aren't some radicals that would like nothing more than to push back against Amarais, but... I can't imagine they'd ever turn away a Mage."

She squeezed her hands together. "You know..." She forced out a mirthless breath of a laugh. "Our lives would've been so much simpler if I had Glacier's looks and he had mine. We might not even be in this mess to begin with, but instead, we had to use each other to survive. It's just... not *fair*."

"Sometimes the cards we've been dealt in life look like a losing hand, but it can also depend on how you play them. I think right now you two are just starting to get better cards. I wouldn't fold just yet."

"Yeah... Yeah, maybe you're right." She picked at Noa's spare pants. "I-I'll let you sleep. I think I want to get something warm to drink if that's okay?"

"I don't mind," he said, waving her off with a smirk. "Go wild."

She stood, giving a quick, polite smile in her short walk to the door before she spun around. "Oh—I don't have any credits on this ID, do I?" She fished it from her pocket as her cheeks warmed with embarrassment.

"Nyx always ties them to a temporary bank account. You're fine."

"Um... but how do you know how much you have, though?"

He gave a half-shrug. "Usually about ten-thousand credits. That's worth—what—twenty cups of coffee?"

Relief spread through her, turning her smile grateful this time. "Thanks."

"Don't stay out too late," he joked, leaning back in his seat again as she left.

Once she was out in the hall, she followed the dim light strips along the floor and ceiling, casting everything in a soft, blue glow. A screen on the wall leading to the connecting car told her how far up her destination was, and she began her trek onward, stumbling into the next section.

Her eyes went wide, drinking in the starry night sky overhead, barely registering the plaque labeling it as the 'Observation Car.' Snow dunes sloped past, skimming the horizon stretching outward toward an infinite sky. A new world outside of the city she'd always known, lighting her soul with wonder.

Cecilia's footsteps turned feather-light in her slow walk to the next car, where she found Crow perched on a stool at the far end. He watched the screens above the bar, most filled with advertisements and talk shows, while he tipped an amber-filled glass to his lips.

She kept her distance, moving along the far side to a drink kiosk, cluttered with icons for various coffees and teas. Cecilia picked out a hot chamomile, pressing her ID to it for a green checkmark. A mug pushed up from a hidden compartment, and the machine filled it with hot water, along with a tea bag dispensing from the side.

With her prize in hand, she took her leave back to the observatory car, picking out one of the aisle seats and letting it steep.

"Enjoying the view?"

She jumped, careful not to slosh the contents of her cup.

"Sorry," Noa said, a hint of a grin tugging at the corner of her mouth.

"Didn't mean to scare you." She leaned forward onto the back of the seat next to her.

"N-no, it's fine," she forced out, a little bit too high-pitched.

"I'm guessing Rune fell asleep?"

"I think so. I'm... surprised you're still awake. You drove here, after all."

She drummed her fingers against the pleather. "Not really tired." Her eyes followed the distant mountain ranges with a slight quirk of her lips like she was somewhere else.

"And what about Glacier?" Cecilia asked.

"Sound asleep as well. What are you, his mom?"

She scowled as Noa pushed off the seat and started toward the dining car.

"Worry a little less. People can't run if they never learn to walk."

Cecilia watched her vanish, leaving her alone again to take in the stars. Every pinprick of light engraved itself into her memory, becoming a sight she refused to forget. A promise of a brighter tomorrow she'd never imagined waking to in Amarais.

5

MIRALTA ✦ 2704-11-13

NOA

Once Cecilia had left for bed, Noa took her place in the observatory car, trading sleep for an ever-changing view. The inky black of night diffused into deep purples, pinks, and oranges, gradually brightening as her mind worked to untangle the thoughts that refused to stay back in Amarais.

The sound of one of the car's doors sliding open perked her ears, followed by the pad of footsteps against the thin carpet until the figure stood in her peripheral vision. "We should be pulling into the station soon," came Rune's velvety tones. "Manage to catch any sleep?"

"Spent most of the night thinking... Decided to take a raincheck on sleeping for a few hours." She watched him frown in the reflection of the glass, angling himself to lean against the edge of her seat with crossed arms.

"Thinking about what?"

"Trying to figure out what went so horribly wrong back at the palace."

His voice dropped to a low whisper, "And your thoughts?"

"Well... Nyx and I had discussed the possibility of dealing with rebels, considering the slow-building unrest, and she managed to break into one of their communication forums to see what kind of activity we were dealing with so we wouldn't get caught without our pants down."

"Which didn't quite go as planned..." he mumbled.

"Considering where we are, who we've picked up, and what we're currently missing, I'd consider that an understatement. But what bothers me the most is that not only did Nyx *not* find anything that would indicate that the rebels were going to act, the evidence actually suggested the opposite. They were specifically waiting until a later date—one that would line up with our dear new regent's return."

Rune gave a low hum, indicating baffled agreement.

"Now," she continued, "either Nyx was wrong, which I highly doubt, given her track record, and an entire band of Amaraian rebels suddenly decided to storm the palace a full week earlier because" —she tapped her index finger to tick off her first assumption— "they suspected that someone malicious had successfully infiltrated their communications and adjusted their plans accordingly, or *none* of the people we encountered during our escape last night were rebels *at all*."

"You think there's another faction."

"Possibly. That's the only one that makes the most sense. Her gathered information alone indicates that they were heavily backing Katerina. They wanted her on the throne, and they were certainly gearing up to make it happen... But then, why were palace sector enforcers flooding the streets? The news broadcasts showed nothing but chaos when the rebels were organized and had at least a chunk of said enforcers in their pockets. We should've seen an organized coup, not—" She stood up, gesturing somewhere in the vague direction of north, where Amarais was still left in upheaval. "Whatever the hell that was..."

His head dipped to his cupped hand. "But wouldn't it be easier to eliminate the enemy if you knew that your champion was going to be off the board for a time? Completely out of harm's way?"

"Yes, but there's one flaw with that idea. The rebels want peace with Miralta."

"I'm not sure I follow. That's what Katerina is here for right now, so what's the problem?"

"Glacier," she said, locking eyes with him. "If the rebels know anything about his father, they would have to assume that he's not only his father's son but that there is very much a chance that he's not half-Bellegardian or whatever else has been tossed around for years that's prevented Cecilia from covering the black hair. The damage was done at some point, and those rumors spread outside of Amarais to people like *us*. Had we not run into him, Glacier would have died with the rest of the casualties, and that doesn't exactly match up with the rebel agenda, does it?"

"I suppose not... Which poses a bit of a problem if we need to get the Soul of Amarais, unless you managed to strike a deal last night."

"He'll gladly give it to us," she said, "as long as both he and Cecilia are handed over in mint condition."

"I don't think you packed any bubble wrap."

"*Cute.*" She rolled her eyes. "But he did try to offer part of the treasury at first since he thought I wanted to sell it."

He raised an eyebrow. "All things considered, that might've been a better deal."

She chortled. "You act like Nyx isn't feeding us seemingly infinite amounts of credits to fund this fool's expedition."

"Still would've been nice to have something to retire on..." he said with a wistful gaze at the horizon.

Almost on cue, the far door opened again, where Crow, Glacier, and Cecilia trickled in. While the two of them stopped, Crow didn't break his stride toward the dining car.

"Good morning, sunshine," Noa called, flashing him a forced smile. He sneered back and disappeared. She turned back to Rune. "Look, I don't know what's gotten into him, but do me a favor and remove the stick from your brother's ass. It's starting to piss me off." She pushed past him to her new captive audience.

"In his defense," Rune started under his breath, keeping at her side. "He came back to the cabin pretty smashed last night."

"Don't blame this on the booze," she hissed. "Fix. It."

She opened her mouth again just as the overhead announcement kicked on, declaring their impending arrival, though Noa didn't think it was fast enough. "All right, we've got thirty minutes. Get some breakfast because once we stop, we're going straight to whatever accommodations Nyx prepared for us. From there, we'll figure out who's escorting the two of you to Corris and establish what our story is. You may *not*, under any circumstances, repeat any of the information we have discussed with anyone else outside of the six of us, understood?"

Glacier stole a glance at Cecilia before his eyes snapping to Noa again. "Can I at least ask *why?*"

"Because if you do," she said, her patient tone going jagged, "I will be sure to make your life a living hell. I might have saved you but make no mistake in thinking that I did it out of the kindness of my own heart. I did it because I saw a payout, and while the two of you are obviously victims of a very flawed system, if you decide to throw me on the tracks, I will take you down with me. Are we clear?"

His lips pressed into a thin line before answering with a begrudging, "Crystal."

"Good. Now hurry up."

She walked around them back toward her cabin, her shoulders sinking with every step down the car's corridor. If she'd been a little more careless, she probably wouldn't have heard the quiet trailing set of steps behind her. When she stopped at her door with her ticket, she spared a glance at Rune.

"That was a little harsh, don't you think?"

Noa sighed, heading inside. "Rune, if I coddle everyone that I make a deal with, do you honestly think we're going to be taken seriously? Look, I get that they're probably still a little shaken up, but we're doing something that is *far* beyond what most people would consider sane. I can't afford to lose control over this situation." She pulled her bag down from the overhead compartment, slinging it over her shoulder. "We get the Soul. We walk away. That's all there is to it. They'll forget about us in a few months, and we'll never see them again."

Once the train pulled into Knighton Station, Noa started scanning the crowd, jumping from black-haired woman to black-haired woman in search of Nyx. A girl matching her petite build sent Noa's hope soaring until she turned to hug a friend, revealing bright green eyes. Not Nyx.

She strode through the morning crowd, her boots emitting a quiet squeak against the smooth, dark green tiles. Her head tilted toward tall, brick archways to the next platform or corridor leading outside, finding Miraltan after Miraltan with the occasional non-green-eyed foreigner mixed among them. Noa spun to catch a glimpse of another with thick-framed glasses, cursing when she saw the dark brown hair.

Rune grabbed her arm, yanking her back into the crowd.

"What? Did you find her?" Noa asked. He didn't answer in escorting her back to the others, but a weight settled in her stomach when she took in how other people in the station stopped around them.

It wasn't until Rune let go and stared up at one of the large monitors hanging from the ceiling that she understood why everyone else had ground to a halt. They were all reading the red ticker tape along the bottom of the screen, plucking Noa straight from the station and dropping her back in that damn Amarais hotel room.

"Katerina Caelius never made it to Miralta," Rune murmured. "Whoever attacked the palace got to her first. She's dead."

Noa's thoughts raced on their way to the apartment building, though the one that stuck at the front of her now-growing list was to shove Glacier and Cecilia inside the unit as fast as possible. Every stray look or stolen glance in Cecilia's direction turned into a pulse-pounding alarm in Noa's ears like they might stop and ask for her documentation or worse—ask if she was okay. The one saving grace is that none of them appeared to notice Glacier. His one damning eye was an afterthought in a place where he looked at home, outside of his growing paleness and unsteady footing.

They were in shock. Noa had gone from kidnapping to babysitting in a matter of moments because their one ticket out had been burned alive in a south-bound car caravan that'd been blown to pieces, along with Noa's hopes of holding the Soul of Amarais in her hands anytime soon.

She flipped on the lights when the door swung open to their new living quarters, landing them straight into the faux-hardwood entry that stepped down into the recessed main sitting area, complete with a TV, a couple faded, green corduroy couches, an overstuffed chair, and a coffee table. The kitchen was through a double-wide opening off to the left, making it a straight shot down the hallway on Noa's right. This left her with four mystery doors that sent her into lockdown mode.

"Rune, Crow," she said, pointing toward the ones down the hall and bordering the sitting area. "Check all the rooms. Block out the windows too."

They dropped their bags and split off before she even finished speaking.

"What should I do?" Cecilia asked, her voice sounding small and frayed. She might as well have shoved a knife straight into Noa's gut, twisting it with the addition of stray tears.

She really needed to break something. Or maybe punch someone.

Noa secured the front door and led the way to the room tucked into the far corner next to the kitchen. She pushed it open to find it empty, save for a plain bed, dresser, and a cramped bathroom.

"Take Glacier in here," she said, ushering her in. "I think you two... probably need some time alone to process all of this."

Cecilia nodded, swiping at her face as she guided Glacier inside and pushed the door shut behind them. Noa tilted her head back and sighed, closing her eyes with a pressing command to collect herself until the searching came to a stop with scraping footsteps.

"What now?" Rune asked.

She dropped her head again while tugging the phone from her pocket. Two missed call indicators sat at the top of the screen. Tapping one, she held it up to her ear, listening to it ring once. Twice. No confused 'hello' or name greeted her, but she picked up on the muffled noises of a street crowded with the morning rush.

"Where are you?" Noa asked.

"That's for me to know, but I'm not in Miralta," Nyx replied. "I tried to contact you earlier, but you weren't picking up."

"Katerina is dead," Noa said, cutting to the chase. "We've got nothing."

The sound of a buzzer, followed by an automated greeting she couldn't make out over Nyx's string of curses. "Of all the—" She bit back a growl. "I've been up all night trying to get back into their security system. I managed to force my way back into the forum server and piece some things together—"

Noa cocked an eyebrow at a quieter male voice that slipped through before Nyx's hand must've brushed against the phone. If she'd been trying to silence any evidence of him, she'd done it a little too late.

"It's another faction, Noa. They were scraping information and hiding behind the rebel networks. There's evidence that it's an extremist group being run by some bastard son of a council member. I dug around and found that they wouldn't claim him, so I'm placing my bets on—"

"That he got jealous of the fact that a bastard prince with Miraltan blood was set to take the throne and went overboard," Noa finished, every word feeding her exhaustion.

"It's a possibility that I'm looking further into, and it seems Katerina fell victim to that."

"So, when will you be here?" Noa asked.

"I already told you. I won't be coming to Miralta. I can't." Each of those words was padded with that same tired edge. It was unusual, especially when Noa had always known Nyx to be the one to not only come up with the plans but have backup plans for her backup plans. She had to have been running herself ragged to fix whatever misstep she'd thought she'd made with the security in Amarais.

"It's okay," Noa said with a tone a little gentler than she'd expected from her own mouth. "We'll... figure this out. You said you got back into Amarais security, right?"

"Yeah, I'm—It's up on my screen now. I backdoored the rebel network again last night and managed to rip the entire database down from the forum too. I can send over the encrypted files if you want to look at them."

"Send that over. Someone here can look through it while you keep an eye on Amarais. I want you to figure out how they operate. Do we know who's spearheading all this?"

"Lucian Scevola, age twenty-six," Nyx said.

"Get me absolutely everything on him. His criminal record to his list of lovers, I want all of his dirty laundry at my disposal."

"Understood."

Noa's shoulders sagged as her sights drifted back toward the bedroom door. "In the meantime," she mumbled, "I have a Mage and an exiled prince to deal with."

"I can arrange more permanent accommodations for them a little further away from Corris, if necessary."

"Later. There's too much going on, and I'd rather lay low for a few days before making any decisions. It's too big of a risk to move them right now. Give me forty-eight hours to scope out Knighton and get a feel for the area. It could be quiet enough that they can stay with us for the next couple weeks while we lose heat."

Crow's sour expression made her grip the phone a little tighter. He motioned to the door, mouthing words that she took as his argument to toss them out. Rune cut him a sharp look, which he bared his teeth in response to before storming out, slamming the door behind him. Rune sighed, slumping into the armchair and rubbing his temples.

"I'll check back with you soon," Noa finally said.

"The files will be sent over in fifteen." With that, the line disconnected.

Noa trudged over to the couch, dropping down by Rune. "This has all gone to hell."

"What did Nyx say?" he asked.

"That I was right about the other faction. They were using the rebels as a cover and outmaneuvered them. And, to top it all off, signs point to it being led by a guy that probably feels cheated out of his supposed birthright."

"So... the complete opposite of..." He motioned beyond that bedroom door to Glacier.

"Yeah..."

"Now what?"

"Well," she said, leaning back, "now we wait. Once Glacier and Cecilia pull themselves together, we decide how to proceed on that front. In the meantime, we lay low and help Nyx with intelligence. We play it like we have for our successes and prepare for the next stop, even if this was a complete and total failure."

CECILIA

An hour passed before Cecilia emerged. Glacier had barely spoken to her, despite all the questions she'd asked. He'd just sat there in the middle of the bed, legs crossed, arms wound around himself, staring at the edge of the comforter. The devastation on his face continued swinging back and forth into denial until she'd told him to get some sleep.

A numbness settled over her, realizing that she'd never see Katerina again. She'd been like the sister she'd never had. She'd been a girl that braided Cecilia's hair while she made up wild stories for her and Glacier back when they were nearing their teens. They'd spent their weekends scouring the palace for secret passageways that didn't exist. She was the one to sneak out and bring them back treats from her rebellious escapades, along with the promise of smuggling them outside the palace wall with her one day. Cecilia would never hear her tinkling laugh or mock ballroom dance in her rooms again.

Even worse, the last of Glacier's family was gone. Cecilia couldn't fix that, let alone fathom it when hers was still out there.

Her vision blurred as she started toward Rune, who fixated on a tablet in the sitting area. "Rune," she said, her voice wavering. "Can I see your phone?"

His head lifted, blinking in confusion. "Why?"

"I want to call my parents." Her voice pitched, nearly cracking. She wanted to tell them everything that happened, that she and Glacier were okay, and that she didn't know what to do next. She wanted to tell them she was terrified and struggling to keep herself together for her grieving friend because she was grieving too. "Please?"

His confusion slipped into pity, ripping the air from her lungs.

"Rune, *please.*"

He slid the tablet onto the coffee table and stood. "Cecilia, I can't let you call your parents. As much as I'd like for you to talk to them, it's too much of a risk."

"What?" She flinched at the small gasp she made. She wanted to be upset with him for saying that—to be angry with him, but she couldn't bring herself to do something like hit him when he'd been nothing but nice to her, unlike his brother.

"If you talk to your parents, and they hear that you and Glacier are alive, not only would it put the two of you in danger, but it would put your parents in danger as well."

"And who's to say they're not already in danger? What's the point then? I can at least warn them—"

"Do you really think they would want people to know that Glacier is alive? That the heir of Amarais is still out there?" His tone turned grim. "Cecilia, do you know there was a rebellion going on to rally behind both Katerina and Glacier?"

She hesitated, shaking her head. "I know there was some sort of rebellion. I-I heard the rumors, but I didn't know... I didn't know anything about Katerina and Glacier."

His body slackened at her reply like a tiredness had gripped him. "Cecilia, it's safer for everyone if you don't contact them now. If there's a safe way to do it, I'll gladly help, but you can't right now. I'm sorry."

What could she say to that? What was she supposed to do? He was right, even if she didn't want him to be. How much was she willing to risk in the name of selfishness? She swallowed down her feelings, ignoring the gnawing sorrow in her gut. It sapped the last of her strength, buckling her knees and dropping her to the coffee table. Her head fell into her hands, and she loosed a silent sob.

Something warm draped around her shoulders, causing her head to jerk up. Rune's hand fell away from the blanket, and he tugged on her arm, helping her up and into what had been his chair. Cecilia tightened the knit fabric around herself.

"I know I can't do much," he mumbled, crouching to her level, "but I can at least make you something to drink. Coffee? Hot chocolate? Tea?"

"What kind of tea?" she asked with a sniff.

The corner of his mouth ticked up. "Let me check the cabinets." He strode into the kitchen and began rummaging around until he returned with a small selection of boxes. "Take your pick."

She searched them for a moment, tapping a fingertip against one. "Please?"

He held it up to read the label. "Good choice," he said with a smirk. "At least, I think it is."

When he turned to go, she gripped the blanket a little harder, forcing out that lingering question on the forefront of her thoughts: "Why are you being so nice to me?"

He paused, glancing back. "Because you deserve better than the hand you've been dealt. Both of you do."

RUNE

Cecilia had curled up in the chair, falling asleep sometime after finishing her tea. Rune's renewed concentration on the data in his hands sped back up, moving from post to post and document to document until the buzz of a text message disrupted him. A check-in from Noa—wherever she was, and then the door swung open to reveal Crow.

His brother took one hard look at Cecilia's peaceful slumber, kicked the door shut, and stormed off down the hall. Rune held his breath, watching the rise and fall of her chest before he gently slid the tablet onto the coffee table and followed.

"You want to talk, or what?" Rune asked, pushing the door shut behind him.

Crow didn't bother sparing him a glance as he pulled off his boots and tossed them into the corner. "Nope. Not really."

"What's your problem?"

"Nothing. Why does it matter?"

"Because you're clearly upset about Cecilia and Glacier, but you're not exactly giving me a straight answer—"

"You know what it is, Rune?" he snapped. "They're useless. We saved them for nothing, and now they're just getting in the way. They've caused nothing but trouble for us since we picked them up. What the hell are we going to do with them now?"

Rune scowled. "They *haven't* caused any trouble. Trouble found them —That's like Noa saying that we've caused nothing but trouble if our problems started showing up and following us around. You're just mad because the job didn't go as planned. Get over it. You need to pull yourself together before Noa brings it upon herself to deal with you."

Crow snorted. "I'd like to see her try."

"No, I don't think you would. Now stop being a complete dumbass and start working with us, rather than fighting against us." He ripped the door open, fists clenched as he started back down the hall.

Noa was standing in the entry now, careful about her every movement with her eyes on Cecilia. When she turned her head toward Rune, she raised an eyebrow, leading the way to the remaining empty room.

"Did you drug her or something?" she asked, pointing her thumb toward the closed bedroom door.

"What? Give me a little more credit than that. We talked. She wanted to call her parents. I talked her out of it and helped her calm down," he said as Noa's arm dropped, and she began sliding out of her jacket. "I think she's trying to hold it together for Glacier, but... she's struggling. I can't fault her for that."

"I can imagine... And what about the *other* problem?" She nodded through the wall to where Crow was undoubtedly still sulking.

"I'm going to need a little more time on that."

"Fine." The word sounded more like a shrug to him than a threat. "And Glacier?"

"He... hasn't left their room since you left. I'm guessing he's sleeping too..." He paused, remembering their short, final conversation on the train. "Noa, he doesn't have anyone left now. As much as Crow can get on my nerves, I can't imagine living without him around. Glacier can't be taking it well."

She ran a hand through her side-swept bangs, framing her face at odd angles. "Well, I told Nyx to give us a couple days before we decided whether or not to relocate them. If we think it would do them good to send them elsewhere, we'll deal with it then. In the meantime, they can sort it out."

"Showing a little extra kindness wouldn't hurt right now, Noa."

"You're too soft sometimes," she said in half-jest, furrowing her brows. "You can play the good guy while I play the hardass."

He shook his head, exasperated with that ever-present wall of hers. Rune still wasn't sure when he had hit it again after months of traveling with her, thinking that he'd made progress just before she pushed him back again. It'd turned into a dance where she would switch up the steps and see if he'd follow along. There was a fear there he'd seen shortly after they first met—one hidden away by hardened layers of her past. One he was certain he'd never pierce through before their luck ran out, but he supposed it didn't really matter.

"Go to bed," he said.

"You going to join me?" she purred with that ever-teasing twinkle in her eye. Just another façade to play off of.

He frowned. "Stop the play-flirting and get some sleep."

Her grin dropped as he left. Rune rubbed at his face and reclaimed his seat on the couch, leaning back with a soft groan. Crow's complaints back in Amarais became a nagging reminder that he'd dug this hole for himself, but he sure as hell wasn't going to lie down in it.

6

MIRALTA ✦ 2704-11-15

NOA

Noa sipped her coffee at the kitchen island, watching Cecilia push her scrambled eggs around her plate at the other end. The past twenty-four hours hadn't yielded the results she'd hoped for, despite Rune's cordial efforts to coddle their charges with tea and home-cooked meals. And Cecilia would emerge from her and Glacier's room, dejected with his barely-touched plates.

Glacier hadn't graced them with his presence once in all that time, and Cecilia spent most of hers staring at the walls or a darkened TV screen once Rune was through with whatever bleak news he'd been watching. Noa had thought they should've been somewhat ready to talk by now, but she'd underestimated that. Perhaps it was her own experience that gave her a poor indicator of when one should be ready to pick themselves up and keep going since she'd always held fast to the mantra to power through the pain.

And something had to give.

"Cecilia?" she asked.

The fork slipped from Cecilia's hand, and she scrambled to muffle the clatter.

"How about..." Noa started, "we take a trip around Knighton and get you some fresh air?"

She hesitated, stealing a glance out the window to the arched-framed panes of the building across the street, separated by stacked pillars. Apartment buildings mirrored the elaborate, artistic architecture that Miraltans poured their hearts and souls into as much as their love of magic. Cecilia shook her head, pushing her plate away.

"I-I shouldn't..."

"If you're worried about standing out, there are more Amaraian-Miraltans here than you think," Noa said. It was a discovery she'd made after her wandering escapades yesterday, much to her own surprise. She'd heard about Amaraians taking refuge in Miralta or going a little further south to King's Republic, but it was still rather rare to see them. Walking past blond-haired and blue-eyed individuals shopping or commuting alongside their dark-haired, green-eyed should-be enemies was a strange yet welcomed sight.

"We could tour one of the universities if you'd like?" she continued.

Cecilia's eyes lit up until they flicked back to that bedroom door.

"Cecilia, sitting around here and not doing anything isn't going to make him suddenly improve. If *you* want to come along with me to help distract yourself, then you should. Don't waste your time doing nothing if that's not what you want."

Cecilia bit her lip, not answering her question with words so much as with that insatiable curiosity. Rune's movement from the bathroom spurred her to keep things moving.

"Cecilia and I are going to get some air," she announced, putting down her cup and starting past her with a mutter of, "Get your coat."

He stopped, the towel he'd been drying his hair with falling to his neck. "You think that's a good idea?"

Noa pulled her own coat off the rack. "There's plenty of Amaraians in Knighton. We'll be fine. Plus, she'll be with me. What could go wrong?" She flashed him a smile, swinging the fur-lined pleather around her shoulders.

"That's a long list," he mumbled.

Her expression shifted to a glare as Cecilia fiddled with the worn buttons on Noa's spare coat.

"Well, since we'll be here for a while anyway, I figure we can get both of them some new clothes that don't belong to one of us for a change." Noa put her hand on the door handle. "Take care of things while I'm gone. Text me if something explodes."

Before Rune could protest, they were out the door.

"Is all of Miralta like this?" Cecilia asked in awe, staring up at the multi-story buildings cresting the overcast skies—a common sight this time of year. A smile tugged at Cecilia's lips as she dropped her head, appearing to scan the holographic advertisements and marquees flickering in the store-front windows below the apartments. They boasted images and blocky text of various electronics, household goods, and fresh produce.

"No." Noa snorted. "Most of Miralta isn't nearly this busy, but they all sing that same song praising handcrafted over mass-produced, art over science, love over war... All that nonsense." She waved a hand in dismissal as they passed a large fountain in the middle of a neighborhood square. An ornate sculpture of a woman stood in its center, holding a large vase encrusted with mosaic glass shards painted shimmering golds and shining silvers while a never-ending stream of water poured from it. Specially-stamped coins littered the bottom, bearing the emblem of their favored goddess—a crescent moon cupping a star.

The surrounding gray brick paths were worn down by the foot traffic of university students, tourists, and the many residents that had fallen in love with this city. That sentiment was echoed by a group of children weaving past, bringing smiles or eyerolls from some and huffs among those with their noses in their phones and seated on benches.

Noa pulled her out of the way, unable to suppress a smirk at Cecilia's wonderstruck expression.

"Why hasn't anyone stopped us?" Cecilia asked. "Is no one going to ask for our identification?"

"They won't ask," Noa answered. "They have good security, not to mention an arsenal of military and a small collection of university Mages at their disposal, being so close to Corris. The various scan checkpoints to get in and out, the constant surveillance, and the quick emergency response time is usually enough to deter most would-be criminals. That doesn't even cover how this city's divided into sectors like Corris to be quarantined at a moment's notice."

"H-how do you know all that?"

Noa arched a brow. "Thief," she mouthed with a tight-lipped smile before she said, "Remember?"

Her expression faltered as Noa pushed through a storefront's glass door, leading them into a shop where the walls were lined with display models dressed in various outfits from streetwear to dress shirts and slacks. All of the mannequins stood towering above cubed shelves that showed off stacks of alternative-colored versions.

Noa grabbed up a wire-framed bag, spinning to face Cecilia. "Get whatever you like. I'll cover it. My clothes aren't exactly *nice*, so don't feel obligated to copy the style." She paused as Cecilia stared, frozen with the overwhelming options, and Noa eyed the unisex section. "Before you run off, do you know what sizes Glacier wears?"

"Oh, um—yes," Cecilia said, half-distracted. Noa handed her phone over for her to type in all the information, and then they parted ways into opposite ends of the store. Cecilia's skittering across the hexagonal white tiles forced Noa to hold back a grin, shaking her head at how she ran a hand along the edge of the shelves to examine each option before Cecilia spun to admire a rose-pink sundress on display.

Noa trekked down the aisles of cubes, gravitating toward the more muted tones. He didn't seem like the kind of person who wanted to draw attention to himself, so she picked out a few charcoal-gray and black shirts, dark pants, and called an employee over to retrieve a couple of fleece-lined jackets from the stock room for her. She strode back over to Cecilia, where she found a bag next to her filled with modest, dull-colored articles.

"You know they have other colors, right?" Noa said, tapping the bag with her boot. "I kind of pictured you finally wanting to wear something a little brighter."

"I... I do like them, but I don't think the colors suit me." She fidgeted while Noa took her slow walk over to the sundress mannequin, reaching to feel the soft cotton for herself.

"You should at least try it on," Noa said, her hand dropping at the sound of the clerk reapproaching. She grabbed Cecilia's arm, whispering, "You're Elodie, I'm Amelia. We're prospective students and old friends. Follow my lead."

Noa dropped the accent she'd used back at the border this time, irritated that Nyx had been going around feeding her resources the narrative that she was Bellegardian or part-Bellegardian. She couldn't exactly change her ID at this point, so she had to work with what she got. Thankfully, she could spin it to include Cecilia's King's Republic origin with Noa's odd appearance.

"Thank you," Noa said, taking the jackets from the attendant's hands.

"My pleasure," the clerk replied. "Is there anything else you need? Or does your friend need assistance with anything?"

"Oh, no. I'm fin—" Cecilia started.

"Could you get this sundress out for my friend to try? She's not convinced that she'd look incredible in it," Noa said. "Honestly, Elodie, you look great in anything."

Cecilia's jaw dropped, torn between Noa and the clerk.

"What size?" the clerk asked, forcing Cecilia to stammer out a reply before she disappeared back into the storeroom.

Noa suppressed a chuckle at Cecilia's growing panic. "Look, you don't have to get it if you don't like it but indulge yourself a little."

"It's not that—It's just... If I wore anything like that back home, I'd either be ridiculed or shamed for calling too much attention to myself."

"Yeah, well, they need to live a little." Noa noted the clerk reemerging once more, and she leaned in close to Cecilia's ear. "If it were me, and I was forced to attend one of your fancy parties, I'd be sure to wear something red that showed a little thigh."

Cecilia's look of horror made it difficult for Noa not to burst into laughter, composing herself once the clerk signaled for Cecilia to follow her toward the dressing rooms. Noa set down her bag next to the other, absently searching through the shelves as a new customer walked in. His bright green eyes narrowed on Cecilia's disappearing form.

Noa bit down on the edge of her tongue. She dropped her head while he moved onto his own shopping, busying himself by tilting some of the price plaques with a tanned hand. Her vision darted to the other shoppers, who all continued minding their own business. It wasn't until Cecilia came back out that the guy's head snapped up again, so Noa spun around to step between them.

The clerk clapped her hands together. "You look adorable!"

Cecilia reddened, her fingertips tugging at the hem of the dress like it might be too short on her.

"We'll take it," Noa said, rooting Cecilia to the spot. "You can wear it on your first day of classes at the university."

"You're students?" the clerk asked.

"Yes," came Noa's easy reply. "The next enrollment period is in a few weeks. In fact, Elodie's a Mage."

The clerk brightened. "No way! What kind of magic?"

"Illusionary," Noa answered for her, cueing Cecilia's hesitant nod.

"Oh, I'm sure you get asked this all the time, but would—" The clerk hesitated. "Would you be able to show me? I'm planning on attending university as well once I'm done with the remainder of my primary schooling. I want to study magic theory."

"S-sure," Cecilia said. She looked around, heading for a gold, crushed velvet curtain pinned against the threshold. Her fingers dug into the fabric as she closed her eyes. A blackness rippled out from her grip, spreading over it until it became a void. Pinpricks of light began to pulse throughout, the curtain turning into a windowpane pulled straight from the observatory car. Noa's shoulders fell slightly, reimagining herself standing under that dome of glass again, watching the snow-capped mountains in the distance in their futile reach for the stars.

A sudden motion from the corner of Noa's eye reclaimed her attention, where she found the guy from earlier slack-jawed, a shirt slipping from his hands.

Noa cleared her throat. "She'll wear it out."

"No—" Cecilia started, choking back Noa's name. "No, Amelia," she corrected. "You don't have to do that."

"Too late. I insist. It's the least I can do for helping me pick out some clothes for my idiot boyfriend. Maybe one day he'll learn how to pack."

Noa feigned exasperation during checkout, trying not to side-eye the guy prowling through the men's shirt cubes and angling his head in their direction every few seconds. Bags in hand, Noa dragged Cecilia outside. Relief fell over her like rain as they started down the sidewalk, only to be disrupted by a "Wait!"

Noa stiffened, turning on her heel with Cecilia to find *the guy*. There he was, cropped black hair and piercing green eyes—eyes set on Cecilia.

"You're an Illusionist," he breathed, an awestruck grin on his face.

Noa twitched, but Cecilia started to nod, uncertainty slipping into her voice. "Y-yes. I am..."

He pulled back a panel of his brown pleather jacket, where it pooled to an inky black around the edges, mimicking her own rendering of the night sky. Cecilia gasped, and he let it go, dropping his arm back to his side. "I guess that makes two of us," he said with a chuckle.

Well, that was unexpected.

"Are you a student?" Noa asked, struggling to slip back into the role of Amelia with this jarring discovery. Encountering a second Mage in just as many days that happens to share the exact same type of magic left Noa reeling, trying to recover that composure in the face of the extraordinary.

"Was," he said. "I took a break for a semester, but I'm considering going back." He never looked away from Cecilia, despite answering Noa's question. Cecilia blushed, tucking her hair behind an ear with a shy smile.

Gods.

"We're actually planning on signing up during the next enrollment period," Noa said, holding out her hand to him. "I'm Amelia." When he shook it, barely sparing her a glance, she had the overwhelming urge to yank him forward and knee him in the gut. Instead, she had to elbow Cecilia, who'd apparently forgotten how to speak.

"E-Elodie." Her hand shot forward, jostling her bag.

"Elodie," he said, repeating it like he was trying out the way it sounded. "I'm Astor." He slid his phone from his pocket with an awkward chuckle. "I know this is a bit forward of me, but could we trade numbers? I'd love to show you around campus sometime."

"Actually—" Noa cut in with a forced giggle. "She lost her phone on the train ride here. The staff haven't been able to find it, so we're on our way to get her a new one."

Astor finally directed his attention to her, his grin faltering.

"But if you give me your number," Noa started, cautious in her next few words, "she can add it to her new phone in a couple of hours." She retrieved her own phone with a sheepish smile.

"Um, sure," he said, his grin returning with that obtainable end goal in sight. He rattled off his number before diverting back to Cecilia. "You, um... Don't have a boyfriend, do you?"

Noa had to close her eyes for a moment to prevent him from seeing how far they rolled back in her head.

"N-no," Cecilia said. Her face was creeping toward the same shade of pink as her dress.

"Good to know." A smirk.

Noa suppressed a gag. "Well, it was nice meeting you, Astor, but we have to get going." She tugged on Cecilia's arm.

He gave a little wave. "I'll talk to you later, then."

Noa took in a deep breath when she didn't see his reflection following them in the windows they passed, glad to be rid of the awkward third-wheel status, but now dreading her next risky task. She almost lost Cecilia when she turned the corner, pausing at the sound of her jog.

"Wait, where are we going?" Cecilia asked. "I thought the apartment was the other way?"

"To get you a phone since you lost yours, remember?"

"Wait, really?"

Noa turned on her heel, causing Cecilia to stumble at the sudden stop.

She held up a finger. "*Yes*, under the condition that you do not, under any circumstances, try to call home. Understood?"

She paled but quickly nodded. "How did—"

"Rune told me."

Noa pressed forward again, every step heavier in their march toward the intersection with painted brick for the automated taxis. This was the part of secret-keeping she wasn't fond of: giving the 'client' a means of botching everything with access to full-on communication. The problem always came down to it being unavoidable, and Noa having to resort to threats or reiterating the truth: that one wrong text or call could end in destruction.

The light changed, and they crossed to step into a small electronics store. Sleek, black, marbled pedestals and countertops were separated with large digital display ads between each showroom phone.

Noa gestured to the wall of popular models. "Pick one. I'll get us more SIM cards while we're here... But I guess I'll need to grab another phone too, so I'm not playing favorites."

"Any of these?" Cecilia asked, her brows knitting together with a weary look with a hand half-pointed toward the large range of prices.

"Yes. And one for Morgan."

Cecilia stared at her blankly before Noa shook her shopping bag at her. "My boyfriend. Morgan. The idiot who didn't pack anything for our trip, Elle."

"O-oh!" she said, recognition flooding her face. "But all of this seems rather expensive..." She bit her lip as Noa began to fiddle with a slim, black phone boasting about every feature imaginable.

Noa shrugged. "Don't worry so much about it."

"You... you didn't have to get me that dress either," Cecilia mumbled.

She paused, letting the smooth shell of the phone slip a little in her hand. Noa didn't have to do a lot of things. In fact, there were a lot of things Noa didn't *want* to do, which is why she always managed to justify the things she *did* want.

"You should want more," Noa wasn't sure if she was talking more to Cecilia than herself at this point, but the surprise on her companion's face was enough for her to keep going. "You shouldn't have to hide what you really want, or how you really feel. You should be able to be you, not what someone wants you to be."

Noa pulled out her ID and tapped it to the pad next to the phone. A chime rang out on the display, alerting her that her purchase was waiting for her at the checkout desk. "So, you pick one yet?"

Cecilia shifted, rubbing her arm before she pointed at the image of the same model. "Could I get the white one?"

Noa tapped the button and pressed her ID to the pad again for a second chime with a smirk. "Let's go then."

7

MIRALTA ✧ 2704-11-15

GLACIER

The room was an abyss. Glacier's abyss. Where only a shred of light peeked through the blinds, falling over his face and the gray, microfiber sheets of the bed that matched the dim sky. The echoing remnants of Noa claiming to take Cecilia out for the day turned into a countdown, where he watched the small, pale numbers change on the blocky digital clock.

Always moving forward. Never moving back.

He told himself that he should get up—that he'd feel better if he showered or ate a little more. But for *what?* For *whom?* The occasional creak of a floorboard was the sole reminder that he wasn't alone in this place, becoming the one answer he could manage to come up with.

But he was alone.

The guilt that weighed on him now had been a temporary relief, knowing that his uncle was dead. Louis could never demand for him to sit at a council banquet or attend another impromptu party as a powerless puppet with a title for him to wield in Glacier's stead. He would never be able to threaten him in his office or over the dinner table, casually implying how he'd get rid of both Glacier and Cecilia once he was twenty. And Kat would never be able to defend him from it all again. No more outbursts of her hurling a glass past her father's head when he made a snide remark aimed at Glacier. No more foolish decisions to travel to Miralta. No more rebellious hopes of secretly negotiating peace for if either she or Glacier were able to take the throne.

Now there was no one left, and there was no throne. He supposed all good came with an evil, but Kat didn't deserve what happened to her. His fists squeezed the sheets into bunches while a shuddering sigh escaped him. It was the sort of pain he tried to recall feeling when his father had passed, but that blurred, distant memory from all those years ago was hard to disentangle from the bittersweet moments a six-year-old Glacier had cherished.

So, instead, he asked himself what either of them might do in his place as he closed his eyes and allowed himself to drift into the dark.

"Seriously? You're sleeping *now?*"

Glacier's eyes flew open, and he winced at the bright light of the platinum, multi-ringed chandelier overhead. Kat leaned over the back of the sofa where he was lying, quirking an eyebrow at his groggy state. She patted the white, subtly patterned velvet, messing up the decorative royal blue, fringed blanket draped across it.

"Get up, loser. You're supposed to be helping."

He sat up, swinging his feet to the plush rug. The faux fireplace radiated heat at the end of the room. Red and orange flames softly crackled to disrupt the lazy falling of snow opposite it, where a double-wide entrance transitioned the great room into the hallway. Familiar, tall arched windows framed the woods outside—a thick mess of dense, snow-dusted trees.

His father's vacation home. It was a place that sat somewhere kilometers away from the nearest town on the eastern coast of Amarais. A home he considered to be more of a real home than the palace.

But something about it now felt... *off*.

Glacier twisted to take in the built-in shelves behind him, lined with trinkets his father had often picked up and tossed from hand-to-hand while Glacier colored in drawings on a tablet on the floor. The pacing, the pondering—it was all normal among the company he kept, though Glacier couldn't remember a word of what had been said now. All that remained were the gentle words and guiding hands of those snatched away, adding to the ghosts that haunted him.

Sluggishness laced his thoughts as he stood, trying to recall which way Kat had gone. He called, but his voice fell into a rasp he coughed out before trying again. "Kat?"

"In the entry," she sang.

When he reached the end of the hall, sure enough she was balancing on a stepladder and lifting a framed, hand-painted canvas off the wall. It was covered by a sheet, but he still knew what lay underneath: a graying man in his late forties, turned at an angle to show off his preferred side. Pale blue eyes painted with the disturbing accuracy looking cold and distant, matching every image Glacier had ever seen of his grandfather. The late King Elias.

Kat climbed back down and unceremoniously dropped it into a storage bin, brushing her hands off on her leggings.

"What... are you doing?" he asked.

"What do you mean?" She frowned, her brows furrowing. "I'm *packing*. Like we talked about. Remember? Are you okay? Did you hit your head or something?"

"No—" A protest that came with an edge of doubt with his hand jerking up to his temple. "I..."

Why don't I remember that? Glacier closed his eyes, attempting to recall any conversation that ended in a planned packing activity.

Her hand fell onto his shoulder, giving it a quick squeeze. "Hey, don't hurt yourself, okay?"

"Sorry, I... don't remember. Why are we packing, again?"

She took a step back, holding her arms out at her sides. "Anything you don't need sitting out anymore. Pictures, paintings, books, little..." Kat paused, searching around the room before walking over to a side table. She picked up a little metal orb with something rattling around inside. "Er...

little things like whatever the hell this is?" It dropped into the bin with their grandfather's portrait, and she freed another bin from the stack next to it, bringing it to him. "Here."

He took it, biting the inside of his cheek. "Um…"

This wasn't *his* house. These weren't technically his things. They all belonged to his family name, sure, but none of it would become anything he'd inherit. It was all temporary.

"Stop stalling," she said, urging him to move. "Take that back to the office, you can start there."

He started to nod, making his way back to the start of the hall until he took in the tree line beyond the glass. Icy cold crept up his neck, suffocating him like it had when he was trapped under the water with a figure dressed in white overlaying that similar backdrop. He half-turned, scrutinizing her navy sweater.

"Something wrong?" Kat's head tilted at his sudden stop.

"There's not a lake around here, is there?" The second it slipped out he felt his face warm with embarrassment. He already knew the answer, but something wasn't adding up still.

Kat began to shake her head—a slow, deliberate movement that added to his shame since she was giving him that look like he'd lost his mind. "The closest thing around here is the ocean. Why?"

"It doesn't matter," he said, his grip on the bin tightening. "Don't worry about it."

He wished he could say the same for himself. He wasn't even sure why he'd bothered asking, outside of a compulsion to justify how his subconscious created that weird, hallucinogenic… *dream?* Whatever it was, he was right: it didn't matter now. Instead, he had a task to complete, despite not quite understanding why it was necessary.

Glacier set the bin down outside the office's double doors, shoving them open to a familiar space where more afterimages greeted him. The memory of playing over at the far window seat as a child resurfaced, recalling how his father would work at the large, stained wood desk directly in front of him—though he had his doubts of whether it was real wood.

Nevertheless, it was backdropped by a wall of well-kept books, all locked behind layers of glass and broken up by more little trinkets.

With a shaky breath, he collected the bin again and took a seat in that cushioned office chair. It was cool to the touch, sapping his strength after the nonsensical idea that it would somehow be warm from recent use. He swallowed down the lump in his throat as his hands glided over the glassy, polished surface, where the built-in computer hummed to life at his touch. Windows began to flicker and pop up on the screen.

Glacier's eyes drifted over to the picture frame sitting in the corner, acting as a counterweight to the lamp on the other side of the desk, where both he and his father were frozen in a fit of laughter, nearly tipped upside-down in his arms. The memory of their contrasting colors had been softened through a child's rose-colored lens, not quite yet understanding the sadness that always seemed to slip into his father's gaze when he looked at him. He knew now that he was seeing the remnants of a woman that Glacier had never known. A woman that he'd loved, and Glacier had never gotten the chance to.

He gently tipped it face-down against the desk, unable to throw it away, but not willing to look at it again in the midst of Kat's little mission. So, he pulled open desk drawers instead. The first held a tablet and its accessories, revealing a collection of pictures when he turned it on—each frame a photo he didn't recall ever seeing. Glacier slid the drawer back into place, moving onto the second drawer to find a heap of clutter. He jumped to the final drawer, tugging on it to find it stuck.

The office chair rolled back in his wake as his knees hit the floor. Another tug on the handle triggered a small red light. Not stuck. *Locked.* Glacier ripped the second drawer open again, spinning the chair back around to reclaim his seat. Among the junk were square keys, all baring a lightly stamped crescent mark. He flipped one over in his hand, frowning before he dropped it on the desk and dug out the rest.

Screw it.

He pressed the first one to the drawer, watching it pulse red, and threw it into the bin. The next gave him the same angry red light. Bin. Then the next, and the next. Ten, eleven, twelve cards—all *red.* His head whipped back to the last card, scooping it up to feel something on the back skim his fingertips. Glacier started to turn it over, only for it to get ripped from his grasp.

"Hey—" He shot up, holding out his hand toward Kat. "Give it back."

She raised an eyebrow, frowning. "Seriously? Playing with keycards? You're supposed to be packing, not snooping around. If it's locked, it's locked for a reason, Glacier." She shoved it into her pocket.

"Please just give it back so I can clean out this desk and move on."

"Nope."

"Then how am I supposed to pack if you won't let me figure out what to pack, Kat?" He threw his arms out to the rest of the room, finding himself at a loss for what did and didn't matter. His hands dropped to his sides again as Kat rolled her eyes. "Wait... do you know what's in this drawer?"

Her hesitation told him enough.

"Spit it out. What's in there? Why is it locked?"

Kat shook her head. "Not yet. I can't let you open it yet."

"Yet?" He drew back, confused. "What? Why? What's in there that you don't want me to see?"

She rounded the desk to stand face-to-face with him, sighing. "It's something you're not ready for. Glacier, there are... there are things that, once we learn about them, it shifts our entire perspective. It changes everything you've ever known and shapes everything you'll ever come to know. Once it's done, it's done. There's no coming back from it."

Her soft, navy eyes were searching his like she was trying to press something into his thoughts he couldn't understand. The only message he got was her pleading.

"So... I'm just supposed to pretend it doesn't exist?"

She shook her head. "I'm not asking you to do that. I'm just asking that you focus on the task at hand for now."

"You mean cleaning out this office?" He forced back his scoff, an instinctive mask for the helplessness rippling through him. There were details of something he was missing, and he couldn't quite grasp it—something *just* out of his reach in the dark of his thoughts. And something in that dark was coaxing him to pry open that drawer.

Kat gripped his arm, giving him a little encouragement that he wasn't sure what to do with. "Give yourself some time."

Time for what?

Kat's hand fell away with a remorseful smile and a nod, slowly backing up as his mind spiraled down into a strange far-off place that also seemed so close. She turned and left, where he could only watch as she took the thirteenth key with her.

8

MIRALTA ✧ 2704-11-20

Noa wasn't exactly excited about having to inform Nyx that it would probably be for the best to keep Glacier and Cecilia under their care for now. She was nearing a week of not seeing Glacier, outside of the brief moments she'd glimpsed him lying on the bed through the cracked doorway whenever Cecilia would bring him something to eat. Each day had turned into another foolish assumption that he would snap out of it, and they'd all be able to discuss plans of where to relocate the two of them, maybe somewhere in Corris soon. At this rate, she and the twins wouldn't be leaving Knighton in the next week, let alone the next *month*.

Cecilia, however, apparently had found a good enough distraction, considering how she'd been glued to her phone with a stupid, giddy smile on her face and would make sheepish requests to go out just about every day. Noa had to refrain from rolling her eyes at the mere thought of Astor and keep herself from telling her to be back by a certain time like she was her mom.

That left her with the final issue of Crow, but he'd been making himself scarce. She'd caught him in the stairwell, making his way to the complex roof, or passing him on the street when she went out for a change of scenery. Noa was pretty sure he never saw her since he didn't bolt the other direction or glare at her, seeing the latter was his go-to behavior before locking himself in his room at night. And while Noa was fine with this, it was a temporary solution to a long-term problem.

"Did you look over the data I put together yet?" Rune asked from the kitchen as she drummed her fingers against the arm of the chair.

"A little," she said, her voice tethering on a grumble without taking her eyes off Glacier's bedroom door. "Have you murdered your brother yet, so I don't have to?"

He cleared his throat, slipping into a hum. "While I'd be amazed to watch you open that door with your mind, I think you might have better luck getting up and opening it using your hand..."

Her fingers stopped moving, and she slowly turned her head, fixing a glare on him.

"All right," he mumbled, pulling out the frying pan from the drying rack. "Forget I said anything."

With her sights focused back on her target, Rune rattled around to make lunch that would be turned away by at least one of the three people left in this apartment, Noa's mind turned that frying pan into a pot instead. One that was simmering on a hot stove, frothing at the top, seconds before it'd spill over.

The imagined scent of smoke eating away at flannel took its place, along with the sting of holding back tears, and the bite of metal piercing her gloves.

Noa shoved herself up from her seat, hands curling into fists in her storm toward the door. She ripped it open, ignoring Rune's protests in his sudden rush to stop her, but it was too late. The mattress was already being upended, sending Glacier sliding off onto the small gap on the other side before she dropped it again. The simultaneous thump of both it and his body colliding with the floor left her panting—whether it was with rage or exhaustion from bottling up her impatience, she wasn't sure, but whatever it was hadn't been satiated yet.

Glacier scrambled to his knees, wincing with his arms over the bed like it was a makeshift life-preserver. "What the hell is wrong with you?" he demanded.

She gritted her teeth. "Stop. It." The blank, confused expression she received in return further ignited that irritation. "Stop spending all of your time in here *moping.*"

And just like when they were first in that SUV together, a spark lit in his eyes. Sharp and sputtering. Until it hit that dim, final glow, and Noa watched it fizzle out of existence. His hands released their tight grip on the blankets. He was surrendering.

She smacked her palm against the mattress, making him jump. "Wake up, Glacier! She's dead. You have to move on. It won't matter if you spend a week, a month, or a *year* in this damn room because it won't bring her back. *Nothing* will, so stop sitting around feeling sorry for yourself and actually *live.*"

Her words might as well have been a slap with his wide-eyed stare and stunned silence. Something in her had gone cold and unyielding, shifting from needing to tell herself not to pity him before to an embrace of the dark void deep within that no longer cared. Noa spun around, pushing past Rune in the doorway and ignoring his calls on her way out of the apartment.

Noa's trip to Corris had taken all of about fifteen minutes of staring at the suburban homes flitting past the window of the train. Her cheek had rested against the cool metal pole while the slim selection of passengers sat and fiddled with phones or tablets. There'd been a freedom to venturing outside Knighton that she hadn't quite expected, but it'd been welcomed. Embraced. *Needed.*

She replayed stupid little things like meeting Cecilia and Astor over and over again, looping their use of magic in her memories. Something coveted by so many and loathed by the rest. Magic was such a wild and unpredictable thing, fickle in its spread as it'd begun to fizzle out. It's why Noa had been so shocked to find someone with it in Amarais, and while she'd been less surprised by a Mage in Knighton, another *Illusionist* had thrown her off enough.

Some might call a meeting like that fate, though Noa wasn't wholly convinced of such a thing. There'd been people studying in places like Corris for years, trying to puzzle out why something like magic appeared in some but not in others. Cases of children ending up with magic and no presence of Mages being recorded in their family lines left many scholars stumped. Was that fate? Or was it a stroke of luck?

There was usually a good explanation for this sort of coincidence, even if it was one Noa couldn't come up with on her own. It worked much like how Mages flocked to cities like Corris, who were trying to preserve the last of their kind. Like how Glacier and Cecilia had been in the palace when she'd been there because she'd broken into their home in the name of greed, among other things that teetered on the verge of sins.

Noa wandered through the city streets, taking in the bitter-sweet scent of coffee from cafés and haunting melodies of slow ballads trickling from speakers tucked into antique furniture shops. The path diverged into the lush university campus lawn, where Corris's museum sat on the outskirts. Her eyes roamed up and down the monuments outside—statues of past great minds dressed in academic robes and holding symbols of their contributions. A scale, a scroll, a tome...

Inside, the light filtered through stained glass ceilings, falling down to the dark marble slab under her feet. Pillars lined the lobby, guiding her forward, despite the recessed, glowing advertisements for other exhibits down the other halls. Noa wasn't here for any of that.

Instead, her sights were fixed on the carved figure at the end, crafted from white stone. But Noa's mind filled in each spot with color, from the hue of her green eyes, the shade of her dark brown skin, and the tint of her black hair overlapping her dress and pouring onto the floor like ink. A Miraltan in the image of their goddess Seraphine's first Seer.

Noa stopped in front of her, gazing up at the box held in her hands where a circular, cobalt-black, brooch-like object rested inside. It was woven in a twisting, knotted pattern that bore an emerald in its center with smaller fragments fanning outward. A counterpart to the piece she'd been searching for in Amarais.

The Shield of Miralta.

That brief thought of Glacier and his green eye made her bite down on her tongue.

"Beautiful, isn't she?"

Noa swallowed back her venom or whatever had gripped her in favor of awe, letting her shoulders drop in the presence of what could be a depiction of the very first Mage. The woman who lingered beside her was patient in awaiting her answer.

"Yeah," Noa breathed, hating how her eyes dropped to the damn box in her hands. She couldn't tell if it was guilt or remorse that mingled with the loathing, but it didn't really matter to her in the end.

"Not many people visit her anymore," the woman said with a wistful sigh. "Many students and tourists pass through these halls to see her once just to say they've done it and never stand in her presence again."

Noa turned her head toward her, taking in the Corris University emblem on the breast pocket of her blazer. Her own black hair was tied back in a braided bun at the nape of her neck, grazing dark bronze skin. A wise, knowing glimmer shown in her crisp, green eyes.

"You work at the university," Noa said, noting it mainly for herself.

A smile tugged at the corner of her mouth. "I used to work here as a guide during my studies. Now I just haunt the halls when I'm not working. But enough about me... What brings you here?"

Noa hesitated, her eyes drifting back to the statue. "A mess of things, I'm afraid," she mumbled.

The woman laughed—a rich, warm sound. "That's the way life feels most of the time. It doesn't get much better as you get older either. I'm afraid it only gets worse." The words rang as a testament to her experience, even though it was laced with a touch of humor. "I do have to say that I've met quite a few people that've come here with the intention to study, but... you don't strike me as one of them."

Noa stiffened, coming back to her senses as her alter-ego a little too late before she decided to let it all go. "You'd be right." She traded her wonderment for wariness, unable to let go of the heartache that came with her first major defeat back in Amarais.

"Well... I wouldn't let yourself be too discouraged by whatever struggles you're facing." Her watch chirped, and she pressed her hand to it with an apologetic smile. "If you'll excuse me, I have another lecture to attend, but it was wonderful talking to you. May Seraphine guide you, Amelia."

Noa's eyes went wide, her head whipping around as the woman started down a corridor. She hadn't given her that alias—she hadn't given her *any* of her names. This woman hadn't just been milling around here for fun— *no*. She'd known Noa would be here and just how to mess with her because she had to have some sort of inkling as to what she was after. That woman wasn't just some university lecturer, she was a Seer.

CECILIA

"You know, as often as you talk about how beautiful the university campus is, I can still think of at least one thing that's prettier," Astor said with a grin.

Cecilia ducked her head, feeling her face heat while her grip tightened on the bridge railing. Her knees bumped against the iron-gliding in her stare down at the tranquil water below. The serenity of this little cut-through park gave her that private, secluded feeling with the tall oaks lining the sidewalks on either side. The only other people disrupting the space were a couple walking the trail along the edge of the pond, admiring the flowers.

She was beginning to wonder if that's how she and Astor looked in their tours through the nearby campuses of Corris and Knighton's universities or during their strolls to and from the little shops, quaint cafés, and tucked-away diners. She chided herself for having the thought but struggled to keep her heart from fluttering in her chest.

This place was like stepping into a dream that she couldn't imagine waking up from. No snow or officers blocked her path during her excursions, and the officers she did see would smile and tip the short bills of their uniform peaked caps in passing.

"You okay?" Astor asked, breaking her train of thought.

"Oh, yeah," she said. "I was just thinking of home. It just feels... so different here."

"I can't imagine that the Republic would be that different. Then again, I've never really traveled outside of Miralta," he said, leaning against the railing.

"I mean, it does have its similarities," Cecilia quickly added, "but I don't think I've seen people so... happy." As relieved as she was to hear that Astor had about as much of a clue about King's Republic as she did, another pang of sadness hit her. It came with a wish that maybe one day Amarais might be able to end up like this. If she and Glacier could figure out a way to return, and he was somehow able to claim his birthright, that maybe then they could shape it into a place of hope instead of fear.

"Then maybe you could—I don't know," he said with a shrug, "just stay here? You clearly like it here, and you're a Mage. You likely fit in better here than back in the Republic, right?"

Cecilia let the thought sit with her for a moment, imagining all the time she could spend exploring every nook and cranny of Miralta, from the nearby cities to the countryside they had passed on the train ride here. She even considered the eastern coast, thinking of seeing beaches that weren't covered in snow.

But her parents would still be stuck up there, likely believing she was dead.

"As wonderful as that would be, I think I'd miss my family too much. Wouldn't you miss yours?"

"I wouldn't know," he started, somewhat indifferently. "My parents died during one of the conflicts with Amarais when I was maybe two or three. Ended up in an orphanage in Corris as a ward of the state until I turned sixteen and finished my required studies."

"Oh, no, I'm so sorry! I didn't mean—"

"No, it's fine." He shook his head, his voice tinged with brightness again. "It's not like you could have known. Plus, I've had the luxury of doing odd jobs and jumping in and out of higher education since then. It's given me a lot of freedom to do whatever I want, not to mention how it's also given me the chance to experiment with my studies in full practice. So it's not all bad." He grinned. "Want to swap tricks?"

"Oh, I-I know next to nothing about what I can do. I can't hold any of my illusions for very long, and they have to be stationary or something basic, like a color. I have no idea how other illusionists manage to do anything past that." She sighed, thinking of how she'd struggled enough recently with her focus on keeping Glacier's eye blue an entire day. "It just takes so much concentration."

"Don't worry," he reassured her. "I'll show you a thing or two that they don't even teach you at universities." He motioned for her to follow with a push off the bridge's railing.

She ran to catch up to him, her heart pumping with excitement. "Really? I mean, you don't have to. You've been so nice to me already."

"Don't be ridiculous." Astor scoffed. "Mages like us need to stick together, Elodie. There are so few of us around now, and even fewer that share the same talents. It's like we were fated to meet." He stopped along the wrought iron fence lining the sidewalk. "Think about it—how many other Mages have you actually met?"

"Um... just you."

"You're joking—" He guffawed. "Seriously? You must be one of the luckiest Mages around for the first one you meet to match your own abilities. I should keep you around for some of that luck to rub off on me."

The words sent Cecilia's stomach somersaulting. She tugged on her hair as he led the way again, keeping her on her toes.

"Where are we going?" she asked.

"Somewhere quiet where we can practice. I'd prefer not to attract a bunch of gawkers."

He pressed forward, past a few more shops before they crossed the street into a housing district. Cecilia took in the tall townhomes with their potted plants hanging from awnings and windows shutters thrown open against brick in varying, earthy colors. Apartment buildings broke up some of the attached units, though the greenery waned, and the muted colors turned dull and worn. Entrance gates began to hang on their hinges, and Cecilia caught herself almost tripping on loose paving stones at least twice. Her pulse fluttered when she realized that there were only a handful of people left milling around, and when she looked back, the sole shop she could find was a small convenience store on the corner.

"We're here."

Cecilia spun around to find him in front of a townhome with faded, brown brick and flaking burgundy paint on the door. Astor pressed his key to the pad by the door frame as she hesitantly jogged up the steps. It swung open to a narrow hallway with cream-colored walls.

"Is this where you live?" she asked as he ushered her inside.

"Yep," he said, a small hint of pride slipping into his tone. "I rent it with a friend, but he's been spending more time at his girlfriend's apartment for the past couple of months."

He moved a little further inside, where the hall met the stairs and dumped them into the living room. He walked around the back of the couch, past the fraying, overstuffed chair, and pulled up the blinds to reveal the brick of the house behind his.

"I know it's not much..." Astor pushed up his sleeves with a nervous smile. "But I can at least say it's mine, right?" Collecting an abandoned mug on the coffee table, he started for the kitchen.

"I like it," she said, meaning it. "It's nice." And it was. Despite the sparsity of the furniture and its used state, it had more character than anything she'd encountered back home, let alone at the palace. The informality of it all caused her to unwind a little, relieved she didn't have to put on a show like she normally had to.

Astor smirked as he set the mug in the sink. "Thanks." He started back into the living room, taking a seat on the couch, where he patted the empty spot next to him.

She smoothed out her leggings as she joined him, watching while he removed a small box from the shelf under the coffee table. He dropped it on top, tossing the lid over to the side before digging through a collection of markers and pens—some still in their original packaging. Cecilia narrowed her eyes at the strange assortment, trying to think of a decent reason for him to have so many, especially when people stuck to tablets. Outside of

some jobs and school courses, no one really used these sorts of mediums—
well, other than wealthy artists.

"Pens?"

He chuckled. "You caught me. I'm a pen hoarder." Jostling his phone
from his pocket, he set it down and tapped at the screen until it displayed a
document that bore a looping, cursive symbol as a figure among the text.

"What's... that?"

It didn't match any language she'd seen in her private tutoring sessions
like the boxy or circular characters of various subsets of Jinwonese text. She
supposed it could've been from Tabir, who's written language consisted of
elongated, shorter height characters. But this one looked too tall unless it
was flipped on its side. Cecilia tilted her head, trying to imagine it. Perhaps
from one of the regions in Esmedralia?

"It's a rune."

She stiffened, instantly picturing Rune. Rune helping her out of the
SUV in Amarais. Rune talking with her on the train. Rune telling her she
couldn't call her parents but making her tea as a peace offering with kind
words. Cecilia shoved the thoughts away, tugging at the hair pooling over
her shoulder. The fact that she'd even thought of any of that *now* was
absurd, seeing how she was sitting next to someone who'd been even more
attentive.

"So," Astor began, pulling out a pad by where the box had been. He
scratched a few of the pens against it, discarding the ones that didn't
produce any ink. "Before you can use a rune, you have to understand how
they work. Judging by your reaction, I'm going to assume that no one's ever
talked to you much about magic in general, right?"

"No, sorry."

"That's okay. That just means we'll get to spend a little more time
together," he said with a playful nudge.

Her hands ripped away from her hair, falling to her lap like stones,
where she switched to picking at her nails.

Astor started to draw on the pad again, this time recreating the image
on his phone with one fluid motion. "Okay, so... think of magic like blood.
When you cut yourself or donate some of it, it comes back, right? It just

takes some time. Our magic works the same way. It's seemingly infinite, assuming we don't lose it all at once. Make sense?"

Cecilia nodded.

"Now, there are different types of magic that work in different ways. Our magic, creating illusions, is categorized as a sustained magic—meaning that we have to concentrate on it to make sure that it continues to exist. That can take a lot out of someone at first, especially when you're trying to make something large look like something else for an extended period of time. You'd be constantly pouring your magic into it, so you'd exhaust your resources pretty quickly.

"That's where the runes come in. You can use them to bind a portion of magic equal to the illusion you want to sustain, making it look like how you want it to for as long as you want, so long as the rune isn't damaged. Naturally, there are multiple runes, each with their own ways of binding spells. Some are used for animate objects, and others are used for inanimate objects, stuff like that. It can be overwhelming at first, but you'll get the hang of it."

He tapped the one on the paper with the other end of the pen. "This one can make it appear like an item is moving, even though the actual piece is completely stationary." Astor closed his eyes, tracing the pen lines with his index finger. The pad slowly began to ripple, color fanning outward from the rune in waves of blue and seafoam. The ocean-like illusion splashed against the side of the pad it was confined to.

Her eyes widened, catching his devious smile before he scribbled over where the rune had been before the image had consumed it, and the small ocean quickly dissolved.

"Your turn."

Cecilia pushed open the door to the apartment, holding her breath until she found the entire place dim. The kitchen's soft glow licked at the edge of the entry as she crept inside and checked the time: 9:08PM. She guessed that everyone beside Glacier was probably out for a little while.

She bit her lip, digging through her crossbody bag to the eyeliner pen she'd purchased on her way home, remembering how the tap of her fake ID against the payment pad had sent a coursing rush of adrenaline through her veins. Why not test out some of her newfound knowledge on her own?

Stepping down into the sitting area, she dropped to her knees on the rug and pulled up the document Astor had given her on her phone. Her shaky, twisting mark with the eyeliner triggered a frustrated noise before she tried again—better this time, even though it was a little stiff.

Close enough.

She relaxed, closing her eyes as she traced it. Her magic trickled out just as easily as it did when she'd been sitting next to Astor, like it was drawn to the magnetic force of this symbol. When her eyes flew open, she was adrift at sea. The rug was her raft in a small ocean that lapped at the edges of the recessed space. A soft, giddy sound of wonderment escaped her just before the door's lock clicked, and her head snapped up to find Noa talking over her shoulder with Rune.

It wasn't until his eyes went wide that Noa's head whipped around, her face going pale as she skidded to a stop. Rune, on the other hand, pushed past her with an expression of wonderment.

"S-sorry—" Cecilia said, scrubbing at where the rune should've been. It took a second before she found it, disrupting the illusion, and shoved herself off the floor. "I didn't think anyone else would be coming home yet, and I—"

"It's fine," Rune said, biting back a bemused grin as he took a step down into the sitting area.

But Noa rigidly shut the door behind them, bumping into the side table along the wall on the way to her room.

"Where'd you learn that?" Rune asked.

"Huh?" Cecilia said, tearing her gaze away from Noa right before she heard her bedroom door shut. "O-oh, well, um... while Noa and I were out shopping, we met this guy..."

"She mentioned that." He took a seat on the arm of one of the chairs. "He's an Illusionist too, right?"

The irrational feeling of guilt overwhelmed her, and she began to shift her stance, looking away. "Y-yeah. He showed me a few things about binding magic to runes this afternoon, so I thought I'd give it a try."

He chuckled. "Well, it was pretty impressive."

"Noa didn't really seem to think so," she mumbled.

"Ignore her," he whispered, almost conspiratorially. "She can get pretty jumpy sometimes. Unpredictability makes her nervous." His eyes flicked down to the floor. "But if you can do this in just one afternoon, I can only imagine what you might be able to do after an entire class."

Cecilia straightened at that, unable to suppress a shy, prideful smile.

9

MIRALTA ✧ 2704-11-23

GLACIER

Glacier propped himself up on the sofa, staring at the flickering flames of the fireplace display. An apt illustration for his thoughts and how they came and went before he could grasp them. He wasn't quite sure how he'd ended up back here, seeing how he couldn't recall laying down for a nap, let alone that nagging feeling in his gut that he was forgetting something.

But... *what?*

In that now-familiar motion, he swung his legs over the side, catching a glimpse of Kat passing through the archway before she backtracked. "Oh, good," she said. "You're finally awake. Now you can help me finish putting the bins in the attic."

"I... thought we were already finished with all that?" A partial lie, considering how he was simply hoping to escape another day of bizarre packing games. How long had it been, anyway? Two days? A week?

"We will by once you stop sleeping on the job." She waited, drumming her fingers against the entry frame.

So, he stood and followed her, rolling his eyes at her pleased smile. She led the way down the hall, leaving a hummed melody in her wake. The lazy, drifting snow in the overcast light beyond the house warmed him to the core in a way he didn't expect—like that indescribable feeling of coming home. It was short-lived though, disrupted by his sudden stop in front of the office double-doors, where that mystery drawer lurked inside.

"Kat?" he asked, jogging to catch up. "When are you going to give me the key back?"

She pressed her lips into a thin line. "Later. Now grab a container." She hoisted one up and started up the pulled-down steps, each one complaining under her weight.

Glacier looked between her and the small remaining stack, unable to hold back a frustrated sigh as he hoisted one of them up. The sound of subtle shifting and clinking of trinkets made him take each step with care until he reached the top to gently drop it on top of Kat's haul.

"Can I have it once we're done with all of this?" he asked.

"No. You'll have to wait."

"Wait for what? I don't understand—"

"Because I told you that you're not ready," she said, jogging back down the steps.

He threw back his head with a groan. "*Kat,* why are we even doing this? What's the point?" Hurrying down after her, he ended up with the second-to-last container shoved into his hands, much lighter than he'd expected.

"Because," she said, grabbing the last one and moving past him, "it's time for you to stop holding yourself back."

He furrowed his brows, spinning on his heel to call up, "That doesn't make any sense."

"Glacier..."

He followed her, dumping his box again.

"Look around," she said, throwing her arms wide. "All of these things are distractions and memories that you've been using to stop yourself from actually moving forward. Don't you think it's time to push it all side and actually *do* something? You shouldn't be sitting around, wasting your life away like Louis wanted."

Glacier bit down on the inside of his cheek and surveyed the sea of boxes he supposed he had a hand in packing and putting away. A shudder-ing, heart-wrenching pang of sadness gripped him, though he wasn't quite sure why.

"You have to move on, Glacier," she said quietly. "Even when it feels like you can't possibly take another step, you have to. You're stronger than you realize—stronger than anyone's ever given you credit for. You just need to find that strength and refuse to back down."

Glacier's eyes opened to the pattering of rain against the windows, accompanied by the soft rolling of distant thunder. His vision blurred with those dreamt-up words echoing through his thoughts.

She shouldn't be stuck in his dreams. She shouldn't be *dead*. Out of the two of them, she was the strong one—the one with a plan, the one that could make people like her without even trying. Glacier *wasn't*. He wasn't his father's son. He didn't deserve to be here when Kat had been the better fit—closer to his father's likeness than he'd ever be. But he already knew that she'd want him to pick up what she'd started—what his father had started, even if he couldn't finish it.

The thunder rumbled again, commanding him to move. His head spun as he sat up, blinking his vision into clarity to take in the rain taking the place of snow, stone and brick in the place of marble, and iron and steel instead of platinum.

You're stronger than you realize.

There was only one way to find out if she was right.

NOA

"Are you serious?" came Crow's sharp reply. "We're seriously not going to discuss what we're doing next? We're just going to sit around and *wait* until *that one* pulls himself together?" He half-heartedly pointed toward Glaci-er's room.

Noa clenched her jaw as Rune stood.

"Quiet," came his short, flat response. It was enough to tip Crow's mouth down in an irritated frown.

Her own voice dropped low. "We're not discussing what we're doing next just in case either of them might overhear. The last thing we need is one of these two accidentally leaking information."

"Then why the hell are we still here, Noa? I thought Nyx said she'd move them somewhere else if we needed her to?"

It was her turn to shoot up from her seat, getting up in his personal space. "Because they're not stable," she ground out. "We're dropping them off in what they consider to be enemy territory, and *you* just want us to leave them here with some cash and a 'good luck out there, kids.' Not only is that stupid, it's unbelievably reckless."

"Not to derail this conversation," Rune cut in, "but since you didn't seem to want to listen to me when you stormed out the other day, I also want to reiterate that you're being too hard on Glacier."

Her eyes widened. *The audacity.*

"So," he continued, "I find it a little funny that you're trying to defend staying here to help them adjust when you—quite literally—threw him out of a bed."

"Excuse me, but when exactly did I ask for your opinion?"

"You didn't, but you know I rarely fight you on things, and I'm also aware that you actually value my opinion, based on the last few times I've spoken up." His face darkened with concern. "Both of them have just lost everything. Their homes, their families—all of it. Not to mention that, despite Glacier being nineteen, he has the weight of a country resting on his shoulders, whether they think he's dead or not. He's grieving. He needs time."

"And?" Noa snapped, jabbing a thumb at her own chest. "Are you forgetting who you're talking to? Don't you remember that I've lost someone too? I don't have the luxury to lay around and feel sorry for myself for a week or more—and if you want to talk about responsibilities, I want you to think about exactly what the hell we're doing here right now."

That spark of anger reflected back in his gaze added weight to his next words, "I want you to seriously consider the difference between someone who's been given the tools to fight back, versus those of someone who's been pushed down whenever they try to stand, Noa."

The three stood silent, locked in a triangular stand-off, waiting for the next move. Crow appeared to be willing to take the next shot, his mouth opening to speak until Noa made a cutting motion to stop him. She tilted her head to the side, eyes unfocusing for a moment while she listened to the slight change of ambient noises. The shuddering of pipes within the unit.

"What?" Crow hissed, his irritation shifting into panic in his wide-eyed stare toward the front door. Rune's body tensed, his focus following his brother's with the same alarm.

"The apartment's water is running," she whispered.

"I'm sorry, what?" Crow demanded. "You interrupted me for *that?*"

"The shower's on, dumbass," she said in a near-growl. "That means that he's finally out of bed, which means that we're closer to leaving."

GLACIER

When Glacier emerged from his room for the first time since they'd been in the apartment, he found Rune sitting on the couch, leaning over his phone and a tablet resting on the coffee table. For a moment, relief coursed through him, glad the sole seemingly reasonable individual would be the one to witness his bravery. That is, until he glimpsed Noa in the kitchen with her back against the island like she was enjoying the view of the next building through the window above the sink.

She didn't move or dare look at him, assuming she knew he was there. Glacier tugged on his hoodie sleeves, biting his lip with an uncertain step backwards.

"I see you're finally up."

He winced, coming to terms with getting caught by Noa, whose head was half-turned to him now.

"Um," he started. "Where's Cecilia?"

"Out. She's been making new friends and wandering around Knighton for the past week or so."

The stab of jealousy that came with those words ebbed into guilt, his heart sinking with the selfish idea that she'd somehow stick around and wait for him to finally drag himself out of bed. It wasn't like she needed him to survive anymore, much like how he didn't have to rely on her to hide himself in plain sight.

"I'd assume she'll be back soon," Noa said, pushing off the counter and striding across the apartment to one of the rooms.

He fidgeted with his hoodie zipper, taking a few cautious steps to sit in the closest chair, praying Noa was right about Cecilia's return. Interacting with a bunch of strangers now had somehow turned into a far more daunting task without anything to discuss or bargain. But the silence that carried on somehow felt even worse, leaving him bouncing his leg as he watched Rune scroll through the tablet.

He couldn't take it anymore. "What's that?"

Rune's head jerked up like he'd been ripped from a trance. "Oh, sorry..." he said, running a hand through his hair. "I didn't realize you'd gotten up." His eyes flicked back to the displays. "It's just a lot of data... Discussion threads Nyx passed off to us, mostly. She's busy with other things anyway."

Before Glacier could ask anything else, Noa returned with a thin, black rectangular object. A brand-new phone. "Here," she said, jerking her arm a little when he didn't reach for it.

"That's not min—"

"It is now. Take it."

So he did, hesitantly turning it over in his palm. "I don't understand..."

"Well, first, I bought you clothes so you wouldn't have to wear Rune's or Crow's—you're welcome for that, but the way—and second, I got you a phone because it would be wildly unfair to get Cecilia one and not you."

"Thank... you?"

"Better," she said with a tight-lipped smile. "Now, the rules are that you can't call anyone from Amarais. It's off-limits. If you let *anyone* find out that you're alive, it's not only a huge risk to them, but a risk to yourself. Outside of that, it would be weird if you didn't have a phone."

Glacier let out a short, morbid laugh. "Wouldn't the people that bombed the palace realize they were missing a body? I don't see why it matters when they already know."

"Because they don't want people to know that someone got away," she said. "Especially not someone who has every right to take all the power back. They haven't announced that you're alive, and they won't. Trust me." She gestured to the air. "If anything, they're probably cracking open the vault and splitting the entire treasury, which isn't exactly how I hoped this would work out."

Glacier started blankly at the phone in his hand. "They can't."

"Sorry, what?" she asked with a slight snort. "What do you mean they can't? Glacier, look, they more than likely have someone who can crack a—"

"You can't break into that vault." He sighed, setting the phone down on the coffee table and closing his eyes. "Because there are—*were*—only three keys and no fail-safe. It's a biometric lock. It's keyed to a person, and the individual that matches has to be alive."

"You've got to be kidding me..." Noa whispered, slowly dropping into the couch. "Well... That's good news and bad news. The good news is that the vault will still be locked, right?"

He closed his eyes again, slowly nodding, bracing himself for her next statement.

"The bad news... is that there's only one key left, isn't there?"

Glacier forced out a breath, putting his head into his hands. The walls of the apartment might as well have been folding in on him, crumbling with the rest of the world. His deal with Noa was quickly falling apart. He couldn't get her what she asked for.

"I'm sorry," he said, his voice muffled while he tried not to lose the remainder of his composure.

"Don't be."

Glacier's head snapped up to find Rune's eyes filled with empathy. "This is beyond your control. None of us could've seen this coming. You can't blame yourself."

I could've told her not to go, Glacier thought bitterly. But that would've ended up with them both dead in the end, and likely Cecilia too. He slumped back in his chair, sliding down into his seat as Noa rose from hers.

"Where are you going?" Rune asked, the two of them watching her pull her coat off the rack.

"Out," she replied, sliding it on and pulling the door open. "I need to think."

10

MIRALTA ✦ 2704-11-23

CECILIA

Astor had sprung for an automated taxi to take Cecilia to meet his friends, showing his sheer determination to win out against the rain. But when she climbed inside and he put in their destination, her chest knotted at the view of the heavy droplets sliding down the windows. The pattering dropped her right back into her and Glacier's room again.

Guilt tugged at her heart as she thought of how he'd barely eaten anything again before she left. Should she be back there with him instead? The idea fell away as the car pulled away from the curb, but the hollowness in the pit of her stomach didn't subside—at least, not until they began to ease into the business sectors. Confusion overtook her, and she turned to gauge Astor's reaction when the businesses began to intermingle with tall, blocky buildings that looked like warehouses and old former factories. He was leaning back in his seat, arm resting on the console without a care in the world.

"Where are we going, exactly?" she asked.

"An old warehouse," he said, leaving her grateful for the confidence in his voice to counteract her unease. "A few of us hang out there during our free time. One of my friends has a father who was planning on selling the space, so he asked if he could rent it out from him instead." He gave a half-shrug. "We sort of have a side-thing going."

"Like starting up your own business?"

"Something like that." The slight hesitation made her weary, though she tried to keep her expression optimistic.

The car came to a stop along the sidewalk outside a narrow street, lined with buildings stacked high with cinder blocks or brick. She was slow to tug up her hood and climb out upon noticing the absence of anyone around. It might as well have been a ghost town, which made it hard to chalk up her shiver to the rain in her jog behind him. Once they were under the alleyway's fire escape, the taxi gave a small orange flash, beeped, and sped off in the call of another passenger.

Astor fiddled with his keys for a moment before a brief green light popped on, and he held the door open for her. Two stories up, strung along the catwalks, were a multitude of cables and light bulbs hung for a warm, moodier glow that didn't fully illuminate the corners. Old, worn office units were half-collapsed along some of the walls while others were set up and filled with various electronic equipment or bins.

The slam of the door falling back into its frame behind her made her jump as Astor called out, "Lark, you here?"

She fidgeted with her jacket zipper as they drew closer to the brighter portion semi-walled off near the back, where it opened into a lounge. A kitchenette sat along the far wall with nothing more than small appliances, a beat-up refrigerator, and a folding table to use for a countertop. Outside of that, there was a cluster of mismatching furniture, all angled toward a couple of large screens—all of them captioned and quartered off with various feeds.

"Well, well..." came another man's voice as he started into view. His eyes were closer to the shade of sunlit grass, rather than Astor's forest hue, lit with a mischievous curiosity that matched his grin. "Why am I not surprised you've been ignoring us for a girl?"

Cecilia felt a flush creep up her neck, biting her lip as she pushed back her hood. His surprise lasted for about a second, at most, before his eyes narrowed. All earlier amusement slipped away in an instant.

"Lark, this is Elodie," Astor said, undaunted by his reaction as he took her arm and brought her forward to stand next to him. "She's a Republican planning to enroll at one of Corris's universities. She's also an Illusionist."

At this point, Cecilia wasn't sure if the tightness in her abdomen was from Lark's unwavering uncertainty or from Astor's still-firm grip on her arm when he could've let go by now. Since her arrival, she couldn't recall a single time in which someone looked at her like *that*—like she was the enemy. It wasn't until Astor had mentioned her magic that his expression eased, but that easy-going nature didn't return.

"Elle," Astor continued, letting go in favor of slipping his arm around her waist and guiding her toward the couch. "Why don't you have a seat while I talk to Lark for a sec?"

After giving him an uncertain smile and slight nod, he flashed her a quick grin and led his friend away behind a divider. Their disappearance was followed by the loud sound of a TV or tablet somewhere that made a muffled noise, accompanied by raucous laughter from maybe three or four people. They quieted at Lark's barking order, but whatever feed they'd been listening to was cranked up a little.

Cecilia toyed with her sleeves, busying herself with whatever was captioned on the TV screens until she came across one that looked... *off*. She squinted, sinking down to the couch as she tried to match up the background and watermarked logo with one of the programs Rune or Crow had been watching in the mornings.

A *private* feed?

She scooted forward, soaking in the scrolling ticker overlapping the display of snow-covered structures. They were talking about *Amarais*.

"TV, mute."

Cecilia bolted upright in her seat, eyes wide as Astor pushed past the group. "Everyone, this is Elodie."

Lark was still frowning, but he said nothing as Astor re-introduced him. "Elodie, this is Lark." He moved onto the next young man with dark skin and black hair that offset his green eyes, who gave a friendlier smile and a small wave before he took his seat. "Everest, Bryn—" Astor motioned to the slightly bigger of the two who remained with bronzed skin and black hair pulled back in a small bun. "And his younger brother, Reed." The final member of the five timidly waved and took a seat with the others, leaving Lark and Astor standing.

"Astor says you're another Illusionist, right?" Everest asked, leaning forward with interest. "That's pretty amazing."

She forced out a quiet, nervous laugh. "I'm afraid that I'm not very good... I'm still learning, which is why I'm hoping to study in Corris."

"Astor's pretty good from what I've seen though," Bryn said with a sly smirk. "Has he been showing you anything? Or is he keeping all his secrets to himself?"

Astor rolled his eyes and made his way over to drop onto the couch next to Cecilia, throwing an arm back over her seat. "As a matter of fact, I've been teaching her quite a *few* tricks. Thank you very much. And I'd say she's pretty quick to pick things up, so don't let her modesty fool you."

Lark began to prowl the perimeter with his arms folded over his chest. "You're fortunate not to be an Amaraian citizen right now, considering all that's going on up there. But seeing how you're a Mage, I don't think you'd last long there anyway."

"Well, there's a reason I've been calling her my good luck charm," Astor chimed in.

She tugged on her hair, trying to hide any blush that might've been coloring her face. "I-I wouldn't go that far. I don't think I'm nearly as lucky as you think, but... I also haven't really been paying too much attention to what's been going on. I just know there was a rebellion..."

It wasn't a complete lie, seeing how the Miraltan news feeds didn't cover much to begin with and recently stopped discussing it altogether. Crow usually rolled his eyes or grumbled and left once the short mention of Amarais was over. Rune often sighed whenever the newscast ended— whether it was out of lack of information or relief, she couldn't tell— and shut it off. It was as if they were holding a collective breath, waiting for something to slip about Glacier still being alive or thieves reported leaving the scene.

But *now*... Now she felt like she should've been paying a little more attention whenever it'd been on since she'd ignored all the details in favor of texting Astor or worrying over Glacier. Now she was fretting over what any of these people knew that she didn't.

Lark sighed. "It seems that they've decided to actively seek out any Mages within their borders. The new regime—or whatever the hell you want to call it—supposedly wants to make examples of them and their sympathizers."

"I mean, they haven't found any so far," Everest said with a snort. "So I'd say they're doing a pretty bad job of it."

"True," Lark continued. "But the bigger issue is that *we* shouldn't have been sending anyone up there in the first place. They'll be the first ones to get turned in. A godsdamned costly mistake..."

"What do you mean 'sending anyone up there?'" Cecilia asked, the words coming out slower than she liked.

Lark opened his mouth, about to speak until Astor's voice cut in, "We," —he paused for a moment, frowning before he started again— "by *we*, I mean certain factions within Miralta that we know of, have an unofficially sanctioned group of Mages that, against their better judgment, sneak across the border into Amarais."

Cecilia's eyes widened in horror. "What? *Why?*"

"It was a program that a handful of Miraltan Mages put together some-time before any of us were born," Bryn said, shaking his head. "I'm not sure when, but it was created to attempt to reach out to any Amaraian Mages that have no way of accessing anything to improve or hone their skills. So, they would hide in Amaraian homes and take room and board in exchange for teaching some random Mage. Reed and I had an uncle who did it. He was convinced he would help. The entire organization believed if they could give them more power—more knowledge in how to use what they had—that they could somehow use it to fight back against their oppressors or something like that, but... he never came back home."

Her chest tightened as his gaze drifted down to the coffee table.

"Not like Katerina Caelius would've actually done anything to fix any of it," he added, bitterness seeping into his tone. "None of those dictators would have. It's almost a blessing that entire family is finally gone. As long as they had all the power and all the money they could ever want—why bother? Why bother trying to change things? Her whole song and dance was likely just a huge ploy to make us think that she was on our side so we'd help support her in her attempt to take over."

She inwardly flinched at the comment, squeezing her hands together in her lap.

"She wasn't even actually supposed to take over, right?" Reed asked. "Didn't the last Amaraian King... Cyrus, was it? Didn't he have a son? Wouldn't that put him as the front-runner?"

"A *bastard son*," Lark said with a snort. "You can't honestly think that they'd allow a half-Amaraian prince to take over. I bet King Regent Louis —or whatever the hell his title—had to have been doing his damnedest to sweep him under the rug for his pretty princess of a daughter to take his place. Gods only know he probably wanted everyone to forget his damn brother existed."

"He was probably the closest to making peace though," Everest said. "You have to give the man credit for that."

"But he didn't." Lark narrowed his eyes at him. "He was assassinated. Probably by one of his own damn council members. They're all snakes. Amaraians can't be trusted, and it's as simple as that." He waved a dismissive hand. "Sure, we had a brief moment of hope, what? Fifteen-or-so years ago? It's over now. The man's dead, and it just proves that they're all corrupt. They'll do whatever it takes to keep things the way they are, which is why we were foolish enough to send any Mages *at all*."

The room fell silent for a moment before Bryn let out a small, soft snicker. "You know... There was a rumor that Cyrus's son was half-Miraltan, right?"

Lark scoffed. "It's a *rumor*, Bryn. If it were true, they would've killed him the moment Cyrus dropped dead. There's no way in hell that he would've made it this long. Not to mention that, despite it all, he'd still be a damn Caelius. They're all corrupt—it's just a matter of *how* corrupt they are."

Cecilia swallowed, looking down at the floor. Her stomach twisted at the pure hatred toward Kat and Glacier. They were *wrong*. Kat would've found a way to fix things if she had a chance, and Glacier wasn't like his uncle or grandfather—he wasn't corrupt. He was kind, empathetic, and eager to help. She'd never seen him behave selfish and greedy like she had seen Louis or his council act.

Everest held out his hands in a placating gesture. "That's why we're going to try to stop anyone else from going, right? Isn't that the point of why we're set up here?" He motioned to the room. "I'm sorry if all of this talk is making you uncomfortable, Elodie. There's just a lot of bad blood between Amarais and Miralta."

"So...um..." she began, "you're trying to convince people not to go?"

"Correct," Lark said, giving her a look of approval. "We're discouraging Mages from continuing to cross the border to Amarais. We've been protesting it for a few years, trying to sabotage equipment, along with impeding communications and travel itineraries. We *need* to stop allowing people to go. It's a huge waste of resources and Mage lives. There aren't that many left to begin with, so we're practically just throwing away whoever's left."

She set her eyes on Astor, who pulled his gaze away from Lark's to meet hers. The words that followed were flat and unempathetic, driving a knife straight through her: "Nothing good comes from Amarais."

Cecilia's heart cracked in half and began crumbling like the glass scattering at her feet back at the palace. *He doesn't know*, she tried to tell herself. He was staring at Elodie from King's Republic. Not Cecilia—not the girl from Amarais who hadn't stepped foot outside of her homeland until over a week ago.

Everest cleared his throat, seemingly catching onto her discomfort and changing the topic to something else she couldn't hear over the echoing memory of glass shifting beneath her. Astor gave her a nudge here and there as the subjects changed, which she tried to respond with a smile or a nod that trailed off after a moment or two. Once an hour had passed, he stood and made an excuse for them to leave.

The taxi ride back to Astor's place was met with an uncomfortable silence. How long could she keep up this façade? How long could she lie to him as friends, let alone if there was the possibility that there might be something more between them? He was the only other Mage she'd ever known—a kindhearted individual that'd been helping her understand her magic. She *belonged* somewhere whenever she spent time with him, but it was never as Cecilia.

When the car came to a stop and Astor climbed out, the rain and overcast skies had given way to a dull blue, though it hadn't taken her dreary feeling with it.

Once they were inside the entry, he shut the door with a look of concern. "You okay?"

"Ye—" She stopped herself, slowly shaking her head. "No."

"Look, I'm sorry if they kind of threw everything at you. I—" He bit his lip. "I didn't want to dump it *all* on you at once, but that's what I've been doing outside of odd jobs. It's part of our own rebellion effort. They originally wanted me to go with them—the Mages who formed the group. I thought it was a good idea until I met Bryn and Reed."

He started a little further inside, slumping into a chair. "They told me about their uncle. He was the only Mage in their entire traceable family line. They would get communications maybe every month or so if it was safe, up until one month when they just didn't come. Gone. Just like that."

Cecilia hovered by the couch before she sat down, letting him continue as he shifted and stared at the floor with a shake of his head. "I feel like no matter what Miralta tries to do, Amarais won't ever change. We need to use what we have to continue to make Miralta better. I feel like that's why we met, so you and I can work together to help protect them from making a terrible mistake. Amaraians just bring trouble with them."

"Is..." she started, her voice a near-whisper. "Is that how you feel about me?"

"What are you talking about?" His forehead creased. "No, no—just because you *look* Amaraian doesn't mean that—"

"Astor, I'm—" She swallowed. "I'm not from the Republic. I... I'm from Amarais." Cecilia closed her eyes, fighting the urge to wave it all off as a joke. She couldn't keep riding this lie anymore.

"What?" he asked, a range of emotions slipping through with an added edge to his voice. To his credit, he didn't shout. "What do you mean you're from Amarais, Elodie? Have- have you been lying to me this entire time?"

When she opened her eyes again, she saw his wounded expression twist into disgust. He shot up, and she scrambled up from her seat. "I-I—"

"I took you there under the impression that you were exactly who you said you were. Under the idea that—" He snapped his mouth shut, running a hand over his face. "Who are you? Is Elodie even your real name? I don't recall that being an Amaraian name."

She took a step back in some poor attempt to escape, but he moved closer. The hot sting of tears threatened to spill as she shrank away from him—as if making herself smaller would help her like it did whenever Louis flew into a fit of rage. "It's Cecilia," she said quietly. "My real name is Cecilia. I-I didn't want to betray your trust, but I escaped from Amarais. And I really did—*do* want to learn magic, but—" Her voice shook, mentally fumbling for something close enough to the real explanation. "Astor, I'm sorry."

He started to shake his head in disbelief, turning away. "You should go."

Her breath was forced out of her lungs, unable to say anything to fix the trust she'd broken. She was too stunned to move either, wishing she could take it all back.

"I need time," he said with a small bite to his tone after another agonizing minute. "Leave."

It was a command, sharp and cold. Cecilia's vision wobbled, but she turned and left. It'd taken more than enough effort not to run outside. Warm tears began to slip down her cheeks as she pulled the door behind her. She'd been so eager to hurry out into the dreary cover of the afternoon that she was let down by the fact that there was no more rain left to hide her misery.

✧

Cecilia stammered out an apology to the second person she'd accidentally bumped shoulders with on her way into one of the city squares again, dazed and finding distractions in every little interaction among the strangers around her.

A hug.

A laugh.

A hand slipping into another hand.

She came to a stop in front of a fountain—one that she remembered passing when Noa had taken her out that first time. When they'd met Astor.

Her chest tightened as she stared down at the little shards of colored glass warped through the water's ripples. She wanted to go home. She wanted to see her family and be wrapped in her parents' warm embrace again. She wanted her life back because, while it'd been a hopeless prison, at least it hadn't also felt so horribly lonely. The lie of being a picture-perfect Amaraian was a far easier narrative to navigate than pretending to fill the shoes of someone she wanted to be.

She'd found someone just like her.

"Elodie?"

Cecilia's head whipped around, blinking away her blurry vision to find Rune. Embarrassment washed over her as she swiped at her face. "Sorry, I—"

"Are you all right?"

Another sob almost escaped when she found genuine concern in his, barely managing to hold it back as he set down his shopping back on the bench beside them.

He reached into his jacket pocket and retrieved a small cloth. "Here."

Sniffing, she paused before she took it and fidgeted with the edges instead of actually using it right away. "Thank you," she whispered. "I-I'm fine, really." She forced herself back into that familiar role of Amaraian Cecilia again. All brave faces and fake smiles.

But his expression didn't change. There wasn't any inkling of relief that she'd convinced him she'd be fine. She even half-expected him to be upset like Astor had, triggering another stray tear that made her press the cloth to her face in a poor attempt to hide it. "Wh-what are you doing out here?"

He shifted his footing, glancing over at the bag. "Well, I needed some air and decided to pick up a few things. Then I found a very distressed young woman crying and thought she could use a little company."

She stiffened, unsure what to make of his slight, sympathetic smirk.

"It's okay if you don't want to talk, but it might make you feel better. You're under a lot of stress right now, and it's not exactly easy to handle all by yourself."

Her mouth wobbled, and she had to duck her head to keep him from seeing her cry again.

"Hey... How about you and I take a walk around the park a couple blocks down? Maybe it'll help clear your head a little, and then we'll go back home, okay? You don't have to if you don't want to, but I think it would help. We don't even have to talk if you don't want that either."

She squeezed the handkerchief. Part of her wanted to go back to the apartment and hide under the covers next to Glacier. The other part of her eagerly wanted to walk with him because it would be so much better than being alone, but that was her selfishness talking.

"Come on," he said, taking a step back so they could walk side-by-side. "Let's get a move on before it decides to rain again."

So, Cecilia walked with him. He shoved a hand in his pocket while his bag swung back and forth in the other, keeping his eyes straight ahead rather than focusing on her like Astor would've. Her shoulders fell, and she set her own sights on the destination ahead.

Soon they turned off into the small park where they ducked under wisteria trees and wound through the gravel path, surrounded by flowers in shades of reds and oranges. A girl sat in the middle of one of the clearings with a tablet and stylus, sketching out a landscape with abstract colors. At first, she was awed by it, but then her thought of it soured when it was replaced by Astor's collection of pens and synthetic paper.

"Um..." she started, biting the inside of her cheek. "Rune?"

"Hm?"

"Have you ever... unintentionally hurt someone you love?" Maybe love was too strong of a word for this situation, but it was the closest thing to say without diving into too much personal detail.

He hummed in contemplation. "Are we talking romantically, or...?"

She cringed, looking down and half-hugging herself.

"I honestly can't say that I have," he said. "But I don't think I actually ever loved anyone I was romantically involved with before. You'd probably get a better answer from my brother, but" —he chuckled— "I don't see that happening, considering he's being a huge pain in the ass."

Her eyebrows shot up. "You're not serious?"

A smile danced across his face. "I know that's hard to believe under the current circumstances."

"Either you're a really good liar..." she said, squinting at him, "or whoever he's dating must be really special."

"I think she's a special case, for sure..." His expression turned wistful. "But I can say that if the guy you're thinking about really loves you, and he knows you didn't mean to hurt him, he'll forgive you. We all make mistakes, and what matters is how we grow from them to make ourselves better."

She hoped he was right, but when her thoughts drifted to Glacier, she realized that there was no way that she could ever mention him to Astor. That brought a different kind of turmoil that she would have to deal with at some point in the future. At least for now, she could agree with Rune, waiting for a chance that Astor would let her make it up to him.

"You good?" Rune asked.

"Yeah..." She nodded. "Yeah, you're right."

"Is this the Mage you've been hanging out with?"

She winced and began to tug on her hair. "Is it that obvious?"

He gave her a small smile, shaking his head. "It just makes sense. You always seem so happy to go out and see him. I'm sure he'll come to his senses and realize just how lucky he is to have you around."

Her hand dropped to her side again, feeling the corner of her mouth tick up in a smile as they turned off the path, making their way home.

11

MIRALTA ✧ 2704-11-24

GLACIER

It was 3:00AM when Glacier slipped out of his room to find the tablet sitting on the coffee table. His hands automatically picked it up, his mind ready to dig into anything that wasn't the hell of being trapped inside his head. He glanced toward the doors to find all of them shut. For once, he was left in comfortable silence, free of the suffocating feeling that came with so many people roaming in and out of the apartment.

His mind drifted to Cecilia as he glimpsed his own dark reflection in the tablet's glass surface, causing him to close his eyes. He stayed quiet when she came last night, her somber, downcast look changing to excitement upon noticing him outside their room. He should have asked her how she was doing. He should have asked if she was okay.

But he hadn't. Again.

He let out a slow, calming breath. Kat would know what to do—what to *say*—to reassure them that they would make it through this. But she wasn't here now. He only had the Kat that resided in his dreams, not the real one. The real one wasn't coming back, no matter how hard he wished it.

The display turned on with the click of a button, threads of posts filling the screen. He settled into the couch, flipping through pages upon pages of usernames, rules, badges, titles, profiles—all of it a heaping mess for him to drown in. So he did, gladly. The only part that surprised him was the number of people communicating in these threads. Thousands upon thousands of users posting, with at least half of that number stuck in a registration queue.

There's no way rebels were the ones that attacked the night we left, he thought, his brows furrowing as he continued to scroll. Everything there pointed toward the opposite. A unanimous decision to hold action while Kat was away, their prime candidate for the new regent. It was all the drive he needed to work into the early hours of the morning, compiling notes until he drifted off with the sunrise.

Glacier grimaced when light shined into his eyes. He held up an arm to shield himself from the trickling stream through the curtains before jolting upright.

He'd fallen asleep on the couch.

His hands began to feel around for the tablet that he *swore* had been on his chest after he'd laid down for a second. Frantically digging through the cushions, he paused, changing course with the horrible realization that it might've slid off onto the rug.

That was when he caught a glimpse of someone sitting in the armchair behind him with a coffee cup in one hand and a tablet in the other. Glacier jumped, throwing a hand to his heart before collapsing back into his prone position on the couch. He sighed and dropped his other arm over his eyes —partially to block the sun, but mostly to try to hide his embarrassment. "How long have you been there?" he mumbled.

"About half an hour," came Rune's nonchalant reply.

The sound of the tablet gliding against the coffee table was enough for him to peek at it.

"And how long have you been out here reading rebel propaganda and plots?"

Glacier's uncovered eye flicked over to witness him sitting back and sipping his coffee.

"You caught me. Happy?" he said, sitting up again. "I didn't want to sleep, and I figured that I might as well be doing something with my time."

"Find anything?"

Glacier paused, not quite sure if he heard him right. "You're... not upset?"

"I'd only be upset if you had managed to *delete* all of the data on the tablet. From the time I spent looking through it this morning, that clearly doesn't seem to be the case." He set down his cup, retrieving it to hold it up with an expectant, "Well?"

Glacier hesitated before he reached into his pocket for his phone, fishing it out and pulling up his notes to hand over to him. Rune took it, not wasting any time to scroll through.

"I don't know that it's much to go off of," Glacier said. "It's a lot of assumptions, and I doubt it's all that reliable since I haven't exactly gotten much sleep lately—"

"No," Rune said. "No, this is actually pretty good... I've been mainly reading through the actual contents, but you went straight for the users and moved from there. It's a different kind of data, but we can use this." He gave him a nod of approval. "Good job."

It took Glacier a moment to register that he was being praised for something he probably shouldn't have been doing in the first place. "Th-Thanks."

"Maybe I should leave my work out more often, so it gets magically done for me," Rune said with a smirk as he reached for his mug again.

12

AMARAIS ✧ 2704-11-24

KOLE

The sun had fallen past the dotting tree line, taking the orange glow with it by the time Kole had arrived in Thassae—a town on the verge of being categorized as a city that rested between Synos at the southwestern border. Buildings here sat a little shorter, halting at three or four stories, but spread out into single homes with short, decorative fences around small yards covered with snow. He'd struggled not to stare at them on the train ride in, having to remind himself to focus on the *why* of being here, rather than the *where*.

The memory of the last time he'd been in Amarais surfaced in disjointed fragments like a freshly smashed layer of ice bobbing to the surface of a pond. All of it was still there, but none of it connected like it once had, and now it was eroding at the edges.

Come on out. You're safe now.

That coaxing, ever-reassuring, gentle tone that he hadn't expected—and rarely heard since—sounded like the soft edge of a dream that ended a nightmare. The warm embrace of Kole's then-small frame had counteracted the stinging bite of the wind against his cheeks during that trek. It was an event that he often questioned the reality of, numb to the idea that his home wasn't among the squabbling, oppressive politics of this place.

The slamming of the driver's door brought him back to the present, where he caught the short flash of blue and blond in the rearview mirror as his head whipped toward Ezra—a neutrally-colored twenty-six-year-old that Kole envied the appearance of. His slight tan from travel only added insult to injury, seeing how Kole struggled to blend in anywhere outside of here and maybe the Republic. But *Ezra*... Ezra could vanish into just about any other crowd with his mussed brown hair and sharp, dark eyes if he kept his head down and his irritating nature in check. But perhaps that would be asking too much...

"Finally," Ezra grumbled, puffing out one last wisp of cold smoke as the car began to heat—a car that Kole had to procure by charming the woman at the rental counter and transferring over a hefty deposit from his fake ID. As dirty as he felt doing it, he would've felt even dirtier allowing Ezra to rub his gloved hands all over the glass desktop with vague, implying gestures before he'd been inevitably approached by security.

"Here I was, foolishly hoping my next job would be *south*, not north..." he continued, sending the car lurching forward and half-sliding through the snow.

Kole scrambled for the handhold, gritting his teeth. "Take it easy," he growled.

He knew he wouldn't, but at least this warning would give him enough of a reason for an 'I told you so' later. For someone a year older than him, Kole had learned the hard way—on more than one occasion—that it certainly didn't make Ezra smarter or more responsible. Assuming he'd grow out of it during their teenage years had been an error on Kole's part, but he supposed that's what made Ezra... well, Ezra.

Once they hit proper traction and pointed straight, Kole released his grip. His thoughts became consumed by the chatter of the radio, each word flat and bleak like the landscape—devoid of human life. Even that had been swallowed by the ever-growing black of night with railway tracks as their guide.

"Be honest," Kole said, glancing over at Ezra. "Do you think he managed to get away?"

He immediately regretted saying anything the second Ezra swung his head around to face him, causing Kole's body to tense with his eyes torn from the road. "Considering he would be hard to miss among the body count, I'm going to assume that the client isn't lying." He tapped the navigation screen. "And this is the last GPS location of the car that left the garage. I think you're just looking to poke holes in this, Kole."

Ezra spun the wheel, taking them off the path and into the blank snowy canvas spread out beyond the rails. Kole's hand pressed against the dash as he leaned forward, peering ahead. A stolen glance at the coordinates on the navigation screen showed they were nearly on top of it right before something materialized in the headlight beams. Ezra stopped the car a few meters shy of the twisted, partially melted heap of metal and plastic and got out.

It couldn't be...

Kole swallowed, fumbling with the seatbelt and hopping out of the car. The charred, blackened, snow-dusted underbelly came into view, along with the twinkling of shattered glass sticking up in patches.

"No bodies," Ezra called back after prying open one of the doors. "But this is definitely her handiwork... Especially after hearing that the client mentioned a woman."

Kole's fist tightened. "It could've been anyon—"

"Don't bother trying to explain this away," he said, circling the vehicle with the sound of glass popping in his wake. "The simplest answer is typically the most correct one."

He started to shake his head, jogging forward to take a look for himself. Crouching down, he saw the melted remnants of the undercarriage, along with whatever was left of the explosive used to detonate it. Kole bit back a curse when he took in the spot it'd been placed.

You sure that'll do it?

Yeah, it'll hit the main fuel line, and the shit ignites in seconds. Trust me.

"She would've taken a sports car if she was riding alone," Ezra said, patting the side of the SUV with a hollow thud. "If I had to take a wild guess, I'd say they're probably still in Miralta... But I have some sources that might be able to help me narrow down where they're heading next."

Kole stood, watching Ezra in his trek back to the car before he turned to look over his shoulders with a devious grin and malicious glint to his eye. "Let's not waste any more time here, shall we?"

A chill ran through him, but he knew it wasn't from the cold this time. Instead, it was one of shock. Of hurt and disbelief. Of betrayal.

Promise you'll stick with me?

Promise.

13

MIRALTA ✦ 2704-11-25

NOA

Noa sighed under the building's awning, breathing in the scent of rain as it smacked against the puddled paving stones. A small smirk tugged at the corner of her mouth as she watched the few people milling about duck into coffee shops and apartment entrances. She checked the time on her phone and tapped Nyx's number.

"Good morning," came Nyx's dull tone.

"Don't sound so excited," Noa said, letting her wry smile slip into her voice. "You're going to make me think you actually miss me."

"I think it's more likely that *you* miss *me*, but that's beside the point. I went through the data Rune sent over yesterday. It took me almost the entire day, but I'll think you'll be happy with the results. It's certainly more than what we had."

"Does it happen to fill in any gaps of why we were ambushed?"

"Yes."

Noa's eyes closed, and her head lightly thumped against the brick, waiting for the explanation.

"I managed to tie Lucian to a username from the notes," Nyx said, "which helped me identify the rest of his associates. Once they rebooted the security systems a few days ago, I managed to get the video feeds back up to keep an eye on them. Fortunately, they're convinced that my program is supposed to be there, so I doubt they'll find us anytime soon. From what I'm matching up, it looks like only the core of the operation was snooping on the site."

"Please tell me you have *all* of their data by now."

"All of it," came Nyx's reply. "Noa, they're all illegitimate children with council ties."

Noa grimaced, piecing together the motive.

"All of them were sent away to boarding school like any good, wealthy parent does with a child they'd rather not put up with for the better part of a year. Considering the heavy curriculum overlap, I have little doubt most of them banned together out of necessity after being deemed social outcasts."

"What makes you say that?"

"Well, not having blond hair and blue eyes probably tops the list," Nyx mumbled, shifting the phone on the other end. "Out of all of them, Lucian is the only one who looks like he belongs. While I'm still digging up the details of their hierarchy, I'm gathering that he's the one taking the lead because he actually *looks* the part, but he's getting shafted anyway."

"You think he gained their trust, and then promised them Amarais because he could be their voice?"

"We have a winner," Nyx responded dryly.

Noa ran a hand through the loose pieces of her hair, chewing on her lip for a moment. "So, they're pissed. Pissed because they were snubbed for their blood or how they look. They decide to lash out, even if some of them end up committing patricide in the process because they feel entitled to the power the rest of their family has, right?"

"Right..."

Noa paused, catching that hang of Nyx's words. "But there's more, isn't there?"

"They went as far as blowing up Katerina's car en route to Miralta," Nyx said, her inflection teetering on caution. "They wanted to shut down any possibility that their takeover might face later opposition from anyone with influence. It's leading me to believe that the agitation I'm seeing through my camera monitoring is due to a certain missing body."

"I mean, I figured as much—"

"No, Noa, I don't think you get it," she said, sighing with a hint of momentary frustration. "Some of the data I've been digging up—some of the conversation and communication logs I've been finding outside of the portal between Lucian and the others—I think they've bought into the rumors about Glacier."

"So? I'm pretty sure there's bound to be a few people buying into rumors—"

"Think about it, Noa. They all have something in common."

She started to frown in concentration before it clicked, and her hand went to her face. "He's the only one in this scenario who was promised a seat, and they're banking on him being half-Miraltan to justify their actions, aren't they?"

"That seems to be the message I've been getting so far."

Her hand fell to her mouth, tapping a finger against her lips. "So what do we do about this now? Do we move them further south toward the Miraltan-Republic border?"

"I don't think that's necessary just yet," Nyx replied. "But I'm trying to connect the dots to the identities of some of the moderators and admins of the portal. I think they're starting up a new one, so I'm hoping to get in touch and gain some trust before we have another go at this death-trap of a country."

"Keep me updated then," Noa said, letting her shoulders drop. "Did you already plot the next leg of our trip?"

"All ready to go, plus two."

Noa hesitated, which seemed to be enough for Nyx to justify her response.

"I'm not getting caught with my pants down again," she said. "I don't want to make another rushed ID turnaround for two people, especially when one of them needs special photo adjustments. I'd rather prepare for the worst and hope for the best."

Noa absently threw up a hand. "Fine."

"Lay low for just a few more days, and we'll pick our next target."

"Please," Noa said with a grin. "I *always* lay low."

Nyx gave a questioning hum in return, hanging up after a clipped, "Sure."

Her smile didn't dissipate though, feeling a little more optimistic than she had the past few days. It put a spring in her step as she jogged back upstairs, swinging the apartment door open to find Rune exiting the kitchen.

"You want the good news or the bad news first?" she asked, kicking the door shut behind her.

He tilted his head in contemplation. "Getting bad news out of the way first typically leaves me in a better mood, so..."

Noa clapped her hands together. "Okay, well, it *is*, in fact, a separate faction that was using the rebels' resources to overthrow the monarchy themselves. The core group consists of a handful of illegitimate children of Amaraian council members and wealthy, influential upper-class. They denied their rights to inherit any titles or positions since they're not full Amaraian."

Rune folded his arms over his chest, following her over to the living room. "Which means that they probably have a pretty good reason to hate Glacier..." he mumbled, and Noa pointed a finger toward him to indicate he was correct. "I take it Nyx confirmed that they know he's missing?"

Noa's eyes flicked toward Glacier's room before she met his gaze again, giving a slight nod. "However, the good news is that Nyx was able to locate the rest of the information on the other members, thanks to your list of usernames. Plus, she said that she's been able to use some of it as leads for info on the rebels. So, good job." She gave him a light slap on his bicep.

His brows furrowed, and he shook his head. "Noa, that wasn't me."

"Huh?"

"I didn't produce the list of usernames," he explained. "I only produced notes over general posts."

Now she was confused. "Then who...?"

"Glacier was the one who looked specifically at the users. I caught him sleeping on the couch yesterday morning. He'd been looking through the tablet."

"Wait- *what?*" Noa's eyes went wide. "Rune, I didn't want him to get involved—"

"So you'd rather he sit back and do nothing?"

"Well- I- *no,* but—"

"You can't have it both ways," Rune said. "He saw it, and you can't exactly undo that."

"Yes, but—"

"He managed to find things that I couldn't. I've been preoccupied. Hell, we *all* have been preoccupied. I can imagine that—out of everyone here—he wanted nothing more than to focus on something else anyway."

Her jaw worked, but none of her protests managed to reach her lips. She didn't want him dragged further into this mess than necessary. Not to mention how he was her only way to get to the Soul of Amarais. At this point, she preferred finding a way to stuff him in a box and retrieve him later since he still had a target on his back.

Rune waited expectantly for her to finally say something, so when she didn't, he kept going, "I'm not sure what's going on in that head of yours, but if you want to actually use your words, let me know." And he vanished into their room.

14
MIRALTA ✦ 2704-11-27

CECILIA

It'd been a little over a day before Cecilia's phone buzzed in her pocket. Her pulse raced when she saw Astor's name flash across the screen.

I want to talk.

So, after warring with herself over breakfast that morning, she met up with him. And he said he forgave her, despite the reluctance in his voice and pleading in his eyes. Her new goal became winning his trust back.

Astor, however, had dropped the topic of Amarais altogether, smoothing out some of the wrinkles it had created in their friendship. She could be Cecilia again—especially since Astor kept correcting himself to call her by her real name, even with her saying that he didn't have to.

A few days of finding their rhythm later, he stopped her just before she left his apartment. He asked if she would head north with him to one of the secret Mage exchange posts near the Amaraian border since two Illusionists could do more good than one in concealing them to sabotage equipment.

"You know how dangerous it is, of all people," he said. "You don't have to give me an answer now, but I'd like one before we leave tomorrow. I'm also not sure that we'd come back to Knighton afterward. Me and the guys have been talking, and we might head to the coast for a while since there are others like us out that way."

The way he'd gripped her hands made her heart squeeze. She was wanted—someone had actually asked for her to join them in something. Two Illusionists setting out to protect any other Mages from suffering at the hands of Amarais like she had. For the greater good.

That high dissipated by the time she'd returned for dinner, where she watched Glacier pick at his plate at the kitchen island with Noa and Rune bickering over something in hushed tones. He hadn't looked at her, let alone anyone else really, racking her with guilt.

If Cecilia said yes, she would be leaving him behind. The little brother she never had—that she abandoned in favor of chasing her own sense of self when he needed her most. Here they were, facing a brand new, uncertain future together, and she nearly committed to running away with some boy with the hope that he'd fill that void in her soul.

When she woke in the morning, she had her answer.

On the front step of his house, she tugged the strap of her crossbody purse and smoothed out the rose-colored sundress she'd worn when they'd first met. She shook a little as she brought a fist up to knock, waiting for maybe a couple seconds before the door swung open. Astor's face lit up, putting on a wide grin that she tried to mimic until his faltered with a darting glance around her. But he ushered for her to come inside anyway.

Once they were in the living room, she realized he'd been looking for a travel bag, much like the one laying in the middle of the floor, nearly packed.

"Well?" Astor asked with a tinge of hope. "Are you ready to go?"

The question made it worse. He knew the answer already, but now she had to make herself say it. "Astor," she started hesitantly with a slight shake of her head. "I... I can't go with you."

His eyes searched her face, like maybe she would somehow give him a different response.

"I'm sorry," she said, her voice coming out a little raspier than she liked.

"I... I don't understand..." he said, releasing a small, nervous chuckle.

"Astor, I'm sorry, but I'm not going with you." The understanding that crossed his features caused her to look away, ashamed by the decision to choose Glacier over him. She wiped her palms on her dress. "I should go."

When she looked back up at him, he took a quarter-step forward like he wanted her to tell her to hold on—to change her mind. Cecilia shifted for a moment and then turned to leave, not wanting to drag this out longer than it needed to be.

That is, until he seized her arm. She gasped in her stumble backward and reached to pry it off. Her skin screamed from the pressure of his fingertips.

"Astor—" she forced out as he pulled her across the room. "Astor, you're hurting me."

He wrenched open the closet door under the staircase, jerking her forward. She lost her balance in the momentum and felt something rub against her face just before she smacked into the back wall. A slam of the door, and everything was dark.

Panic clawed up her throat as she spun around, fumbling for a handle as her face began to burn. She threw herself against the door once when her pulse pounded in her ears and felt around for her purse. It was gone. Her hand went to her face where the burning was—a friction burn from the strap.

"*Astor!*" she screamed, slapping her hands against the door. "Astor, let me out!"

A sharp *thump* made her trip and fall over a pair of shoes.

"Shut up!" he growled. "Do you really think you have the right to deny me anything? You knew *nothing* when you met me. I taught you *everything* you know." The sound of footsteps moving away made her breath quicken. "*Fate* brought us together. I was even willing to overlook your appearance because of our magic. You can't just leave—Not when you and I have a duty to protect everyone like us."

"Astor, please—"

"*No,* I don't think you understand that *you* were made for me."

She cupped her hand over her mouth, muffling a sob while she listened to the shuffling of his packing. Her mind went straight to Glacier, telling herself that she couldn't leave him here alone; to Noa, with her rough kindness that she didn't have to give; and Rune—Rune, who had given her encouragement at possibly her lowest point in life, being nothing but kind and patient, even when his brother hadn't been.

I've made a huge mistake.

Her head jerked up as light flooded the small space, the door was thrown open, and Astor roughly pulled her to her feet again. She cried out from the tight grip on her arm.

"We're going," he said sharply. "And you're going to do exactly what I tell you, understand?"

She nodded, and he dragged her toward his bag. No more miscellaneous items littered the floor, which meant that he was packed and ready to leave. Too bad she wasn't. Her eyes snapped over to the coffee table, where her purse lay partially open with her phone peeking out.

The second he bent to pick up his luggage, Cecilia kicked in the back of one of his knees, sending him forward. He let go in favor of trying to catch himself as she sprinted for her bag. She slid the phone out the same moment he had the back of her dress, ripping her backward and shoving her to the floor. The phone flew out of her grip, spinning across the faux-planks with a heart-wrenching thud against the baseboard by the stairs. She quickly scrambled to get up, crying out as she was knocked down again, and Astor pinned her.

"Get off of me!" she screamed, flailing in her attempt to escape.

"You ungrateful bitch."

She gritted her teeth and jerked her knee up as hard as she could. A gasping yell escaped his lips as her strike landed between his legs. His grip loosened, and with a shove, he toppled sideways. The sickening crack that followed sent a chill through her, but she was already scrambling for the phone.

The device shook in her hands, jittering and slipping with every nerve in her body. Cecilia looked back over her shoulder, wobbling as she made a half-hearted attempt to stand. Astor, however, continued lying there, his upper half-obscured from the angle of the couch. She froze, her hands curling around the phone while she waited for him to twitch or groan or *something*.

Seconds ticked by, but each one became a minute in her mind, along with the chant of a name. Her fingers finally pressed against the phone's screen, searching for the contact entry labeled with an 'R.'

"Hey, Elodie," came that warm, familiar voice after the second ring.

"Rune—" she said, choking at the end of his name. Her own voice sounded high and strangled to her own ears as she slumped against the wall.

"What's wrong?" he asked, his tone immediately shifting to concern. "Are you okay?"

Her eyes stayed pinned on Astor's limp form. "No," she whispered.

"Where are you?" he asked, his voice calm and even but firm. "Are you in immediate danger?"

"I-I don't think so- I—"

"Cecilia, I'm going to text you something. I need you to click on it. It'll tell me where you are, okay?"

She nodded before she remembered that he couldn't see her. "O-okay." She tore her phone away when it buzzed, tensing before she saw a message with a link. When she tapped it, an image of a map appeared, and her location was marked with a pin. Her vision blurred, coming with a pang of relief.

"I'm on my way. Do you need me to stay on the phone with you? Are you going to be okay?"

Cecilia hesitated. "I... I think so."

In truth, she had no idea, and she was horrified of what might come next.

GLACIER

The rumble of the dark sky matched the distorted hum of Glacier's thoughts: sorrow, grief, anger... *Kat.* No one had the right to rip her away like that, even if they saw it as justice through a warped lens.

The tranquility that the main room of the apartment had originally offered began to drift into maddening silence, like he'd asked a question purposely left ignored. But there wasn't anyone around, not in sight anyway. His head turned to the window again, watching the clouds roll in. After he'd collected his jacket from his room, he pulled the apartment door shut behind him with a soft, nearly inaudible *click* that left his heart racing.

His high crashed once he stepped out onto the street. Temporary freedom because he'd never be truly free. He'd always be shackled to something: his meaningless title, his wretched luck, his mismatched eyes.

Tugging up his hood to try to hide them, he kept his head down and hands in his pockets. The wired sensation of the crisp, pre-storm air against his skin raised goosebumps down his arms. He wasn't even sure where he was going, but he didn't really care. Each person he passed became another nameless, faceless entity that came and went faster than anyone he'd known, but even they vanished in a blink of an eye—so what did it matter in the end?

Block after block passed by in a blur with the flash of crosswalk signals and scrolling signs that advertised gadgets or reupholstered furniture—all of them might as well have read, 'wrong way' since no route was correct. No route would take him back home. No route would—

He gasped, stumbling into an alleyway with a firm grip on his arm and his back pinned against the rough brick. Noa stared back at him, her expression hard and eyes alight with a flicker of—annoyance? Anger?

Whatever it was had been enough to let his own boil over. "What?" he spat.

"What do you mean 'what'?" she snapped. "What the hell do you think you're doing?"

"What does it look like?" He gestured to the sidewalk. "Am I not allowed to just take a walk?"

"Not without telling anyone where you're going," she said sharply.

"So it's okay for everyone else to come and go as they please, but not me? I'm on house arrest?"

"Well, you weren't before, but you're about to be. You're just *asking* for trouble roaming around by yourself."

He almost scoffed. "So?"

"Don't be stupid. You just don't get it, do you? I'm getting the feeling like you almost want to die at this point."

"So what? So what if I do? Sorry if that's an inconvenience for you, but I don't see why I should be alive when *she* doesn't get to be. If the world was fair, it would've taken me instead."

"So now you're just going to throw your damn life away? That's the answer?"

"No." The word came out sharp and forceful.

"Then *what?*" she asked, her tone on the verge of exasperation. "What are you going to do? Sit around and keep feeling sorry for yourself?"

"I want them to pay!" he said, his voice echoing down the alley. He swallowed back his own surprise at the outburst and pushed through what was left of his rage-fueled words. "I want the people who killed her to pay for what they've done. She didn't deserve to die."

Noa didn't so much as flinch. She rocked back on her heels ever-so-slightly, folding her arms over her chest with thoughtful, narrowed eyes. There was an uptick at the corner of her mouth that grew into something sinister, replicating the chills he'd felt earlier. When she took a step forward, his stomach dropped.

"So, you want revenge." The words velvety and casual. "Fortunately for you, you're talking to just the right person to help." The glint in her eye sent his palms straight against the wall like he could somehow sink into it to escape whatever version of Noa had unmasked herself here. "I think it's time we have a talk, *little prince.*"

He tensed at the sudden buzz coming from her pocket, snapping her expression to surprise. Grumbling, she pulled out her phone with a frown and brought it to her ear. "This is Amelia." Her eyes bore into Glacier's again until she closed them with a sigh.

CECILIA

Cecilia sat against the baseboard with her knees against her chest and her phone in her hands, thinking that the map might show some sort of indicator out of her peripheral vision while she waited. It didn't. Between that and Astor, her pulse pounded in her ears, anxiously preparing for move-ment that never came. But she was still too terrified to move. Shouldn't she be waiting outside? Shouldn't she have *run?*

She squeezed the phone, her eyes going wide with the realization that Astor mentioned having a roommate. What if they decided to come back and check in or pick something up? What if—

A knock sent the phone tumbling from her hand and onto the floor. She suppressed a startled cry and winced as she picked it back up. Every creak of the floor sounded painfully loud on her way over to the entry, where she sucked in a sharp breath and peered through the peephole.

And exhaled, fumbling with the door for Rune.

His shoulders fell upon seeing her, but she stepped aside like she was inviting him into her own house. She dropped her face to the floor and tightened her grip on the door handle, waiting for him to do *something*— declare judgment on whatever she'd done? She wasn't sure.

Instead, he stopped in front of her and gently pried the door from her hand. "What happened?"

She swallowed, trying to force down the tears welling up again, and hunched in on herself as she guided him to the living room. Astor was still there. Just *there.*

Run. Go. Leave.

"I—" Her voice wavered. "I didn't want to hurt him. I—" She clapped a hand over her mouth to stifle a sob.

"What happened?" he asked again, his tone prodding but gentle.

"He asked me if I would go with him up north..." she whispered, looking anywhere but either of them. "I told him I couldn't. And... he got really upset."

Rune gave a small nod for her to continue out of the corner of her vision.

"He- he locked me in the closet—" Warm tears slipped down her face, barely catching the surprise in his blurry features before it turned to fury with each new word. "He yelled at me, saying that I owed him for teaching me and that I was made for him. When he finally let me out, I saw my bag and went for my phone, but he pinned me to the floor—I shoved him off of me and- and—" She buried her face in her hands. "I'm sorry."

"You were defending yourself," he said calmly, causing her hands to fall from her face in search of his reaction. "It's okay." He reached for her, but she jerked away, tensing until he drew his arm back. "You didn't do anything wrong."

"He's dead... I *killed* him."

"He didn't have the right to treat you like that. You were defending yourself—you did nothing wrong." He shook his head. "You didn't *belong* to him because you don't belong to anyone." He pulled his phone from his pocket.

"Wh- what are you doing?"

"Calling Noa."

She lunged forward, grabbing his wrist with both hands, pleading, "N-No! You can't! Please don't tell Noa—she'll be livid—"

He gently pulled her hands off, his voice dipping into soothing reassurance. "She won't be angry. Just calm down and let me call her. Trust me, Cecilia."

She bit her lip, nodding. Everything fell out of focus, and a dull ringing sang in her ears, over the sound of Rune moving into different parts of the house and answering with a 'yes' or 'no' to whatever questions Noa asked. Kitchen cabinets opened and closed, and the bathroom light flicked on as she ran her eyes over the floor to Astor's shoes. She met his now-dulled green eyes and whipped her head away with shaky breaths.

Cecilia's eyes squeezed shut, trying to blot out the image of blood covering the corner of the coffee table—a place where he'd compared it to magic a couple of weeks ago.

"Hey."

Her eyes flew open to take in Rune's hand running through his hair. "She said she'll be here in fifteen." His eyes searched hers before a brief drop back down to Astor, making her stiffen. "You really didn't do anything wrong, Cecilia."

Instead of arguing, she hugged herself and braced for whatever Noa might say.

RUNE

Noa had let herself in like she owned the place, not even sparing either of them a glance before she stood over Astor with her hands on her hips. With her back to them, her shoulders fell a little like she'd let out some inaudible sigh.

"Do you need my help?" Rune asked, despite knowing that he'd have to take Cecilia back to the apartment first. She'd had enough trauma for one day—let alone a lifetime—but taking her back would eat up time. Time that was better spent packing up and ditching their apartment or leaving Miralta altogether.

But Noa waved a hand. "No. I have what I need." She stepped over Astor's body, grabbing Cecilia's purse and tossing it to him.

He tried to hand it off to Cecilia like it was a peace offering, but her hesitation almost made his fingers dig into it. Unfortunately, that anger didn't have anywhere left to go now, seeing how the target of said rage was dead.

"Take her home," Noa said. "I'll be there soon."

Rune ushered her toward the door, guiding her out onto the street. He kept his phone at the ready on the walk back while Cecilia clutched her purse to her chest. Whether she was shivering because of the chill in the air or from the trauma, he wasn't sure, but something told him she didn't want to talk about it. So the long stroll was endured in silence.

Each block they passed turned the sky a shade darker or triggered another roll of thunder overhead until the two of them made it to the apartment building's entrance. Small wet dots formed on the pavers right before they ducked inside.

When he pushed the apartment door open, the two remaining residents swung their heads toward him. It was as if he'd interrupted a tense stand-off with Glacier leaning back against the kitchen island and Crow mimicking his stance using one of the sitting area's chairs.

"Cecilia?" Glacier asked, pushing away from the counter. "Are you okay?"

She bolted toward him, falling into his arms with a sob while Rune shut the door.

Glacier looked up at Rune with wide eyes. "D-did something happen? What's going on?"

Rune bit down on his tongue, unsure how to answer. "I don't think she wants to talk about it right now."

"Talk about *what?*" Crow asked.

"Don't start," Rune snapped.

"What?" he asked, pointing a finger at Glacier. "This one comes back from a walk with Noa, suddenly wielding an attitude, and now the other one is a sobbing heap for whatever reason. So, yeah, I'd like to know what's going on." He pushed himself away from the chair, heading straight for him. "And where the hell is Noa? She just dropped him off and left."

"You need to back off," he said, adding a warning edge to his voice. "Now is not the time."

His eyebrows rose. "Oh, so now it's inconvenient for *you?*" He let out a breathy laugh. "I'm sorry, I forgot that we play by *your* rules—"

"That's enough—"

The door swung open again, and the whole room paused to shift their attention to Noa. She shook out her hair and tugged off her jacket, drizzling water around her boots. "Might as well have just walked instead of wasting money on a damn taxi," she grumbled, kicking the door shut behind her and tossing her jacket on the rack. Her focus fell on Glacier and Cecilia— the latter pushing out of her comforter's arms and wiping away her tears.

"All right," she said, smoothing her hair back. "I believe it's time we finish our discussion now that Cecilia's here too."

Rune frowned, tilting his head in question as she advanced.

"I've decided to give you both a choice."

Crow's eyes went wide with disbelief, shooting Rune a look of outrage. "*What?*" Then his outburst was turned to Noa. "You can't seriously be considering this right now! Not when—"

She spun to face him, fury in her eyes. "Shut the fuck up, Crow." He stopped dead in his tracks, frozen to the spot while she prowled closer. "You've done nothing but challenge me since we left Amarais. I don't know what your problem is, but I don't really give a shit. I don't care that the job was botched, and I don't really care for you calling my authority into question because of it."

Crow's jaw tensed, like he was holding back a retort. Fear crossed his face, despite staring down someone who was several centimeters shorter than him. After a moment, he moved around her and tore out of the apartment with a slam of the door in his wake. Rune immediately locked eyes with Noa, her gaze boring into him with the silent command to deal with him. So, he let out a short sigh and followed.

It only took him a minute to catch up, finding Crow ducking under a pathway of awnings just outside. He grabbed his arm and pulled him up against one of the buildings, despite Crow trying to shake him off.

"We need to talk."

Crow scoffed. "Funny."

"No, it's really not."

"Rune, nothing I say is going to godsdamned matter, so piss off—"

"Are you pissed because we've picked up stragglers?" he demanded. "Or because of the job?"

He didn't answer, turning his head away in protest.

"*Crow.* I'm done dancing around the damn problem," Rune growled.

"Honestly? Both," he finally said, whipping his head back around. "We shouldn't be sitting around, babysitting when we have better things to do. We don't have time for this shit—"

"We're doing the same damn thing we've done before to lose heat. Having two more people around shouldn't make a difference."

"Wasn't it enough to flirt with Noa back in Bellegarde?" Crow asked. "Or are you feeling like you might as well try your luck with Cecilia too because who the hell knows when we'll get caught?"

Rune drew back in surprise before setting his jaw in irritation. "That's not at all what's happening here—"

"Cut the shit, Rune. You act like I haven't noticed you being extra nice to her."

"Because she's *grieving*, you dumbass," he said. "Aren't you forgetting that I've been going out of my way for Glacier, too? Not to mention that—even if that were true—she's been seeing someone else."

"Oh, please—"

"I think both you and I know that this is you taking out your frustration of our last job and this entire situation on whoever you can. I get it, you're pissed. But we're supposed to be a team, remember?"

"Team, huh?" Crow sneered. "How are we a team when you're constantly sucking up to Noa?"

"Because she's right, Crow. This isn't our show. This was our ticket out."

"Just like our last 'ticket out'?" He made mocking air quotes.

"You know this is different." Rune shook his head. "We chose this—"

"Wrong! *You* chose this. You chose this just like the other one!"

"So you're saying that you would've chosen differently?" he asked, watching Crow's mouth open and shut again, halting his argument. "Because I don't think you would've, but if you want to blame me, then blame me. You can choose not to help and complain while I drag us both along to whatever end we finally find."

Crow glanced away again, rubbing his arm like he was tending to a wound.

"You don't have to say it," Rune said quietly. "I know we've run out of options. We're in a corner that neither of us like, but we have to manage with what we've got. I just need you to trust me."

15

MIRALTA ✧ 2704-11-27

GLACIER

Three short tumblers clinked against each other as Noa set them and a bottle down on the coffee table. "Sit," she ordered, nodding to the couch.

Glacier exchanged nervous glances with Cecilia before they followed her command, settling onto the cushions while Noa popped the top off the liquor. She held it up with a raised brow.

"I'm not—" he started.

"I don't care if you're not twenty yet," she said. "I just know that I'm going to need at least one drink to get through this conversation, so if you want one too, I'm not going to stop you." She nodded toward the glassware. "Now, do you want a drink or not?"

He hesitated, finally shaking his head, which Cecilia copied. Noa rolled her eyes, pouring a glass for herself and leaning back in her chair. Her lids drifted shut and took a sip. "Now, which one of you is going to tell me *The Origin of Magic?*"

Glacier went rigid as Noa flicked open one eye, clearly watching their paled expressions.

"Well? I'm not stupid enough to believe that both a prince and his personal attendant don't have enough of an education that they somehow haven't heard the story at least *once*."

Cecilia tugged on the hem of her dress. "It's considered an act of treason to tell it..."

"But you *have* heard of it," Noa said. "And you're not in Amarais."

Cecilia shrank down, but Glacier remained unyielding, contemplating Mrs. Angelis's history and culture lessons. It was one of the things she'd shuffled into their curriculum with the caveat that they were never to breathe a word of it. Something just for them—a small taste of magic-based knowledge that she'd abruptly stopped when his uncle had decided that Kat should be tutored with them as well. Even that barrier was broken with time and trust, especially with the reserved chuckles and comments about how Kat's questions and stubborn behavior reminded Mrs. Angelis of Glacier's father.

Back then, Glacier had thought nothing of it. His Miraltan blood shouldn't make him an exception like Cecilia with her magic. It hadn't been until he'd become a teenager that he'd considered if his mother had been a Mage, though he had no evidence, let alone anyone that would've told him the truth.

That had been a topic his father had always skirted around, but Glacier had gleaned as much as he needed from the soft, sad look in his eyes whenever he cupped his head in his hands. He'd covered it up with a smile, but there'd never been joy there. Only remorse and a firm grip on the one fragment of her he had left.

"There are... certain things better left to discuss when you're older," his father had said before giving him a kiss on the forehead. "Now go to sleep."

Now whenever Glacier closed his eyes the world was filled with nightmares and pain instead of dreams and wild ideas of magic. All his safety had fallen away—his protectors taking swords pointed at him so he could live. He scoffed at the thought that he was someone special. Glacier, the Prince of Amarais—a title that everyone had tried to pry from him because it was the sole shield he carried once everyone else was gone.

Did any of it really matter now? After all, everyone thought he was dead, didn't they? What more did he have left to lose?

Glacier closed his eyes, recalling the way Mrs. Angelis had sat so close in front of him and Cecilia that both of her knees had brushed theirs. That tight-knit cluster of chairs had been pulled to her desk against the wall with her tablet hidden from view in case anyone burst through the classroom doors.

Her voice merged into his as he repeated it for Noa now. "Avaria was once a united kingdom with no borders, ruled by a single King whose name has since been lost to time."

When he pulled himself from the memory, he found Noa settling further into her seat, motioning for him to continue with a tip of her drink.

"During the time of his rule, many parts of his kingdom were seemingly isolated, though they were always somehow well cared for. He was a kind and generous ruler who loved his people and was well-loved by them in return. So, when he requested that each region send a handful of representatives to attend his court, they unquestionably obliged, despite knowing that the journey would be perilous.

"Between them and their destination were foul creatures that emerged from the dark, ravaging the land at night. The people called them shadows, stalkers, creatures of the night, daemons, takers of souls. Even with many well-trained soldiers at the ready to defend them come nightfall, there were almost never enough weapons with the proper blessings to deter the creatures. Scholars and priests often exhausted their energy imbuing such blades with marks supposedly torn from daylight, saying if these things should fail that their only hope of survival would be to pray to the gods for the sun to rise.

"The King sought to bring as many people together as he could to figure out a way to drive the creatures back, once and for all. Many didn't survive the months of travel, but those who did spent even longer deliberating, planning, and conducting trials of how to eliminate the threat. However, everything they theorized and tested had failed.

"They had all but given up, and the King had begun to consider sending his faithful subjects home. That is, until a young woman appeared at his court. She called herself the Messenger, claiming to be blessed with the gift of hearing whispers from the goddess of magic. She was the first

Seer to walk Avaria—gifted by the same goddess who had blessed the weapon-making scholars and priests: Seraphine.

"Initially, the King was skeptical as to whether or not the creatures had somehow adapted to take on human form. So, he tested the Messenger for weeks before she was finally able to earn his trust. She would give him advice on how to defend his new city—on how to best prepare for an attack that later came to pass just as she had predicted. Soon enough, the two became inseparable, the King and the Messenger, protecting Avaria with whatever power they had.

"But one the day, the Messenger brought a proposition to the King. She offered him, along with a select few of his choosing, a fraction of magic from Seraphine. The King immediately saw this as an opportunity to finally drive back the dark, assuming it was anything like the Messenger's own power. Power that pushed the creatures away from her like ripples on a lake. However, she warned that he should be cautious in whom he chose to receive these gifts with him, knowing that power can change a good soul into something far more menacing than the creatures they fought.

"So, the King deliberated, selectively narrowing down his chosen few within his court, and when he was ready, he left his chambers. Outside, he found a small group already waiting for him. They had heard the rumors of the Messenger's proposed gift and had come asking for the blessing of magic for themselves. None of them were the ones the King had selected, so he refused their requests, reassuring them that their talents lay elsewhere. Outraged when they couldn't change his mind, they attacked him—killing their King in a fit of rage before scattering back into the court to avoid being caught.

"When the Messenger had heard of the King's death, she rushed to where he had been laid in his chambers. She mourned him, weeping until she gathered the strength to take up his mantle for the kingdom that she had grown to love. It was the Messenger who declared the King's parting to his people, announcing that traitors dwelled amongst them and that no one was to leave until the culprits were caught.

"Thirteen members of the former King's court came together, all from different regions of Avaria, and all with unique skills. Wanting justice for the man who had brought them all there, who had done everything in his power to try to save their world, they took it upon themselves to seek out the traitors.

"Eventually, they apprehended the culprits, bringing them before the Messenger to ask what should be done. She replied that it wasn't her place to decide since she wasn't the chosen ruler of Avaria—not the one who had sought the blessing of his peoples' gods. However, the same applied to them, so the thirteen decided to leave it to a vote, asking for the court to sentence them for their crimes. It was an answer that pleased the Messenger, finding remnants of the former King's qualities in their actions.

"She later called the thirteen court members back to her and, with Seraphine's blessing, gave each of them the blessings meant for the King and his chosen few. Along with their power, she commissioned thirteen emblems to be forged as symbols of their newly sanctioned regions, empowering them to continue the King's just reign within their own regions of Avaria. This divided the world into thirteen countries, each finally able to combat the dark with Seraphine's magic—a force that spread like wildfire once it was lit.

"It left the now-fractured kingdom of Avaria stronger than ever before, still ever-united under the banner of the former King's hopes to protect and strengthen his people, as well as the thirteen new rulers' guide to continue his legacy. The darkness eventually receded, giving way for the people's gifts to be used for creation, rather than war, breathing new life into a once hopeless world. A world that the Messenger faded from, just like her King, fated to be lost to time as well."

When he finished, Glacier's mind couldn't help but stick to the part about the emblems, leaving him with a sinking feeling that was only further exacerbated by Noa. She swirled the liquid around in a smooth, circular motion, a tired, satisfied smirk on her face. There was, after all, a reason why Louis locked away the Soul of Amarais, hating the implications of magic somewhere along their family line that came with it—not that Glacier's grandfather had treated it any different. But it was just a *symbol*. It didn't bestow any power or do anything special, which made him question why Noa was bothering with it in the first place.

"That wasn't so difficult, was it?" she asked. "However, I'm afraid that the ending is a little... *off*."

He frowned, feeling a prick of irritation at her critique. "Sorry, but that's the only ending I know. I'm sure there are many different endings, but that's the only one I was ever told."

She leaned forward, pushing her glass onto the table. "I've had the... perhaps the unfortunate privilege of hearing or reading most—if not all—of the endings for myself," she began, holding up a finger. "But there was one in particular that I was always sent back to. Everything leading up to the end—the finishing off the evil forces, the magic—is all true. However, in the version I was taught, the Messenger continues to mourn the loss of the man she loved once Avaria is split. She lost the will to continue. She wanted to die. But Seraphine would only grant her peace after she finished one final request...

"Saying, 'one day, in the distant future, when magic dwindles from the people, the dark will rear its head again. The foolish descendants of those who sought to destroy the foul creatures will hope to control them, bending them to their will.' While the Messenger didn't want to believe this, Seraphine told her that magic would one day need to be restored from its waning state, or Avaria would face destruction at the hands of its own people—their hearts filled with corruption, only caring for themselves.

"So, the Messenger complied, creating a vault—*the Vault*—tucked away in a place where only few could find. This became the place where the next wave of magic sleeps, waiting for a champion to unlock it through the blessing of the thirteen members of the King's court. Someone to give the power back to those who would wield it with the same restraint and loyalty."

Glacier's expression turned uneasy, hesitating as her fingers started for the collar of her shirt. "You don't mean..."

She didn't even have to bother saying anything, instead tugging a small cord up over her head that was followed by the soft, clinking sound of metal. She tossed it on the table in front of them, and his stomach dropped. He wasn't sure if he should laugh or run. She actually thought it was real—

that some old tale with dozens of different endings was *real*. Cecilia's hand clapped over her own mouth, her eyes going wide.

"You're insane," he finally said, almost as if it were a realization. He couldn't even bring himself to look at her, staring only at the three relics strung together. Three that would've been four, had it not been for the heaping mess he was in.

"Funny," she said. "That's what I told the Seer who gave me the first one."

His head jerked up at that, finding her all business now—her playfulness from earlier long gone.

"A *Seer* gave you..."

"Yes. He—" Her voice faltered, and her gaze flicked back to the relics. "He gave it to me before he died. He told me that I was the only one who could do it. That I *had* to. I guess I'm the only one who can."

Despite knowing little about Seers, he'd caught on that they were lesser versions of the Messenger through that story and other little bits of reading that had mentioned them. They were somehow able to see or hear whatever Seraphine wished them to, which gave him pause over whether or not a Seer would have a motive to lie to Noa like that.

"They're keys," she said, breaking through his thoughts. "The thirteen emblems given to the original rulers weren't just symbols. They're keys to the Vault—one that no one's ever opened."

"How..." Cecilia started, her voice quaking. "How do you even know it's real?"

"The Seer I knew was like a father to me," she said, sounding somewhat distant but keeping her tone firm. "He gave me all the information I needed, telling me that it was all true. The only thing he couldn't tell me was the location of the keys and the Vault. He just told me that I would know when the time came, and I decided to take his word for it." She pushed herself out of the chair, moving to stand across from them as she reclaimed the cord of emblems and pulled it back over her head. "So, I now leave you both with a choice. You can either stay here and wait for me to return. In which case—seeing as how you're the only one that can get to it —I'll collect you before I plan on launching a second attempt to retrieve the Soul of Amarais, as promised. Or you can decide to come with us, which would assist us in expediting our collection, in turn, fast-tracking a way for you to reclaim your kingdom." Noa folded her arms over her chest and shifted her focus to Cecilia. "And it would reunite you with your parents faster too. So, what will it be?"

Cecilia's head turned like she was looking to him for his answer, and Noa snapped her fingers. "No," she said. "You get to make your own decision. You are your own person. You're not just Glacier's little assistant or tag-along."

Cecilia fidgeted with her dress again. "I... I don't want to be alone," she said. "I want to go wherever Glacier goes. There is nothing left here that I want more than for the two of us to stay together."

Noa drew her arm back, hesitant but seemingly accepting of that answer.

At first, Glacier considered Cecilia, though the reasoning was partially due to guilt. She could actually *learn* here. She could finally be a Mage for however long it took before Noa returned. Then again, she'd been so upset when she'd come back with Rune that he wasn't sure if that's what she truly wanted or not now.

So, what about him? What would he be doing here? Would he try to blend in among the students here? Would he need to keep himself barricaded in another house again? Would he be left alone to finish his grieving with no real results? *Would Kat go with them if I was the one who died?*

"I'll go."

The sound of the door opening tore Noa's attention away from them to Rune and Crow standing on the threshold.

"Oh, good. You're back." That devilish grin reappeared as her sights drifted back to Glacier, bringing back that unsettling image to the Noa he'd encountered in the alleyway. "Pack your things. We're leaving first thing in the morning."

16

MIRALTA ✧ 2704-11-28

NOA

Noa dropped her chin further into the collar of her jacket, attempting to suppress a shiver in the foggy, glass-topped Corris train station. The bench had finally started to warm right before the hiss of their ride's breaks echoed from the platform.

She was beginning to regret agreeing to Nyx's text asking if a 7:00AM departure was fine. Seeing how they needed to put distance between them and a body, she hadn't seen any harm in saying yes until she'd watched Glacier's head dip at least twice in the last five minutes sitting next to her. Each jolt awake had resulted in his boots sandwiching the new travel bag at his feet.

Cecilia kept her head down to fidget with her own travel bag's strap. The woven fabric turned her skin a brighter white every time she squeezed it. Rune's cut her a sideways look and frowned, likely because he was either actually concerned, or he was worried about having to bunk with her and Crow again.

Noa narrowed her eyes at the brother on the end, who stared at some distant point near the platform and then locked her sights on Rune. Noa raised a brow and gave a slight nod in Crow's direction, earning an inaudible sigh before Rune mouthed, 'later.' Later then.

The overhead speakers called out their automated boarding call, and Noa stood, leading the way with a brief glance back at Glacier to make sure he stayed close. Losing her key's key in the crowd was the last thing she needed right now, but they made it to their cramped cabin without incident.

She pressed her lips together as she shoved her bag into the overhead compartment, noting how the space had been halved. If she held out her arms, she could almost touch the other side. The theory gained a little more traction with Glacier brushing up against her to store his own bag, cursing quietly as it fell against his chest.

"Didn't sleep well?" she asked.

His shoulders tensed before he heaved his luggage upward. "Not really..." he mumbled, curling his fingers along the lip of the rack as his head turned toward the window.

Another swath of platform spanned out the other side, where another train was boarding. A girl with braided black hair and coal-black eyes jogged across to get in line right under the sign that boasted an imminent departure to Bellegarde. Noa could already imagine the plush, indigo, damask-print carpeting and breakfast selection of all-you-can-eat croissants she'd gorged herself on their ride from Roth. Then again, she supposed she might be able to fill that void with pancakes, assuming this train didn't stiff her with a bland substitute of oatmeal instead.

"Do you actually believe in what you're doing?" he asked, sounding slightly weary but genuine.

She gently bit down on her tongue in consideration. Such a complicated answer for a yes or no question, especially when she looked down at her hands, picturing them covered in blood. A Seer's blood.

Please—

It'd been the one word she'd been able to get out before he cut her off. Maybe it was because he knew that she was on the verge of letting out a sob and decided to spare her the humiliation. Or maybe it was simply because he was too damn stubborn, but he handed her that wretched, yellowed key from around his own neck.

Seeing that piece of plastic with the new stain of blood resting in her palm had made her stomach drop. The faint tune he'd always hummed hadn't floated through her mind when he'd instructed her to open his desk —a desk cluttered with slim packages of real paper, glues, tweezers, and small blades.

A small fortune's worth of supplies sat here, and yet she dug around it all for a small, velvet box with bald patches at the corners. She squeezed the container just to keep herself from hitting him with it. *This* hadn't been what he needed. What he *needed* was a first aid kit—a doctor, stitches, *something*.

She'd dropped back down to her knees in front of him in his slumped state against the wall, and he opened it for her when she tried to hand it to him. Inside sat a looping, silver emblem with red agate gems. Each one might as well have been the same glimmering red seeping from his abdomen.

Noa's hand moved to her chest where that emblem rested now, hidden under her shirt with two of its siblings. To her, Glacier's question wasn't so much about what *she* believed, but what she *had* to believe because she didn't have any other options. Even if that old bastard had finally lost his godsdamned mind, she promised herself that she'd do this for him.

"Yes," she finally said. "It feels like the more progress I make, the more I end up second-guessing myself."

"What makes you say that?"

"I... may have run into another Seer in Corris." The vivid image of standing next to that woman in front of the Messenger's statue had lingered in her mind for days, a haunting reminder that this may or may not be what she was expecting. "I ran into her the day I tossed you out of bed. I'm... sorry, by the way. I shouldn't have taken out my frustration on you like that."

He rubbed his arms, looking away. Noa had to admit that Rune was right. She couldn't compare her coping to his. They were different. She couldn't expect him to get right back up like she did—to liquify his grief into anger. The growing need to hit someone overpowered the feeling to lay down and surrender.

"Do you know self-defense?" she asked abruptly.

His brows knit together before giving a hesitant shake of his head.

"It's something you should probably learn," she said. "Especially if you plan on facing the terrorists back in Amarais. You probably weren't ever taught anything like that so it would be easier to get rid of you later, right?"

His hand moved to the back of his neck. "Not really any point in protecting someone that's the only thing between you and officially taking the throne."

"Then when we're not in a cramped train compartment, we'll be spending our mornings teaching you how to defend yourself."

He gave her a weary look in response. "*You're* going to teach me?"

"I wouldn't underestimate me if I were you."

CECILIA

"Have you been to Southaven before?" Cecilia asked, the remnants of Corris giving way to dewy green hills obscuring Knighton in the distance from the window.

Rune tilted his head in recollection and tapped the side of the tablet in his hands, leaving her to wonder if Crow would've chimed in if he were here. He hadn't said a word the entire morning, not even to Rune unless it'd been in private.

"Twice, I think. I remember going to a South-something when I was fairly young, so I don't remember much, but it seemed familiar the last time I was there a few years ago. Crow and I had stayed about a month for a job."

"How was the ocean?" she asked, imagining the frigid eastern coast of Amarais before it dissolved into the lapping ocean waves confined to a notebook on a coffee table. A coffee table now tainted with blood.

It must've shown, noticing how Rune's expression changed from thoughtfulness to concern.

"Sorry," she quickly added. "I've just never seen the ocean before. I-I shouldn't have asked..."

"Cecilia... I understand if you don't want to talk about it, but you shouldn't let what happened hold you back from the things you like. You shouldn't restrict yourself from meeting new people and seeing new places because it reminds you of *him*. He wanted to control you when he was alive, and you stopped him. Don't let him control you now."

Her vision blurred, the faded green carpet of the cabin losing its leafy pattern. "How?"

"Be your own person," he said. "You don't have to be anyone but yourself. Then you have all the power, and no one can take that away from you."

17

KING'S REPUBLIC ✧ 2704-11-28

CECILIA

When they crossed over into King's Republic, Cecilia allowed herself to wander the train, eating a little in the dining car with Glacier at lunch and later sitting with him in the observation car to take in the view of the countryside. Most of it was farmland, broken up by patches of forests or smaller towns they briefly stopped in. Solar panels lined the roofs of farmhouses while people tended to checkerboard squares of land with large machines. It was far different than Miralta's lush, green landscape, let alone Amarais's vast white blankets of snow over every centimeter of terrain.

That didn't even include the variety of *people*. Each populated little nook had its own feel, some of which she couldn't place, all with clusters of people that were far from the blond-haired, blue-eyed ones back home. Whites and soft grays had been replaced by a myriad of patterns and colors while suits and fine dresses had been exchanged for plain denim pants, cotton shirts, and plaid button-ups. As they passed one farm, Cecilia could've even sworn one man's arm glinted like metal in the sun.

The further they sped away from Amarais, the more she realized just how vastly different their world had become. How different the two of them were in comparison. They were truly on their own.

"I'm sorry for not being there when you needed me," she finally said.

"Don't be," he replied. "We... we were both trying to cope. I just wish I hadn't spent so much time doing nothing..." He forced out a short, mirthless laugh. "I don't even know what I could've done anyway... But neither one of us can bring her back."

It took her a moment before she turned to him, pulling him into a hug. He didn't hesitate to return it as she buried her face into his shoulder.

"We're in this together," he said.

She nodded against him, not quite willing to let go right away. She was anxious in every sense of the word about the future, trying to hold on to the one familiar person she could with the knowledge that Kat would no longer be around to protect them. Cecilia finally drew back to see the tiredness in his eyes.

"I think I'm going to go rest for a bit," he said, getting up from his seat with a small, reassuring smile. "I didn't exactly sleep much last night, and I think it's starting to catch up to me."

"Have a good rest, then."

With that, he exited the car, leaving her alone to take in the sun dipping closer to the edge of the horizon. She stood, her body feeling heavy after a long couple days with little sleep as well, deciding to follow Glacier's lead. Her journey back to her own cabin was short, and she found it empty.

She retrieved a blanket from the bottom compartment and slid out the second leaf of the seat, extending it to create more bed space. Turning the lights off and tapping the window to shade it, she curled up in the dark, letting herself drift with the image of the pink, evening Republic sky fresh in her mind.

Two hours passed before Cecilia woke to passengers passing through the hall of the car. It was more rest than she'd expected to get anyway, and she decided to venture out for dinner. She folded the blanket and dropped it onto her seat right before a thud sounded against the cabin door.

She jumped as it slid open, and Crow stumbled inside. He half-fell over the bench on the other side of the cabin, slumped over for a few seconds longer than she anticipated.

"Are... are you drunk?"

"*No!*" His protest was slurred, which didn't do anything to help his sad struggle to stand. He started trying to kick off his shoes but gave up to sit on the floor, where his head thumped against the seat cushion. "Yes..."

Crow tried again, sighing and swaying before he fell down on the seat. He leaned up against the outer wall of the car and stretched his legs out over the entirety of the bench. Once he appeared to be situated and no longer in need of potential assistance, she cautiously started for the door, glancing back to see if he might tumble back onto the floor before she left.

"I'm sorry," he mumbled, halting her, "...for how I've been treating you two." His head fell against the headrest, eyes half-lidded in a drunken stupor.

"Well," she said, "for what it's worth, I'm also sorry that I blinded you back in the library." That recollection of her panicked moment tearing down the curtains to escape Crow's menacing presence in the supposed safety of the palace felt like such a far-off memory now.

His head jerked up in surprise, his arm flailing outward at the sudden motion to steady himself.

"Let's just call it even," she said. "I'm not here to cause trouble."

He relaxed, slowly dipping back against the cushions. "I can see why he likes you."

She turned to the door, rolling her eyes. He could think what he wanted about her and Glacier.

"Knowing him my whole life, I don't think I've ever seen him look at someone the way he looks at you," he said, his words trailing off near the end. "Even if he tries to deny it..."

Cecilia stiffened, sure that she misheard him. Her hand went to the button anyway, sliding the door free. She almost didn't hear the click of it shutting behind her with her pulse thrumming in her ears. Crow *had* to be lying. This was just another tactic because his anger had been thwarted by Noa, right?

She shook her head. It was ridiculous—wasn't it? Her thoughts were torn, pulled in two different directions as she remembered Rune's comforting actions and then Noa's flirtatious behavior. Cecilia bit her lip. Even if Crow was telling the truth, she had enough to focus on right now, and the last thing she wanted to do was make an enemy of Noa.

18

KING'S REPUBLIC ✧ 2704-11-29

GLACIER

Glacier woke, grappling with his phone to find it was 4:00am. He'd slept through dinner. Throwing his arm over his face, he sighed, reconsidering sleep when it always ended up turning into a prison. A prison that traded his memories for a make-believe version of Kat—an ominous copy that left him feeling uneasy, like he'd forgotten something important.

He pushed himself up and tapped the window for the shade between the glass panes to adjust, vanishing to reveal the waning night sky's purplish glow.

"You're supposed to be sleeping."

Glacier tensed, whipping his head toward Noa with an eye cracked open. He frowned, huffing slightly as he rapped his knuckles against the window again to shade it. "Shouldn't I be saying the same thing to you?"

She threw back the covers and tapped it to reveal the sky once more. "No point in trying to sleep now," she said, peering at the plains stretching out to the edges of the forest. "I hoped that you might just pass out until a reasonable time, but I figured that was probably asking too much when I came back around six to find you dead to the world."

"I don't think that means that *you* have to stop sleeping..."

"Please," she said with a roll of her eyes. "I'm not human. I don't need sleep."

"Funny," he said dryly, pulling on his shoes to follow her into the hall. His voice dropped to a whisper, trying not to disturb the other passengers. "Where are you going?"

"You didn't get dinner, and I didn't feel like eating until now. So, I suppose *we're* going to the dining car. Doesn't seem like I can get rid of you anyway..."

"You realize that you could've just put me with Rune and Crow, right?"

She gave a short, clipped laugh. "Yeah, because that would've gone over well. While you might manage okay with Rune, I'm pretty sure pairing me with Cecilia might not be the best idea. She's probably scared to death of me by now. Aside from that, I think the more important point is that you're quite literally the key to the key I want."

His mind tripped over her comment regarding Cecilia as she started through the next passage door. "I know you're a little terrifying sometimes, but—"

"Glad we're on the same page."

"But why would Cecilia be scared of you?"

She stopped, and Glacier almost smacked into her before she spun around. "She didn't tell you about what happened yet, did she?"

"No," he said, eyeing her suspiciously. "Did you... did you do something?" The way she brought the whole thing up made Glacier nervous that Noa might've been the one to upset her, but he didn't think Cecilia was *afraid* of her from their recent interactions. Timid? Definitely. Outright terrified? No.

She chewed on her lip in contemplation before responding, "No. I want to give her the opportunity to talk to you first. Give her a couple of days. If she isn't ready then, I'll tell you."

Although he wasn't thrilled about it, he gave a reluctant nod, and she led the way again. The corridor through the cars eventually gave way to the dining car, lined with booths along the sides, two-person tables down the middle, and a bar counter in the far corner. A dimmed screen rotated through the options of toast, eggs, bacon, waffles, oatmeal, and pancakes, the latter of which Noa didn't hesitate to select with a cup of coffee.

Whatever little machine that laid hidden behind the wall whirred to life, manifesting a hot plate in the window for her to take once the shutter retracted. Even when Glacier had traveled by train *once* back in Amarais, there'd been a chef to do all the cooking, but he supposed that perhaps that wasn't as desirable or feasible for this sort of mass transit over time.

After he'd made his own selection of oatmeal and diced apples, he slid into the booth across from her, gliding against the smooth pleather backing. "Am I actually going to meet Nyx in person when we reach Southaven?" Glacier asked.

She nodded, continuing to cut apart her pancakes like she might drop dead if she didn't eat them fast enough.

"Why didn't she meet up with us back in Miralta though?"

She gave a half-shrug, washing everything down with her coffee. "Don't know. She just said that she couldn't make it. Could've been some flags at the border that she didn't want to trip and decided it was safer to stay put. I can't really say that I disagree with the idea since I don't want her to compromise herself for the sake of waiting together until things settle down again."

He chewed thoughtfully, absently tapping his spoon against the rim of his bowl while he surveyed the tree-dotted horizon in its warm glow. "And where are we going after Southaven?"

"Don't know. Won't know until we get there."

"Wait, what?" Glacier asked, cringing as the handle of his spoon hit a little too hard against the bowl, so he shoved it back into his food. "Why? How do you *not* know?"

"Nyx has the itinerary," she said. "She's the one that examines all our outs and decides where to go based on timings and openings. It's why we ended up in Amarais when we did. She predicted, based on past behavior, that the entire palace would be preoccupied with Louis's demands for entertainment, so we'd be able to get in and out without being noticed."

"But that didn't work out as planned..."

Noa sighed. "Yes, but that's mainly because we were left with three possible places to search. Not to mention that all the building plans were difficult to map out because of the restrictions and versions, so she eventually had to tap into the feeds and grab what she could while leaving as little evidence of intrusion as possible. *Hell*—we weren't even positive what the piece looked like at first, considering there are a couple other countries with a similar white-silver-platinum and blue emblem as well."

His shoulders dropped, resting an elbow on the table as he reached for the back of his neck. He wasn't sure why *he* felt embarrassed when he wasn't the one to lock it up. "I don't think anyone has seen it outside of the vault since my grandfather died before I was born. My dad hated talking about him, but Louis... He seemed to believe that Elias was practically a god. Never seemed to be good enough to please him either." His hand fell away, leaning back in his seat and folding his arms over his chest. "Can't say I'm disappointed I never met him, considering that he probably would've killed both me and my father himself."

Noa watched him for a moment, slowly chewing the last of her food before mirroring his initial movement. She leaned back, half-tossing an arm over the bench's backing with a scrutinizing gaze. "How you managed to go this long without shoving one of those assholes down a staircase is beyond me."

He chortled in surprise, recalling a moment in which Kat had motioned like she had been about to do just that in the foyer while Glacier had looked on in horror. "I'm pretty sure Kat would've beaten me to it."

The corner of her mouth ticked upward. "If it's any consolation, I've come to realize that family is who you choose. It's not dependent on the blood you share. Your blood relatives may reject you or you might not have any left in the world, but you can still have a family." She plucked up her coffee cup, tracing circles with her thumb near the handle as she set her sights on the sunrise.

Glacier thought about the Angelis's as he returned to his meal, remembering all the little promises he'd made with Cecilia that made her the sister he'd never had. They were the only people he had left to go back to if they'd welcome him. He just hoped Noa was right, and that they were okay right now, wherever they were.

NOA

Later that morning, Noa had gathered everyone in the larger of the two cabins, where Crow had brought in his plate piled with eggs and bacon, barely getting in his order before the menu swapped to lunch. He'd taken a seat on the bench across from her near the window, and Cecilia had perched on the edge of the opposite side, leaning away as he scraped his fork against the glazed ceramic.

"Aren't you hungover?" Noa asked, narrowing her eyes at him. "I could've sworn I saw you shoving your way into a bathroom earlier, followed by loud retching noises."

He stopped his chewing long enough to shoot her a glare.

"Anyway," Rune said, clearing his throat from where he stood, leaning against the window. "We'll be arriving in about an hour, so we should probably discuss what we'll be doing."

"I talked to Nyx a little earlier," Noa said. "She said that her train was delayed for some reason, so she made reservations for us to stay in a hotel for the night under our current names. It's not exactly ideal, but she'll be meeting with us first thing in the morning. From there, we'll start the next leg of the trip."

"But we don't know where we're going?" Cecilia asked hesitantly.

"None of us know, so just roll with it," Noa replied. "Enjoy the ride, not the anticipation of the destination."

She worried her lip, shrinking down a little.

Noa stretched. "I'm just glad we're on the express route. I'm already sick of being on this train. I'm ready to be somewhere I can actually walk."

Crow scoffed. "I don't think letting a psychopath like you out on the streets of King's is a smart decision."

"Did Rune finally give you that much-needed attitude adjustment?" she asked, her voice slipping into a faux syrupy-sweet tone. "Or do I need to kick your ass when we get off this train?"

Rune frowned. "Don't make me separate you two."

"We came to an understanding," Crow said, pointing to his chest with his fork—a gesture in which Noa deemed incredibly stupid if she wanted him dead. "And I understand that while you may be in charge, you *need* me."

"That so?" she asked, arching a brow.

"I didn't say anything like that—" Rune said.

"*I'm* the professional thief," Crow said with a confident smirk. "You're *not*. Simple as that." He set his plate off to the side and dropped his arms to lazily rest against his knees.

She leaned forward, her voice dropping to a near-purr. "I believe you're issuing a challenge."

"Please leave the competition for when we get off the train," Rune said.

"Shoplifting!" she declared, pointing a finger into the air like she had made a discovery.

"Oh, you're on—" Crow thrust out a hand to shake.

"Do *not*," Rune growled.

She took it, lifting her chin with the utmost confidence that was followed by Rune's despairing groan.

"If either of you idiots get caught out-stealing each other. I'm leaving you."

Noa had to resist grabbing Glacier by the arm and pulling him along through the train station, hating how he gawked at the Corvian-Bellegardian architecture. Tall, wide windows curved with the domed ceiling, along with pale bricks supporting latticed glass skylights and decorated patterned walkways.

Instead of getting upset, a small smile crept onto her face, trying to grasp that feeling she'd experienced the first time she'd lost herself in a sea of Republicans—becoming another face in a melting pot of the other twelve countries. Her spark of wonderment extinguished when she caught a glimpse of a figure moving past one of the signposts and into the crowd. Noa would've known that silhouette anywhere.

"Hurry it up," she called over to Glacier. It was enough for him to push forward, keeping close behind everyone else while she picked up the pace, brushing shoulders with Crow. "No shoplifting," she whispered.

"What? Scared you'll lose?"

"No."

All signs of teasing fell away, replaced with concern. "What's wrong? What's going on?"

"Later. I need to talk to Rune. Hang back and make sure the other two don't get split off from us."

She jogged ahead to walk alongside Rune with a quick glance back to see Crow bringing up the rear.

"You good?" Rune's brows knit together.

"Actually, *no...*" she mumbled. "We have company."

His eyes widened, briefly darting around the wide corridor until his phone buzzed in protest. Noa caught the linked address just before he tapped it.

"Don't say it, just lead," she said. The last thing they needed was to announce where the hell they were going.

He brought up the map as they left the building, stepping out onto the crowded sidewalk and heading straight for the intersection. The smell of the sea air brought an excited giggle from Cecilia, but Noa's stomach clenched in protest.

"How do you want to handle this?" he continued.

"Well," she began. "I have a theory I'd like to test, but I'd need you to trust me."

He was quiet for a moment, before he said, "All right, I'll bite."

"Okay, let's get to the room. I'll lay it out for you there."

Each storefront-cluttered block they passed became another few minutes of plan formulation gone. She'd tried to focus her attention on the reflections in the windows to where Crow peered behind them with his hand tight around his bag's strap. Her concentration split the moment the docks came into view up ahead, dead-ending the street with traffic poles at the start of plastic, wood-patterned planks that led to private boats and docks. A prime view of the commercial carriers rested a little further up the curved shoreline, crawling with people.

Noa's heart hammered a little harder in her chest as Rune stepped into the revolving glass doors of what had to be their hotel. She had to stop herself from following him in favor of keeping her head down. She waved her hand to Crow, signaling him to coral the others around the elevator bank while Rune approached the front desk. They left temporary indents in the plush navy-to-royal blue oversized rugs in the lobby's sitting areas, matching the nautical theme blended with the Republic's national colors. She suppressed a grimace when her boots scraped against the grout of the mosaic tiles in the elevator nook, noting how they'd tried to make it look like seafoam.

Rune's swift return didn't leave her any time to examine much more, handing over the entire pack of keycards. "Rooms next to each other." Then he hit the button, and they rode it skyward. Each numbered plaque on the wall was about a two-second gap for a walk and half a second to run, leaving them with about sixteen seconds to prepare for someone to emerge from the elevator. She'd have to count the stairs later.

"Your room," she said, holding out the first key to Crow, who took it and started inside just as she held the next out to Glacier. He opened his mouth as if he was about to question her but snapped it shut before following Crow inside. Noa offered the final one to Cecilia, who stole a glance at Rune before her shoulders fell.

"Cecilia," Noa started as she shuffled toward her new room. "Can I have a moment to talk with you first?"

She blinked, a little surprised. "Oh," she replied, dropping her bag inside. "Sure."

Noa moved to the next room, pushing it open with a motion for both her and Rune to go in ahead of her, and kicked the door shut behind them. At least the walls and bedding were white, and the curtains were already drawn, leaving sleek, modern, boxy fixtures diffusing soft light off the coffered ceiling.

"I need you to do me two favors," Noa said, not bothering with a preamble.

"Um..."

"Don't let anyone leave your room until I say so, all right? I need everyone in one place, so do whatever you have to do to convince everyone to stay put."

Cecilia's baffled expression didn't instill much confidence, but she nodded anyway. "O- okay."

"Now, my next request is going to sound... even weirder, but I need you to trust me. I promise I'll explain later."

Rune shifted his footing—an indication that he was potentially catching on to what the plan was. Noa, however, hoped that this gamble was right, along with her assumptions of why she'd seen Ezra back in the station.

19

KING'S REPUBLIC ✦ 2704-11-30

NOA

Noa crept out into the hall around 4:30AM, feeling for her phone and room key in her jacket pockets as another door popped open to reveal Cecilia.

"Go back to bed," she said, keeping her tone firm but unbothered, despite being anything but. "Stay in the room like I instructed."

"Noa—"

She narrowed her eyes, tilting her head in warning. "Look, if I'm not back before Nyx arrives, tell her what I had you do. She'll understand what's going on."

"I don't know what Nyx looks like. How will I—"

"Crow does. And Nyx knows which rooms we're in. Now lock the door and wait for one of us to come get you."

Cecilia lingered another moment longer before the door clicked shut, and Noa waited for the latch of the secondary lock. After that, the only sound Noa could make out on this floor was the muffled thumps of her boots against the carpet. The lobby was just as quiet with a single person manning the front desk, who gave her a small wave as she left.

The cool, foggy, early-morning air coiled around her—smothering her. Traffic was sparse at this hour, one of the few people she passed was a man wearing grungy overalls and waders, whistling an upbeat tune that made Noa's stomach churn. Most of the other dockworkers and fishermen were either already in the port or preparing to set off with their cargo.

She retrieved her phone again, slowing when she passed the vehicle poles and stepped onto the boardwalk. Her screen told her that her destination was dead ahead, marking a little shack down a gravel path a little further northbound. At this angle, she could make out the digital padlock on the entrance, but the extra-wide double doors on the opposite end were flung open to its private dock.

She sucked in a breath, bolstering herself as she followed the side of the building. A little prayer was the best she could do as the muddy ground dipped closer to the water, forcing her to leap onto the dock. The good news: it didn't collapse. The bad news: the yawning maul of the storehouse was pitch black, like an everlasting night ripped straight from one of the other nightmarish stories in *The Origin of Magic's* pages. Shadows teemed along the edges of the room, shifting and fluttering.

A lantern flicked on to her right, illuminating a workbench under a tool board with contents neatly organized on pegs. A scuffed, metal rowboat hung from the ceiling, strung up by cables and pulleys. Oars hung on a display along the back wall like trophies. Various storage bins and miscellaneous repair parts lined the final wall opposite the workbench. Every single item's location seared into her mind before she fixed her sights on her target again.

"Good morning, Noa." Ezra leaned up against the workbench, wearing that familiar, shit-eating grin. "I decided to bring a friend if that's all right."

He motioned over to the chair in front of the oar wall, where a man sat with his hands bound behind him and tape over his mouth. Those mismatched eyes darted between her and Ezra, who hadn't spared his hostage a glance.

"Rather ballsy of you to break into the Amaraian palace," he mused. "And not only did you somehow manage to walk out alive" —he began to circle Glacier's seat, causing him to go rigid before dropping his hands to his shoulders— "but dragging the prince with you... Even I'm impressed."

Glacier leaned forward, trying to put distance between the two of them as Noa's fingernails dug into her palm.

Ezra chuckled, casually walking toward the storage wall. He was baiting her to go for him. "I don't suppose you'll be so kind as to tell me what you're trying to do? It's been what? A few months? You never call... you never write..." He prowled back toward her, minding the gap that split the dock in two where the rowboat hovered near the ceiling.

"Funny," she responded flatly. "It's almost as if I don't want to talk to you."

"Noa, please—" he said, radiating faux amusement. "Just think about all the good times we had together." His mocking smile vanished. "Oh, wait. There weren't any. It's almost like you ripped everything out from under me just when I thought I might have it all. Now look" —he gestured at her, disgusted— "the star pupil, throwing everything away. You always were an ungrateful bitch."

"Last time I checked, you were the bitch," Noa said. "But sure, I'll take it. Now stop wasting my time and either tell me what you want or get lost."

"You know, I was instructed to give you a *choice*. You could either kill this sad excuse for an Amaraian" —he pointed a thumb behind him, and Glacier's eyes went wide— "or I can kill you myself before I do the honors. My final shot at redemption to prove that I was robbed of my rank."

"You can keep the damned title, Ezra," she spat. "If you honestly thought I really wanted it in the first place, you're a complete dumbass. I just wanted to kick your ass in front of everyone because I had the opportunity."

His eyes darkened. "It's a good thing that I didn't plan on actually giving you the option anyway." He pulled an object from his pocket—a thin, palm-sized bar that a blade slid from with a flick of his wrist. A faint *click* locked it into place like a door shutting on her, sealing her fate.

"Round two," she mumbled, lunging forward.

She ripped a tool from the wall, not really caring which one, and hurled it at him. He feigned to the side before he went for her, gasping as he was suddenly yanked back by his hood. Flailing, he swung the knife around, catching the back of Glacier's hand. He stumbled backward, a mess of black hair obscuring his features before dark brown eyes shone through where green and blue had been, along with a black rune now broken by broken skin and a trail of blood.

Rune ripped the tape off his mouth.

"What the hell?" Ezra seethed.

Noa shoved her body into him, knocking him to the floor and sending the knife flying.

He roared, throwing her off him. "You cheating bitch!"

She clawed at the floorboards in her slide toward the water, shoving herself to her feet mere centimeters from the edge. Ezra matched her speed, the two of them hurtling toward the knife, but Rune got there first, just in time for Ezra to tackle him against the wall—the force of the collision causing the bins to sway. Before Ezra knew what was happening, Rune kicked the knife to Noa, and she scooped it up, hurling it into the water in one fluid motion.

"Swim for it, bitch," she taunted.

Ezra growled, shoving Rune down in favor of his true target with bared teeth. She tried to sidestep his run at her, putting herself closer to the damn bin wall—a mistake that nearly knocked the wind out of her when he feigned passing by and snapped back to pin an arm over her throat. Her back smacked into the containers, and she gritted her teeth as Rune sprinted toward them again.

"I *will* snap her neck if you come any closer!"

Rune's boots skidded against the planks, squeaking to a halt. Noa was at least thankful that he appeared to take Ezra's words to heart. She knew he'd been letting that fury simmer for years, allowing it to fester like an untreated wound from every time he'd snarl at her like he'd been slighted. Those words made her next action that much easier.

Instead of kicking Ezra in the balls—not to say he didn't deserve that, but he'd absolutely see it coming—she twisted to kick the lever off to his left. The pulleys whirred, and the rowboat dropped behind him. He whipped his face around, tensing in surprise as she reached out for the tacklebox teetering on the small table next to the bins and smacked it against his head.

He fell like a stone to the planks, and she gasped, gulping down air as she dropped the box next to his prone form. That malicious light in his eyes and cocky smile were gone now, replaced by shadows and the orange hue of the rising sun.

Sinking Ezra's body into a shallow grave under the dock sounded rather poetic for such a shallow human being. Noa couldn't recall him ever wanting anything more than things of surface value like beauty, praise, and the joy that came with inflicting pain on others.

"Won't they find him?" Rune asked, ducking his head on the walk back. "He's not that deep."

"They will," she whispered. "But there's no avoiding it. The best it'll do is buy us a few hours, which is enough for us to get the hell out of here."

"Republic patrols are going to start swarming the place. They're going to have to start piecing *something* together."

"They'll start to look, and then they'll be told to stop. That's how this works. Once they discover he doesn't have any legitimate IDs, it'll throw up a red flag. People more important than the local detectives and authorities will shut down the investigation. They'll make up some random identity, some fake story for the press, and sweep the whole thing under the rug. Done—problem solved. Ezra doesn't exist, he never existed, and he will continue to not exist once he's discovered."

Rune grimaced. "You can't be serious."

"We're ultimately disposable, Rune. I would think that you and Crow would understand how this works. Even though we were in completely different positions, do you not believe that the same would've been done for either of you?"

He said nothing, though his begrudging look told her that she was right.

"We don't have any time to waste," she breathed.

"Why? Ezra's dead. You just said that'd buy us time—"

She shook her head. "Yes, for our *escape*. But I was right that he was here for Glacier. He was trying to use him to lure me out, which *mostly* worked. He must've managed to pick up our trail in Amarais, which means that he probably had the last GPS coordinates of—"

"Of the damn SUV."

"Exactly," she said. "And the one flaw with Ezra being in Amarais is that most people there likely wouldn't have talked to him. They certainly didn't want anything to do with us while we were there under false pretenses."

"What are you getting at? I'm not sure I follow if Ezra wasn't able to track us himself—"

"There's an Amaraian with him." She shoved her way through the revolving doors of the hotel. The two of them remained quiet until the elevator doors slid shut.

"There's *two* of them?" he hissed, his question laced with fear.

"Yes," she said through gritted teeth. "And if Ezra doesn't report back very soon, he's going to know something's wrong. Not to mention how pissed he's going to be if one of Ezra's final communications confirmed that Glacier's half-Miraltan."

A chime ended their conversation, and Noa stalked down the hall with Rune on her heels. "Get them. I'll get your stuff," she said, pointing toward the first room.

He went to knock, but it swung open to Cecilia, who moved past him and straight for Noa as Rune made his way inside.

"Noa, I—"

The elevator dinged at the end of the hall, and Noa sliced an arm through the air to silence her. Her heart raced, picturing the doors opening to Ezra's *very* pissed accomplice, but instead, a woman took his place. Her black hair was on the short side, falling midway between her chin and collar bone. Thick-rimmed glasses framed her lighter face, the lenses glinting off the overhead ceiling lights. She wore a cross-body bag that was slung over her shoulder, the bulk of it hanging at her back with her hands tucked into her jacket pockets. She might as well have been an angel descending from the heavens.

"Don't look at me like that," she said with slight irritation as she came to a halt next to Cecilia, who glanced between them.

"I could kiss you right now," Noa said.

"Pass."

Noa caught the look of confusion crossing Cecilia's face. "Nyx, Cecilia. Cecilia, Nyx." She pressed her room key to the door, pushing it open. "Inside, now. Both of you."

"Any particular reason why you're spouting orders?" Nyx asked, following along anyway.

"I need you to do me a favor."

Nyx folded her arms over her chest, rolling her eyes. "I thought we've been over this before…"

"I'm being serious this time." Noa huffed, fishing her phone out of her jacket and tossing it to her.

She caught it, flipping it over in her perfectly tailored, gloved hands to view the screen. Instead of tapping through it, she raised a brow and held it up for Noa. The display showed an incoming call.

Shit.

"You want to take this or let it go?" Nyx asked.

She held out her hand, a silent request to give it back. "I need you two to give me five minutes alone."

Nyx nodded, placing the phone in her hand and motioning for Cecilia to follow her out into the hall. The second the door clicked shut, she drew in a sharp breath and put the phone to her ear.

"What the hell have you done?" came the voice at the other end of the line.

"It's called self-defense," she replied, her voice tinged with anger.

"This isn't funny. You were given a choice—Where is he?"

"If you honestly think that *Ezra,* of all people, would actually give me a choice, you're more of a dumbass than him."

"Tell me it isn't true, Noa."

She could hear the rage held back through gritted teeth, but she refused to answer. Instead, she went for the merciful response. "Go home, Kole." And hung up. She only took a moment to compose herself before she let Cecilia and Nyx back in, the latter of which gave her a look of suspicion.

Noa handed her the phone again. "It's being tracked. I need you to run it and ditch it when you lose him."

"I can do that," Nyx replied. "Who am I looking for?"

Noa's eyes flicked to Cecilia, hesitating in her answer. "An Amaraian. Typical coloring. However, he'll probably suspect something's up if he follows the tracker and doesn't see me... Which is why I need you to do me another favor, Cecilia."

Cecilia shifted uncomfortably, turning to Nyx. "Can- can I see your hand?"

Nyx paused, shooting Noa a questioning look before she complied. She held out her left hand, which Cecilia took after grabbing her eyeliner pen from her pocket and pushed up the sleeve of Nyx's jacket. She drew out a looping, elegant-looking rune on her wrist, lightly tracing it with her fingertips. Noa watched Nyx's features change, shifting to match her own. Her black hair changed to a dull brown, her near-black eyes lightened to a chocolate hue, and the colors and styles of her clothes subtly shifted to somewhat resemble the ones she was currently wearing.

Cecilia stepped back, and Nyx looked down at her hands, flipping them over with wide eyes at seeing her gloves missing. Then she moved to the mirror, touching her face—well, *Noa's* face.

"Creepy," she breathed, pulling off her glasses and leaning closer.

Though the voice didn't match the body, Noa still felt unsettled. "Yeah, that's... pretty unnerving..."

Nyx took a step back and swung her bag around, putting her glasses away, acquiring a hair tie, and collecting a frosted bag that she tossed to Noa. Inside the bag, she found several smaller bags, each packed with an ID, a couple of SIM cards, and tickets.

"I have a few more in the works to burn through," Nyx said. "But that will be once we get there. I'll ditch our shadow first and take the next train out." She reached for the door. "You owe me." She jerked it out of the frame, starting out into the hall.

Noa shot forward, catching it before it shut behind her. "Don't do anything I wouldn't do," she said, immediately regretting what *should* be a request to stay safe.

Nyx smirked, mirroring one of Noa's admittedly arrogant, obnoxious expressions that made her wince. She'd brought this on herself.

The smirk fell away, replaced by Nyx's resting face merged with her own. "I'll assume you didn't actually mean that."

20

KING'S REPUBLIC ✦ 2704-11-30

KOLE

Kole bit back a scream at the beep of the call ending. He threw the phone against the white, rumpled comforter, where it bounced once before landing against the pilled fabric. He paced the threadbare carpeting while running his hands through his hair. She was actually doing this. Noa was protecting this half-Miraltan *mutt*, and godsdamned Ezra had likely pushed her too far this time.

"You *idiot!*" Kole swung back around, grabbing up the flimsy desk chair and hurling it across the room. He couldn't tell if the outburst had been meant for Noa or Ezra, but he didn't think it really mattered anymore. One of them had decided to go play with fire while the other had stabbed him in the back.

A Miraltan in Amarais masquerading as a prince.

Promise you'll stick with me?

"Why?" he growled. "You had *everything*, and you *left*—You threw it all away, and for what?" His fist collided with the vanity mirror, and it buckled. Shards tinkled against the dresser, but a few smaller pieces came away in his hand. He barely felt it, overshadowed by the pain lancing his heart. A warped, broken version of himself stared back.

Kole shoved away from the vanity and collected his phone, blood dripping onto the sheets. He ripped open the door to the dim hallway and sprinted down the stairwell at the far end, spilling out onto the street. Gray skies greeted him as he stalked away from the building and pulled up Noa's location—a small dot that was already on the move.

Cursing, he dove down an alley, cutting across intersections right before the signals changed. Block after block, he pushed his legs to carry him toward her a little faster until he turned a corner. That was when he saw her silhouette in the crowd. He pushed past pedestrians and sidestepped a bicyclist who brushed up against his jacket sleeve. She turned the corner up ahead, and he shot forward in pursuit.

But when he caught up, his eyes went wide, searching for that familiar form. Kole spun around before he checked his phone. The tracker's signal was lost. The dot was *gone*.

NOA

Noa's heart steadied once she climbed the stairs and stepped into the second floor of the luxury car, where overstuffed, faux-wood-framed furniture sat bolted down to the royal blue carpeting. She jogged toward the velvet-covered bench stretched under the window facing the terminal, dropping her bag by her feet.

Crow whistled somewhere behind her. "Nyx really pulled out all the stops for this ride, didn't she? Speaking of—"

"Quiet," Noa said. No sign of Nyx, but no Kole either. She reached for her phone, and her hand curled into a fist, remembering *Nyx* had it. Rune nudged her elbow and tilted his phone for her to see.

> Clear.

Noa puffed out a sigh of relief and swayed as the train crawled forward. They were leaving. Nyx was fine. And Ezra was dead.

"What's going on?" Glacier asked, frowning as Noa turned around. "You said Nyx was going to meet us. We have our new IDs and everything, but she's not here."

"She was for a few minutes..." Cecilia said, worrying her lip.

When Noa kept her sights pinned on Cecilia, Glacier's voice turned sharp. "Well? You and Crow went from talking about stealing to everyone being locked in hotel rooms, and now Nyx just... suddenly isn't boarding with us? Some transparency would be nice if we're going to tag along for whatever the hell this is."

"Yeah," Crow said, stepping up next to him—she would've raised her brows if she hadn't been biting down on her tongue to keep everything from spilling out. "You said you'd tell me later. It's later, Noa."

She grimaced. "They caught up to us, Crow. I saw one of them in the station yesterday."

Crow blinked a couple times before his eyes went wide. "*Shit.*"

A slow-growing panic spread onto Glacier's and Cecilia's faces like water washing over the rocks along Republic shoreline. The prime view of it all emerged in the windows behind her three judges, threatening to take her with it.

"Who?" Glacier asked—a hesitant question he would regret. But there was no point in drawing it out.

"Volkov," she answered. No special delivery. No dramatic reveal. She'd simply placed it in front of him, waiting for whatever reaction he'd give her. She got about what she thought she would.

He chortled. "What? Is this some kind of joke? Because it's not funny. The Volkov aren't real—"

"They are *very* real," she replied, taking a menacing step toward him. He recoiled, and Cecilia shrank back with him. "And I would know because I was one."

Their pale faces matched the foamy laps of the waves that remained in the too-quiet car. Cecilia looped her arm through his, trying to pull him back, but failing. He was rooted to the spot—either because he was too afraid to move or because he felt that need to keep standing his ground. She couldn't tell, but it also didn't matter.

Cecilia's voice wobbled, breaking the silence since escape wasn't an option. Her panicked blue eyes strayed to Rune, dropping to his now-bandaged hand. "Is- is that why—"

"I recognized a man in the station when we arrived," Noa said. "And I had a suspicion about why he'd suddenly bother showing up in King's, so I told Crow to bring up the rear. After my *test*, I'm led to believe that our vehicle back in Amarais gave one last signal that I had assumed the new management would check out for themselves. They would find the remains of the SUV, write it off, and call it a day. However, what I didn't consider was that one of them might do some digging and find information on the Volkov. They likely decided that they couldn't risk the possibility of a certain *prince* returning, so they contacted someone to finish the job."

Glacier's eyes grew wide, but that didn't stop Noa from pressing forward.

"So my test was using you as bait—and by *you*, I mean Rune. I asked Cecilia to make him look like you, albeit a bit taller, but it was enough to do the trick. We confronted him, and now we know there's a contract on your head. One that the Volkov will pursue until it's completed."

"You could've gotten Rune killed," Cecilia whispered.

"What the hell, Noa?" Crow demanded.

"Quiet, Crow," Rune said sharply. "She told me the risk, and I took it anyway. If we had just locked ourselves in for the night, it's very possible that he would've just broken in and dealt with *all* of us."

Crow flinched. Noa's stomach twisted at the display, especially since Rune was defending a type of test she'd created for him. She hadn't been sure how he'd react when face-to-face with life or death, but he'd passed, doing everything she'd hoped for to shift the less-than-ideal conditions to their advantage. He'd even kicked the knife to her, knowing full well that if she'd chosen to keep it that it could've backfired on him.

"He said that he was supposed to give me a choice," Noa said. "I could either kill Glacier or suffer the consequences. Instead, he decided to bait me and got too cocky. So we killed him."

Crow's jaw dropped. "The two of you *killed* a Volkov? Wait, if he's dead, then what was with the rush?"

"There was a second one with him," she said. "One that he was supposed to check in with but never got the chance. Instead, the two of them used some resources to track my phone, and I got a call from the other one when Rune and I got back to the hotel. He was *pissed*. I figured he would be, so I asked Cecilia to do one last party trick when Nyx showed up to send her off looking like me with my ticking time-bomb of a phone."

Cecilia's hand cupped her mouth, taking a step back as everyone turned to her.

"I didn't tell either of you in the first place because I had hoped that it wouldn't come up again. The *only* reason why these two and Nyx know is because it's how we met. I was leaving the Volkov and somehow picked up stragglers." Noa broke into a faux smile, fearing it might be on the edge of manic. "So here we are—a car full of killers, thieves, and royalty. What a combination!" She threw her arms up, collapsing into the window seat.

"So..." Glacier started, his voice shaking. "Not only are you telling me that you're supposedly the only person who can open this *Vault*—one that nobody knows where it is to restore magic based on some old storybook— but you're also Volkov. A member of *the* Volkov—that group of killers-for-hire that people poke fun of online that nobody believes is real."

She propped her arm on the armrest, placing her chin into the heel of her hand. "Yep. It unfortunately seems that way, doesn't it?"

GLACIER

"There's a group of assassins trying to kill me," Glacier mumbled. It was mostly to himself, as if saying it enough would allow it to sink in, but Cecilia had the unfortunate honor of listening to his ramblings in their little corner of the cabin. Noa, Rune, and Crow had kept to the opposite window, where the former two conversed in hushed, casual tones, and Crow stared up at the ceiling, half-sprawled out on the seat next to Noa with the occasional contribution.

What kind of hell had he fallen into since that day back at the palace? Had he and Cecilia made a mistake? Would he be dead right now if they had stayed in Miralta? All of his questions ultimately converged, leading him to the one that bothered him the most: why couldn't he get Kat out of his head? Instead of blurting out any of those, he asked, "Where did you learn to glamour people like that? I didn't think you knew how."

She fidgeted, refusing to look him in the eyes. "I... I met someone," she whispered. "Back in Miralta. He was an Illusionist."

"He taught you?"

"Yeah." She swallowed before she continued, discomfort creeping into her voice. "Glacier, he- he started out really nice, but then... I mean, I could tell he might be a little uncomfortable with me looking Amaraian, but... He tried to abduct me. He asked if I *wanted* to go with him to another part of Miralta to help him, and when I told him no, he got really upset. We fought, and... and I defended myself..." A tear rolled down her face.

He immediately pulled her into a hug. "It's okay," he said, feeling her squeeze back.

"It was an accident," she forced out through a shaky sob and slipped from his grasp. She took a steadying breath and swiped a hand across her face. "But I was scared, so I called Rune. And then Rune called Noa, and..." Her eyes unfocused like she was only now just piecing something together. "Oh, *gods*..." Her hand went to her mouth.

"She..." he said with a grimace. "She got rid of him, didn't she?"

"I'm so stupid," she mumbled.

"I can't say I wouldn't have tried to write it off if I was in your place," he said. "I'm just glad you're okay. I don't know what I would've done if you'd disappeared too."

"I really should've been there for yo—"

"Cecilia, don't. It's fine. Neither of us were prepared for this. We were just trying to keep it together." He huffed out a bitter laugh. "I just wanted to disappear, but now I might just get my wish..."

"Don't talk like that," she said, shaking her head. "No one's going to let that happen."

He sighed, running a hand through his hair. "This whole thing is insane."

Cecilia glanced over toward the others, her gaze lingering before she turned back. "Yeah... it really is."

21

CORVIA ✦ 2704-11-30

NOA

The sky began to take on an orange hue by the time their train arrived in Strada—Corvia's capital and the smallest, southernmost country in eastern Avaria. Each digital placard counted down to the second for arrivals and departures, and the large station clock suspended above the archway out of the terminal gleamed in the sunlight as if it were freshly polished.

Time progressed mercilessly here, even leaving magic behind before it could abandon them. It's why Nyx had skipped marking Cecilia as a Mage on her new ID—a move that Noa could agree on, especially once she'd witnessed one of the checkpoint guards sigh and pull a would-be entrant off to the side for special registration. His colleagues shook their heads when the Mage merged into the crowd again, garnering a few stray pitying looks from the violet-eyed natives. A dying subset of humanity walking among them, but already written off as obsolete—obsolete because they'd been replaced by medicine, machinery, and technology as a whole. So, in a sense, Corvia was the antithesis of Miralta.

Noa's shoes tapped against the bronze-flecked deep purple that transitioned into scraping against fresh brick pavers—all of it probably redone in the last year if she had to take a guess. Suited businessmen held phones up to their ears while traveling students in logoed sweatshirts stretched or leaned against friends, but all of them patiently waited for the local commuter train.

"*Guten Tag!*"

Her head whipped around to Crow. He was grinning, but it was more of an arrogant, playful grin, rather than one filled with excitement like she'd half-expected from Cecilia. The people around them exchanged glances, nervous smiles, and some of the students giggled, huddling a little closer together.

She dropped her voice low, leaning closer to him. "See, now *this* is why there's an international language—it's so people like *you* don't look like idiot tourists by poorly attempting to speak like a local."

The grin dropped, dipping into a frown. "*You've* been conversing with locals in Roth and Bellegarde—"

"Because *I* actually know the languages."

If you want to blend in, regardless of how you look, you need to learn the language.

Why?

People are less likely to turn on you if they consider you one of their own.

Truth. It'd gotten Noa overlooked for things on more than one occasion since people had assumed she was a native of most places—either with mixed parents or adoptive ones. The same could go for here too, considering how if it weren't for the eyes, Noa would be able to blend in as a Corvian just as easily. Bellegardian was the only one that tripped her up the most with its silent letters and strange pronunciation systems that didn't translate all that well from its written form into her mind. She absolutely faked it to the best of her ability whenever she needed to utter a single word in that language.

The commuter train pulled alongside the small platform and the doors slid open. People trickled out and reshuffled to make room for the next batch of incoming rush-hour traffic, leaving only standing room. Noa's body screamed in protest from her lack of sleep the night before, and she sulked as she wrapped her arms around Rune's chosen pole. He didn't pay her any attention, favoring his phone instead for what she hoped were directions.

"I'm spent," she mumbled.

"Cry more." Crow gave her a smug look, and she narrowed her eyes to slits.

Her immediate wrath was disrupted by Glacier's slight stumbling into one of the other poles, where he and Cecilia kept close. A passenger that'd bumped into him turned to apologize, hesitating at the sight of his green eye and then Cecilia before he forced out the nicety, though it was laced with remorse and confusion. That strong correlation and assumption that Miraltans wanted everything to do with saving magic perhaps ran a little too deep with all the history and stories.

Glacier kept his head down once the train began moving, and Noa ripped her eyes away, looking up at Rune. "Are we there yet?"

"Does someone need a nap?" A teasing smile danced across his face.

"I will kick your ass in front of all these people."

Rune shook his head and continued messing with his phone. Crow grabbed onto the pole and leaned over her to look at the map in his brother's hand. She shot him a glare, but he didn't notice, spouting off a casual, "What stop are we?"

So she punched him in the side. He winced, and Rune frowned.

"Get your armpit out of my face," she hissed.

"Maybe you should get your face out of my armpit."

"Don't make me separate you two," Rune warned. "We're only a stop away."

She straightened, slapping on a fake, sweet smile. "Don't worry. I won't do anything until I know there are no witnesses."

"See?" Crow threw his arm over her shoulders. "We can get along."

"If you don't remove your arm in the next five seconds," she said in a painfully cheery voice, "I will shatter your arm the moment we step off this train."

He jerked his arm away right before the train slowed, and Rune led the way out onto the large, diamond-patterned paving stones that made up the promenade. Every three or four large slabs gave way to intricately designed, circular beds of flowers or tall plants, and benches breaking up the spaces in between. Sleek, high-rise buildings climbed skyward on either side, plated with large, glittering windowpanes reflecting the orange-pink horizon. The building entrances didn't capture that same simplicity, instead looking more like the insides of old clock towers had been torn out and cobbled together in archways.

Cecilia gaped at the structures, her head turning to follow the twisting bronze sculpture that towered over the park near the middle of the strip.

"Keep up," Noa called, startling Cecilia before she jogged to catch up.

Their hotel continued with those muted, serene tones. Brassy, metallics spread throughout the lobby with splashes of dark purple and black furniture. A piano played somewhere on the opened floors above them, but all she could find were other guests walking past the balconies and the large waterfall chandelier twinkling above her head. Rune collected the room keys from the kiosk while Noa led the rest of their little group to the elevators. The scent of lavender tumbled out of the elevator car before they even stepped inside, overwhelming her. She didn't even notice that Rune had tapped the keys to the sensor and selected their room until the doors slid open again, the cards dangling in front of her face.

She sorted through them, frowning as they strolled down the hall. Six keys, all for the same room. Noa frowned, thinking that it must be a mistake until they reached a door at the end. She pressed a key to it, shoving it open to a spacious living room. Coffee-colored modular furniture sat in front of a floating electric fireplace wall that divided it from the kitchen. She started forward, past the wall of doors that must've been bedrooms, and dropped her bag next to the plush chair. The moment she fell into it and kicked her feet up onto the coffee table, the world around her vanished, immediately replaced with dreams.

GLACIER

The soft flickering of a fireplace roused Glacier again, and he sat up to that all-too-familiar scene of snowy windowsills and decorated shelves. That lingering feeling of forgetfulness refused to yield, despite giving it a few minutes, as if it might fade along with the drowsiness of sleep. When it didn't, he called out for Kat.

The faint call back prompted him to stand, and he started down the hall toward the office. Its doors were wide open, but the lights were off. The noise of Kat tapping something against the desk made him peer inside to make out her darkened frame in the chair—that damn key in her hand. Her shoulders fell as she snapped it against the mat, and the chair rolled back. When she started for him, she brushed away her hair like she was avoiding looking him in the eyes.

It wasn't until she stood in the threshold next to him that she said, "You can open it now if you'd like. But you should know that it's not something you can lock away again once it's done."

He moved forward anyway, taking a seat and picking up the key. Her shadowed face peered back at him in the doorway—her blue eyes filled with what he thought was guilt.

"You won't like what you find, Glacier."

It was enough to give him pause, debating if what he was about to discover was worth knowing. Equal parts dread and curiosity compelled him to reach down to that drawer, where it blinked green in answer. A small tug slid it free.

"I'm sorry," she said in a near-whisper before he plunged into darkness.

Glacier shivered and opened his eyes to his breath curling out in cold wisps. His mouth tugged down in a frown while he stared at the dim emergency lights lining the palace hallway. He was home, mere steps away from his room, but he might as well have been standing outside with the chill. Frost crept up the windows, fighting against the inevitable melt around the edges.

As a water droplet fell against the windowsill, a delayed drip echoed after—a sound coming from behind him, back where the source of the cold seemingly stemmed from. Swallowing, he began to turn, searching for the source of the noise.

A dark pool spread across the tile, partially obscured by shadow, but at its base lay a woman. Lifeless, emerald green eyes stared back at him, and black hair hung over her pale face. Then another drip—coinciding with a droplet falling from the thin, sharp instrument dangling over her, tucked into a man's hand. Glacier knew that shape towering over her, despite being unable to make out his features. Where had he seen it before?

The man stepped forward, dagger raised. Everything came into sharp focus as Glacier took a step back, throwing up his arms while ice climbed up his throat, ripping the air from his lungs like cold water.

Glacier gasped as he shot up in bed, throwing a hand to his heart. It fluttered around like a bird trapped in a cage while he shoved away his sweat-soaked hair, half-expecting Noa to be standing over him with a knife. He shook his head and rubbed at his face, warring over the afterimage of the man in his mind's eye—the same figure that had stood over him when he'd been trapped beneath the ice of his dream back in Amarais.

His hands dropped to his lap as he took in a few final deep breaths and mentally kicked himself for not examining the back of the key. He'd felt it though—his fingers had indented in the grooves where a V sat trapped within a triangle. The symbol for Volkov.

He glanced over at Cecilia, finding her still sound asleep, and carefully swung his legs over the side of the bed. Every step across the laminate might as well have been that horrid dripping from that knife. Glacier pulled the door shut behind him, falling against it with a sigh.

"Aren't you supposed to be sleeping?"

He jumped, biting down on his tongue as he whipped around. Noa sat on the padded bench lining the windows. Instead of ducking back inside like he immediately wanted to, he drew his hands up into his sleeves and stuffed them under his arms, halfway hugging himself. "Do *you* ever sleep?" he asked in a low whisper.

Glacier couldn't recall her retreating to a private bunk on the train, let alone if she'd managed to get any sleep back in Southaven, considering her little stakeout to send Rune out into the streets—much like how he'd slipped outside back in Miralta. The action sent goosebumps pricking at his arms now, imagining how easily someone else could've dragged him into an alley. Not to mention that if Noa had decided to give up on all this key-collecting nonsense, she could've killed him then or—hell, she could've done it back on the train from Miralta when they'd sat down for breakfast together. He'd been sitting face-to-face with a killer eating pancakes.

She shrugged, turning back to the window. "Sleep and I don't tend to get along very well. You afraid to sleep because of some idea that I'll come in there and kill you now?"

When he didn't answer right away, disturbed by the casual way she'd asked, she glanced back at him, prodding for a response.

"Honestly," he said. "Yeah." That was only the half of it.

"Well, don't be." She rolled her eyes. "If I wanted to kill you, I wouldn't do it in your sleep. I prefer my victims to be fully aware about what's about to happen and *why* it's happening."

"That's... reassuring..."

"Plus, there's that small issue of you being the key to the vault and all, which I sort of need."

"But you don't need to open it if you just kill me so they take you back."

A sudden, sharp laugh escaped her, muffled by her hand slapping over her mouth. "Don't be stupid. I burned that bridge the second I walked away. Offering that to me was just a way to clean up this mess quietly. They were banking on me being a dumbass and actually *wanting* to go back."

"And... you don't?"

"Hell *no*. I left for a reason. I knew exactly what could happen when I left, but I did it anyway. I had a new goal, so here I am."

"But... why? All because a Seer said so? That's all it took?"

She chuckled, her eyes fixing on the floor as she pushed back her hair. "I hated every minute of being Volkov. I didn't have any control over anything. I was told what to do, where to go, and who to kill. It wasn't *my* life—I didn't have a life of my own. There was always someone else pulling the strings. I was just a weapon, not a person, so if I wasn't useful, then I was better off dead."

Disposable. His heart squeezed, understanding that sentiment all too well. The horrid flash of that man coming at him with a dagger reemerged with that thought. "Um..." he started, not sure why he felt compelled to ask. "Is there... was there someone that went to Amarais about nineteen years ago? A member of the Volkov, I mean."

Honestly, the man might as well have been Louis with the sheer animosity rolling off him in thick waves, but the keycard's stamp against his fingertips told him otherwise. Mrs. Angelis had mentioned that his mother died when he was around a year old, but he'd always assumed that she'd died in an accident. The dream indicated otherwise, despite it being a dream. But it matched up with the information he'd been told about her being kept in that wing of the palace—that same hall where that Miraltan woman laid dead.

"I... think there's only one person that it could've been at that time..." Noa said. "But he's the only one who could say for sure. Not that he will. We don't keep records of any of the jobs we do once they're done, and we don't talk about it unless there's a breach of contract. That's rare, of course, considering the price for breaking a contract is—well..." She let the word hang in the air. "Needless to say, people tend to make sure they're good and ready before they want people swept under the rug." She paused, locking eyes with him. "It... wasn't your father, was it? I thought he died when you were older? Unless I'm misremembering the news..."

"My mother."

"Ah..." She shifted uncomfortably. "I'm sorry."

For someone usually so flippant, it was jarring to hear something that genuine. She cleared her throat, rubbing her hands on her leggings before she stood and started for the kitchen. The light turned on above the sink, and she began busying herself with something just out of view.

"What are you doing?" he asked, slowly rounding the counter.

"Coffee." She waved an arm in front of the faucet, filling the pot. "Then we start teaching you how to fight. So, for our first lesson, let's start with the basics of self-defense."

She flashed him a smile that he couldn't help but return with a smirk.

22

CORVIA ✧ 2704-12-01

NOA

"You know, it would be nice if you maybe *didn't* kill Glacier in the living room," Rune said, strolling past them to the kitchen.

Noa stopped herself from rolling her eyes, mainly because she might have just knocked the wind out of him. Glacier grimaced from his prone position on the floor, holding a hand to his chest.

"Look, maybe if he didn't try to act like a badass and attempt to outwit me, I wouldn't have to take him down a few notches," she called over to Rune, who looked unconvinced.

Glacier propped himself up on his elbows. "Please tell me we're done for now..."

Sighing, she offered him a hand and pulled him to his feet. Her lesson plan had hit a snag after a few linked questions that diverged into retaliation behavior. It started with him asking, "Like this?" about five times, her correcting him with each one, and then him just *going for it*. New or not, taking it easy on him wasn't exactly beneficial if he could eventually find himself face-to-face with Kole, and while Kole played more defensively to offset Noa's brash actions, Glacier would still be outmatched.

"Yeah, you're dismissed," Noa said, deciding that maybe she'd been a little too rough with him from his wince. "Go get breakfast." She padded back into her and Rune's room to change, undoing her hair tie and shaking her hair free with the thought that he'd need at least another day to rest before they started again.

She surveyed the room and collected a few of her strewn-about articles to tuck back into her bag, a little disappointed she was repacking after all her hard work of convincing Rune to kick out his brother for her. It was a completely selfish tactic after he'd roused her in the living room when dinner was delivered, but she'd smacked straight into that heart-wrenching dread of curling up in bed alone.

Solitude had been the one thing she'd begged for when she set out on this crusade, but now she was trying to fill that void with whatever temporarily fit. The irony of swinging from keeping everyone at arms-length to faking something a little more flirtatious wasn't lost on her since both were just as unfulfilling. One had been to protect herself, and then the other added another layer to put on a show to get what she wanted—a rough, awkward, too-intimate dance with Rune as a partner she hadn't fully trusted when their train stopped in Bellegarde.

By the end of that original three-week trust exercise, comprised of doing stupid couple things like holding hands in public and letting him put his arm around her waist without smashing his head against the pavement, she'd realized that she'd sort of *enjoyed* it. Mainly the part about putting on a show and making people uncomfortable with personal displays of affection, but also the connection of partnership sans tension that she'd had before all *this*—something that she'd fallen into much faster with Nyx.

She zipped up her bag and chewed on her lip. Nyx, however, had made it clear that she would rather die than share a room with either twin, but more specifically, *Crow*. The brief image of the four of them sitting outside a quaint Bellegardian café with heart-shaped wire chair backs and grated iron tabletops while she and Rune had been sharing a *flamiche* floated to the forefront of her thoughts. Crow had made some snickering comment Noa couldn't remember the details of, except for how it'd gotten a growl from Nyx. An empty glass later, his eyes were wide, blinking past the fresh stream of ice water dripping down his face while she folded her arms back over her chest and drummed her fingers against her sleeve in irritation.

"Look," Nyx had said later when she and Noa were alone, "just because we have them on board to help this shit along, it doesn't mean I have to *like* them. You don't have to like them either, but we all have stakes in this: we can't go home. So we might as well get our shit together for a few thefts and buckle in for the ride." Whether or not the twins had grown on Nyx had yet to be seen after that, but they'd managed to pierce Noa's initial barrier.

Noa headed back out as Rune laid out a tray of bagels on the counter, straight from room service with its fancy bronzed tray. Cecilia leaned forward on her barstool, frowning at Crow while he opened and closed nearly every cabinet door.

"Really?" Noa asked flatly. "What the hell are you doing? The silverware's in the drawer, dumbass."

"I'm not looking for the silverware, I'm taking *inventory*," Crow said, slamming another cabinet.

Rune looked like he might've been biting down on his tongue right before he grabbed up a dishtowel and snapped it at Crow. He danced away after a couple of hits.

"*Ow*—Okay, stop! *Stop!*" he yelled.

Cecilia giggled, trying to hide her amusement behind her mug. He narrowed his eyes at her as he plucked a bagel off the tray and jammed it in the toaster. "Apparently it's a crime to see what I'm working with just in case we get ambushed."

Noa rolled her eyes. "We're not getting ambushed. No one knows we're in Corvia."

"*Yet*," he added, pointing a finger at her. "If we end up spending a week here scoping the place out, I'm going to lose my damn mind thinking that the Volkov are trickling into the city to kill us and dump our bodies in some Corvian compost facility."

"We're eating," Rune grumbled.

"Yeah? Well, I'm *living*."

Glacier stepped up to the counter next to her, looking a little unsteady. Noa bit her lip, trying to ignore that tiny flicker of remorse for being a little too hard on him earlier. That thought was further solidified with a knock at the door that made both him and Cecilia jump. Noa jogged off toward it, checking the peephole and pulling it open for Nyx, who tossed her a box.

"Give me a little more warning next time," Nyx said, dropping her bag by the couch on her way to the kitchen. "I'd prefer to enjoy the accommodations I reserve for myself instead of letting the rest of you reap the rewards. At least then I can shove you in closet-sized cabins."

"Like you didn't do that from Corris to Southaven," Noa complained, shoving the door shut while she pried her new gift open.

Nyx picked out a bagel on the tray, rounding the counter for the toaster right as it popped up. Retrieving the toasted bagel halves for herself, she shoved the other into Crow's hands and started for the cream cheese. Crow's jaw dropped, and Noa suppressed a snort as he gestured wildly at her with wide eyes at his brother in some sort of telepathic communication.

"Who did you room with during the ride to Southaven, by the way?" Nyx asked, prying the lid off the container. "Rune? Or did you shove everyone in the other cabin to have it for yourself?"

"Glacier," Noa responded, immediately forgetting the question when she pulled back the protective packaging to find a new phone. "Oh, hell *yes*." She almost missed the scrutinizing look Nyx shot Glacier, who took a half-step away and bumped shoulders with Cecilia. Then Nyx's head swung around, aiming at Rune while Crow grumbled and pushed down the toaster lever again.

"Huh…" Nyx mumbled.

Noa dumped the box onto the counter and leaned up against her. "It's beautiful. I love you."

"Gross." Nyx's face crinkled, turning away from her in favor of Glacier again. "I'm Nyx, in case you haven't already figured that out. You must be Glacier, and I met Cecilia back in Southaven, so now that we have that out of the way, let's go ahead and get started."

She dusted the crumbs off her gloved hands and carried her plate over to the living room, setting it down on a side table to sort through her bag. Tugging out a thick cylindrical tube, she unscrewed the cap from the top and slid a tightly rolled, black mat onto the coffee table. It appeared like a cheaper desk blotter with its glossy sheen before faint, blue text trickled across it and little activity windows began appearing in the corners.

Noa slowed as she started past the furniture, stopping across from Nyx's seat in the middle of the couch. Covian news and metrics took over each new popup, spouting off various data while the others began their journey over to join them. Crow fell into a chair Rune leaned against, and Cecilia perched on the arm of the couch, keeping a safe distance away from Nyx, despite her being completely engrossed in whatever she started tapping through.

"So how are we doing this?" Noa asked.

"How about let's start with *where* the Strength of Corvia is kept first?" Nyx suggested, her tone taking on an inkling of irritation.

"*Verfahren der Historica*," Glacier said, stepping away from his spot at the counter. "It's where Corvia displays most of its prototypes for various engineering advancements, and—" He hesitated, clearing his throat once the entire room stopped to stare at him. "And other... historical items."

Nyx panned back to Noa, who tensed.

"Do you recall when you said I could have whatever I wanted as long as it helped get the job done?" she asked.

Noa raised an eyebrow, trying to figure out where this was going.

"Well, as of thirty seconds ago, I decided that I would like an assistant."

"Um... what?"

She pointed a gloved finger behind her, toward Glacier, who stiffened in surprise. "I'd like an *assistant*."

Noa sputtered, "I- *Okay?*" Well, *that* was unexpected. It wasn't exactly like she could tell her no anyway.

So, Nyx waved him over. "Come sit down over here. You won't be able to see anything from there."

He glanced around, shuffling over to the couch to sit next to her.

"Plate." She held out her right hand toward him, her left busy with the display's keyboard.

He stared, confused as he looked to Noa for guidance, which she gave by flicking her eyes in the direction of the bagel plate sitting on side table.

After a brief moment of scrambling to hand it over, Nyx slid it across the coffee table, covering seemingly less vital information before she continued.

"Glacier is, in fact, correct," she said. "I honestly assumed that you would've skipped over most information about foreign countries in your curriculum, but you seem to have proven me wrong."

"Know your enemy," he replied.

Nyx smirked. "That's my kind of teacher. Because of the constant innovations, they have multiple parts of the building dedicated to certain eras. Each can be quarantined off fairly easily in case of breach or theft. Naturally, we'll be overriding these functions, but there's always the chance that someone can manually override the system to force a lockdown. That control is *here*."

She pointed to the main hall of the museum. "It's for the security teams to quickly access near the main entrance of the building, as a fail-safe. Now, the best way to ensure that no one is wandering around the museum—outside of regular security and staff—is to naturally go at night. However, that's also typically when certain protections are enabled. One of the few exceptions is during a special event when attendees are allowed to take private tours with a guide, who are kept to a strict schedule to avoid interfering with another group."

"So," Noa started. "You want us to go during an event?" Her eyes slid over to Rune with a grin. "When those areas aren't off-limits, and we can slip in and out between tours."

"What kind of event?" Rune asked.

Nyx pulled a lilac-colored envelope from her bag, dropping it onto the mat. A brown, wax seal flecked with shimmering slivers stamped onto the back.

"Is that *real* paper?" Noa asked, giddy at the thought.

"No," Nyx said. "It's all that synthetic garbage. It still looks and feels pretty real, but even real paper is a little too much for these rich bastards. The wax seal is real though."

Rune reached for the envelope, stopping when Nyx pulled out a smaller bag from her collection. She motioned for him to continue, not sparing him a glance. Noa watched intently, eager to hold it in her own hands.

"Look alive," Nyx called, barely giving her enough notice to catch a card—a new ID. Nyx passed out a few more while Noa flipped her own over to absorb the details of her new alias.

"King's Republic this time, huh?" she asked, feeling satisfied with the choice. "Finally realized that it's difficult for me to pass as Bellegardian?"

"No, you can still pass for it."

Noa scowled.

"I—" Cecilia spoke up, her voice catching. "I'm nowhere close to passing for Bellegardian, though. Not to mention that I can't even speak it. I can only speak International—that's all Amarais uses."

Noa frowned at the realization that Cecilia had been given an ID. "She's going in with us?"

"I'll get to that," Nyx said.

But Rune had already pushed off the back of the chair, tugging the ID from her hands. Nyx didn't protest, instead watching with a hint of interest.

"Cecilia," he said. "You don't have to know Bellegardian to be a citizen because we're married." He handed her both IDs, and her eyes went wide, darting over the information as her face reddened.

"Wait, *what?*" Noa asked with a short laugh. "If Rune's new persona is married to Cecilia's, then who the hell am I? I'm clearly not Bellegardian since mine is from King's."

"The mistress," Nyx said. "In for a good time with his clone to steal the town." She smirked over in Crow's direction.

He nearly choked. "No—" he said, standing up. "Hell no. You're putting me with *her?* That is absolutely the worst idea you've ever had."

"What?" Noa asked in a sultry, confident tone. "Scared I'll beat you to it?"

"Oh, you're on" —he tilted her hand to read the name on her ID— "*Laila.*"

"Good," Nyx said. "Then the two of you will work your way past the guards, avoid the tour guides, and collect the key without setting off any alarms. Meanwhile, Cecilia and Rune will be mingling in the main hall to keep an eye out for anyone going for the manual override and listen in for any important information circulating among the partygoers."

"But I-I can't use magic while I'm here though, right?" Cecilia asked. "What if something goes wrong?"

"If something goes sideways," Nyx replied, "then use whatever you have at your disposal. Other than that, you and Rune have the easy part. It's good practice when you can't actually wear someone else's skin. You're ultimately just the alibi for Rune in case there's a lockdown and anyone starts asking questions because they saw Crow elsewhere. As for him and Noa, they need to avoid that to begin with by making sure they don't get caught."

She pushed another invitation across the table for Crow. He immediately grabbed it up to tease Noa, who tried to rip it out of his hand.

"Won't they notice the duplicate on the guest list?" Glacier asked. "Or what about the cameras? They would have some sort of facial recognition, right?"

Nyx smirked. "I knew I made a good choice with you. You actually have a brain, unlike the rest of these idiots. According to the itinerary, there will be two name-takers. The 'real' Mr. and Mrs. Dupont will go in first via one line. From there, I'll remotely uncheck them from the list for Mr. Dupont and Ms. Vance—the alternative plus one—to be checked in on the opposite side after a wave of guests has trickled through."

She pulled up a list of camera locations in the building. "As for the cameras, those will be flagging them as false positives for a match, much like how I've tricked a few government databases into claiming that all of us are different people. Anything else you want to try to poke holes in? I'd prefer we do it now, so we have the chance to fix it, especially after what happened back in Amarais."

Glacier bit his lip, drumming his fingers against his leg for a moment. "No... It seems like it should work... Since you're planning on accessing the guest list and the cameras, I'm assuming you'll have access to the building's main system, right?"

"Correct. They're all connected, so I'll be able to weave in and out of them, as needed. I plan on turning off the security node for that room. She selected a blueprint, pointing to where the Strength of Corvia sat on display. "And I'll have the cameras looped in and around the room during the time of retrieval just in case anyone in the control room is actually watching the feeds. Noa and Crow will duck out early, and Rune and Cecilia will leave at the end of the night with the rest of the guests."

She pulled up a few documents, each with matching ID photos, quickly typing in a series of numbers that triggered various chimes from everyone's pockets.

"That's your homework," Nyx said. "The party is tomorrow night. You'll have the rest of today to learn who you are. Stick to the script about your identity, and you shouldn't have any issues. Only improvise when absolutely necessary. Clothes will be delivered tomorrow morning, and then we'll make sure nothing requires any adjustments. Good?"

"What about the relic?" Glacier asked, pulling his eyes away from the blueprint. "Won't someone notice it's gone during the next tour group?"

She reached into her bag again and handed him a small box. Confusion clouded his features until he popped it open, and then his eyes widened, darting from Nyx to Noa.

"How— Where did you—"

"When I saved you," Noa started, "I took a calculated risk, and you asked if I had done something similar before. There are others out there that I've done the same for, and while they don't have direct access to the keys, they're able to help in other ways."

"And one of them," Nyx continued, taking the replica Strength of Corvia from the box, "happens to be a former notorious art forger." She tilted the round, bronze gear-like piece in the light, illuminating the amethyst bars that evenly split the circular form into sections. "By the time anyone notices that this is a fake, we'll be on the other side of Avaria." Taking the box back, she tucked it inside again and held it out for Noa. "Anything else?"

Glacier shook his head, and a smile danced across Noa's face. "Then let's go get ourselves another key."

23
CORVIA ✧ 2704-12-02

CECILIA

My name is Kylie Dupont. My husband is Marc Dupont. We just got back from our honeymoon where we toured southwestern Valentia. I met him in King's, where we met through friends while I was going to university. He's an engineering investor like his mother, Claudette, and he'll take over her investments and business holdings when she retires.

"Relax," Rune whispered into her ear.

Cecilia squeezed her satin black clutch, glancing out the window of the town car. He shifted away again to put a little space between them—something that shouldn't really matter since they were technically married, but relief coursed through her as he leaned back and tugged at his tie. Outside of that subtle gesture, he'd taken everything in stride so far—from changing in the specially-reserved hotel room to opening the car door for her like a gentleman and making small talk with the driver, he fell into his given role much easier than her. The problem with it all was how confused it left her, unsure of where Rune ended and Marc began.

Her reminder of why she was sitting there with him became her new mantra: this was to help her and Glacier find their way home a little faster

—not to indulge the fluttering sensation she felt whenever Rune talked to her.

"Sorry, nerves," she said, smoothing out the long, black skirt of her dress flecked with gold. The princess cut of the bodice was trimmed with velvet lace around the shoulders and sleeves—something she'd never been allowed to wear back home because it would be above her station.

"You'll do great," he said softly as the car rolled to a stop in front of the building, a hulking classical-looking structure with layered arches basked in gold lights. It stuck out in the midst of modern glass monoliths as if it was the final historical monument left standing.

Rune stepped out, and she tucked her lacy velvet glove into his outstretched hand. Together, they moved forward to fall in line behind the other attendees. She scanned their faces, taking in the variety of styles and swearing she'd been transported back to King's Republic. Only a couple of Corvians stood in the line parallel to theirs with shimmering violet eyes that crinkled at the edges when one of them laughed at their partner's joke.

Cecilia relaxed the grip on her skirt some. At least she'd blend in a little better here after being surrounded by Miraltans and then Corvians on the way to the hotel, though she was certainly in the minority of lighter coloring. Her head turned back around as they stepped forward to a greeter with a tablet, and Rune handed over their IDs for her to scan.

That was it. It was over.

"Right side," Rune muttered into his comm as they started through the thrown-wide double doors.

"Got it," came Nyx's reply.

"Then we'll take the left," Noa said through the earpiece. "Signal when you want us to move, Sloth."

Cecilia gaped as they stepped into the spacious foyer before the ballroom. A large chandelier was held from several crisscrossing cords, its design a spiral of reflective frosted shards. Under it sat a fountain, built with multiple steps, matching the direction of the chandelier, like a spiral staircase. Water softly bubbled from its center, trickling down the path to the coins littered at the bottom, all from different places. They had no value before, but now they were priceless pieces in this museum dedicated to the ever-present march of time.

She squeezed Rune's arm as they circled it and passed some of the attendees milling about, hugging, and saying hellos. Her mouth went dry. How many of these people *knew* each other? What if they were recognized as intruders?

"You all right?" Rune asked, putting his free hand over top of hers.

She loosened her grip, fearing she might've been holding on a little too tightly. "Sorry, I—"

"Marc! There you are!" An older woman—Cecilia guessed maybe late forties or early fifties from the stylish gray streak in her brunette curls—waved as she strode toward them, wearing a bright smile that emphasized her kind, dark eyes. She grabbed Rune's arm, turning him toward her. "Don't you look *dashing*—even better than your picture."

"Abigail, I assume?" he asked with a charming smile. "It seems my mother hasn't wasted any time bragging about me to her friends."

"You can't blame her for being proud of her son," Abigail said with a chuckle. "He's moving up in the world." Her eyes moved to Cecilia. "And who is your lovely friend?"

"Kylie, my wife," Rune answered, glancing over to Cecilia with a new gleam in his eyes. It wasn't soft and caring like she usually found but prideful, like she was a prize to show off. "Kylie, this is my mother's dear friend, Abigail."

Cecilia gave a small bow of her head at the introduction, a reflexive palace nicety she thanked her own mother for forcing into every minuscule action.

Abigail clapped her hands together. "You are *gorgeous*, dear. Far too good for this boy, I'm sure."

"I-I wouldn't go that far," she said with a nervous laugh and heat creeping into her cheeks.

"Marc, dear, would you mind if I borrowed her for a little while? I'm sure she'd love to meet some of the other young ladies here. You know, get to know some of her new peers."

Panic pulsed through her, looking up at Rune with pleading in her eyes. She was *not* ready to navigate this on her own.

"I'd prefer to keep her close—" he said.

"Don't be ridiculous. I'm sure you had her all to yourself during your honeymoon. I'm sure she'd love nothing more than some time to herself, so she won't have to dote on you in front of all your associates." She took Cecilia's arm and pulled her away. "I'll have her back in an hour!"

Cecilia glanced back in horror, watching as they left him at the door and began weaving through elegant, deep purple furniture around small tables.

"Just relax," came Rune's voice through her comm. "Keep an eye out, but act like how you would behave at any other event in Amarais." She bit down on her tongue, only thinking of how her sole job had been to follow Glacier around like a shadow.

"Abigail isn't working with us," Nyx's voice added. "She's really a friend of Claudette Dupont, who's the one that got us in, but Abigail only knows the cover story. Just stick to the script, and no one will bat an eye."

"I'll be over on the far left," Rune said. "Near the back with the new money. If you need me, you'll be able to find me there."

Abigail stopped when they reached one of the sitting clusters, where they stood in front of two women who weren't much older than Cecilia. Whatever they'd been discussing came to an abrupt halt, and their smiles fixed into something a little more forced. The one in the deep green dress stood first and tucked a lock of her coppery hair behind an ear. Her hazel eyes looked Cecilia up and down before extending a pale hand. Her companion—a woman with dark brown, heart-shaped face framed by near-black curls with coal-colored eyes—took one more sip of her drink, which almost matched the orange of her dress. Both appeared to be around her age.

"This is Alaina," Abigail said as Cecilia reached for the Taliean girl's outstretched hand. "And Mandla."

The Mharuan girl popped up from her seat and slid her glass onto the table with a too-cheery smile to greet her.

"This is Kylie, Marc Dupont's wife."

Cecilia's stomach flipped, unsure if she was more uncomfortable with the use of that fake name or the reiteration that she was married to a guy she knew almost nothing about. That glint in his eye mere moments ago had been Rune, but also *hadn't*, leaving her with the question of if that was simply him in his element or—

"It's a pleasure to meet you," the two of them said, their clashing voices ripping her from her downward spiral of thoughts.

"It's lovely to meet you too," Cecilia replied, sounding a little too timid to her own ears.

Abigail motioned for a waiter, who handed her a tablet of wine selections that she picked the most familiar sounding one from before he scurried off, and they all took their seats again.

"So, where are you from?" Alaina asked, that Taliean lilt slipping through a few more of her words.

Cecilia swallowed back the fear that maybe *she* had an accent that would immediately dismantle Nyx's well-crafted story. "I'm from King's Republic. I met Marc through some friends when I was at university." She glanced over her shoulder at Rune, hoping he'd look her way and she could make some excuse to join him again, but the return of the waiter blocked her view, handing off her drink.

"He is definitely easy on the eyes..." Mandla mumbled, craning for a better view. Cecilia felt heat creep up her neck.

"What did you study?" Alaina asked, undaunted by Mandla's distraction with a hint of scrutiny.

"Historical preservation," she replied, the lie coming out easily this time like an answer she would've prepared for a questioning Amaraian council member that Louis would've drilled into her to cover himself.

Alaina raised an eyebrow. "Really? Any particular focus?"

"Book preservation and restoration."

Even Mandla's face brightened at that. "Seriously? That's quite a career to get into. I've heard that if you're really good, you can make *bank*." She lifted a glass up to her with a grin.

"Thank you," Cecilia said, pushing back a lock of hair to avoid nervously tugging at the strands. "And... what about you two?" Her eyes flicked over to Abigail frowning down at a phone and a nervous warmth began to work its way through her. Had they been found out already? Did she miss Noa and Crow's entrance, and they'd been caught?

Mandla laughed. "Oh, I studied a few things here and there when I was abroad in Talie for a few years. It's how I met Alaina, but I admit that I was far too busy with other things..."

Abigail stood suddenly, giving an apologetic smile. "Sorry ladies. I need a few moments." She started across the room, heading over to the panel on the wall next to one of the security guards—the one she recognized from Nyx's camera feeds with the specific instructions to look out for as the emergency override—and passed it, vanishing around a corner. Cecilia almost released a relieved sigh and covered it with a sip of her drink.

"I think," Mandla continued, "I got smashed and smashed just about every guy on a yacht before Daddy caught me."

Cecilia almost choked.

Alaina let loose a tinkling laugh. "I remember how she locked herself out of our rooms once while I was still in one of my engineering classes. She started frantically messaging me to let her in. I think I sprinted across campus, only to find her gone and later discovered that one of my floor-mates took her out to his boat." She rolled her eyes. "And then she started drunk texting me all night until I picked her up. Gods."

"I can't help that I like what I like," Mandla said in mocking defense. "And I like to have fun."

The lights dimmed, quieting Mandla's chuckle as a spotlight illuminated a circular platform on the far side of the room, cueing the welcome speech to begin.

CROW

Nyx's voice rang out over comms, "Pride, Gluttony. Now."

Crow straightened his tie, smirking as he offered Noa an arm. "Laila."

She looped a velvety-gloved hand through, and the two of them turned the corner, starting up the left side with the straggling parties. Annoyance prickled through him with her slower stride up the short flight of steps because of her dress—an unadorned black thing that she complained about the entire walk there. He didn't quite understand the problem, outside of the length, but then again, he wasn't the one wearing it.

They'd made it inside right as the lights were dimming in the ballroom, which meant that they'd be free of tours for at least the next ten minutes. He took a sharp turn and popped the latch of the roped-off hallway for Noa before taking the lead again down the softly lit corridor. Each recess and nook displayed a pedestal with a bust of some old dead dude or casted replica of a tool that he'd learned about in school. Every plaque boasted nonsense about paving the way for the future, but he didn't have much time to read any of them before they moved on.

A couple more turns later, he motioned for Noa to back against the wall again, waiting for yet another camera to swivel back in the other direction. Nyx's murmur in the comms sent him forward, but Noa ripped him backward, sending him stumbling through a door that she pulled shut behind her. She slapped a hand over his mouth just as he opened it to protest, and that was when he heard the distant sound of footsteps thudding against carpet.

A shadow passed in front of the door, cutting out what little light they had as Noa dropped her hand. Once the noise faded away, Noa flicked on a handheld light, smirking.

"What?" he asked. "Is this the make-out closet?"

She took a step closer, and he jerked back, falling into the shelves behind him.

"Would you like it to be?" she asked in a sultry tone and chuckled while she pointed her light upward to an air duct. "It'll be a little faster." She pressed a finger to her comm. "Sloth, are the vents monitored?"

"Yes, but I can disable that."

"Would you?" She tugged on the hidden cords of her dress. The fabric slid upwards, folding near her waist to reveal black leggings.

He followed her lead, popping up the upper folds of his suit jacket and snapping them into place over his crisp, white shirt and tie. The last thing he needed was a damn tie getting caught on something.

"Done," Nyx finally responded.

"Age before beauty," Crow said, locking his fingers together to offer her a lift.

"I will strangle you in your sleep tonight." Noa gave him a tight smile, lightly smacking his cheek a couple of times before propelling herself up.

CECILIA

Cecilia clapped with the thundering applause of the other attendees when the ceremony was over, dropping some sort of unspoken command to get up and mingle. So she stuck close to Mandla and Alaina, finding every opportunity to turn each introduction around to avoid talking about herself too much. It struck her as odd that Mandla kept stealing smiles with a guy a couple groups over whenever Alaina looked away, busy with someone else. When Mandla went in search of another drink, Cecilia nudged Alaina, asking if she knew him.

"Oh, that's Carlisle—my fiancé." She smiled and waved at him, which he returned and went back to his colleagues. Her expression faltered.

"Did... you two meet at university too?" Cecilia asked.

"Sort of. He said that he wanted to help fund my work, and I told him I wanted to move to Corvia after my studies. We both knew each other from a summer engineering program in a wealthy part of Talie. I'll admit, I think he feels a little slighted for postponing the wedding until after my graduation. It's not until the spring, but I'm so close to the end that I don't want to try to focus on a wedding and finishing up my courses at the same time."

Cecilia nodded, and they made their way through a few more introductions before she found an opening to break away. Her thought of slipping out into the museum garden for some fresh air was shoved aside in favor of privacy in the powder room. So, with a glance back at the manual override and finding the guards still surveying the crowd, she vanished inside. Relief gripped her when she discovered the stalls were empty, and she locked herself inside one with a sigh. Her peace lasted all of a minute, broken by the sound of two sets of heels clicking on the tile as the main door swung back into the frame.

"I don't know why Abigail bothered to introduce her to us." It was Alaina's voice. "She's obviously just a trophy wife."

Cecilia froze, afraid to make any noise to alert them to her presence.

"She seems nice though," replied Mandla noncommittally. "I don't get why a Dupont would bother marrying someone that wasn't more in line with the business."

"Housewife. Degree is likely just for show. She'll probably never use it. Honestly, he'll probably just get rid of her in five or ten years when she starts to look over thirty."

It hurt more than she wanted to admit, feeling like the snap of a hairband against her knuckles after being pulled past its limit. It always came back to this—about how she was different. It could be her looks, it could be her magic, it could be *anything*—all of it stemming from some sort of lie she had to tell to make it easier for everyone else to swallow. She was only good at dodging the truth and putting on a fake smile.

A liar.

But she wasn't useless, was she? Cecilia bit her lip. She had magic—magic that she'd used to save Glacier. That counted for something, didn't it? And maybe she was a liar, but she lied to protect others too, not just herself.

"Envy?" Rune asked over comms—asking for her by her new alias and her liking the way it sounded. "Where did you go?"

Envy.

She was Envy. Not timid, scared Cecilia. She wasn't bound by the same rules here. She could be *whoever* she wanted. A small smile tugged on her lips. Envy the Mage. Envy the liar. Envy because she could be *anyone*.

She pushed the door open, catching the stunned expressions of Mandla and Alaina in the mirrors as she strode over to a vanity. The rush of the tap gave them both enough time to shuffle through their clutches, absently messing with their makeup until she flicked the excess water from her hands. Cecilia grabbed a towel, staring them down.

"Maybe," she began. "You should consider paying a little more attention to yourself, rather than scrutinizing someone else next time? Seeing how Mandla and Carlisle have been eyeing each other all night whenever you're not looking, I'd say there's something going on there." Each word struck home, fueling Alaina's fury as she slowly panned to Mandla. "Enjoy the rest of your night. I'll be spending mine with my husband."

She turned on her heel, a prideful smirk pasted on her face as she strode out, listening to the irate shouting as the door swung behind her.

CROW

Crow caught the vent cover right as Noa dropped to the floor, down into a stream of moonlight coming from the back windows. It gave them a decent view of the main hall activity through the gaps in the privacy hedges on the east side, but the greenery was close enough no one would see them—he hoped.

Shimmying the rest of the way out of the vent, he passed Noa on his way to the south-side windows while she began placing small round objects along the base of the pedestaled case in the middle of the room. Demagnetizers. Most devices ran on electronic seals and sensors, including the vents, but most were keyed for specific functions to keep handymen and locksmiths in check.

Theirs, on the other hand, were programmed for just about anything. Nyx had explained as much when she'd dropped them into his hand back in Roth, telling him she would gut him if he lost them. The only way he would've lost them was if he'd been the one swindling the illegal gambling shack's digi-card tables with Rune and Noa.

It would've been an easy bet over money since these demagnetizers had to have cost an average year's salary as a wage slave. But instead, he used them to crack a high-tech safe and giggled like a child with a new birthday present as he did it. It'd been worth freezing his ass off after huddling on a storage building's tin roof for an hour. Plus, he supposed the slumlord gang hoarding the Embrace of Roth deserved it—a win-win, honestly.

"Eyes on the prize," came Noa's voice over comms, indicating they were ready at Nyx's order.

Crow's eyes, however, were on one of the cases up against the wall, where he found one that displayed an antique sword. Runes ran up and down the blade, along with one carved into the real leather at the handle. It might as well have been ripped straight from a story told over dinner to drown out the wail of sirens down the street in his old apartment. He'd always thought he might encounter one back in the museums at home, but if there had been one, it hadn't been on display. His hands almost grazed the case, imagining the blade's corrosion cutting through thick shadow, though it could've tasted blood too.

He pulled away, jabbing a thumb toward it as he rejoined Noa. "There's a rune sword over here if the apocalypse happens tonight," he said, a joking smile dancing onto his face. "At least we'll be able to fight our way out."

Noa rolled her eyes. "Hopefully it won't come to that."

He pressed his gloved hands against the glass, waiting to pull it free.

"Ready?" came Nyx's question.

Noa retrieved the key's replica, spinning it around in her hand to match the angle of the original. "Go."

RUNE

Rune relaxed at the sight of Cecilia anxiously weaving her way through the crowd.

"Sorry I didn't respond," she whispered with a nervous smile and a glance over her shoulder. "I was trying to ditch my new *friends.*"

"Feeling better?" he asked, slipping his arm around her waist. To his surprise, she didn't tense up like she had whenever he'd touched her on the way in.

"Yeah, I think I am."

Nyx's voice cut through relief, putting him back on alert. "Disabling security matrix in sixty seconds. Greed and Envy, watch for override."

He headed for one of the waiters, flashed him a dashing smile, and plucked two glasses of champagne off his tray. The more props to blend in, the less suspicion they would draw while refusing to mingle with the rest of the patrons—just a couple trying to catch their breath. Cecilia followed his lead, casually sipping on champagne during the painful wait for something to possibly go sideways. That wait was over the moment Rune's eyes landed on Abigail near the entrance, talking with a man in a suit. An emblem emblazoned on the breast pocket. Security.

"Did Abigail say anything to you earlier?" he asked, pinching the stem of his glass so hard he thought it might snap.

"No... I mean she seemed a little preoccupied, but... You don't think—"

"Thirty seconds," came Nyx's voice.

"Watch the controls. Act natural." He ditched his glass on another tray on his way to Abigail, and he forced that easy-going façade like there wasn't a problem that couldn't be solved by throwing money at it. "Something wrong, Abigail?"

The security guard frowned at the interruption, and she whirled around in surprise. "Oh, Marc—Unfortunately, yes..." she said, half-turning back to the guard.

"Ten."

Rune's mouth twitched, feeling the seconds slipping away.

Abigail tapped at her phone to pull up a document, gesturing to the guard. "I had specially ordered some *very* expensive gold rose bouquets for some of our retiring benefactors, and this man claims that they never arrived."

"Now."

A relieved laugh bubbled up into a casual chuckle. "Let's see if we can't find someone who might be able to locate them, shall we?" he asked, his eyes falling on the manual override—where it remained unoccupied—and motioned for Cecilia to join them.

NOA

"Now," Nyx said, and Crow lifted the glass box off the pedestal.

Noa quickly placed the replica overtop of the original and slid the latter out, letting it fall into place on the stand. Once her hands were clear, Crow clicked the box back into place and removed the demagnetizers while she tucked the Strength of Corvia into her clutch.

"Clear," she whispered into comms, giving him a smirk. "Let's go." She started for the vent, pausing as her eyes caught on another case.

Inside sat a book. A real, paper book. Its cover was a deep, inky black with red trim, and yellowed pages, indicating its age. There wasn't any title—no fancy foil lettering. Instead, it was blank. Blank like how she prayed the inside would look, despite knowing it wouldn't be. The more she considered it, the more she felt sick, thinking of her hands slick with blood and the first key.

"Pride."

Her head whipped around to find Crow watching her, halfway to the vent with a hesitant expression and a slight frown. "Leave it," he said.

She nodded, forcing herself to follow him, despite the heaviness of each step. It persisted as they backtracked through the vents, the halls, and down the steps in their proper formal wear. Crow's hand hovered on her waist until they turned the corner after refusing the valet in favor of a nearby establishment before they would return—well, until the *real* Duponts returned.

"Pride and Gluttony, out," Noa mumbled into the comm, and she got an affirmative reply from Nyx.

"Back there," Crow whispered, tucking his hands into his pants pockets and glancing over his shoulder, like there was something following them. "Was... that what I thought it was?"

An uncomfortable silence settled between them, disrupted by the sound of their footfalls against the sidewalk. She hadn't expected him to recognize it, but he and his brother were thieves after all—and most highly-skilled thieves were procurers for the desperate and the wealthy. However, fear lurked in his features where she'd half-expected to see the greed or gluttony to choke on more money.

"Yes," she finally answered in a near-rasp, keeping her eyes forward.

He cursed. "Who thought that keeping one of *those* on display would be a good idea?"

"It's coming from the same logic of keeping a rune blade on display," she replied. "They're all just old artifacts at this point, right? Just cogs in the wheels of progress." She regretted how flippant it came out.

"*Dangerous* cogs, Noa."

She rounded on him, hissing, "Clearly we both understand that, but to *them*—the archivists that work that damn museum, the government, maybe all of Corvia—they just see something old and archaic. Something that can't possibly be used as a proper weapon anymore as long as it's behind glass. And, between the two of those items, I think both of us know which could still cause plenty of destruction."

"We should go back—"

"No," Noa said. "Trust me, I want to go back too, but we can't. We have to keep going. If we manage to live through this—if all of this shit is real—we'll deal with it then, but not *now*."

"You know—" he started, forcing out an uncomfortable laugh, "you know that comment I made back there was a joke, right?"

She turned, picking up the pace again. "I'm starting to realize that fate has a funny way of keeping our mouths in check."

RUNE

"Thank you *so* much for helping with this, Marc." Abigail pulled him into a hug before moving onto Cecilia. "And you too, Kylie. I'm so glad I finally got to meet the two of you tonight."

"No problem at all," Rune replied with a dismissive wave. "But I think we're going to duck out a little early. We have a train to catch first thing in the morning."

The older woman frowned. "Where could you possibly be rushing off to now?"

"Back to King's for business," he said, putting his arm around Cecilia. She stiffened, reverting back to her original anxiousness that left him feeling guilty. "A short stop on the way back home to Bellegarde."

It seemed to be enough for her to let them go with brief goodbyes before the car pulled up along the curb. He emitted a quiet sigh once the doors were shut, glad to take off that mask and shed the stress that'd come with feeling like he'd been overstepping his bounds with Cecilia all night. Silence flooded the vehicle on the way back to their secondary hotel, broken by the sounds of car doors opening again, the greeting of the desk clerk, and the elevator.

When they made it up to their suite, he gestured for Cecilia to take the bedroom while he tugged off his blazer jacket and tossed it over the back of the sofa.

"Rune?" She lingered in the bedroom doorway, fidgeting with her gloves.

"Is something wrong?" he asked.

"N-no, I—" she said. "I was just wondering... you usually have Noa with you on these types of things, right? Are you two—Never mind." She turned as a huffed out a small, surprised laugh.

"What? No- *No*. We're not together. We just work well together. Nothing romantic. I honestly think she finds it an excuse to feel like she isn't alone."

"Sorry, I was just a little curious, I guess." She pushed down on the door handle, lingering like she might add more before the door clicked shut behind her.

Rune stood there for a minute, his thoughts torn between if he'd seen a flicker of relief, or if that was what he'd wanted to see.

24

CORVIA ✧ 2704-12-02

GLACIER

Glacier watched as Rune and Cecilia climbed into their town car on the outdoor camera feed displayed on the mat. Once they were gone, his vision drifted over to the haphazard pile of corded keys on the edge of the coffee table while Nyx began closing several small, blue-lit windows.

"Now *this* is how it's done," she said, somewhat grumbling. "Far better than Amarais."

He pushed one of the remaining windows off to the side, where it framed the view of a private tour taking a minute to hover around the Strength of Corvia's case. They moved back into the hall, leaving shadows promptly cut by the door closing outside the frame.

For a moment, Glacier felt like he was somewhere else, leaning forward and staring at this same mat, but watching himself jog up the stairs of the main foyer instead. "Did you have access to the security systems there?" he asked, the vision fading away. "Back in Amarais, I mean."

"Yes, and I also made sure to get back in the second they restarted the systems, so hopefully they believed all the processes left running were supposed to be there. Considering how they haven't noticed it, it seems to be working, and I doubt they'll bother looking into it since none of them are familiar with the infrastructure anyway. And no, I won't let you see it."

He bit down on his tongue and fidgeted with the ribbed knit of his hoodie sleeves. She'd seen right through his want to check on who might be roaming the halls in his absence while they waited on the Volkov to finish what they'd started.

"You're not prepared to see the aftermath," Nyx said. "Not yet. It's only been a couple of weeks. Noa seems to think that you're ready to jump on the revenge train, but I don't think you've had nearly enough time to process everything. Plus, she told me that you've been skipping out on sleep." She pulled up another window of data, her eyes flicking off to the side the moment he leaned a little closer to try to read it. The window collapsed. "Stop it."

"I thought you wanted me to help you," he said. "You're giving me mixed messages."

"I'd like you to help, but you're no good to me if you run yourself ragged."

But he *hadn't*—Noa had seen to that when he'd gotten up early that morning to practice again, and she'd told him to take the day to rest. Resting meant idleness. Idleness meant room for his dark, creeping thoughts to consume him. That special place where Kat's memory rested and had kick-started this vicious cycle to begin with.

"Do you want to talk about it?"

He stiffened, surprised and a little confused.

"About what happened in Amarais," she added. "Do you want to talk about it?"

He hesitated, narrowing his eyes at her with suspicion. "Don't take this the wrong way... but I don't think you actually care about the hell I've been through. I don't exactly expect you to either since we've known each other for all of two days."

Nyx sighed, closing her eyes, pulling off her glasses, and pinching the bridge of her nose. "And *you* don't take this the wrong way, but you're right. I'm not emotionally attached to whatever you tell me, but if you want to talk about it, I'm your best bet. Getting things off your chest might make you feel better, and well..." She set down her glasses, ticking off each person on her fingers. "Cecilia is clearly in the same boat as you, and you're both sinking. Then we have Rune, who shields himself with a mask of serenity and tries to let everything roll off his back. Noa, who claims that she had *no* emotions—which is a load of shit by the way. And finally—the pièce de résistance—our resident dumbass, Crow." She deadpanned back to him. "Well?"

His shoulders dropped, and he stared down at the void of the computer mat again. Wouldn't it all just sound like complaining? What was the point of telling her when she'd probably scoff and brush it off?

Nyx grabbed her glasses back off the table and leaned back against the sofa. "Fine. If you don't want to talk, then I'll start. You should know that I'm not here to make light of your situation, much like how I've treated any other individual Noa and I have relocated along the way."

There was a pause like she was considering how to begin, a thumb absently tapping against her lips as she set her sights on the skyline beyond the wall of tall windows. "My father died when I was twenty-one," she began, and Glacier's heart sank, leaving him with a fuzzy image of his own father. "He wasn't exactly young, but he wasn't old either. It took a toll on my family. He grew up with a weak heart, and my mother was aware of it before she married him, but they still planned to do whatever it took to hold it at bay. I'm convinced she died of a broken heart a few months later."

Glacier tried to imagine his own parents in that position, wondering if it would be better or worse to have known them for that long before losing them. "Were you close?" he asked quietly.

She lifted a gloved hand, tilting it from side to side. "I never got along well with my mother. She always treated me like I was made of glass, so we fought a lot over what I could and couldn't do."

"Is that why you wear the gloves? I don't think they'll exactly help you from getting sick or anything if you never take them off."

Nyx let out a short, clipped laugh. "No. No, I don't have a heart problem like my father or some auto-immune disorder. I was a perfectly capable child. Nothing to indicate I'd meet an early grave. These weren't a gift from my mother or anything."

"So... paranoia? About fingerprints?"

"Not completely useless, are you?" Her eyes shone with a glimmer of pride. "Back to my father though... We got along pretty well, better than me and my mother. He'd scolded her for being too protective." She gestured toward the mat. "He encouraged me to get into electronics, though he tried to push me more into engineering. I broke a lot of things to see how they worked and put them back together again."

Her smirk had turned reminiscent, slowly dropping from her face altogether. "But my talents clearly lay elsewhere, so I played along until he passed. I don't know if it was simply me lying to myself, or if I just wanted to make him happy. It wasn't until my mother died that I packed up and moved myself to the other side of town—I was almost twenty-two. They probably would've had me sent to a mental hospital if they found out I was freelancing."

"Set up shop as a therapist?" he teased, which rewarded him with a renewed smirk.

"Information broker," she corrected. "I did just about everything in terms of data. Pulled public records for background checks all the way to digging up things that people buried or tried to erase. I'd find it all for the right price. Well, until I found something that someone was desperate enough to keep hidden. Funny thing is that I didn't even think much about it, not until Noa showed up in my office." Her eyes met his, allowing him to fill the silence with what she left unsaid.

"She was there to make sure it stayed a secret," Glacier said cautiously. "But she decided not to kill you."

She snorted. "Well, when someone breaks into an office that only a handful of people know the location of and says they're Volkov, you nearly shit your pants and either *run* or try to talk your way out of it. Needless to say, I had very low expectations of making it out alive if she was telling the truth, so I offered her a deal: whatever she wanted in exchange for letting me live. I threw the entire world in front of an oncoming train to save my ass, and do you know what she did?"

He hesitated, slightly amused by the irritation in her voice. He started to shake his head, trying to imagine Noa actually threatening Nyx face-to-face after seeing how they interacted for even a short period of time.

"Dumbass sits in *my* chair and kicks her feet up on *my* desk. Then she proceeds to tell me to continue. I was completely dumbfounded at this point, shocked and awed that my mouth actually got me out of trouble for a change somehow. So... we talked."

"About the keys?"

"No- no," Nyx waved that away. "She didn't know shit about that yet I don't think, but she was done killing. She wanted a way out, and the more people she could hide away in exchange for favors when the time came for her to walk away, the better. I agreed to helping her, and... then she vanished for a week. It took a couple days before considering that maybe I had a bad dream or some really good drugs—like I made the whole damn thing up until I found her in my office again. Only this time, she's casually eating at my desk like she owns the place and snooping through my things."

He put his hand up to his mouth, attempting to stifle a laugh. Nyx glared at him. "Oh, *ha-ha*. Very funny that Nyx keeps finding a killer in her office, ruining her life," she said with a roll of her eyes. "She came back to have me fake my own death and move out of the city, which we did. However, I stayed in touch with my stronger contacts when I moved across the countryside, then out of the country into Esmedralia for a while. What was left of my immediate family knew that I was alive, but I was confident that they'd sound like they were in denial, much like whenever they talked about my parents. Just another case of 'dead, but here in spirit.' Guess that puts us in the same boat since I'm not going back. Not while the Volkov are out there."

"For what it's worth, I'm sorry," Glacier said after a moment. "I can't imagine choosing to leave the only thing you know."

"Yeah, well," she mumbled. "Sometimes that's the only choice we're really given. We can either choose to lean into it or fight against it while it drags us down."

He bit the inside of his cheek. "And what about Rune and Crow? How exactly did you two meet them? They're both thieves, right?"

Nyx paused like she was considering how to frame her answer. "Those two are... rather complicated. They weren't running as thieves when they reached out to me for my services. We had only started talking just after I met Noa, and it made me anxious to discuss anything with them. Rune was my point of contact, and he made it clear that he'd be open with me. However, I... initially rejected his requests."

Glacier's brows knit together. "Why...? What do you mean they weren't running as thieves?" From what he had seen from them tonight, they seemed comfortable with it, not to mention Crow bragging about it on the train. While he could picture Rune doing honest work, Crow didn't seem like he fit the part.

"They had been thieves sometime before we met, but they were in a situation that I think is better for them to explain in their own time. It's not really my place to say. All you need to know is that they were stuck in a position they wanted out of, and I decided that we needed all the help we could get after Noa dumped the whole magic-Seer-keys shit on me. So, I told them to meet Noa on a train that was on its way to meet *me*, and I let Rune convince her himself since she didn't know they were coming. Trial by fire seemed like the best way for them to prove their worth."

"I'm assuming it went pretty well?"

She released a short, bitter chuckle. "She got pissed at me. She only let them join with the rule that they had to follow her rules, and she gave them one opportunity to prove themselves. If they screwed up, they were on their own. Clearly, they passed, and so here we are, all betting our lives on the idea that Noa really can do what that Seer claims she can do. The worst that could happen is we die, but we don't really have anything left to live for."

The truth of those words scared him. He didn't have anything to return to at this point, other than trying to reclaim a country that didn't want him and reuniting Cecilia with her parents. Sure, revenge might be enough of a reason to push him to go back, but what would happen after that? What would happen if everything Noa said was real?

"And you believe her?" he asked.

Nyx tilted her head in contemplation. "If you had asked me after the first key we stole, I would've told you that it was all just four idiots chasing their last high before the world crashes down on them. But... now?" She hummed as she rolled up the mat, and each little blue-framed window winked out. "Now, I'm not so sure... It's funny, the further we go, the more I actually believe her—the more I actually think that maybe there will be some light at the end of the tunnel or some happy ending where we manage to all make it out alive. Not that it'll happen, but the hope is there." She slid the mat back into its tube and capped it before eyeing him. "Are you falling for it too?"

Back when he recited the tale in Miralta and asked Noa about it on the train, she sounded more resigned than convinced. She was at least willing to use it as justification to do whatever she wanted, but did he believe it? Or was he along for the ride with the hope that she'd help him?

"I don't know."

Nyx tucked the tube into her bag and stood. "Don't worry. You'll have plenty of time to doubt yourself. For now, you should get your things. We'll be leaving soon." With that, she went to collect the rest of her belongings and left him with more questions than answers.

NOA

Everyone met up at the departure station around midnight, fighting off exhaustion. Noa shoved her hands in her jacket pockets, relishing the full weight of four keys now hanging around her neck. Part of her was irritated that it should be five, but she reminded herself that she had all that she needed for it, minus a strategic plan to acquire it.

Patience.

Patience, however, wasn't something that Noa was ever good at. Slow and steady wasn't quite her pace either, not unless it came with progress. Moving to a new destination just to sit around in an apartment or hotel for a few weeks was the exact opposite of that in her mind.

A shuttle train arrived—an odd choice on Nyx's part due to the lack of private cars or overnight cabins. Table booths lined the walls with a handful of them occupied by other passengers through the dozen cars. They settled into one of the empty ones, claiming back-to-back booths where she boxed Glacier in against the window and Nyx took the seat across from her.

"Where are we going?" Noa asked, stifling a yawn. She caught Glacier's sideways look, and she shot him a glare. His head whipped back around to stare out the window instead.

"Tabir," Nyx answered, pulling out her phone.

Noa's head hit the back of the seat with a groan and dropped her arms against the tabletop. "Gods, that's going to be a long train ride…"

Nyx continued to tap on her phone. "We're actually not taking a train there. It's faster to go by boat, so I booked a luxury, multi-room cabin on the ship departing from Port Cameron just outside Corvia's border. It'll be almost two days by boat and a half-day by train through Mharu."

Noa sat up straight with a jolt. "Wait, what?"

Nyx frowned. "Did I stutter?"

Her mouth worked, unable to immediately form a response once she felt Glacier's eyes on her again, but this time he leaned against the window to put distance between them with a weary expression.

"Why can't we just take a train up and around? Aren't there plenty of other routes we haven't exhausted yet?"

"Yes, Noa," she replied with a hint of caution, heavily mixed with suspicion. "But we're all clearly tired, and we're going to need time to recover once we get there. A train isn't exactly easy to sleep on…"

Noa wanted to argue that a boat wasn't exactly easy to sleep on either, but it sounded like a flimsy argument when Nyx was aiming for speed.

"And I know the faster we go, the sloppier we might get, but faster is actually better in this case. The alternative would be to take a north-eastern line back into King's, go all the way *around* the coastline of King's into Mharu on the complete opposite side, and then have to travel for at least another couple of days southward to Tabir since it's at the tip of the damn peninsula. The trip could eat up the better part of a week by then, versus a couple of days."

Noa's mind frantically searched for any other options.

"Is a boat okay, Noa?" Nyx asked, her tone turning forceful with slight irritation.

"Yes," she replied, wanting to snatch the words back out of the air the second they were out. Since she couldn't do that, she hid her discomfort with a tight-lipped smile. *Hell no. No, it's not okay.*

"Okay," Nyx replied, slowly returning to her phone.

Her palms began to stick to the table, and she began praying for the gods to strike her down before she was faced with climbing aboard a watercraft. She narrowed her eyes at Glacier again, and he pressed a temple to the window, feigning boredom—like she somehow wouldn't notice his scrutiny. She moved her hands to her lap, rubbing them on her pants and slid down into her seat while she listened in on the other booth's idle chatter and tried not to think about Port Cameron.

25

KING'S REPUBLIC ✦ 2704-12-02

NOA

Crow's face lit up at the hulking vessel in the harbor, illuminated by the canopy lights. "We're taking a cruise? Hell *yes*."

Noa walked with Nyx, who called over her shoulder to Crow, "Don't get too excited. If I catch you stealing, I'll throw you overboard myself."

Noa wished her heart would keep in time with the Glacier's footsteps directly on her heels, glad that he was keeping close, but she was dreading coming up with an excuse to ditch him once they were on board.

The funnel of the security checkpoint turned agonizing. Each beep of the ID scan and bag sweep added another bead of sweat trickling down her back. She gripped her bag strap in their trek up the ramp—each creak making her tense up until she stood on the main deck. Nyx led them to the lobby, up one of the staircases, and past the gold-tinted geometric-patterned walls to a door at the end of the hall.

It opened to a room about half the size of their former hotel suite with eight slim doors, which Noa guessed were for one or two bathrooms and the rest for small bedrooms. She started for the closest door, sliding it open to find a small mirrored-door closet, a night table the width of the open floor space, and a narrow bed up against the circular window.

As the others trickled inside, she cringed at the padding of footsteps halt behind her.

Glacier.

"There's enough space here we could practi—" he started as she rounded on him.

"Not until you sleep. Sleep first. We'll pick up again in Tabir."

"But—"

"Goodnight, Glacier." She shoved the door shut, feeling her pulse hammering in her fingertips as she pulled away. His final look of baffled frustration lingered in her mind's eye, but she shook it off, dropping her bag and struggling out of her jacket.

Each movement left her off-balance until she dropped onto the bed and crawled over to wrap her knuckles against the window, calling the shade. After that, she curled into a ball, taking slow, even breaths, and prayed for sleep to take her, even though she knew it wouldn't.

GLACIER

Glacier dumped his things into one of the small rooms before he joined anyone left awake in the common space. Crow was sprawled out on the couch to watch the news into the early hours of the morning while Nyx worked on her tablet, occasionally shooting Glacier a disapproving glare until she headed to bed. The murmurs of the TV managed to keep him distracted long enough that he hadn't noticed Crow nod off.

He twisted around to take in Noa's door, wondering how likely she was sleeping right now instead of pretending to keep Nyx happy. There was something else that nagged at his thoughts, calling his attention to her strange behavior up until she'd shut a door in his face. So, he crept toward her room and gave a small pull on the handle.

It flew open, automatically gliding the rest of the way in the track. Light poured out around him as Noa shot up from the middle of the bed, her eyes wide with surprise for a fleeting moment before hardening. Anger wasn't the only thing radiating from her—there was something else there too. Cecilia's quiet ramblings about learning magic left him with that final clue that pieced it all together—the mention of Noa's reaction to her small, illusionary ocean.

"Get the hell out!"

"Noa, are you hydrophobic?"

"Don't be ridiculous," she snapped, the rest of her fury drowned out by Glacier's irrational action of shutting the two of them in the room together.

At least, he told himself it was irrational, but the only irrational part about his reaction was that he hadn't just *left*. His initial thought had simply been to not wake Crow, followed by that horrible, familiar grip of fear. Not that *he* was scared, but that *she* was. He might as well have been looking into a mirror at a younger, newly-orphaned version of himself—surrounded but so very, *very* alone.

Glacier started toward the bed, trying not to flinch back as she stood a little taller on her knees. She was more afraid of looking weak than of him, donning a mask to hide what he'd already seen.

"I said—" Noa's voice darkened as he reached for her, but it only took a small shove for her to lose her balance. Her wobbling had been from fear, wrapped in a thin layer of rage. And now that rage dissolved into shock right before he grabbed the folded duvet at the end of the bed and draped it over her.

Glacier dropped to his knees next to the mattress and lifted the edge of the blanket to peer into the dark. That scared child inside of her stared back.

"You don't have to be a badass all the time, Noa," he said softly. "It's okay to have a weakness. It's okay to be scared of something. You're still only human."

Her eyes searched his as he started to push away, hoping that she'd take some comfort in the embrace of the duvet. But before he had the chance to stand, he jolted as fingertips dug into his arm.

"Wait—" she said, panic absorbing her features. Her mouth worked like she was trying to say more but couldn't force the words out. He could take a guess at what they were though: *I don't want to be alone.*

Glacier shifted, leaning into the edge of the mattress. "I'm not going anywhere," he whispered.

She didn't let go like he had thought she would, but her grip relaxed. His fingers twisted the sheet, thinking of what to say next.

"It... um... probably seems weird that I did that," he continued with a breathy chuckle. "I used to be afraid of thunderstorms. They're rare in Amarais, but we got a couple one year when I was younger. My dad used to make a blanket fort for the two of us, and we'd watch something on his phone until I fell asleep. It was like the rest of the world didn't exist anymore. It felt safe."

Noa remained quiet, like she was waiting for him to fill the silence again. The fact that she wasn't speaking made him wonder if she ever had any family memories like that. Had she only ever known the Volkov? His heart ached with the thought, but something within him gave a small nudge, telling him that they weren't alone anymore, even if they felt like they were. Everyone with them would help keep each other afloat. They didn't have to be afraid.

"I won't let you drown," he said quietly.

Relief spread over her features, giving way to exhaustion. Her eyelids drooped, and her grip slackened. Her breathing went rhythmic, and he shuffled backward, freeing himself from the cover of the blanket and Noa's arm.

His head swam when he stood, begging for sleep as he started back into the common area. He grabbed the remote off Crow's chest, turned off the TV, and scrubbed at his face on the way to his own room. Once his head touched the pillow, his mind pulled him under.

Glacier woke to the familiar flicker of the fireplace. He laid there, staring up at the ceiling with his hands resting on his stomach like it might calm the uneasy image of that Miraltan woman covered in blood. When he finally pushed himself up, he rubbed his face and started toward the hall, his foot catching on a wide, thin curl at the corner of the rug. Frowning, he kicked it back into place and glanced around the room for something large that might've moved to cause it. Nothing.

Glacier shook his head and resumed his trek to the office, where Kat sat in the chair again, turning the white plastic square over in her hands. Her eyes met his as she placed it against the desk, revealing an emblem boasting a crimson-colored V.

"I was starting to think that you weren't coming back," she said somewhat jokingly as she rose to her feet.

"What do you mean?"

Her smile faltered. "Never mind," she said, moving aside as he started for the chair. "It's nothing."

He brushed it off, dropping into the seat and tugging on the drawer to find that blinking red light. A sigh of relief escaped him, glad that nightmare was still locked away, even if he now knew what lay inside.

"Do..." Kat started, "do you want to talk about it?"

No, not really. He pulled open another drawer, rifling through its contents to avoid the question.

"How—" she said, her words catching when he didn't look up, "how much were you told about your mother?"

Glacier tensed, letting one of the metal baubles he'd found slip from his hand back into the drawer. "Not much," he mumbled. "Just that she loved me." It sounded hollow to his own ears, accompanied by a familiar numbness. A numbness that came from being robbed of the time they should've had together, essentially making her almost nothing to him.

"I... want to show you something."

She beckoned for him to follow when he looked up. Kat led him down the next hall and pulled down the attic steps, standing aside for him to go first. It creaked as he hurried his ascent, both curious and confused about packing everything away to revisit it again. The light turned on, illuminating the bins, totes, and white sheets draped over the rest of the clutter before Kat's shadow joined his along the wall.

When he looked back, she gestured toward a covered, thin, rectangular item leaning up against a few containers. The thing had to have been around three-fourths of his height. Dust stirred under his feet as his shoes scraped the floor in front of it, treading a portion of the attic that'd been left undisturbed for so long.

He glanced back to get a nod of confirmation, and he pulled the sheet away. It fell from his hands, dropping to the floor to reveal a painting that shouldn't exist. A man and a woman stood, half-wrapped in each other's arms, staring into each other's eyes with *love*. Glacier knew both of them—the blond man was a younger version of his father, and the woman had been the Miraltan woman he'd encountered in that nightmarish thing locked away in the office.

More dust stirred out of the corner of his vision, replaced by Kat. "Just after you were born," she said, "back when no one knew about you yet, Uncle Cyrus visited us. I remember asking him if he would ever get married —mainly because I had heard dad complain about it."

He swallowed back the lump in his throat, unsure why he was feeling choked up by the sudden memory of the two of them back at the palace, standing side-by-side in the hall of kings and queens that had come before them.

"He asked if I could keep a secret," she continued, "so of course I told him yes because I wanted to know. What sort of kid says no to a secret?" She gave a short, quiet laugh. "He told me that he had met the most beautiful woman in the world, and he was going to marry her. I asked if she was as pretty as a princess, and he said she was prettier. So, I called him a liar since I thought there was no such thing, but... I was wrong."

A somberness fell over the room, accompanying the brief moment of silence. "He wanted to make her Queen of Amarais. Cyrus did everything he could to fight back against Amarais's council, and he still tried to reach out to Miralta—to bridge that gap of hate after generations and generations of pulling away from magic and anyone that wanted anything to do with it. No one even really knows why it started or how, but now all the reasons are gone. We just teach our children to hate out of tradition and fear that we might be wrong.

"Somehow these two found each other and saw past it all. Against all odds, they managed to see each other for who they really were. And I can say for certain that at least one good thing came out of it." Her head moved slightly, catching his attention so their eyes met. "You."

His shoulders fell, and he let out a bitter laugh. "I'm nothing, Kat."

"You know that's not true. You know that your father made sure there was a place for you the moment you were born—a place for a prince that would become Amarais's first king with Miraltan blood. He wanted to end all the fighting and strife—to see Amaraians like Cecilia be able to freely use their magic for the benefit of the country, rather than having to hide themselves away."

He started shaking his head. "I'm not like him. I- *You* have always been more like him than me."

"But you *are*, Glacier. You're like *both* of them. You know how to demonstrate grace under pressure, and you have the willingness to fight back. You just need the proper tools and the know-how to use them."

She moved to stand in front of him, forcing him to look her in the eyes. "Stop doubting yourself. *You* were made for this, not me. Now take what's yours."

26

RUNE

Rune's phone fell into his lap as Nyx emerged from one of the bathrooms, eyeing him on her way to the main door.

"Where's Crow?" she asked. "Not that I care or anything. I'd just like to at least know he's accounted for and not pulling the boat apart."

Rune chuckled, watching her stop in front of the display as it rotated through various on-boat shopping and dining. "He said that he was going out to explore the ship and find breakfast. I think that he's probably scoping out where the bar is for tonight."

She rolled her eyes and tapped at the panel. "Lovely," she said dryly. "Well, I'm having room service delivered for breakfast, so he's missing out."

He smirked and stretched, his smile fading away when his eyes flicked over to Noa's room. "You think she's okay? She's been asleep for a while now. That's not exactly like her."

Instead of echoing the sentiment, Nyx shrugged and tapped one more button before turning back around. "I usually just leave her alone unless she tells me otherwise. You afraid she doesn't want to cuddle with you anymore?"

Despite her bemusement, he scowled. "No, she just didn't seem like herself when we boarded, so I'm concerned. As a *friend*." He scolded himself as Cecilia floated to the top of his thoughts. She deserved better than him, even if he considered himself at least better than Astor.

As a grifter, Rune didn't believe he was all that redeemable, but she made him want to be a better person. Despite her naivety, she was kind, bright, and enthusiastic about seeing new places and learning new things—all things that had turned faded and gray through the lens of someone who was taught to assume the worst in people, rather than the best.

Nyx waved a hand. "Yeah, yeah... Whatever you say." And stifled a yawn on the way back to her room. A *click* of the latch catching signaled his solitude, and then another put him on alert again.

Cecilia emerged, padding into the living area from the second bathroom and drying her hair with a towel. So Rune scooped his phone back up, trying to keep himself from staring.

"Why'd Nyx leave?" she asked, twisting to look at her door. "Is she not feeling well?"

"I think she's monitoring a few things before breakfast," he replied, absently checking through the weather reports. "She's having some food delivered to the room for those of us who would prefer to stay in the cabin."

"Oh, okay." And then she took a seat across from him.

Rune shifted uncomfortably, clearing his throat and trying to maintain focus on his device, not really paying attention to what he was pulling up, outside of it being news. He caught Cecilia's head tipped to the side, and he clutched the phone a little tighter, afraid to tilt it further up because it was hard to tell if she was angling to see what he might be looking at or if she was watching *him*.

"Um..." she started. "This... might be a bit intrusive, but are you from Bellegarde?"

His head jerked up in surprise.

"I mean," she quickly added, ringing the towel on her lap, "you already know that Glacier and I are from Amarais. I'm just... sort of curious to find out where everyone is from. And maybe hear about what those places are like."

Rune couldn't help but chortle. "What gives you that idea?"

"I- well- I—" She reddened. "I just sort of assumed that you were because of the darker hair and eyes, the lighter skin, and how Nyx seemed to always give you and Crow Bellegardian IDs."

"You're close," he said, setting the phone back down. "We're not from Bellegarde, but our mom was immigrating to King's when she met our father. He was a third- or fourth-generation immigrant. They settled down somewhere in the north-western part of the Republic that was mainly populated by other former Bellegardian natives. We lived in a small townhouse—it was barely enough space for three people—so I'm sure they lamented when they discovered they were having twins."

"Are- are they still around at all?"

He leaned back, closing his eyes for a moment with a nearly inaudible sigh. The memories rushed back in, but he no longer felt the need to brace for impact. Each one of them used to have a bite, but the sting was gone thanks to each layer of new experiences.

"They're not around anymore. Not for us, anyway. Our mom walked out on our dad when we were three or four. He didn't really know how to take care of us, but he tried... at least, at first. Eventually, he just started coming home and drinking every night. Pretty sure he drowned himself in work after she left, so Crow and I pretty much fended for ourselves by the time we were old enough." He shrugged after catching a glimpse of Cecilia's sympathetic expression. "It was never perfect, but we had each other."

He ran a hand through his hair, dodging her pitying expression. "That was pretty much how it was until Crow and I were... maybe eight, I think? Our dad left for a month on an extended business trip to somewhere on the other side of King's. I guess he had a whirlwind of a trip because he came back with a new wife."

Cecilia's jaw dropped, and he tried to stifle a laugh.

"W-what?" she sputtered. "A *month* and he married someone?"

"Yes," he said, trying to suppress a grin, "and he also failed to mention that he had twin boys."

Her eyes widened in horror. "How- how do you not tell someone that?"

He shrugged. "I'm not sure. I know she was pissed when she stumbled into her new home to find us, but it was all directed at our father. She followed him around from room to room, arguing with him, yelling at him, threatening him... He eventually locked himself in the downstairs bathroom. I think he fell asleep in the tub.

"Crow and I lost track of them since we ended up invested in some stupid game on the upstairs landing. We avoided going downstairs until we were hungry and couldn't hear any more signs of her wrath. She'd been in the kitchen, waiting on a kettle to heat. The way she looked at us then... was different than when we'd been introduced. There was a tiredness about her—whether that was a result from her verbal tirade or from the realization that she lived there now, I don't know. but it'd replaced the shock and fury that I'm... now convinced was never meant for us. Before we had the opportunity to bolt back upstairs, she made us sit down at the table and fixed us dinner. A motherly gesture from a stranger in our own home."

Cecilia leaned forward in her seat, her damp hair cascading over her shoulder in tendrils. Those blue eyes searched his features for any inkling of what might come next. But this was the part where Rune normally stopped. That was supposed to be the end of his sob story to anyone who bothered asking since those people more or less knew the rest. That was the beginning of who he was now, flourishing into an unruly mess of paint covering a once-detailed canvas sketch of who he could've been.

However, Rune was Rune. And Rune wasn't in King's anymore. He was drifting somewhere between there and Mharu, barely holding onto the one person he had left while greedily hoping to pull in another.

"She told us to call her Corrine," he said, letting that greed consume him, despite that knot that formed in his stomach. "She didn't want us to call her 'mother' or refer to her as our stepmother. She hadn't ever planned on being one, so I think she hated the titles. But she still acted like one—to us, at least. Corrine wasn't all that fond of our names, saying that they were too similar, like we were supposed to mirror each other instead of playing off of our strengths. So, she gave us new ones. She pulled them from her favorite old parable called 'The Wizard and the Merchant.'"

Cecilia's brows furrowed before slowly shaking her head. "I haven't heard that story. I assume the wizard is just a Mage before Mages really had a name, so the whole thing was probably censored in Amarais."

"He was. I'm... not very good at storytelling, but I can summarize." He hummed for a moment, recalling how Corrine used to tell it and focusing on her theatrical declaration of the high points. She'd drape herself in one of the threadbare throw blankets and hunch over slightly for the part of the wizard. The memory of Corrine's eye dancing with amusement from his and Crow's quieted giggles brought a smirk to his face.

"It's about a hermit wizard and his pet crow that lived in the woods, settled amid a few small towns. He spent his spare time carving warded sets of stones to protect the homes of his town-dwelling neighbors and then would make his yearly trek to distribute them. He didn't really need much money since he was self-sufficient and asked for just enough to make an occasional trade.

"But one year he ran into a merchant, and they struck a deal. The wizard was an older gentleman, and the trip would leave him weary. So, he gave half of his stock to the merchant, allowing him to make an additional profit along his route, which would save the wizard half the journey. But after they parted ways and the wizard passed through a few towns, he heard from another traveler that had come from one of the merchant's stops that he had been selling the stones at outrageous prices for *one*—not even for the full set of four. This enraged the wizard, and he decided to teach him a lesson.

"On his way to the next town, the merchant encountered runes carved into several trees. Of course, he didn't know what they meant, but he knew that any sort of magic like that was valuable, so he carved the bark away while thinking up a gimmick to sell them. But, as he continued along, his dog growled at the back of his wagon. Irritated because there was nothing else around, he hushed the dog several times before it huffed and laid down while the merchant kept carving.

"Wards and runes tucked among his other goods, he rolled into the next town, ready to set up shop again. As per usual, the local guild asked him to pay the fee for setting up his cart, but when he pulled out his coin purse from his wagon, he found it empty, save a single coin. A coin that was quickly snatched up by a crow—the *wizard's crow*." His smile turned sly, pleased to see Cecilia staring back in awe. "I think it's a pretty good reminder to keep to your word or pay the price, but it's also a good lesson to be cautious of distractions and greed."

"Rune and Crow," she marveled. "The distraction and the thief."

"Yep." He chuckled. "Corrine decided that I would be Rune, and my brother would be Crow. She realized that I was the more social of us, and how I ran interference while Crow got away with whatever act we'd planned to reap the rewards. I originally found it odd that she almost seemed *proud* of that. It wasn't until later—after she decided to leave our father and take us with her—that we discovered she was a thief."

"Wait—What?"

"Corrine was a professional thief and con artist. And when we were eleven, she moved the three of us to an apartment in the capital, Kingsheart, where she trained us in her profession."

"Your *stepmother* taught you two how to be thieves?" Her eyes were wide with disbelief.

"Yeah, pretty much." He chuckled. "She would take us out on weekends to some of the busier shopping districts to show us how to pick pockets, shoplift, rig street performances—all the basics. The only rules she enforced were that we couldn't steal or con anyone who seemed to have anything less than us, we couldn't hit the same area twice within a certain time frame, and we couldn't pull anything near where we lived. It was too risky and would upset the neighbors.

"Plus, having your neighbors think of you as upstanding citizens really works in your favor if the authorities show up and start asking questions. We even went out of our way to help them from time to time, so the entire complex was pretty friendly toward us. Afterwards, we'd hop on a train to the other side of the city and run a small con with a few other kids our age. That's how we ended up meeting most of our associates."

"Is... that how Crow met the girl you mentioned back on our walk in Miralta?"

He nodded, hesitating before his voice took on a reminiscent quality. "Yeah. The three of us got along pretty well, and we stuck together as the rest came and went. I don't think she could really stand Crow much at first, but now it's hard to think of one without the other. They became more and more inseparable as we planned bigger jobs with Corinne's advice..."

The coffee table warped in his vision as he considered what came next. He tried to push the memory back down, but it forced its way back up, telling him that it would soon be his fate too, after all. "Well, until she, um... couldn't give any more advice."

Cecilia tilted her head slightly, her brows knitting together. He decided to stare at his phone, lost in the depths of the screen that transported him back to his cracked bedroom window. The old man that lived above them had whistled as he watered his plants hanging on the fire escape, obstructing the view from Rune's bed. He hadn't really cared then, unlike all the other times he'd griped about it because the leafy monstrosities seemed preferable to staring at his bedroom door that always popped open.

The mattress sunk down at his back, partially turning him up to find those familiar, purple-tinted eyes fixed on him. She'd wrapped her arms around him and buried her face into his neck. Crow dropped down on his other side and gently collapsed on top of them both. The weight had been a welcomed comfort.

We'll find our way through this. I'll help you two make it to the other side like you both helped me.

"Corrine... encountered a job that proved to be her last."

"Rune..."

He cleared his throat, pressing forward anyway. "Corrine's friend watched over us until shortly after Crow and I turned twenty. After that, she had to leave to take care of a sick parent back in Esmedralia, so then it was just the three of us. We were left to come to terms with the final lesson she taught us. You don't live to be Corinne's age without eliminating as much risk as possible. Other than that, you just got to rely on a lot of luck and borrowed time." The lump in his throat left him unable to look Cecilia in the eyes.

"But... you still kept going anyway," she said. "Was the risk worth the reward?"

He paused as one particular item surfaced to the forefront of his mind. "Corrine had stolen something for a client once... but she held onto it for a week after. I heard her on the phone with someone a couple of times, saying that she was still in the process of getting it, which I knew was a lie. So I asked her why she was putting off selling it because I'd overheard the price. It was the sort of ransom that would've paid the bills for months—a score that every thief dreams of running away with. It was the sort of thing Crow and I kept chasing even after she was gone."

A younger, more arrogant version of himself had asked that question with his sights set solely on the money. Credits were the end goal. Nothing else had mattered then. It's why he'd been surprised to see Corrine's expression darken.

"She took me into her room and got it out of her closet. I... I actually *laughed* at her when she showed it to me. Then I told her she was being stupid because it was just some *book*—a real, paper book, which warranted the value. Who doesn't want a first edition or that last volume of a set to put on display in a fancy office or personal collection case?

"She yelled at me for being careless and flippant before explaining that it was... a grimoire. After she dragged me into the kitchen, she called in Crow and told us what it was used for. We watched it turn to ash in the kitchen sink while she messaged the client. She told me that she'd been torn on selling it because it wouldn't be her problem anymore, and she'd walk away with enough credits to stay comfortable for quite a while.

"I'd be lying if I didn't have nightmares for weeks after that, knowing that it had been in the next room over while I slept—knowing that someone was hounding Corrine so they could buy it. There are... some things worth risking for money, but others..." He slowly shook his head, catching the disturbing hint of curiosity on Cecilia's face. His stomach twisted.

"What, exactly, is a grimoire?" she asked. "I've heard of them, but—"

"Something that if you ever come across, you run from as fast as you can. Never, *ever* touch one, Cecilia."

She shrank back and guilt washed over him.

"Trust me when I say that you're better off not knowing what it can do."

The silence between them lasted for a few beats before Cecilia cleared her throat and changed the topic. While part of him regretted mentioning any of it in the first place, the other part of him latched onto the slim possibility that what Noa had told them of her role in collecting all these keys might be real.

And if he ever ran into another grimoire anywhere near Cecilia, he would destroy it in a heartbeat simply because the alternative would be far, *far* worse.

GLACIER

Glacier woke to a muffled knock against the suite's main door. The sound of Nyx, Rune, and Cecilia starting up a conversation after that forced him to get up. He swayed when he stood, gathered his clothes and toiletries, and slipped out to clean up.

When he returned to the common area, there was a small stack of plates on the coffee table. He started for them, noting a towel left in the doorway of Crow's darkened room. His eyes shot over to Noa's door, finding it still closed.

Nyx's head lifted as he approached. "Took you long enough," she said, pointing her fork toward the dishes. "Grab a plate." She glanced behind him as he took a seat. "Weird that Noa isn't up yet... She's usually wide awake by now."

He stiffened, an alarming thought blaring out everything else when Rune shrugged.

They didn't know.

She hadn't even told Nyx about her fear. That explained her defensive behavior last night, and he'd been the only one to discover her vulnerability.

"She woke up last night," he said, letting the lie slip out. "I hadn't gone to bed yet, and she mentioned that she was feeling a little seasick. She probably overslept."

He began to collect a couple pastries he didn't recognize, along with a small helping of some red and pinkish-orange jams, which he assumed might be strawberry or raspberry and maybe peach. After snatching a cup of yogurt and what looked like Taliean bread pudding, he picked up a spoon and forced a smile. "I'll just drop a plate on her nightstand, so Crow doesn't wander back in and take it."

Glacier tried his best to ignore Nyx's suspicious look as he started for Noa's room. He just hoped that his unfamiliarity with what he assumed was a Mharuan breakfast selection, his only offering since it was based on the ship's destination, didn't bring her ire down on him.

So, he slipped in with a light warning knock. She was still under the blankets, which gave him pause after depositing the plate. He debated lifting up the covers to see if she was all right but decided against it in favor of privacy.

When he stepped back out and began to load up another plate with his own breakfast, he considered if there was anything else he could possibly do to help ease her stress. It was a thought he dropped almost immediately since he figured he'd only make things worse.

"How long will we be in Tabir?" Cecilia asked Nyx as she pulled apart one of her pastries. "Or are we staying in Mharu for a little while before then?"

"We won't be staying in Mharu. Just taking a train through. The hope is that we spend as much time in Tabir as we did in Corvia, but that's dependent on Noa."

Glacier's chewing slowed while he absently ran his spoon through his yogurt. The thought that they might end up stuck in Tabir for weeks left him with a sense of dread. What if the Volkov followed them? A sickening sensation replaced what hunger he had.

He gently set his spoon down, swallowing back one of the few bites he'd taken. No one seemed to notice that he had nothing to add to the conversation as it prattled along in lighter tones, contrasting the creeping dark corners of his thoughts.

Glacier quietly set his plate back down and retreated back into his room, earning a stray glance from Nyx. The door slid shut behind him, and he flopped onto the bed, staring up at the ceiling. For the first time in three weeks, he imagined he was back home, staring up at the ceiling of his room instead.

As much as it'd felt like a prison, he missed it. At least there, he knew what dangers lurked and how to navigate them. But now he was in the middle of the ocean, completely unfamiliar with where they were heading or if they'd even make it there.

And he began to wonder if he should try to make the best of it.

NOA

Noa's eyes flew open at the resounding *click* of her door sliding shut. She threw back the duvet, sat up in bed, and froze. She'd completely forgotten about where she was until that moment: *the hell cruise.* She ripped the covers back over her head again, ready to bury herself when she caught a glimpse of the food sitting on the nightstand.

Glacier.

She dug her fingers into the soft sheets, wondering who all he might've told about her phobia. Noa grimaced as she recalled his reaction the night prior, wishing she could've eliminated that pitying look he'd given her. Then again, he'd given her food. She jerked the plate off the nightstand and pulled it into her cocoon of blankets.

Fighting back nausea, she shoveled down what she could, slowing when her thoughts intruded again. Glacier's reaction had been the opposite of what she had expected from *anyone* on board since she'd pictured all of them poking fun at this fear. Weirdly enough, it'd been unnaturally calming having him nearby, which only further played on her anxiety now.

Noa chided herself, shoving the thoughts away like her plate back on the nightstand again. She was getting soft. She couldn't afford to be soft, especially not *now*. So, with deep, even breaths, she closed her eyes and tried to lull herself back to sleep, forcing Glacier from the forefront of her mind.

27

ASTRAVNY ✦ 2704-12-04

KOLE

Returning home without Ezra had been... *strange.*

It's not like Kole hadn't ditched him before out of anger or frustration, but the fact that he wouldn't be trailing in behind him after deciding to split off along the way had finally sunk in. As much as he'd disliked him, there was still some small part that grieved. But a bigger part grieved the loss of Noa.

The clatter of the iron gate broke him from that prison, trading a set of invisible bars for real ones until he turned around to face the hulking mansion against a darkening sky. His face stung from the wind that picked up and carried away a flurry of snow off the sagging roof, over the courtyard, and into the fir trees, adding another fresh layer of white. The once deep-red shutters dipped toward the empty flower boxes, its color nearly matching the black tulips that had once licked at the windows. Now thick, plastic boards covered cracked and broken glass on most of the first floor.

The scene wasn't unfamiliar in Astravny, a nation sitting on the cusp of turmoil ever since King Elias took power and cut off trade to the eastern coastline. Miralta had hesitated traversing disputed Amaraian-Astravnian waters, and Talie had been forced to turn back when the Amaraian coast guards claimed they were drawing too close.

So, a country built on advanced alternative manufacturing and trade had all but collapsed overnight. Half the country migrated inland, abandoning those ports in favor of the southern routes to Bellegarde and King's Republic or the west for Jinwon and maybe Roth. He'd seen those apartments and offices himself once, barely occupied by those who fended for themselves by fishing before the sun came up and scrapping whatever remained of the outdated tech in the snow-flooded cubicles of the port buildings.

The promise of stipends became a joke. It was a promise Astravny couldn't keep, which is why it'd fallen into a pattern of every person for themselves. That also meant that the beggars he'd passed on the streets weren't his problem.

Instead, his problem lay on the other side of the large door, looming in its tall, curved frame. He twisted an old-fashioned key in the lock and gave it a shove, grimacing at the groan it let out. Kole stepped inside to the soft flickering of the electric faux-flame bulbs set within the bronze, classical chandelier hanging over the base of the staircase fanning out toward the entry.

He brushed the snow off his coat on his way to the steps, halting when a figure appeared on the landing. Even without the help of the staircase, he'd tower over Kole by the way he carried himself—his head always held high with a purpose or angled down in disgust. The silver at his temples stood out against his dull, reddish-brown hair in the light, but that gleam didn't reach his eyes. Instead, those dark-gray irises examined the empty space around Kole and then narrowed on him with a silent order to follow before he continued his path across the landing.

Kole swallowed and started the ascent. One door was left propped open, its light spilling out onto the dusty crimson carpeting. The source of the glow actually brought heat, which poured out from the fireplace tucked inside. His master had ripped the original electric one from the stone frame with the complaint that there was a perfectly good chimney being wasted.

That'd been the first time that Kole had questioned whether or not his master had always lived in the cold, noting how his appearance didn't match that of Ezra or Noa's Astravnian features. After that, he'd tried imagining his master as a boy from Talie because of his hair, Bellegarde because of his eyes, or King's Republic because he didn't quite belong in either. It was something he'd left to speculation because he had never dared to ask.

His master kept his back to him now, a curtain panel tucked into his hand while he peered out the window. It was as if he expected Ezra to run out of the woods any second now, cursing about being chased by wolves or accidentally setting himself on fire.

The curtain fell back into place. "Shut the door."

Kole did as he was instructed, telling himself the sweat beading at the base of his neck was from the fireplace. When he turned back around, he knew without a doubt he'd lied to himself. His master's hands dug into the headrest of his pleather chair with his eyes closed, almost in contemplation.

"Where's Ezra?"

The unnerving calm sent a shudder through Kole before he answered, "Noa killed him."

An uneasy silence blanketed the room, causing every muscle in Kole's body to tense. Silence meant disapproval. Disapproval resulted in punishment. This was something Kole had been on the receiving end enough times that he had the overwhelming urge to throw up.

"Then she made her choice." His master's tone skimmed the surface of his anger, barely masked with serenity. He opened his eyes, which seemed to pierce through to Kole's blood-soaked soul. "I have little doubt that Ezra pushed her. That always had been one of his glaring flaws."

"What now?" Kole asked, barely above a whisper.

"I assume the target is with her?"

He nodded, not wanting to push his luck by accidentally speaking out of turn.

"Then tell the client that we're dealing with a delicate situation. We need more time to ensure that the problem is contained. If he doesn't want word getting out that the target is still alive, then he'll be patient. In the meantime, let Noa go for now." His eyes fell on a desk ornament, a thick resin crescent that Kole didn't recognize. "Assist the others in finishing up their jobs."

"Just—" Kole started, a little stunned by his response. "Just let her *go?*"

He was certain that this man would be furious. Kole had felt that sting of betrayal back in Amarais—that sting that had boiled over into rage back in King's, but it ultimately cooled to grief. Maybe *devastation* was the better word for it, seeing just how alone he was now, but their master didn't feel remorse for the loss of Ezra. So how could he be so calm with Noa going rogue?

"She'll assume we're coming after her in immediate retaliation," he said. "So, she'll get sloppy. We just need to give her enough rope to hang herself with, and once she realizes the error of her ways, we clean things up. When that time comes, you can dispose of the target yourself. Until then, do what I've asked."

Kole understood that cue for dismissal, so he turned to place his hand on the door handle.

"Oh, and Kole—"

He froze, squeezing the handle even tighter.

"Be sure to choose a second in command before your next task."

"I will."

His heart continued wildly pounding in his chest as the door pulled shut behind him. Not only had he managed to step out unscathed, but he'd been *given* a position he'd never chosen to fight for—let alone had the ability to *win*. Ezra had sunk his claws into this title until Noa had challenged him.

Why'd you do it? Are you insane?

She'd shrugged, but there'd been a tenseness to her that waned as the month drew on in her new seat. A tenseness that Kole wasn't sure would leave him now, compounded by fear. It was how he usually ended up paired with Noa after that, but now there was no Noa to pair with.

What had once been six apprentices under their master was now four. Kole was the highest-ranking one alive, though he never considered himself the strongest. He always played it far too safe for his master's liking. That didn't even begin to address Kole's issue of not trusting the final three apprentices he had to pick from, almost like there'd been an imaginary line between Noa and the rest, separating those who'd learned via trial by fire and the others who'd been able to manipulate their way through with ease.

He bit the inside of his cheek as he strode across the landing, moving to the opposite hall. Each candidate he considered brought doubt. Kole crossed into his room and tossed his coat over a chair in the corner, soaking it in moonlight. When he turned back to reach for the light, he swallowed back a yell.

Wide, dark eyes stared back at him, jittering with excitement. "Ezra's dead, isn't he?"

He cycled that fear into anger, standing a little taller and beckoning the barely contained serenity he'd faced mere moments ago. "You shouldn't be sneaking up on people," he growled. "Especially after one of us doesn't come back."

She recoiled, an inkling of fear appearing before a feral grin distorted her features. Ice crept up Kole's spine.

"It's your turn to choose a second now, isn't it?"

He hated how giddy the question sounded, but he managed to keep his composure in check. "Get out."

She took a couple steps back, her sights pinned on him until she darted down the hall—quick and silent as a shadow with a flag of inky, blue-toned black hair streaking behind her. He swung the door shut, switched on the light and spun around to check the rest of the room before he exhaled. A bed, a dresser, and a desk. All untouched. No other lurking shadows.

For a brief moment, he imagined walking into Noa's room down the hall, thinking how it'd been left the same. Anger—or maybe sorrow—ignited that desire to wander down there and begin picking it apart. For answers. For closure. For a reason that explained all the pain she'd caused, even though he was certain that it'd only bring more hurt.

It all came back to that damn prince—a title he didn't deserve. And as much as he wanted justice for Noa's actions, the one thing he wanted more was Glacier Caelius dead.

28

MHARU ✧ 2704-12-04

NOA

Noa emerged from her room about fifteen minutes before they docked, stepping out to some petty argument between Rune and Crow. Nyx raised an eyebrow and frowned with a hint of bafflement, but Cecilia and Glacier simply watched the back and forth between brothers in Crow's final sweep of the kitchen, taking whatever he wanted.

Glacier hadn't told any of them.

A surprising but welcomed development in the midst of her turmoil that would ultimately save her from denying anything he would've leaked. She hadn't exactly been *nice* to him up to this point either, aside from a touch of sympathy.

"You feeling okay?" Nyx asked, folding her arms over her chest as she stepped up next to her.

"Um... yeah, just..." Noa shrugged. "Felt really tired."

Nyx hummed, seemingly accepting her answer before she started out the door, leading the way off the deathtrap of a watercraft. Noa hurried after her, sticking behind as close as she could until her boots hit concrete, and she regained a second shadow.

She glanced back to find Glacier, and she narrowed her eyes. "You didn't tell them?"

He frowned, catching up to her side. "No... why would I?"

Noa hesitated, trying to determine why he wouldn't have—something that took far too long to come to the conclusion of. "Are you *blackmailing* me?"

His eyes went wide. "What? Noa, if I were blackmailing you, I'm pretty sure you could—I don't know—leave me for one of your former *associates* to deal with me. Seeing how the only thing between me and them is *you*, I'd rather not piss you off."

Deciding not to draw it out into an argument that might backfire on her, she mumbled, "Fair enough."

Glacier rolled his eyes.

"Don't start getting sassy with me," she warned, "or I might actually leave you for dead."

The checkpoint funneled them into the train's shuttle station, where they fell in with the mix of other Republicans that'd traveled with them. They pushed their way over zig-zagging, round-tile patterns set into the cement, mimicking simplistic, foamy waves. Noa shook her head, silently bidding each watery reminder a 'good riddance' as they boarded the next shuttle.

"So," Nyx began, eyeing Noa's stifled anxiety yawn, "are you two going to stay up for the next three days now? If anything, I feel like you two over-slept somehow..."

Noa flashed her a lazy, suggestive grin. "I mean, I certainly feel refreshed." A flat-out lie since she felt like she'd been hit by a train, but she tossed in a wink to sell it.

"Spare me the flirtatious attitude," she said dryly. "You can't have this. You can *never* have this." She motioned to her entire upper half.

"Not with that attitude."

Crow brushed past their booth, sporting a taunting smirk. "Oh, good to see you're still alive."

"Glad to see you didn't fall off the boat, bitch," she replied, lacing her tone with fake cheeriness.

"Sorry, but I wasn't spending a whole lot of time on deck for that to happen. I was far too busy spending it in other people's beds."

Cecilia stopped short behind him, gaping in horror, and Rune shot him a glare.

"Oh, please," Nyx said, gagging.

Rune ushered Cecilia into her seat, snapping at Crow with an order to take his. Noa at least got a touch of amusement when she glanced back to find a disgusted expression on Glacier's face.

She suppressed a laugh, turning back to Nyx as the train started moving. "Where's the next drop point?" she asked. "Is it the next station?"

Nyx pulled out her phone, nodding in answer. "I got a message saying that our *goods* were dropped off about thirty minutes ago. After that, we'll get on the train to Tabir. It's a bit of a tight window, but we should be able to make it."

"Do you guys have the one from Mharu?" Glacier tapped his chest with a pointed look at Noa, indicating her keys. "Wouldn't it make more sense to go for that one since we're already here?"

Nyx shook her head. "I'm trying to get a hold of a couple of contacts to deal with that one, so it would be better to circle back to it later. Not to mention that the more randomly we move around to collect them, the harder it'll be for anyone to track where we're going or what we're doing."

"So..." he drummed his fingers against the table. "Exactly which ones do you have? You have the Strength of Corvia, obviously, but I didn't really recognize the rest."

Noa locked eyes with Nyx. Noa sighed, quietly listing off each one. "The Strength of Corvia, Roth's Embrace, the Hope of Bellegarde, and the Sword of Astravny."

"So nine more to go," he mumbled, almost more to himself. "But... do you even have any idea where the Vault is?"

She bit the inside of her cheek, feeling even more ill-prepared. "I mean, not *yet*, but we're working on it."

He frowned. "Please don't tell me that you're just hoping to stumble onto it by the time you get the final key."

Nyx shook her head. "We've been calculating some leads, however, you're more than welcome to assist if you have any thoughts that might point us in the right direction."

That sounded like a manipulation tactic if Noa had ever heard one, but he began sliding down into his seat, his head listing to the side in thought.

Noa cleared her throat, decided to take advantage of the opportunity. "Seeing how we don't have much to do on the way to Tabir, we could discuss it tonight. Want to throw a few ideas around?"

"I'll pass," Nyx said. "If you and this one" —she half-heartedly gestured toward Glacier— "want to discuss, go for it, but I'm hoping to catch some sleep between now and then."

"Suit yourself." She shrugged.

"Plus, I'd rather not join the insomniac club you two are starting. One of you is going to pass out during the worst possible time, and then I'm going to be pissed."

"Oh, don't worry. It'll be Glacier."

"Hm, what?"

Nyx sighed, and Noa shot her a bemused smirk.

GLACIER

The inset gold lines cutting through the hexagonal jade tiles of one of Mharu's international stations fanned out in front of Glacier like the starting point of endless possibilities. As sleek and bright as it was, his feet dragged when they passed under thin gold arches.

By the time they'd made it into a small four-person cabin, he was so exhausted that his head lulled against the window once he'd dropped into his seat. He tossed and turned during the last night on the ship until he started hearing voices in the common area. Even then, he laid there for a while, thinking about home. About the version of Kat haunting his dreams. About whether or not Noa was okay. And especially about the keys and the mess he'd fallen into.

He jerked out of his drowsiness as Noa yanked the cabin door open. The vague recollection of her mentioning something to Nyx floated to the top of his mind, though blurry and warped.

"Jumpy much?" Noa teased.

"Let him sleep," Nyx said from the seat across from him, barely looking up from her tablet. "We have a few hours until we reach Tabir."

"What time are we getting in?" he asked, rubbing at the side of his face.

"A little before 2:00AM," she replied. "There shouldn't be much, if any traffic at the checkpoint, so processing should be quick."

He bit back a groan. At this rate, he wouldn't make it without passing out. "Is there anything you want me to do before we get there?" His eyes flicked down to the tablet.

"Sleep."

Once again: not the answer he was looking for. Not with whatever morbid dreamscape he'd created.

She tapped at the tablet. "We can deal with everything else tomorrow once we're settled in."

Noa stretched out on the bench next to him, wearing a taunting smirk like this was some sort of sleep-deprived competition. Regardless of what she thought, he needed to move just to stay awake for his own sanity. It would allow him to potentially consider the location of the Vault, among other things that Nyx had mentioned off-hand, especially if she considered him to be one of the more knowledgeable people here.

Glacier stood and started for the door, ready to pace through the cars with these thoughts until he was yanked back down to the bench.

"Oh no you don't," Noa said.

"What? I want to stretch my legs. Is there something wrong with that?"

"New rule. You wait until I patrol the train once it's left the station. It'll only take about five minutes, but you're not walking around alone until then. If any Volkov decide to slip on board, they'll definitely get on at the last minute before it leaves to avoid alarm."

"Fine," he said, trying to keep the begrudging tone from his voice. Once she leaned her head back and closed her eyes, he folded his arms over his chest.

The rhythmic sound of Nyx's tapping against the tablet melded into a shift in scenery as the train started forward, and Noa took her leave. City lights against the evening sky lit up large murals, then apartments and row houses before dropping into one-story dwellings. It collapsed into open fields of tall, wild grass, dotted with shrubs and the occasional tree against the moonlit horizon.

Glacier absently pressed the side of his face against the cabin wall, taking in the low hum of the train. Every wonder flitting past the window became some sort of bizarre comfort, stemming from something deep within him he couldn't quite name.

Glacier woke to the sound of snapping—specifically, Kat snapping her fingers a few centimeters from his face.

He slapped them away. "What is wrong with you?"

"You can't just keep ignoring me, Glacier." She threw her hands in the air.

He pushed himself up, cringing at the fuzziness weighing on his mind. He'd assumed that she would sit down to discuss whatever she meant, but instead, she left.

He blinked, staring at the doorway. "What?"

No reply.

Letting out a frustrated sigh, he stood and started after her. He stumbled and grabbed the door frame before he glanced back. The rug was partially curled back again. With a frown, he kicked it back into place again and jogged down the hall.

"Kat, I don't understan—"

"Look at this," she said, motioning to the rug in the foyer. "What the hell is this?"

His slowed. It was curled up at the corner too. "It's... a rug."

She shot him a glare. "Thanks, I would've never guessed. Now would you like to explain what's *wrong* with it?"

Glacier furrowed his brows and tapped it free to lay flat again.

Kat paled—her expression shifting into one of horror. "You—Glacier, you can't just—"

"I can't just *what?* Kat, it's just a rug. It's not the end of the world if it gets a little messed up."

"You're missing the point. Gods, give me strength." She stared up at the ceiling.

"Oh, stop being dramatic."

"Excuse me?"

"Kat, you were just talking to me about my parents and having me pack up a bunch of stuff without any reason why. Are you seriously losing your mind over a *rug* now?"

Her hands balled into fists for a brief moment until she clapped them together. Then she closed her eyes, let out a breath, turned, and walked several paces away, locking her fingers together on top of her head.

Glacier's ears perked up at the sound of her mumbling something, but he couldn't make out any of the words before she spun around to march toward him again. This time, her gaze was lit with fiery determination.

"All right," she said. "So, in order for me to help you, I need you to start asking the right questions. And in order for you to start asking the right questions, I need you to get your shit together."

Questions?

Did she want him to ask about the rug?

"What's me getting my shit together have to do with the rug?"

She put her head in her hands with a disappointed sigh.

Decidedly *not* the rug then.

"Okay," she said, her voice muffled before she pulled her hands away. "So *this*" —she kicked the corner of the rug back again— "is going to continue to happen, plus a lot of other little things until you start to accept the reality of your situation."

Well, that was... unhelpful.

He gave a slow, nearly imperceptible nod, like he understood and nudged the corner of the rug back into place again.

Kat's lips pressed into a thin line. "Glacier," she said with a deadly calm. "Is there *nothing* about this entire situation that seems wrong to you?"

"Is this still about the rug?" he asked in a frustrated near-whine.

"No—Just shut up about the rug for a second and look at *me*." She tapped her chest. "Is there anything wrong with me being here? Right now."

He hesitantly began to shake his head. "No. The only thing weird is the way you're acting."

She folded her arms, drumming her fingers against her sleeve. "What did you have for breakfast?"

"Wait, what?" he asked with a chortle. "Seriously?

"Well?"

He opened his mouth to answer, but closed it again, feeling that fuzziness wrap around his thoughts. The answer was right there—he could feel it—but it was trapped beneath something muddled and obscured.

"I..."

"Now tell me the last thing I had you do."

"You took me up to the attic to look at that portrait."

She raised an eyebrow, signaling that she had made her point somehow. A point that he still didn't quite understand.

"You need to figure out how to break down that barrier you're keeping up, or else you're going to have bigger problems." She brushed past him, heading back into the hall. "Stop avoiding it."

<h1 style="text-align:center">29</h1>

MHARU ✧ 2704-12-04

NOA

When Noa returned a few minutes later, Glacier was sound asleep against the cabin's wall.

Good.

She carefully sat down next to him, setting her sights on Nyx.

"If your intention was to trap him into falling asleep," Nyx mumbled, not bothering to spare her a glance, "you should know that it probably took him about three minutes before he crashed."

"Actually, I was being serious. I don't want to risk him walking around the train by himself unless I've swept it myself."

Her eyes flicked up then, part of the screen still reflected in her glasses. "What? You actually have a heart?"

"I don't know that I would go *that* far," Noa said with a snort before nodding down to the tablet. "So, what do you got?"

"Well... I've been trying to connect some of the previously collected data from Amarais to actual people, but all the admins and moderators seem to have covered themselves fairly well. The only good lead I've managed to get is that they've opened a new portal." She handed the device off to Noa, who took in the open conversation between Nyx and a couple anonymous users on the screen.

"I offered a couple of deals in exchange for assistance, but none of them want to risk it." Nyx shrugged. "I can't really blame them. At this point, it's a matter of persistence and finding the right person to prove my trustworthiness to."

"Did you mention *him* at all?" Noa gave a small jerk of her head in Glacier's direction.

"No, I'd prefer to keep our cards close to the vest for now. We don't know for sure if they'd back him like Katerina. Saying and doing are two different things. Considering how a small fraction of supposed 'rebels' killed her, and she was *supported*, there's quite a large risk involved. At the very least, I'd like to get back into the portal to feel things out, so we can formulate some sort of plan to rally the rebels behind him. It's a possibility we can utilize them to storm the palace."

"Help us make a path straight to the Soul of Amarais and liberate the country all in one go..." Noa mumbled. "Why can't you just fool the sign-up process like you did the last time?"

"There are more manual checks now. Previously, there were a few somewhat manual checks before for filtering, but now it's strictly invitation-only. They're the ones that hand you your credentials, you don't generate your own. Plus, you have to wait in a queue like a checkpoint. First-come, first-serve."

"So they're approaching people and making them wait in line for vetting?"

"Sort of... It's more like a chain of who you know, from what I'm understanding. Like... one person vouches for two people, who get queued, then those people vouch for one or two more each. It webs out from there. As long as they pass the checks, they're in, but because I can't prove that I'm Amaraian, they're assuming that I'm here solely for war profit rather than humanitarian assistance."

Noa frowned, eyeing Glacier.

"Trust me," Nyx said. "It would be *very* easy to name drop, but then we'd also have to give proof of life, an explanation of why we have him, how we have him, and what's in it for us. After that, we could end up handing him over, only for them to kill him, making all of this for nothing. The safer way is to play the long game, and in order to play the long game, we need to give as much truth as possible without mentioning *him* or the Soul of Amarais."

Noa clicked her tongue as she handed the tablet back to her. "Fine, but you do realize that the Volkov aren't going to wait around for us to play the long game, right? They're going to want to get rid of us sooner, rather than later, which means that I don't know how much time we have left." She pointed a thumb at him. "Having this one with us has definitely eliminated some of the time we might've previously had. Now that he's with me, I can imagine they'll be twice as aggressive in pursuing us."

Her mind momentarily stumbled over a possible idea to buy a little extra time, giving her enough pause that Nyx noticed and motioned for her to continue. "I... Look, when this whole mess started, I thought that I could flip two of the Volkov to my side. But I burnt that bridge with one of them when we left Amarais."

Nyx raised a brow. "Let me take a wild guess... Was one of them that Amaraian back in King's that I led away?"

She grimaced. "I chose him as my second in command. Ezra must've done the same after I left the Volkov. Kole..." She sighed, trying to think of the best way to phrase it. "He's good at covering someone, but he's not good leadership material. He's cautious, which can be an advantage and a disadvantage. However, I think his driving force here is that he believes a Miraltan killed his parents—that's what he told me when we were younger. They were probably a Mage from the way he described it."

"You don't sound all that certain..."

"I... don't know anymore. I'm not sure if that's what Kole *remembers*, or if that was what he was *told*. But if it was the latter, then it might be enough to beg him off."

"You want me to dig."

"I don't know what you'll find. He left his real name behind when he left Amarais, so he never told me it. That also means that I don't have anything else to give you outside of maybe a couple of time markers."

"I've had less to work with before," Nyx said. "I'll see what I'm able to find. I guess my only question is what if it's true? What if a Miraltan actually did off them?"

"Then... I guess there's nothing I can do to help him see past the hate. He's clearly upset with me, so I don't think there would be anything else I could do to convince him."

"That's quite the risk to try to flip him to our side, but... it could work in our favor. You mentioned that there were *two* Volkov though. I'm assuming the second wasn't Ezra."

Noa huffed out a laugh. "No. The other one is a complete wildcard. If I run into her, I'll either have a brief opportunity to convince her that I have her best interests in mind, or she'll kill me on the spot. There's no in-between."

Nyx's hand went to her forehead like she was about to massage away a headache. "And you couldn't have picked a more predictable option?"

"Now where's the fun in that?" she asked, a slow, teasing grin pulling at the corner of her mouth.

GLACIER

Glacier jolted awake to someone shaking his shoulder. Noa held her hands up. "Don't panic," she said. "We're just pulling into the station in a few minutes."

He rubbed his eyes. "Why didn't you wake me earlier?"

"Seriously? Maybe because you haven't been sleeping. I don't believe you for a second that you slept a full two nights on that boat."

He stood, hissing at how stiff his body was from leaning against the wall. Noa pulled down his luggage while he stretched.

"So you're allowed to forgo sleep for a couple of days at a time, but I can't?"

Noa shoved his bag into his arms, and he stumbled back a little.

"I think that you're forgetting our occupations are vastly different," she said. "I know my limits from years of experience, and you clearly don't know yours." She worried her lip as he slung his bag strap over his head.

"Are you having trouble sleeping because of what happened back in Amarais?"

He froze. It wasn't something he had expected her to ask. In that moment, he was transported back to the palace, telling Kat to be careful and giving her one final hug.

"I don't want to talk about it," he mumbled.

Deep down, there was a part of him that did, but the time, place, and people were all wrong. The one person who he wanted to talk to now no longer existed outside of his dreams, but that was a distorted mess of its own.

You can't just keep ignoring me, Glacier.

Maybe that was his problem. Maybe it was because he didn't want to face the truth and just *talk* to her in his dreams to figure out what his imaginary version of her wanted that he was still struggling with. There was something he was missing, and dream-Kat seemed to know it.

"Well, not sleeping isn't an option," Noa said, "just so you know. You need to rest, even if you hate what you see when you close your eyes." She pulled her own bag down and led the way out of the cabin. "Come on. Nyx is waiting for us in the exit car. Get your ID ready."

He jogged after her, picking through his pockets to find his ID as the train began to slow. When they met up with Nyx in one of the exit cars, she and Noa exchanged hushed words that he hadn't bothered listening in on. Instead, he was thinking about Kat and the strange riddles she'd given him to solve. He was supposed to start asking her the *right* questions. But what was he supposed to ask?

The train stopped and the doors opened, taking his thoughts with the surge of offloading passengers. He bumped into Noa, sucking in a breath as people flooded past. Nyx fell in line behind them, turning into an afterthought as he looked around for the others. Cecilia, Rune, and Crow had ended up on the opposite side of the terminal, where they were already passing through the checkpoint toward the blue-teal intermittent drapes overlapping the sandy brick wall leading to the exit tunnel.

Glacier's heart pounded a little harder in his chest as they approached the scanners, noting the wheel-like emblems on the security workers' uniforms. He kept his head down as he submitted his bag for inspection.

Noa scanned her ID, earning a flash of green before she reclaimed her bag, and he stepped up to touch his to the sensor. The card felt slick in his hands, nearly shaking from the pulse thudding in his fingertips. But it came up green. He determined that it must've been anxiety talking as he collected his bag and turned back just as Nyx pressed her ID to the scanner.

Red.

His stomach dropped, but Nyx appeared completely unamused—even a little annoyed—as the guard motioned for her to head down to the end.

Glacier gasped as he was yanked back, scrambling to catch himself while Noa dragged him away from the influx of people.

"The hell..." she mumbled when she let go of his arm, slowing to glance back to where Nyx had been taken.

"What was that about?" he whispered. "You haven't had any problems like that before, have you? I assumed that she would have the best one out of all of ours."

She shook her head. "I'm not sure what the hell is happening, but I'm not thrilled with it."

The others waited near a blue-painted bench along the wall, where Cecilia and Rune gave looks of concern at Nyx's absence while Crow bounced up and down slightly with impatience.

"Where's the other short one?" Crow asked, shoving his hands into his jacket pockets.

Glacier glanced back at the security booth as the guards there consulted their devices. One of them was going through her bag, but she continued waiting with her arms folded over her chest. He turned his attention back to the group with a helpless shrug.

About a minute later, Rune's shoulders dipped a little. "They're letting her through now."

Everyone's eyes fell on her as Nyx worked her way over to them.

"Just a glitch," Nyx said with a shrug, leading the way into the tunnel. "Let's hurry it up."

30
TABIR ✧ 2704-12-05

NOA

Noa watched Glacier's bedroom door as it drew closer to 6:00 AM. She'd expected him to fake sleeping for about an hour or so before he joined her, but he hadn't. Noa had even peeked inside at one point to see his head half-buried in a pillow next to Cecilia.

She sighed, turning her gaze to the window while she twisted her hair. There was always a strangeness that came with having someone new to talk to, but this case felt... *different.* She threw her arm over the back of the turquoise, low-backed couch with a huff, settling into it sideways while chiding herself for getting attached.

She thought back to how Rune had defended him in Miralta. He was right. She and Glacier both understood hostility but in different ways. Maybe having someone to commiserate with gave her a form of comfort that differed from her flirtation with Rune and business talk with Nyx. Those connections left out a lot of real feelings—feelings that Glacier had seen and didn't judge. He'd given her sympathy she'd originally refused to give him.

She wondered if she'd broken that slow-building trust early on with her behavior since he'd refused to talk to her when she asked on the train. But, then again, Nyx said that he did the same to her back in Corvia. Maybe that was also why he'd gone quiet after mentioning the *Verfahren der Historica*. Noa understood attention often being a bad thing, and him being silent was probably how he combatted it, unlike her reaction to find a way to rebel.

The thought reminded her of what she'd decided to do when she first met Nyx: show mercy to those who would've been her victims and eventually seek revenge on those who'd hired her—hired the Volkov to sweep their problems under the rug. *Problems* like Nyx and Glacier, who'd been completely unaware that they might be hunted.

Her nails bit into her palms right before she tensed at the quiet thump of a door hitting its frame. Her head swung back toward Glacier's room, where she caught his hand dropping from the handle.

"Is it too late to get started?" he whispered.

And Noa smirked.

GLACIER

Glacier winced, squinting up at Noa from the floor.

"Now *this* is why—" she started, stepping over him.

His hand shot forward, wrapping around her ankle. He yanked it toward him and took in her wide-eyed flicker of surprise—surprise that shot through him as well before she smacked against the geometric, star-patterned rug.

Glacier shoved himself up, horrified. *Why the hell did I do that?*

A weird sensation akin to déjà vu had spread over him right before it happened like he'd just *known* she would step over him. The problem he had with that was that she'd never done it before. Maybe there'd been something a little more arrogant about her movement this time? That had to be it.

Noa pushed herself up. Her brows furrowed in a display of confused irritation, and he scrambled to stand, feeling flustered.

"Are you okay?" he asked. "I don't know why I did that. You'd clearly beaten me, and it was over—I shouldn't have done that. I'm sorry."

She jerked forward and grabbed a fist-full of his shirt before he was steady, ripping him back down to her level. He pitched back as she leaned in a little closer with her eyes almost narrowed to slits. His mouth went dry.

She's going to kick your ass. Again.

"You're pretty damn lucky I held back from my initial reaction of kicking you in the face," she said with a deadly calm that he could've sworn was softened around the edges. "Because that's exactly what I would have done had I not been reigning myself in."

"I'm sorry," he repeated as she finally let go of his shirt.

Noa stood, rather than dealing out additional threats, but he didn't move. Instead, he waited for her to leave or give him some sort of indication that he was dismissed. She put her hands on her hips, seemingly scrutinizing him until her shoulders fell, and she offered him a hand.

"If you do that in a real fight," she said. "You'll regret it. Trust me, that's how I broke my nose once." She pulled him to his feet and tapped a sock-covered foot against his shin. "Kick the other leg next time."

Then she started for the kitchen, leaving him standing there, stunned. He blinked while she started filling the coffee pot, certain that she would've given him more of a lecture instead. Glacier pushed back his hair, trying to shake it off as Nyx padded out of her room.

"Oh good," she said flatly. "I was afraid you two might actually be resting."

"If you *must* know," Noa said, starting the coffee maker. "Glacier actually slept until six, so if you're worried that he'll mangle whatever precious data you give him, it won't be out of complete sleep deprivation."

Nyx stopped to stare him down, freezing him to the spot.

"Huh," she mumbled before she continued her trek to the room's service panel. He paused, taking in her clothes for a moment before whipping his head around to peer out the window. Sandy streets and palm trees. And yet Nyx was wearing a long-sleeved shirt, dark skinny jeans, and her trademarked gloves.

"Um," he started. "Won't you be hot if we go outside? You realize it's mostly sand out there, right?"

Nyx frowned at him. "Are you questioning my choice of attire?"

Noa's eyes went wide, locking with his and giving him a small, almost imperceivable shake of her head.

"No," he answered, glimpsing Noa's relief.

Nyx slowly panned back to the screen. "That's what I thought."

So, he began pushing the furniture back into place to keep himself from saying that she was asking for a heatstroke.

"Noa," she said once she was done and started for the kitchen. "Would you please get the resident idiot and his brother up? I'd like to discuss our plan of action for today." She plucked a mug out from the cabinet. "And Glacier, I'd suggest waking Cecilia yourself to spare her from Noa."

Noa groaned and let go of the coffee pot handle. "Can't I at least have my coffee first?"

"It'll take five minutes, tops."

She grumbled and made sassy gestures on her way to the twins' room while Glacier dusted off his hands on his way back to his own.

He pushed open the door and rounded the bed, giving Cecilia a small nudge. "Hey, Nyx wants to talk to everyone. I think you might have a couple of minutes to clean up since Rune and Crow aren't up yet."

"Okay," Cecilia said, stretching. "Give me a minute to get dressed." She propped herself up on her elbows. "Did you sleep okay?"

"A little." He put on a small smile for her benefit. In truth, he hadn't gotten the result he wanted from his dreams, but maybe he was making some progress.

"Well, it's certainly better than nothing," Cecilia said with some relief. She pushed back the blankets, and he made his way out to give her privacy.

He wandered back out to the living room to see shadows moving in the next room over. Noa had thrown back the comforter and dragged one body out of bed with a thud.

"What the hell is wrong with you?" Crow shouted.

She ignored him and crawled across the mattress to the next form, then leaned down like she was whispering something into his ear.

Rune twisted his body to look up at her, sounding disgusted. "Gods, Noa." He threw back the rest of the comforter and strode out of the room, rubbing his arms.

"What?" she pouted in her scramble to follow. Crow threw out a leg to trip her on the way out, and she kicked him, earning a hiss. "Do you not like the sweet nothings I whisper into your ear?"

He rounded on her, lowering his voice. "Believe it or not, 'good morning, Daddy' isn't how I like to be woken up."

Glacier rolled his eyes at Noa's uncontrolled grin.

Nyx set her mug down on the counter. "I'm suddenly no longer interested in my coffee." She started over to the couch, pointing to Crow's prone form. "And would you get your useless body off the floor? At least move your ass to the couch."

"Make me."

Nyx shot Noa a look—a silent command that sent Noa prowling back in his direction.

Crow immediately scrambled to stand. "I didn't mean it—I didn't mean it!"

She halted, staring him down as he slipped out the door and hugged the wall in his escape, refusing to break eye contact. He fell over the arm of the chair, sinking into it. "You know," he said. "*I* certainly wouldn't mind being woken up like how you woke Rune up."

"Oh, I'm aware, and that's exactly why I didn't say it to you." She moved to collect the mug off the counter, and Nyx paused. "What?" Noa asked. "You said you didn't want it."

"Karma," Crow said with a grin.

"It's fine," Nyx said, narrowing her eyes at Crow. "I have another sucker I can take a cup from later." His grin vanished.

Glacier spun around at the sound of the door opening behind him, and Cecilia stopped short. "Oh, sorry," she said. "I didn't mean to take so long."

"You didn't," Noa said, gesturing to the sofa for her to take a seat. "These two just woke up."

Cecilia hurried past Glacier to take her spot on the end, and Glacier dropped onto the cushion next to her. Surprisingly, Noa fell back onto the seat next to him, flashing him a brief smile before Nyx cleared her throat.

"Due to recent events," Nyx said, "we've been left with no other option but to speed up our current timeline."

"Oh, hell yes!" Crow pumped his fist. "Finally!"

"No, not *finally*," she snapped. "Speeding things up means that there's more room for error and worse odds. We can't stack the deck if there's too little or no time to prepare. Not to mention that we currently have the *very* pissed Volkov after us, so we don't have much of a choice now. If we screw up, we die, and if I recall, lack of proper planning is how you got into this mess in the first place, *Crow*."

He looked away, avoiding Rune's gaze. There was something there Glacier couldn't quite place, but he didn't exactly have the time to puzzle it out before Nyx started up again.

"*Now*, I believe that we're here for the Wheel of Tabir. We have two options."

"Is a good old heist one of them?" Noa asked, her voice tinged with genuine curiosity.

"Wouldn't it have to be a heist?" Glacier asked. "Unless I'm mistaken, the Wheel of Tabir is held by a specially licensed curator and stored in a private facility with several more of Tabir's prized artifacts, right?"

Nyx nodded before fixing her sights on Noa, where bafflement gave way to sudden understanding. "Too risky," Noa said. "Let's go with the second option."

"What's the second option?" Cecilia asked with a frown.

"Nyx, could you get me the replica?" she asked as she rose from the sofa, getting a nod before Nyx slipped into their bedroom. "I have someone that owes me a favor here who also happens to have access to the Wheel. There's almost no risk involved, not even for said individual."

"Are you sure they'll even agree to it?" Glacier asked. "That seems like a *lot* to ask in exchange for whatever your favor was. They could end up in jail."

"Trust me on this one."

He didn't miss the hint of doubt there, but he also didn't get the chance to press further as something flew over his head, sending him ducking into the cushions.

Noa caught a thin box, holding it up in a wave goodbye. "I'll be back later," she said, starting for the door. "I'll call you if something goes terribly wrong."

And with that, she left.

31

TABIR ✦ 2704-12-05

RUNE

Crow had muttered something on the way out of the suite sometime after Noa's departure. Rune guessed he was probably sore about Nyx calling him out, but he'd also been left without a reason to stick around and plan for a job. So, Rune chalked it up to the idleness.

He'd settled into the couch by the time Nyx tapped his shoulder, saying that she needed to run some errands. Cecilia's face lit up from the kitchen, and Rune had to hold back his amusement when Nyx caught her starry-eyed look.

"You're babysitting," she'd told Rune, despite Glacier's pensive expression about the prospect of leaving the hotel.

The overhead sun felt nice on his skin after all the cold and rain, but Nyx didn't let any of them stop to enjoy it. They started down the unpaved main road, moving around a taxi and bumping into street vendor carts butting up against storefront windows. Designer clothes cluttered most of them, advertised that each thread was woven with magic—likely a marketing scheme, but unsurprising to find here. Unfortunately, the other unsurprising postings he caught flashing or scrolling in most of those same storefronts were signs written in elongated Tabirian script and International characters that read, 'no modders.'

"No modders?" Cecilia whispered.

"Tabir isn't all that fond of those who replace parts of their bodies with something mechanical," he said quietly. "Probably something to do with how some people believe it removes a fragment of your soul."

"Really?" Her brows furrowed. "I read that mods were for medical purposes, even though they're not really allowed in Amarais. Is that not true? Miralta certainly wasn't like this, but they have restrictions on mods too…"

He hesitated, reminded of some of his jobs back in the Republic with a few individuals that had sported mods. One had replaced his legs, bragging about how much it had cost him, even though his original ones had worked perfectly fine.

"There are some who participate in it a little more… recreationally. But most only go through procedures to acquire mods because they have legitimate medical conditions. Some places aren't very fond of the idea, but Miralta is certainly more on the progressive side. I think their documentation system is more just to keep tabs of modders since they understand some do it out of need—like to help a person walk again or be able to see— rather than *want*, so they can turn themselves into something inhuman. Modding in itself isn't bad. It's just dependent on the person doing it, much like magic."

Rune quieted after that small dig at Astor slipped out, but Cecilia gave a solemn nod as they continued past other weathered, beige-brick buildings and past one of the many corners packed with vibrant pinks and greens of desert flora.

Nyx led them through a circular hub that parted the buildings, opening up to a bubbling, decorative pool. Teenagers sat along the tiled rim, giggling as they showed each other their phones and took pictures while traffic pulsed through from one cut through to the next. Each path split out like spokes on a wheel, giving Rune pause as to whether or not Nyx knew where she was going or just guessing since he was already turned around and longing for the city blocks of Kingsheart.

"I just need a moment," Nyx told Glacier before she vanished inside a shop with tinted windows.

Rune glanced up to the striped canopy overhead, already leaving the street rather shaded. He hummed, eyeing the Tabirian lettering before he noticed Glacier's thoughtful, far-away look at the door.

"Something wrong?" Rune asked.

"Oh—um, no," he said. "It's nothing. Just thinking."

Cecilia's boots ground against the sand as she nervously glanced between them and tucked a blonde lock behind her ear. Rune bit his lip, considering filling the silence, but Nyx emerged another moment later.

"Hopefully that was quick enough," she said, leading the way again. "But the next stop should be a little more entertaining for the rest of you." She pointed a finger at Glacier. "However, *you* need to stick with me."

Rune cleared his throat. "I thought we agreed that we weren't going to take them anywhere dangerous."

"Oh, we're not. But since he's my assistant now, I'll be needing him to assist me with this particular errand. The two of you can occupy yourselves while you wait."

"And what, exactly, are you doing?"

"I like to call it information management." She spun around to face him, holding up a round, plastic token that she pressed against a small panel on the wall. It flashed green, and a voice came over the small intercom attached to it, accompanied by a small, red light near what had to be a camera.

"How many?" came a deep voice.

"Four," she said, holding up just as many fingers. The door next to the pad clicked to unlock, and Nyx pulled it free.

"Welcome back." The red light flicked off.

Rune grabbed the door on her way in, holding it for Glacier and Cecilia to step in ahead of him.

"Ah, Nyx!" said a man behind a half-glass partition in the cramped entry. He was medium toned with black hair, much like most Tabirian citizens, and tall. His dark eyes managed to brighten in the dim lighting of what felt more like an elevator car than some sort of storefront—assuming that's what this was. Rune eyed the door on the opposite side, trying to make out some sort of glow from the other side without any luck.

He pressed up against the charcoal panel wall with a frown, finally realizing that this guy knew Nyx by her official alias, rather than a fake throwaway name. *Odd.*

"It's been a while, Fadil," Nyx said with a slight smirk. "How are things?"

"Better now that you're here," he exclaimed, throwing his arms wide. "And you've brought friends—" He quickly tapped the desk his heavier-set companion manned. "Rashidi, give them the VIP bands. Nyx will probably want to talk to the boss."

"That's exactly why I'm here," she said. "But I think my friends will want to enjoy the facility while they wait."

"Ah, yes. Of course, Rashidi—"

Rashidi gave an unenthusiastic grunt that matched the baritone of the voice from outside, and he slid open the small window. "Arm," he said, and Nyx put her wrist through for him to secure a band around it. "It'll be removed on your way out. Next."

His eyes set on Glacier, who glanced toward Nyx before starting forward to get his, followed by Cecilia and Rune. The man slid the window shut again once he was finished and began tapping something into his terminal.

"Enjoy!" Fadil said before he pushed a button on his handheld panel. "The first one's on us."

The door at the far end of the room split apart, clunking as Nyx started toward the stream of silver light pouring in. A grand staircase covered in blue-green diamonds, spades, hearts, and clubs cascaded downward to glittering silver tile pathways to people hovering around large tables with holographic games and kiosks with spinning icons on screens.

Rune caught up to Nyx. "Did you just take us to a casino?" he whispered. As if in answer, one table group threw up their hands and cheered, triggering a flurry of lights and mini, holographic fireworks spouting from the center.

"I would hope so, or we're in the wrong place."

"I'm assuming Fadil meant that the first game is on the house then?" he mumbled, scoping things out for himself. It reminded him of casing a building by taking a casual tour and mingling with strangers, except this time he was with two new charges. He glanced back at them when they hit the bottom of the stairs. They bumped shoulders with each other, wearily making their way down behind them. He grimaced the second it dawned on him. "And we've brought two Amaraians to a casino, which are illegal in Amarais."

"Well then it's a good thing we're not in Amarais," Nyx said with a shrug. "I have to catch up with the owner to make sure things are going smoothly. Plus, I have some other questions for him that might help us out. You and Cecilia... find something fun to do."

She tapped Glacier's shoulder and motioned for him to follow. After a hesitant look at Rune, he nodded for him to go, and Glacier jogged to catch up.

Cecilia tugged on the hem of her shirt next to him. Being dressed in streetwear into a secret casino filled with patrons in designer clothes definitely marked them as *other*. He considered ushering her over to a quiet corner, but his contemplation lost him enough time for a man to slow in front of them. The scent of strong, citrus cologne mixed with alcohol forced Rune to suppress a gag, amplified by the revulsion he felt when the guy began leering at Cecilia.

"Well, well..." he said with a crooked smile and a malicious twinkle in his glassy dark eyes. "How about you join me at the tables, and I get you a drink?"

Rune threw an arm around her, pressing her against him. "Sorry," he said coolly, "but she's already taken."

The man took a slight step back, faltering before he scurried away. Once he was out of sight, Rune started pulling his arm away until Cecilia grabbed it and held it in place.

"Something tells me he won't be the only one here to try that," she mumbled. "And I'd rather not be ogled."

He leaned in as close as he dared with the hope he wasn't making her uncomfortable. "And something tells *me* that this won't stop them..."

"What sort of people even know about this place?" she asked. "The entrance is practically a hole in the wall."

"It's probably a membership-only or club casino to lock it down since it doesn't look like a place that deals well with troublemakers. But since we're here... Do you want to learn how to play the odds at a few games?" He smirked down at her.

She chewed on her lip. "Well... I've already broken just about every other law, so I guess what's one more?"

"That's the spirit."

GLACIER

A man lounging in a blue-velvet chair with a tablet barely spared them a glance when Nyx stopped in front of him.

"Name's Nyx," she said. "I'm here to see Daxton. This one's with me." She jabbed a thumb in Glacier's direction.

Glacier tugged at the collar of his tee-shirt as the guy peered up, his expression flat as he took them both in and tapped something into his tablet. After a moment, he motioned to an arched, silver door, where a woman dressed in a suit stood.

Nyx nodded and they made their way inside. It opened into a wide hallway decorated with frosted glass water fixtures cycling along the walls, barely muffling the echoing of their footsteps as they approached a wheel-like intersection that matched the others they'd passed through earlier. The only difference was that this one lurked below ground with faux natural light reflected off the ceilings and looping videos of an overcast sky in the central dome.

Their guide led them straight through to a set of simplistic, dark brown double doors—no silver, no blue. The woman rapped her knuckles against it, pressed her badge to the sensor, pushed it open, and stepped off to the side. With a mumbled word of gratitude, Nyx led the way in, and the door clicked shut behind them.

Dark floor-to-ceiling curtains lined the walls, broken up by glass-front bookcases and classical works of art that must've cost a small fortune. This small office was a tranquil sanctuary tucked behind the loud and glitzy atmosphere of the casino. All to hide away a man a few years older than Glacier and Nyx. He absently dug his fingers into his reddish-brown hair while his tortoiseshell-framed hazel eyes darted over something on the desk. This guy was *Taliean*, not Tabirian.

"Daxton," Nyx interrupted.

The man jumped, nearly knocking off his glasses. "Sorry," he said, his voice lacking that Taliean accent Glacier had expected. "I was informed that I had guests, but I've been doing some rather heavy reading and couldn't pull away." He stood and started around the desk. "Go ahead, take a seat. I've done nothing but sit all day." Daxton motioned to the low-backed, overstuffed chairs in front of the desk as he leaned against the corner.

Nyx didn't waste any time taking the seat closest to him, so Glacier claimed the other, catching Daxton following his movement with a hint of curiosity before he cleared his throat.

"So, what can I do for you, Nyx?" he asked while he plucked up a loose mechanical component from his desk and began to fidget with it. Glacier had mistaken it for a strange decoration until he noticed the other miscellaneous parts along that corner. More were strewn out on top of a short cabinet further past Daxton, obscured by the pattern of the Tabirian fabric spilling over the cabinet doors.

"I wanted to see how you were doing since I happened to be in town," she said, "and to ask you a few questions if you don't mind."

"Of course," he said, cutting his last word a little short with his eyes on Glacier again.

"Oh, don't mind him. He's my new assistant. You can say anything in front of him that you would normally discuss alone with me."

His fidgeting slowed, and his smile grew less forced, drawing in a touch of warmth. "And does your assistant have a name?"

"Call him Morgan."

The name from his first fake ID. A good cover since Glacier wasn't exactly a common Amaraian name. Maybe fifty or a hundred years ago there were more, and even more before that, though likely in Miralta instead. It was a name drawn from the world—something which most

Amaraians deviated from—and inspired by the cold that most Miraltans now tried to avoid.

"Pardon the curiosity but are you Miraltan or Republican?" Daxton tilted his head slightly.

The fact that Daxton hadn't even listed Amaraian as an option both stung and gave him some relief in knowing no one suspected it. "Miraltan," Glacier answered, deciding to keep to Morgan Hawthorn's documentation.

"One of your parents must be feeling rather fortunate right now, considering all that's going on up north," he said, pointing to his own left eye. "But I doubt that's what either of you are here to discuss."

"Correct," Nyx said. "I'm actually wondering what you can tell me about Wilton Arrington."

Daxton released a long, heavy breath. "That's quite the request. Do you care to be a tad bit more specific?"

"Back when I was relocating you, I asked you for a list of people that you thought might have you targeted, which ended up being quite a few between your work and research. Arrington's record is probably the cleanest by far, so why did you add him to the list?"

"Well... for starters, I worked under the man for years—" He gave Glacier an apologetic look. "I was in the Republican Intelligence Agency."

And your real name isn't Daxton, Glacier thought. This guy was another would-be victim of the Volkov. He nodded, signaling for Daxton to continue.

"He was my direct superior, but he ultimately took interest in hiring another technical supervisor. Said supervisor also tended to stay late with him, while I typically wrapped up and went home to pursue my pet projects." He held up the mechanical piece.

"Who's to say they weren't just breaking workplace rules with their one-on-one time?"

Daxton chuckled, shaking his head. "I'm positive that wasn't the case. I suspected favoritism, but nothing quite to that extent..." He stared down at the part in his hands, turning it over. "Call it whatever you'd like—a gut feeling, intuition—but it felt like they were conspiring against me. Like I was causing them problems somehow, and they weren't quite sure how to get me to leave."

Nyx leaned back in her seat. "So, you think he wanted to push you out the door? That doesn't really explain the jump to make you permanently disappear."

"I really don't know," he said with a sigh. "There was something he was doing. I could never quite pin down what it was, but... I don't know. Maybe it's something I could look further into for you if you'd like?"

She shook her head. "It's fine, Daxton. As long as you're convinced, then I can have someone else look into it. I'd rather not risk you coming back from the dead. However, I do have some additional research I'd like you to see to instead."

His face lit up at her request. "By all means, I'd be happy to help."

32

KING'S REPUBLIC ✦ 2704-12-05

SHANE

"Six days, Jinko," Shane Delacroix hissed. "We're only behind by *six* days."

Jinko Matsuoka kept her eyes narrowed dead ahead, refusing to acknowledge him. The resounding *click* of her high heels on the linoleum tile drove any oncoming employees against the walls, where they ducked their heads and hurried past. Tablets were clutched to suit jackets and phones pressed to ears—anything to keep out of her way.

Normally, it would've given Shane a decent chuckle to see such a small woman cause so much fear. Honestly, it was something he admired. It's what had caught his attention when she'd been hired on, despite her resting bitch face that made it difficult to read her—a skill he was admittedly too dependent on. But when he saw her hand tighten around the round, mini hologram projector in her hand, he understood that she was pissed.

He ran a hand through his dirty blond hair again, betting it was sticking up at odd angles by now since he couldn't loosen his tie. Not in the middle of the workday and certainly not before he stood in front of his boss.

Jinko cut off his path with a sharp turn through a door. The wide interior windows on either side gave him a brief glimpse of what he'd be walking into before he slinked in behind her, passing the digital placard that read, 'Director W. Arrington.' The room greedily grasped at the natural light backdropping the desk from the high-rise windows. Shadows loomed toward Shane from the shelves bracketing the walls on either side of the desk, neatly lined with binders of synthetic paper records, personal trinkets, and work-provided devices.

A man in his late thirties sat reading arbitrary data panels and that morning's news, pushing the windows around with a pale hand while his coal-black eyes trailed over each meaningless word. His coffee-colored hair took on a blueish hue as Shane shaded the windows to the hall, and Jinko slapped her projector on the desk, locking up everything he'd been messing with.

"Southaven," she said. "Six days ago."

He leaned back in his seat, removing his horn-rimmed glasses to spin between his fingertips. Shane stopped next to his coworker and stared down at the projections Arrington was taking in: ID images of two Bellegardian-Republicans. Mirror images of each other with two red data boxes connecting them to their profiles.

Shane's mouth twitched slightly in disgust, but he swallowed back the irritation the second Arrington changed targets from the pictures to Jinko. This was *his* find. Not *hers*.

"Would you care to explain why it took your team six days to find them?" he asked before flicking his eyes to Shane. "Or do we need to start taking disciplinary action?"

Shane flinched, suddenly no longer wanting the attention he'd craved before. "The tech who found them in Southaven explained in a report—" Jinko rolled her eyes as Shane fished his phone from his pocket. "A report I foolishly left on my *desk*" —he cursed himself, gritting his teeth as he swiped through the device— "that there was a discovery of them being flagged as false positives in the system. It's not all that unusual, seeing how clusters of people in certain areas of King's can look very similar, but she found a discrepancy in the data. So, she alerted both Jinko and I the moment she came across the footage in the station. None of the other techs had even bothered to look twice, despite us emphasizing that it was rather critical."

Jinko made a short noise of annoyance, causing Shane to bite down on his tongue before he continued. "We haven't seen either of them for *months*, the fact that it only took her six days before finding their trail again should at least be acknowledged."

Arrington rose from his desk, smacking his palms against it so hard the sand pendulum shook at the epicenter of his mini, spiraling zen garden. Shane shrank back.

"And who's to say," Arrington said, his voice darkening, "that *she*, along with all of the other techs, hasn't been missing them going in and out of stations, public streets, and *gods only know where else* over the past few months? You don't know if they've missed any of it because you only know what they've *found*."

Jinko raised her chin a little higher and her mouth twitched like she was holding back a smirk. "I've already sent two agents to Southaven to investigate," she said as Arrington slid his glasses back on and returned to his seat. "If they're still there, we'll find them."

So, not wanting to be outdone, Shane said, "And I've assigned the same tech to hunt through all of Southaven stations' footage. We'll be able to tell where they went from there if they left."

"Report back the moment you receive any more information," Arrington said, returning to his usual, gruff calm. "You're dismissed."

Jinko pried her device from the desktop and strode out without another word. Shane should've followed suit, but he lingered for another moment, trying to force out some sort of explanation that would paint him and his underling in a better light somehow. Unable to think of anything, he finally turned and left.

ALYVIA

Alyvia Watson popped her head up over her curved, standing monitor at the sound of footsteps clattering through the doorway to the office. Her supervisors had returned to their domain. Jinko furrowed her brows on her way to her private office, her pulled-back, black hair brushing the back of her blazer with each movement until the door slammed shut behind her. Alyvia ducked down, barely catching Shane tugging on his tie and scanning the rest of the room with his copper eyes, darkening with each step before he vanished into his own little retreat.

Alyvia glanced down the empty aisle she sat in, recalling all the chuckling and chatter over where to head out for lunch after she'd gotten verbally ripped into by Jinko—a complete reversal of the metaphorical pat-on-the-back Shane had given her moments prior before he had to take a call. Then everyone had left—both supervisors and techs. Not that any of the techs went out of their way to invite her to lunch anyway. Between keeping to herself and always keeping her head down to pump out work, a social life wasn't exactly at the top of her priority list.

Shane reemerged from his office, and she slid further into her seat, preparing for the worst. He knocked twice on Jinko's door and pushed his way inside, calling the window shades on his way in. Alyvia sighed and rubbed her temples.

Never good enough, huh?

Her eyes flicked over to the sandwich she'd sprinted down to the cafeteria to get, left partially eaten since her stomach went sour after a couple bites. A badge sat next to it, the clip bent after one too many accidental trips through her apartment building's washing machine. But her little, bright face still beamed on it. A feeling she was far from able to replicate right now.

That'd been a hopeful Alyvia. An Alyvia fresh out of college, willing to put in the time to prove herself—willing to prove that she had the mindset for a technical job, instead of the magic-loving Miraltan she appeared to be. Those dark green eyes on that badge mocked her now with that enthusiasm. She blew a lock of black hair from her vision and nudged the sandwich container off her desk and into the trash with a dark-skinned hand.

Maybe she'd made a mistake by deciding to study and later work in Kingsheart. Maybe if she'd gone for a job in Miralta's government instead, things would be different. Maybe if she'd listened to her father's suggestion of pursuing magical-related studies, she wouldn't need to work so hard. But would she be happier?

She pictured herself waiting for her first train to Kingsheart, giving her parents each a hug goodbye before she'd climbed aboard and watched the cities and suburbs of northern King's flit by. Everything familiar slipping away like sand in an hourglass.

Alyvia jolted upright at the sudden sound of Jinko's office door reopening. She started tapping at her desk's keyboard screen again as Shane emerged, his mouth set in a grim line. He shuffled back to his office, letting the door lightly bounce off the frame to sit popped open. She tried to shake off how he'd looked directly at her before he disappeared, instead pouring her focus back into the footage. Leaving her alone again in a sea of empty desks.

33
TABIR ✧ 2704-12-05

NOA

The sand-dusted white stones of the cul-de-sac glowed in the midday sun, lighting Noa's path dead ahead to the house with red shutters at the very end. It matched all the other homes in the neighborhood known as 'The Oasis'—a quiet, beachside reserve for the upper-middle class that had once been Noa's home away from home. An escape. A haven. A place where she'd pretended that she could've been someone else, rather than a killer.

Noa hovered in front of the door, her fist poised to knock as if she was some stranger instead of some semi-casual former resident that slipped in at dusk and out at dawn. Her arm dropped.

Screw it.

She made her way past the brown shrubs and pink desert flowers along the pavers leading to the side of the house, where a dread-inducing view of the large, community lake butted up against the back deck's privacy fence. Praying the code still worked, she punched in the numbers for the gate's keypad and received a happy chime. Relief washed over her, glad to ditch the waterside and—walk straight in to find the pool.

Shit.

The recollection of sitting in a far-corner lounge chair while her companion chatted from the water brought a pang of longing. They'd talked for hours about places they'd hoped to go—including places Noa had been to but kept to herself. There was always an unspoken line not to touch on anything personal, even though they'd been picking up on the aspects that set them apart.

Phone calls, nervous habits, sad looks. Whenever their talks began teetering on something more serious, Noa would feel a tug on her chair poolside lounge chair, sending her scrambling in an attempt not to be yanked into the water.

Noa slid a demagnetizer from her small crossbody bag and pressed it against the sensor at the edge of the window, popping it open for her to climb inside. Cool air rushed to greet her as she searched around the living room for her would-be target. The sounds of chopping, clattering, and occasional beeping coming from the kitchen told Noa to take her time. So she did.

She ran a hand along the electric fireplace mantle, frowning up at the muted TV's news ticker's minor input of Amarais before moving on to the weather. Noa sighed and reached for the tablet resting on the round wicker coffee table, half-covered in fabric swatches on a ring. It lit up with squares of magazines and half-completed sketches of models in gowns, suits, and street fashion clothing.

Noa's grip tightened on the device, transported back to when she'd retrieved something from down the hall as a phone rang.

I'm a little busy right now, Baba—No, I'll have to call you back—I told you I wasn't having this discussion again—Because it's a job. *Don't bring Mama into this—*

The scent of warm vegetables and spices began to permeate the air, pulling Noa back to reality, accompanied by a gasp. She jerked her head up to see a tall woman dressed in a long, sheer, lime-colored cardigan over a tank top and leggings with a hand knotted in her near-black hair.

"Good gods, Noa," she said, releasing a breathy laugh. "Are you not capable of using the front door like a normal person?"

Noa flashed her a charming smile, placing the tablet back on the table.

"You know me, Shani," she said with a playful shrug to hide her nerves. "I'm more of an 'ask forgiveness' sort of person."

Shani chuckled, shaking her head as she strode over to her. Her umber eyes peered into Noa's with a warm smile that melted her heart. Just like the first time they'd met, back when Noa had been that sharp twenty-year-old killer on her first solo mission. Meeting Shani at a party mingling in the same group as her target had turned into Noa's first opportunity to dig up information by proxy, only to discover that Shani knew next to nothing about the guy. And yet Noa ended up talking with her late into the night anyway.

They'd left to visit a late-night café and roam the streets talking about art and its many forms, almost like they were two wandering college students. After that night, Noa wasn't sure if it'd been fate, luck, or the idea that they were both like-minded souls, but they'd found each other again. They found someone else to get lost in—to become someone else around because they didn't want to be themselves. No mess. No problems. No past. Only the present.

Shani ran a hand down Noa's arm—like brushing daylilies onto a fresh canvas—tickling her skin with the light, trailing touch.

"Did you swing by to catch up?" she asked in a husky purr that threatened to catch everything in Noa on fire.

"There's someone else," Noa blurted, surprised to hear it coming from her own mouth.

"Oh."

Why the hell did I say that? It's not like it was *true*, not with Rune keeping her at arm's length and Nyx having none of her advances. The only other person she'd come remotely close to finding common ground with was—

Nope. Do not even consider that one.

Noa cleared her throat, rubbing away the goosebumps. "I'm... actually here for that favor you owe me."

"I see." She pulled the sheer fabric over herself, pinning it down with her crossed arms. "I didn't exactly expect you to come back for pleasure anyway, seeing how things ended last time... I just... guess I hoped things could go back to what they were." A slight smile tugged up at the corner of her mouth before it faded away again.

And she was right. The last time Noa had been in this living room, it'd been with two more people than Noa had been comfortable with, and she'd forced herself not to pace over the speckled woven rugs. Every carefully crafted lie and avoided admission between them had crumbled the instant Shani's mother's name had been placed in front of Noa as her next target. She was a witty, intelligent woman that pestered Shani as much as her father did about her supposedly low standards of settling for fashion design over research, civil service, and politics.

The problem with said careers is that one could easily end up with a target on one's back, assuming they weren't careful. Fortunately, Noa had Nyx there to explain that while she and Shani stared each other down with remorse, unsure who had hurt the other more.

The solution was simple: fake the death of Shani's mother and send her elsewhere. And Shani made the executive decision not to tell her father.

"The last thing I need is for him to try to pick off digging around in whatever place she'd left off and someone hunting him down too," she'd said. "So, no, I won't tell him. I can keep this secret for however long we need to."

Noa had prayed it'd been sooner rather than later, but now was the time to rope her father into this, even without him knowing.

"So, what do you need?" Shani asked with a touch of weariness.

"For you to crank up the charm with your father," Noa said. "I need you to take the Wheel of Tabir for me."

Her eyebrows shot up and she shook her head, almost like she had heard her wrong. But before Noa could repeat it, she said, "Okay, I'll do it. If that's what you want, I'll get it. I'm actually planning on seeing him tomorrow."

Noa retrieved the box then, holding it out to her. "I figured that you might need this to help minimize problems."

Shani took it, puzzled as she popped it open and blinked. "This is..." — she let out a breathy laugh of disbelief— "a rather convincing fake. I don't suppose you have a way to tell the difference between the two?" Mischief danced in her eyes, throwing Noa somewhere in a rift of time held ever-still.

"Shani, I'd be dead by now if I couldn't tell a real from a fake."

She bit her lip to suppress a laugh as she snapped the box shut. "Then I'll have it for you tomorrow. We'll meet at our usual spot?"

"The usual spot."

On her way back, Noa took her time wandering the city streets while the shadows crept in. The archways lit one by one in response to the dipping sun, making a path for those closing up shop to head home.

Home.

She'd always heard that home was a place you chose. Somewhere safe you could always return to in the care of those you loved. Noa had let herself believe it was here, or maybe that little old shop where she'd been given her first key. Now, she didn't have either—both pieces of her life she couldn't go back to. Neither were what they'd once been, so now they were a memory to hold onto of what once was.

Perhaps that was why she'd told Shani that there was someone else. Because it'd been an easy way to cut her free from Noa's tangled mess of a life. Or maybe—just *maybe*—the person Noa was lying to was herself.

34

KING'S REPUBLIC ✧ 2704-12-05

Alyvia's bag dropped to the low pile carpeting of her studio apartment about an hour later than usual. The door echoed in its frame, setting off her neighbor's dog barking two doors down. A feeling of homesickness choked her, prodding through her blazer jacket as she tugged it off.

After changing into a baggy tee-shirt and sweatpants, she put together a sandwich for dinner and took her seat in front of her docked tablet at her desk. Alyvia swiped through news articles detailing New Year's celebration dates for various regions of King's Republic, times for neighborhood festivals and firework shows, a notice that the United Council Hall of Avaria and its archives would be closed to the public for the rest of the year, travel forecasts, and scarce details on Amarais's decision to remain closed under its new regime.

Her finger hovered over the last tile before she tapped to close out of the list and leaned back in her seat. She brought a knee up under her chin, hugging her leg with a sigh.

Maybe she'd made a mistake in coming to Kingsheart—in fighting the good fight to prove herself in a role that the world enjoyed holding just outside of her reach. Maybe she should have listened to her father's advice, but she could already fabricate the words he'd wielded against her, cupping her face in his hands like he'd always done when she was a child.

You can't go back. You've worked so hard, Alyvia.

Tears blurred her eyes. He was right. She wasn't a quitter. She swiped at her eyes, welcoming that rush of determination.

Alyvia pulled up her network settings and routed her traffic to a point along the eastern coast of the Republic. The dots ran back and forth across its bar, blinking in unison on completion. She cracked her knuckles and began running through the facts.

First: her targets were agents. She had seen them in the building before —she'd even ridden the elevator with them once. One always seemed pensive and stand-offish while the other appeared calm and collected. But something about them didn't quite *feel* like agents—not like the ones she had encountered reporting to anyone else.

Frowning, she moved on. Second: these two reported to Arrington, and they disappeared often for assignments. So, due to Arrington's divisional status in the Department of Intelligence, she conjured up one of the few conclusions that fit: they were likely spies.

Her fingers lightly drummed against the keyboard. Something still didn't quite sit right with her about them, but she shook it away. Alyvia sat up straight, typing in one of their names.

If Jinko and Shane were going to block her from digging into potentially vital information, then she'd get it through other means. There was no way she was going to keep working with her hands tied, just *hoping* to stumble onto what they wanted again. If Arrington wanted them brought in, this was now her sole option. So, she sucked in a breath and hit submit.

Her eyes scanned the screen for a moment, flicking back up to the search box to double-check her spelling. She resubmitted it, and then quickly typed in the other name.

"What the hell...?" she whispered.

A jumble of names matching the random combinations of either their given or surnames populated the screen, none of them that exact match she'd been looking for. She pulled up the public records site, dumping their names into that too.

    0 results.

She stared in disbelief as her back thumped against the chair.

But they were *real*, so how were they not in here? She'd looked them up after the first time she'd run into them and found most of their data classified. They *should* be in here now.

She bit her thumbnail while bouncing her legs up and down. Now came the question of whether or not she should dig around where she didn't belong. Doing some light after-work research with public databases was one thing that might get her questioned, but her curiosity threatened to latch onto her like a vice—much like it had back in her college days. She'd spent late nights on supposedly secure networks for anything from casual chatting about brute-forcing data entry into the chain coffee shop down the street to ghost stories about people vanishing off the internet as if they hadn't taken a break from their alter-ego hacking account.

Her hands dropped into her lap. There had to be another way to do this, even if she hadn't found it yet. The risk wasn't worth the reward in this case, even if it would be at the cost of her sanity. If it was confidential, then it was confidential. She reached to close out of the portal and paused, finding another icon active in her tablet's taskbar. The command console.

She tapped it with a frown, and then her eyes went wide. *"Shit—"* Adrenaline pumped through Alyvia as she pulled up her network settings and mashed the button to disconnect. The lines halted, but her heart still kept up the pace. She began scrolling through it, trying to ignore how her hand shook.

The sudden snap of the lights turning off made her jump and slap her hand over her mouth. A dull beeping from the hall sounded in tandem with the neighbor's dog, accompanied by soft, blue light creeping under her front door. She launched herself up from her chair, sending it spinning as she climbed onto her bed and peered out the window.

The entire neighborhood was dark, flickering with faint traces of emergency power.

The rolling blackouts, she thought.

She forced out a shaky breath and a nervous laugh. After nearly collapsing on the bed, she crawled her way back to the desk right as her phone buzzed. The screen illuminated the words 'Private Number,' giving her pause before she reached for it on the second ring.

It stopped.

Then it was followed by a shorter pulse to indicate a text.

Callisto, correct?

An icy chill spread through her. Those fond, rebellious college memories instantly collapsed into a manifestation of dread. She quickly typed back, trying to channel her fear into anger at the intrusion with the use of her old handle.

Who the hell is this?

Someone who'd rather not see you get caught.

She stared at the stalled console window on her tablet.

Not very nice to go through other people's things.

Well, I'm not here to make friends. I'm here to do business.

Retired. Sorry.

Considering your search history, the probability of you exiting retirement is high, which means that your odds of getting caught shoot through the roof.

You going to call the authorities to break my door down?

Seeing how you work with them, no. But there
might be someone who decides that you know
too much and may consider a more…
permanent solution.

Alyvia's hated how slick her phone began to feel in her hands as she
fumbled with the keys again.

You're saying that someone would try to kill me?
Over these two idiots?

Those two 'idiots' were swept under the rug for
a reason. Having you pull their information out
of the shadows will cause more problems for
quite a few people. Why do you think they want
them found without alerting all of King's? Why
bother pulling down every piece of information
related to them? Think about it.

Wait—had her own department taken all of it down?
The phone buzzed in her hands again with another message.

They were disposable, and they knew it. That's
why they're running. If you're not careful, they'll
do the same to you.

Why? Then what am I supposed to do?

I'd like to make you a deal. Exit retirement and
I'll lend you my resources. I need assistance in
hiding the two of them. In exchange, I can help
you find some of the answers you've been
looking for, according to your files.

Alyvia racked her brain for anything that might've been compromised
on her tablet. Over the years, she'd dabbled in a lot of things that interested
her: puzzles, geocaches, shady research topics…

Care to be more specific?

You've been looking for a missing family
member, correct?

She dropped the phone on the table and ran her hands through her hair. Now that she knew exactly what mini-project had been found, she had to ask herself a very important question: would this be worth it? She'd be risking a lot for answers that she had tried to find for *years* before this. Who's to say that this wasn't just a con?

She grabbed up her phone again.

> I've checked everywhere online. There's nothing.

> I have offline sources as well.

Alyvia scowled. Great.

> I see. Unfortunately, I'm not fond of working for information brokers.

> Consider it working 'with,' rather than 'for.' Associates.

She rolled her eyes.

> No thanks. I'm not exactly comfortable with you breaking into my devices and knowing everything about me, and the only thing I know about you is that you're somehow invested in these two.

> *Call me Nyx.*

Her eyes went wide. There was no way.

> THE Nyx? Prove it.

A link appeared in answer, showing an encrypted file type. She let out a breath, glad that she had backed up her phone that morning since this one might very well need to be destroyed after tonight. A tap of the file, and it began its installation, ending with a chime when it was ready. She pressed the little blank square, and it brought her to a new message interface.

This is my personal encrypted communication network, Alyvia Watson. I know that your handle was Callisto before you retired to go into government work, namely the King's Republic Intelligence Agency. Your direct supervisors are Shane Delacroix and Jinko Matsuoka.

As for your family, your mother is Myra Watson, and your father is Ryland Watson—formerly Ryland Everett. Would you like me to continue?

If this *wasn't* the real Nyx that she had heard so many rumors about, then she was talking to a really convincing fake. Hope surged through her. Alyvia might actually be able to get her answers after all.

No.

She drummed her fingers against her phone case for another moment to formulate the rest of her reply.

If I do this for you, I'll need to know what I'm covering up. I can't clean what I don't know is there.

I'll tell you everything you need to know and nothing more under the condition that you tell no one. You'll have to play dumb and act like you're trying to help. Point them in the wrong direction on purpose if you have to in order to throw them off. Do we have a deal?

Alyvia bit down on her tongue. She was gambling her job—possibly *more* if Nyx was right.

Under the condition that we are associates like you said. You give me the information I ask for, and I give you what you request in return. If I can't get what you want, then I can't get it. I can't risk being exposed.

That's what I like to read. I'll drop some more files and software to this account. There are a few chat rooms in here as well, so don't hesitate if you have questions.

I'm the only one with your personal information, so the rest of my associates shouldn't cause any problems. They have a code of honor not to exploit each other, considering the line of work.

I'll expect periodic updates once the initial information dump is complete. In the meantime, get some sleep, Callisto. That seems to be a struggle among my resources recently.

You don't want me to binge energy drinks and write a fifty-page report?

Bold of you to assume I have the time to read something like that. Summarize or send vocal reports. Keep to the point and pace yourself. Don't do too much too quick to avoid suspicion. We have some time.

Goodnight, Callisto.

The green circle next to Nyx's name faded to gray, an indication that she had been left alone again. She rocked back in her chair, staring up at the ceiling. She was so screwed.

35

TABIR ✦ 2704-12-06

NOA

Noa sat on the edge of the circular raised-stone flowerbed in the center of Shani's favorite shopping wheel, colored by rioting bolts of fabric spilling out of doors and into walkways where tubes of the stuff leaned up against walls and windows.

And here she was dressed in street blacks and charcoal grays, thinking of Glacier. Their morning session hadn't resulted in any more surprises like the last—in fact, he'd been slow to respond to much of anything and ended up asking her to repeat or re-demonstrate a couple times. She'd started to wonder if Nyx's brief mention of taking him to meet with Daxton had anything to do with it, but Nyx herself hadn't noted anything else. It seemed unlikely Nyx would've missed something that he'd decided to keep to himself, but Noa wasn't sure what else it *could* be.

She shoved the thoughts away the second Shani came into view in a loose white top tucked into light blue slacks. Noa stood to greet her as Shani lifted her sunglasses to rest on her head, like night greeting day. The weight of regret settled on Noa when she looked up into her face to find that ever-present slight smile.

Perhaps in a different life, the two of them would've helped each other carry the burden of all their insecurities, hopes, and dreams. Maybe *that* Noa would've asked Shani to join her on her suicidal mission—a thought that Noa almost rolled her eyes at because she'd want her to stay put and out of harm's way.

Shani's smile turned teasing after she plucked the thin box from her bag, holding it like she might jerk it out of Noa's reach. "You'll come back to explain to me why you needed this later, right?"

A slightly nervous, exhausted chuckle slipped from Noa as she started to shake her head. Before any words could make their way out, Noa felt the press of Shani's lips against hers and the smooth surface of the box against her hand. When Shani pulled back, Noa was almost certain there'd be a dent in the thing from how hard her thumb dug into it.

"You deserve so much better than me," Noa whispered.

She chortled. "And here I was just about to say the same to you with my selfish little goodbye kiss." Her eyes softened to something more remorseful like she knew full well what Noa was heading into. "Good luck, Noa. Tell whoever's lucky enough to have you that I wish them good luck too. They'll need it."

GLACIER

Glacier and Nyx twisted around from the couch at the sound of the hotel door swinging open.

"You got it?" Nyx asked, standing up next to him as Noa tossed something across the room in a blur.

The box from yesterday.

Nyx caught it and popped up the lid while Noa casually leaned against the back of the couch with a prideful smirk. Glacier rose to take a look for himself, careful not to brush shoulders with Nyx as she flipped it over and held a light to the back.

The silvery sheen didn't glow white like all the platinum he'd been exposed to, but the Wheel of Tabir dazzled with brilliance anyway with its turquoise gemstones, sparkling throughout what reminded him of an old-fashioned spindle whose spokes had been laced with thread.

Nyx clicked her light off and handed it back over to Noa. "Pretty good use of a favor."

"Good enough to put us at five now," Noa said, tilting it around like a mirror in the light. "Eight more to go."

Crow dropped his arms down against the back of the couch next to Noa.

"Hot damn." Crow whistled, bumping up against her. Her face scrunched up. "Two keys in—what—four days? That's a new record."

Nyx narrowed her eyes at him. "Don't get used to max speed. I have some catch-up work to do, and we'll be taking a long train ride to our next destination to try to keep any wandering psychos off our trail."

He slumped over the cushions with a groan.

"Oh, please," Rune said, dropping his bag by the front door. "Don't act like you didn't hunt down some entertainment yesterday."

Cecilia made a choking noise from the chair at Crow's lazy, smug grin.

"What is *wrong* with you?" she said, clapping a hand over her mouth the second it tumbled out. Her eyes widened, darting between Noa and Rune.

An abrupt, bubbly laugh poured out of Noa. "Gods, Cecilia, out of all the people here, I'm incredibly proud of you for saying that."

Rune tried to stifle a snicker, and Crow cut Cecilia a sharp glare. "Oh yeah, little miss perfect? You want to throw down?"

"She's got a point, Crow," Rune said. "You jump into bed with so many random strangers I'm surprised you're not disease-ridden by now."

"Hey, I—"

"All right, kids," Nyx said, clapping her hands together. "That's enough. Pack up. It's time to get the hell out of here. You'll have more than enough time to bicker on the way out of here in your own train compartment."

Crow's head swung around to face her. "What? Didn't shell out for the entire car again?"

She shook her head, rolling her eyes as she started to her room. "No, not when I need peace and quiet for research time. I don't have time to deal with sticky-fingered drunks."

He grinned like she'd complimented him.

"I don't care for your face either."

The grin dropped to a frown, and he narrowed his eyes at Rune. "That means she doesn't like your face either."

"At least she tolerates me," he replied with a shrug.

"Rune's also prettier," she said.

Crow gave her an incredulous look. "But we're *twins*—"

"Wait," Noa said with sudden, mock surprise. "You're *twins?*"

"Go to hell." He shoved off the couch, grumbling as he followed Nyx and split off for his own bag.

Noa smirked, seemingly too absorbed in her own self-praise that she didn't react to the minor back-and-forth with Rune and Cecilia when she got up too. He'd stopped to lean in the bedroom door frame, whispering something that turned her cheeks pink and made her fidget with her hair again.

Glacier tensed, biting the inside of his lip before he trudged toward them, but Noa beat him to the end of the couch, cutting him off.

"Nyx said you met with Daxton yesterday," she said. "I'm assuming she didn't let you give your real name, right?"

"Don't worry. She didn't."

"Did he say something weird? You were pretty distracted this morning."

"No. We just... talked." He shrugged. "She got some information from him, and then she locked herself in her room for the rest of the night."

"So... what's bothering you?"

"Nothing." It came out a little too quick, but he tried to sidestep her anyway.

She mirrored him, blocking his path. "Glacier, if this is related to information that Nyx might need, you can't just hold onto it."

"It's not *for* Nyx—" He lowered his voice to a whisper. "It's *about* Nyx. Now drop it."

"And *what* about her are you talking about? If you have a problem with her, let's put it to rest now—"

"I don't have a problem with her—"

"Then what's going on?"

"I... think she's keeping a secret."

"Then I probably already know it, so just tell me what you think it is."

He hesitated, rubbing his arms with a wary glance in Nyx's direction. She hovered by the door with her phone in her gloved hands, barely even registering Crow dropping his bag to do one final ransack of the kitchen.

"Well?" Noa asked.

He struggled to find the best way to phrase it without sounding accusatory. "Um... is Nyx a modder?"

Her eyebrows rose. "What? That's ridiculous. She's just a hacker, not some modder—"

"I don't mean like—Like a full-body mod junkie or anything like that, but... She told me that she had some sort of condition when she mentioned her family. And then she got pulled from the line at border control, avoided all the anti-modder shops yesterday, and just happened to skip out on traveling to both Amarais and Miralta—one country that outright forbids modding and the other that requires detailed documentation. It's not exactly something you can hide all that well like magic."

She frowned, shaking her head. "Then what's modded, Glacier? Her *mind?* That's just about the only abnormal thing about her."

"Her right arm."

Noa's eyes went wide, and she turned to stare at Nyx, who looked up from her phone. "Hurry it up," Nyx ordered, frowning at Noa's gawking. "We don't have all day, you two."

NOA

Noa ran her hand up and down her bag's shoulder strap while they waited on the station platform. The wavy silver mirror strips along the pillars reflected her blank expression—the one thing she hoped would be enough not to give away the absolute embarrassment she felt.

How had she not noticed that before? Was it because she'd ignored it in favor of using her? Or was it because Nyx had put up such a good defense that Noa had brushed off her strange behavior?

She stole a glance at Glacier lingering beside her in the archway between the idling trains with his hands tucked into his sleeves and shoved under his arms. Whether he'd been lost in thought or the pattern of the tiny turquoise circles of the floor tile, it'd been broken by her attention. Her stomach clenched as his eyes met hers.

Noa whipped her head to face forward again, clenching her bag strap even tighter as Nyx's boots softly crunched against the grout.

"You seem... tense..." Nyx mumbled.

"I turned down sex with a really hot woman because I'm a dumbass."

Glacier's jaw dropped in the mirrors—a somewhat choppy, comical image that she wished she'd found funnier at that moment.

Nyx cleared her throat to stifle a chuckle. "That... checks out."

The boarding call couldn't have come at a better time, sending Nyx to continue on ahead of them.

"Smooth," Glacier whispered.

Noa punched him in the arm.

"*Ow*—"

"Look, just because I need you *alive* doesn't mean that I need you *unharmed*," she said, jabbing a finger at him.

He began rubbing at the injury. "I can't wait until I can kick your ass."

"Oh, that'll be the day," she muttered.

After playing with the window shade some in the cabin to avoid staring at either of her roommates, Noa couldn't stand the view of the stationary platform any longer. Her eyes began to linger on each person that passed, checking to make sure they weren't watching them. So, she toggled the window shade one last time and leaned forward, trying not to stare at Nyx's arm.

"So... Valentia, right?" she started, her words sounding awkward even to her own ears. "That's what the ticket says. Um, unless it's a quick pit stop..."

Glacier's hand went to his forehead with a small, mostly hidden grimace she tried to ignore.

"Well, we happen to have someone that will help us gain access to the Vision of Valentia," Nyx replied. "Which I hope will work out in our favor, considering we only have a couple weeks before most transit shuts down for the year with all the New Year's celebrations. It's something we should be able to take advantage of too..." She clicked the button to turn on her tablet. "However, I have some other work to deal with, so we can get into details later."

"Um... yeah, sure," Noa said, shoving herself to her feet. She had to get the hell out of this room. "Glacier, we're going over to the next car for a bit."

His hand dropped to reveal his brows knitting together. "But I thought that you didn't want me to—"

"I said you're not allowed to go out *alone* until I inspected the train. You won't be alone. You'll be with me. Let's go." She jerked her head toward the door.

He dragged his feet against the carpet on their way through the hall. Once they made it to the dining car, she craned her neck to peer over the dark, high-back booths.

"Did you want a drink or something...?" Glacier started before she grabbed his arm and hauled him over to the table tucked into the corner.

The pop of the far door sliding open caused Noa to glance back, but the two women passengers continued passing through, chattering about swimwear on their way out.

"Sit," Noa said, letting go of him before she dropped into the seat with its back against the window. He did, even though it was with a frown.

"I think you're right," she said. "About Nyx, I mean."

He reached for the back of his neck. "Um, well... even if I'm right, I really don't think she wants us to know."

"I think you're right about that too."

"But what if she's flagged at Valentia?" he said, a small tinge of fear lacing each word that followed. "We can't just pretend like it's nothing, can we? What about if we make it back to Amarais? There are sensors and scanners to pick up on modifications in checkpoints leading in and out of the palace sector of Synos if we try to sneak back in. If security were to catch an alarm tripped for that, they're not going to ask questions to find out if her mods are medical, recreational, or just flat-out *lethal*. And you said she's the one with all the plans, right?"

"Yes, but what about Cecilia? If she was able to fool everyone as a Mage, we can fool the tech shit—"

Glacier shook his head. "And what if we can't? They're not going to give her the benefit of the doubt like Cecilia because Cecilia actually *looks* Amaraian. Hell, if it came to that, I'd honestly be the best distraction because I'm pretty sure everyone I talk to is convinced I'm Miraltan anyway..." He looked away, pulling his arms off the tabletop and onto his lap.

Noa jerked a little as the train started forward. She didn't regain her composure as quickly as she regained her balance. Instead, she held her tongue, trying to figure out the best thing to say to him. "Let's just... focus on one thing at a time. We'll worry about Amarais later."

"Yeah..." he mumbled, shifting in his seat.

Now what the hell was she supposed to say? Noa ran her palms over the faux wood grain of the table, trying to imagine them sitting somewhere else. A flash of a dining table took its place, which she forced into a memory of a desk before it all fell away with her hands curling. Every conjuring of familiarity left such a bitter taste in her mouth that perhaps it was easiest to leave him alone with his own lonely recollections.

"Well..." she finally said. "At least we'll get to enjoy Valentia, right?" Her attempt at a carefree smile faltered when his eyes narrowed on her again. "What?"

"Noa, you do realize that the Vision of Valentia is in *southern* Valentia, right? The island portion?"

Her heart plummeted. *Oh. Shit.* "Please tell me you're joking."

"I'm not. And—gods, you're going to hate this..."

"Hate *what*?"

"The museum's primary entrance is via the canals."

Manic laughter threatened to crawl up her throat. Everything started to feel hot. *Can't breathe. Can't breathe. Can't breathe—* "*What?*" The question came out a little too loud, especially with how hard her hands hit the table.

Glacier jumped, gripping the edge as he whipped around like he was checking for anyone else in the car. "Just- just calm down," he said, hesitating and letting go of the table's edge as if he considered reaching for her hand to comfort her—something she could imagine him doing for Cecilia. "You'll be fine."

"*No.* No, I will not be *fine*. There's no way I'm risking falling out of *two* boats to get to this damn thing."

"But you won't be alone because you'll have Rune with you, right? Or maybe Crow—"

She guffawed. "Oh, *no*—There's no way in hell I'm making a fool of myself in front of Rune. Gods, and if Crow found out, I'd never live it down."

"Then wh—"

Her hand shot across the table, latching onto his arm like it had a mind of its own—like the night he'd checked on her on the ship. She would've equated the feeling to an anchor, but it was the reverse—a life vest to keep her afloat since she never believed flying too high had been her problem, not with the weight of everything around her firmly tethering her to a life she never asked for.

"You'll go with me."

He tensed. "I-I'm not sure how you're going to convince everyone we should pair off, but... I'll do it."

Her elbow thumped against the tabletop as she relaxed. She hadn't expected him to give in so easily, and it left her with a torrent of lingering questions she'd been too stunned or unsure of how to ask before. "Um..." she started. "Did... you make up that story back on the ship? The one about your father?"

"No," he said in a near whisper. "That was really something he used to do... Back before I understood that there were scarier things to worry about."

"Like... Louis?" she asked, watching how he avoided her gaze again. "Did he threaten to get rid of you?"

He shrank down in his seat, and she thought he might pull away and leave before he answered. "I don't think a day went by where he didn't."

"Even as a kid?"

The silence that followed told her more than he could've ever said. The distrust and pain that radiated off him rooted from that question—one that she no longer hoped he'd answer because she'd want to find a way to reanimate Louis to kill him all over again.

But she got a quiet reply. "I think... I think the way he first looked at me said it all. If it weren't for Cecilia's magic and my title, I think he would've found a way to get rid of me sooner. I think the only other thing that would've been able to damn me is if I'd happened to be a Mage too."

Her heart ached at the numbness that came with each word. That faraway feeling of her younger self standing face-to-face with her master for the first time paled in comparison to that. At least she'd been treated like a tool, rather than a problem.

A short, mirthless laugh escaped Glacier. "I mean, I don't see why any of it matters anyway. I'm just a means to an end, right?"

"Glacier, you're a *person*, not just a key." She hated how he'd gone back to not looking at her like he couldn't accept what she was saying as truth. "No one deserves to be treated like that, especially for something you don't have any control over. You can't choose who your parents were or what you look like. What matters is that you're smart, observant, determined—*kind*. Incredibly kind, despite all the shit you've gone through."

He squeezed the arm she'd refused to let go of, keeping his head down as she continued.

"No one here is going to think any less of you or compare your life to ours. We've all been through our own specially catered hell. Plus, out of everyone here, I think I'm probably the one who might relate the most with how you've had to survive through your childhood. I'd like to think that if we'd met when we were younger that we might've been fast friends."

He chuckled. "Somehow, I doubt that since we barely get along now."

She patted his arm and drew back. "I don't know. I think that we're beginning to understand each other a little more. Who knows, we might actually be friends before we make it to Amarais. Maybe you'll even be nice enough to let me crash there before I settle on world domination."

Glacier covered his mouth, but he couldn't extinguish the light in those mismatched eyes. Noa grinned, giving in to the infectious amusement—glad for it.

36
MHARU ✧ 2704-12-06

A pair of dark green eyes stared back at Nyx from her tablet screen—those of a fair-skinned Miraltan with coal-black hair. Alyvia's missing person. Her aunt, Juniper Everett.

Nyx drummed her fingers against the side of the device with a hum. Alyvia hadn't been lying about telling her she'd vanished. Nyx's search for this woman was already rivaling her research on Kole after several more dead ends. It made sense now why Alyvia had given up, realizing that this would take a lot more resources than she'd originally hoped for.

Sighing, she tapped away from Juniper's profile to her small collection of notes she'd gathered between her own results and the document she'd copied from Alyvia's machine. First, she had the connection of Alyvia's father, Ryland Watson né Everett, who'd previously lived with Juniper in east Miralta. Second, according to Alyvia's notes, the two had fallen in with Mage smugglers. Third, Juniper was also a Mage.

The dots weren't difficult to connect here, but the issue became timing, much like how Noa had only been able to give her timing for Kole. And Alyvia had been too young at the time to provide enough details. Nyx just hoped that there were still some records floating around, but the sole saving grace in all this was Alyvia's mention of a journal. A journal lost in an ocean of cluttered data. Finding it would be hard enough but unlocking it would be a whole other problem.

Nyx scrubbed at her face and readjusted her glasses before typing in a few commands. Her search program popped to the top of her application stack, and she set it to run through several queries. If one of these could lead her to details of where to find the journal, then maybe she could find it within a week. And if she wasn't so lucky...

She cringed at the idea of shipping this off for someone else to deal with, worrying over a potential breach of trust. She had someone far better at finding people who didn't want to be found, but that could cause more problems than she needed right now. Nyx leaned back and contemplated her next approach.

Kole drifted to the front of her thoughts, and she began pulling up the public records within the Amaraian government database. Noa had told her that he was twenty-five, making him two years older than both her and Noa. Then she'd mentioned that he'd been about eight when his parents died.

Nyx chewed the inside of her cheek—seeing the potential overlap in answers if she hunted for connections to both Juniper and Kole—and dove into her rabbit hole of filtering and un-filtering data. It wove her in and out of possibilities until she was leaning back against the bench with her legs stretched out to the other side of the cabin. Too many options remained on the table when she finally hit a wall of exhaustion, leaving her frustrated with vague notes under multiple death records.

Criminal records it is.

If she'd crossed the border and stayed with a family, then she would've either made it back home or that family would've been arrested. So, Nyx began sifting through arrests and warrants tied to housing Mages. She clicked her tongue as she adjusted the date range—again and again and *again*, swapping between hundreds of results or none.

She frowned at the gap in arrests that coincided with the seven-year reign of King Cyrus Caelius, realizing how much harder it'd be to find

Juniper if she'd been lost in that time frame. She could've easily been a victim of one of late King Elias's loyal subjects, and her host family could've survived or—worse—suffered her fate.

Her head lulled against the back of the cushioned wall after a few more pages of records, and she pulled off her glasses to rub her eyes. When she replaced them and called the shade at the window, no light trickled in. Instead, she drank in the view of the velvety night sky blossoming from purple past the tall grass.

Perhaps some sleep would do her good. At least then she could pass the time to clear her mind while her device worked to pick up the cold trail that Juniper Everett had left behind.

GLACIER

"Please tell me you're joking," Kat said, folding her arms over her chest from her spot on the opposite sofa.

"It's a legitimate question," Glacier said.

"Asking me to tell you what you're supposed to ask isn't how this works. I *can't* tell you."

"And why can't you tell me? How am I supposed to know?" He stood, throwing out his arms.

She shoved herself up to mirror him. "And I already told you how—I told you everything without actually giving you the answer. Glacier, you need to come to terms with what's happening."

"I don't *know* what's happening! We're just going in circles here!" He started out of the room, tripping over the rug with a curse and kicking it back into place.

"Gods, Glacier—Would you stop and *really* listen for a second."

He continued toward the office, ignoring the sound of Kat jogging down the hall after him. Glacier pushed down on the handles and nearly smacked into the doors when they didn't give. "Did you lock the doors because you're pissed?"

"Nope," she said, with a heavy dose of mock-cheer. "Congratulations, the rug problem has now spread to the doors."

He bit back a grumble and gave them another shove. They parted and he stumbled inside. "Having a couple of slightly stuck doors isn't that bad of a problem, Kat."

"And I told you that it's just going to get *worse*. First, it's the rugs, then it's the doors, then the paint will start peeling off the walls and the furniture will begin deteriorating—"

"All of that can be fixed," he said, taking a seat at the desk and pulling open the drawer with the stash of keys like it would somehow be able to give him the answers Kat wasn't volunteering.

"*Glacier,*" she snapped.

His head jerked up, paling at the fury behind those blue eyes. She'd never raised her voice like that at *him* before. It'd always been directed at someone else. He slid the drawer back and dropped his hand onto the armrest. "I'm sorry... I don't... Kat, I don't understand why this is upsetting you. I don't know what I can do to fix it."

"Just... think, okay? You know that things are happening when we aren't talking, right? Think about... think about Cecilia."

He frowned. "What... about her?"

"What's the last feeling you remember in relation to her?"

A strange question to ask, let alone answer. His mind struggled to seek out that intangible emotion, overlaying Cecilia's image on memory-collected backdrops of palace halls. He closed his eyes, picturing her standing in front of him, but the scenery tried to shift—threatened to change with how it blurred at the edges, warping into something foreign he didn't recognize.

She stepped forward—her face painted with that weary, pitying look that rippled through him with the sting of a slap. He dropped his head, staring down at her uniform-issued black flats.

Glacier—

The soft, tinkling sound of her voice contained a lilt of concern, sorrow, loss—paired with understanding and dread. He reached for his cheek, feeling a phantom touch resting there until his hand cupped over another. A blink and the flats were replaced with scuffed boots. The voice turned a little huskier and warm like how Kat might've described her favorite drink.

It's okay. I've got you.

That reassurance rocked through him, grounding him—tethering him to something he couldn't quite place. Glacier unconsciously began to squeeze that hand, and the world appeared to bottom out beneath him. The voice shifted to a different tone on that same scale. A voice he still didn't recognize, but it enveloped him and dragged him downward.

We've *got you.*

Downward into an abyss of silvery stars.

Glacier jerked his head up, opening his eyes to Kat next to him while she leaned against the edge of the desk. He slowly released a pent-up gasp as a shaky sigh, unable to describe that fear-laced familiarity.

"Well?" Kat finally asked.

"I... um..." He tried to recall the question—something about what he'd last felt around Cecilia, right? "Bitter-sweet? Like..." He didn't want to refer to it as them drifting apart. Not without context. Not when she wasn't even here to defend herself or prove him wrong. "I don't know."

Glacier started to shake his head, trying to ignore how Kat's face fell with disappointment. She reached for him, and he flinched, thinking she was reaching for his face. Instead, her hand landed on his shoulder.

"It's okay. Just... keep trying. You'll make progress."

He bit his lip, staring through her to the drawer. "And... what do the other twelve keys go to?"

She hesitated and shook her head. "Don't worry about those. They go to things that will make themselves known in time. You need to try to remember first. The rest will fall into place after."

37
MHARU ✧ 2704-12-07

GLACIER

Glacier woke to the darkness of the cabin with his heart pounding in his chest.

It's okay. I've got you.

He *knew* that voice, even if he hadn't recognized it in his dream. His head rubbed against the pillow, turning to lock eyes with the only other person who'd be awake at whatever odd hour it was—something impossible to tell through the darkened windowpanes.

Noa moved first, sliding out from under her blanket without disturbing Nyx's curled-up form against the seatback. Glacier copied the motion, swinging his feet to the floor and felt around for his boots.

He bit back a hiss and threw up his arm as they stepped out into the hall, where they drank in the fresh orange of the horizon.

"I'm honestly kind of impressed you're managing to get proper sleep now," she whispered with a grin while she grabbed onto the handholds above the windows. Her eyes glinted a honeyed amber, darting over the patchwork squares of farmland flitting past.

"And... were you waiting for me to wake up?"

"What? *No.* Gods—I just thought you would've woken up earlier, and I didn't want to disturb anyone. So I stayed in bed." She gave a half-hearted shrug and pushed past him into the next car.

He spun around and followed, jogging after her until she wandered into the observatory car and fell into a seat. She threw her feet up over the backrest in front of her, leaving the chair on the end of the aisle open for him.

Glacier slowly dropped into it before he hazarded a glance in her direction. "So... is there any particular reason why you're always awake?"

"Nope," she said. "It just comes with the job. Sort of important to make sure a target doesn't escape. But I guess now it's to make sure no one else gets to their target..." Her eyes slid over to him, and he sank down into the jade cushioning.

The faraway dotting of houses and farm machinery became their quiet source of entertainment for the minutes that followed, letting Glacier's mind spin in time with the bulky crop harvesters.

"Do you miss it?" he asked.

"Hm?"

"Your old life. Do you miss it? Sure, traveling is... sort of nice and all, but..."

"No," she said with a chortle. "No, I don't. As exhausting as this is, I don't think I'd trade it. Not now, at least."

"What about your family?" He watched for her reaction out of his peripheral vision, noting the way she bit her lip. "Your parents?"

"They died a long time ago," she said matter-of-factly the second he asked his follow-up question. "There's not really much to it. I barely remember them, but I remember we were poor, and we struggled to pay for anything. They died so I could live. Lucky me. Lucky enough to survive until Myron found me."

The shadowy figure from his dreams blotted out all his other thoughts, inking out that hazy image through the ice of that frozen lake. "Myron?"

"Yeah," Noa said. "I was five when the older couple that'd taken me in knew they had to get rid of me. It'd only been a couple months, but they barely had enough income to sustain themselves. One day Myron had shown up on their doorstep and took me off their hands. I expected him to dump me off in the next town over or something, but he brought me back to his house instead. That's where he introduced me to my new family—a couple of boys a little older than me. Ezra and Kole."

"So... is Myron the head of the Volkov?"

"Yep."

"But... weren't there any others?"

"A few, but they all came after me."

"No, I mean—" Glacier gave a low, frustrated hum. "Weren't there any other *older* Volkov around? That seems a little strange if it was just him. I don't think a single person could somehow keep that sort of business alive on his own, right?"

"I..." she started, pausing as her eyes seemed to linger on her scuffed boots. "I have a theory as to why he was the only one around. He and I... we're not all that different. It took me a long time to realize that we know how to use people to get what we want. We know when we see something that we think we should have—something we believe we *deserve*—that we'll stop at nothing to take it for ourselves. We don't settle. And we hold onto it for dear life once it's ours."

While the words brought Glacier discomfort, the exhaustion behind each one told him a story that contrasted Myron's. The keys, the vault, Nyx's planning, Rune and Crow's thieving, Cecilia's magic, all her collected debts and favors—it all compounded to her goal: power.

"I think he killed all the Volkov before us," she continued. "I think he killed them all and decided the only way he could keep that top spot was to take in godsdamned children that would view him as a father figure, so they'd be less likely to challenge his authority. It's not all that different from how your uncle bullied you into submission. But the biggest mistake Myron made was assuming that if he pushed me down enough, eventually I'd stop getting up. Instead, when he'd finally put the pressure on the right spot, I left."

No, not power, Glacier thought. *Freedom.*

"And what... what did he do to make you leave?"

"You remember that Seer I mentioned?" she asked.

He nodded, unable to reply with the sickening feeling that he knew where this was going.

"His name was Lazarus. I started doing delivery jobs for him when I was eight for credits. He became more of a father to me than Myron ever could, and when he found out, I think he realized that Lazarus was the one person that kept him from controlling me. So, he... he left him to bleed out on the floor of his own shop. I found him, but I was too late. Bastard wouldn't even let me try to help him—like he *wanted* to die. He just insisted that I take the damn key he had, told me to collect the rest, and find the Vault..."

Glacier fidgeted when she brought a fist to her mouth and stayed eerily quiet for a moment while she blinked back what he swore were unshed tears.

She cleared her throat. "I burned his body before I left. I told myself I'd grant him his last wish as my true surrogate father, even if I thought it was absolutely insane."

"I'm... sorry for your loss."

She scoffed. "I'm not even sure I deserve that sort of sentiment after how I treated you when you lost your cousin. He probably would've shamed me for being so disrespectful..."

"Do you ever dream of him?" The question slipped out at the mere mention of Kat. Maybe what he was going through was normal. Maybe it was stress or grief or—

Noa hummed and started to shake her head. "Maybe once or twice? Nothing super noteworthy. Why? Are you having dreams with Kat in them?"

He hesitated, reaching for the back of his neck.

"It's probably your mind's way of coping," she said.

His hand dropped back into his lap. "I... was honestly avoiding sleeping because I was afraid she'd be there, but now... Now I don't know. I think I'm failing horribly at trying to compartmentalize."

"I don't know. I'd say you're holding yourself together pretty well, all things considered. We're stealing thirteen emblems in the hopes of unlocking some mythical Vault with a handful of Volkov hunting our asses after all."

He chortled. "Thanks for the reminder."

"Look at it this way—" She stretched and shot him a smirk. "At least we'll go down together, right?"

38

KING'S REPUBLIC ✧ 2704-12-08

ARRINGTON

The executive chair complained as Director Arrington leaned back and watched the holographic projection dancing over his morning news feeds. The lack of updates the past few days had left him pensive. Disposing of a couple of reckless thieves should've been an easy task, but with their current elusiveness, he needed a way to lure them back...

The soft sound of the door catch pulled his attention away from the profiles to Shane, who slinked over to one of the seats in front of him.

"You're late," Arrington said, nearing a growl as he swiped all traces of the twins away.

"My apologies," Shane said with a hand pinning down his tie in his short, slight bow before sitting. "Jinko decided to intercept me on the way here, and... unfortunately, we haven't managed to acquire any new information since you've decided to dedicate Watson to searching for them. All her time has been spent scrubbing the footage from all the Southaven stations, and I think there might be a better way if we'd just let her—"

"No."

"But—"

"I think you fail to understand that her background could cost us a valuable resource," Arrington growled, leaning forward. "That is precisely why I'm telling you to drop it."

"But we can't even give her access to their old files? What if it could help her track them? I discussed her issues with her the other day, and she's going off of nothing. It's just going to take her longer to find them now, which is the exact opposite of what we want. We don't know how much they might've figured out before they left."

Arrington steepled his fingers and stared out at the now one-way windowpanes dividing them from the hallway. Each slow-walking employee deepened his frown. With the right initiative, any one of the people around them could unravel what was happening in front of them, but there were always ways to put a stop to it. Everyone had a weakness.

"Have her continue with her current task," he finally said.

"W-what? Why?"

Arrington stood and began slowly pacing behind the desk, cutting through the pale stream of light spilling onto the drab, gray carpet. "Do you recall the deal they took? More specifically, the reason *why* they agreed to the terms?"

Shane hesitated, tilting his head. "N—Wait..." A short laugh. "You don't mean to—How do you even know it'll work? You can't just arrest one of their former colleagues without some sort of reason. And who's to say they'll come back for them? They had to have destroyed all ties with each other. No criminal in their line of work wants to associate with someone that defected to the government."

Arrington stopped and leaned against the edge of his desk, facing his small one-shelf private collection of books. "That doesn't mean that neither of them wouldn't come back to try to break one of them out. I've noticed that there was one particular thief that they appear to have a history with, so I think we can put pressure there."

Shane scowled. "How, exactly, do you want to catch this thief then? We'd need something to hold them long enough to draw these two out... something potentially publicized to warrant the Intelligence Agency's involvement..."

"I know how to proceed. In the meantime, see that Watson continues her search. I'll make the appropriate correspondence and update you during the next time we reconvene for your *review.*"

"Of course," Shane said, shooting out of his seat with a pleased smirk.

Arrington held back a sigh. "And inform Jinko to make preparations for next week. She's far more organized than the two of us at the moment, so I trust she won't mess it up."

"I'm sure she'll be pleased to hear it." With that, he headed for the door, reaching to tap the window shades back off.

"Leave it," Arrington interrupted, pushing off his desk. "I'll need some privacy for my call."

"Yes, sir." And he was gone, prowling back down the hall to leave him in peace.

He ran his tongue over his teeth and unlocked his top desk drawer. Small containers of memory cards, adapters, and synthetic paper clippings slid forward. He reached past them to the smooth case of the device shoved to the back and pressed the power button. His fingers left fresh trails along the phone screen until he found the number he'd been looking for.

It rang once. Twice.

Arrington fit in a single tap of his shoe against the carpet before an answer.

"Fontaine."

He could hear the lazy grin in the way the man on the other side of the call tossed out his own name, the final syllable elongated by what had to be him stretching.

His eyes flicked to his desktop clock. 9:37ᴀᴍ. And this man was still in bed.

"I need a favor," Arrington said, ignoring the lack of professionalism—clearly that was too much to ask.

"It's been a while, hasn't it?" he asked. "What can I do for you?"

"I'm calling about that woman I asked you to keep tabs on a while back."

"Hmm..."

Arrington's mouth set into a thin line as he actually tapped his foot this time.

"Ah, yes. That's right—*the bitch*." His voice sounded like he had pulled the phone away for a moment. "No, not you, dear. There's another bitch." A woman murmured something, and then a man chuckled in the background.

His hand curled into a fist. "I'm not here to join your pillow talk, Fontaine."

"All right, all right—" There was a rustling sound, followed by complaints from both of his playmates before a door shut. A sound of a stifled yawn cut through his question, "What about her?"

"I need you to send her on a high-profile job—not some small-time crime. I need to be the one with the jurisdiction to bring her in. With enough publicity, I'll have it."

"I see," he replied, sounding a little preoccupied. "Any particular reason why?"

"Nothing you need to worry about."

"Fine, fine... Exactly how fast do you want this to happen? You realize that high-profile doesn't exactly happen overnight. Plus, if I give her everything she needs, it'll be pretty damn suspicious."

"How fast can it be done without drawing suspicion then?"

Fontaine hummed in contemplation. "Well... if I'm not mistaken, the New Year's gala will be happening next month. It's a rather nice opening for her to nab something that isn't featured in the main showcase. And if you want to go *big*, there's nothing more valuable than the museum's typical centerpiece." A glass clinked on the other end of the line, like he was pouring himself a drink.

"I can work with that," Arrington said. "If you need about a month, then take a month. I assume I'll be receiving an anonymous tip with more details later. And should she manage to succeed, you'll also be sure to set up a proper drop-off point so I can dispatch my people, correct?"

"Naturally," he said, the sound of the glass warping his voice. "I wouldn't leave you out in the cold like that. I'll make the arrangements and pass along the details in the next couple of days."

"See to it." He immediately hung up, dropped the phone back into the drawer, and wiped the offending hand on his pants.

At least that was one problem solved. Now all he had to do was wait.

WEATHER

Weather Blackburn jogged away from the commuter train's small platform, weaving her way between parents out with their children to run errands and university students circling cafés for study spots. She brushed her too-dark brown hair out of the way of her violet-hued eyes with a sigh.

Almost there.

Despite the encroaching winter chill, the sun had her in a chokehold between the dark gray hoodie and washed-out black jeans she'd thrown on this morning to keep herself looking inconspicuous in a packed train of early-rising salary workers.

Bumping against a few with designer handbags and fitted tailored suits had been easy, especially when she'd been quick to flash each of her victims an apologetic smile. All while the little device in her pocket copied ID data. They'd been none the wiser, either giving her a kind, reserved smile in return or one that teetered on the edge of something a little more predatory —an immediate signal for her to move on.

A few hours of jumping from train to train had finally earned her a seat and then her final destination: the pawnshop. She just hoped that her bag of goods would earn her some extra credits after sitting on it for a few months since she was out of things to sell. She'd finally realized how bleak things had gotten when she'd been eyeing her small stash of unopened makeup this morning with the thought of how much she might be able to mark it up.

At that point, she might as well have considered cutting off one of her hands with how vital both were to her trade. Quick fingers and good looks were fine on their own, but a day didn't go by where she didn't somehow manage to swindle a few extra credits with a damsel in distress act—glittery eyeshadow and all.

But when she passed a Corvian café, the scent of crisp potato pancakes and fresh soup made her stomach growl. She dipped her head, pressing forward with the promise of a large container of soup to eat off of for a couple days if she had more than enough for rent on her way back. Weather tried to recall the last time she'd actually eaten something that hadn't been scraped together in her kitchen as a sleek, black car pulled up against the curb further ahead.

Two men stepped out onto the sidewalk, sporting suit jackets with rolled-up sleeves and crimson-colored dress shirts with no ties. She aimed herself toward the storefronts, trying to give them a wide berth before one stepped in front of her. The other moved to box her in.

Damnit.

"Can I help you?" she asked, batting her lashes once as she tucked a lock of hair behind her ear.

"Get in."

"Sorry," she said with a wince, "but my parents told me not to get into vehicles with strange men. Now if you'll excuse me—"

"Giovanni wants to have a word with you," came the man from behind her, a tell-tale Republicanized variation of a Valentian accent bleeding through, branding him a native of the Republic's eastern coast.

She bit back her annoyance as she turned on a heel to face him. "Look, I'm sure he would, but I'm afraid that I'm on a bit of a tight schedule, so—"

"And so is he," he said sharply. "Now get in."

Her face twitched ever-so-slightly while she weighed the possibility of bolting down the street. Unfortunately, she was fairly certain she couldn't outrun a car. Not that she'd tried it before since her sole option to test her escape had been a security vehicle idling outside some boutique storefronts she frequented shoplifting from. "Fine."

She slid along the smooth pleather seats to the other side and tested the handle. *Locked.* The chorus of doors shutting sealed her fate, even before the driver pulled back onto the brick pavers.

"So..." she started, smoothing out her jeans like it was a fine dress. "Do any of you lovely, strong men care to explain why dear Gio has sent you to fetch me, or am I just in for a surprise?"

"He wouldn't say," said the one next to her. "Just said to bring you to his office."

Lovely...

Weather intertwined her fingers and glanced between her captors as they navigated down street after street, passing taxi after taxi. The idea that Giovanni Fontaine had sent anyone out to hunt her down made her stomach churn. Soup was out of the question now.

There'd been a time when she'd realized Giovanni had been eyeing her like a prize—a far cry from what she actually was. Weather couldn't be won because she'd have to be broken first, and she'd been broken and pieced back together so many times that she'd only gotten faster at figuring out where every fragment fit. Well, that, and the issue that Giovanni hated her mouth.

Every snide comment or flippant remark she'd made snuffed the light out of his eyes in an instant, which she quite enjoyed. However, his carefree, playful persona would vanish in favor of control, and the monster would do battle with her instead. Word for word, threat for threat—a lethal dance that she was always outnumbered in.

Why she'd taken a job from him nearly a year ago, she didn't know. Perhaps it was arrogance in thinking that she could go toe-to-toe as a street thief against a rich boy that wanted to play mafioso. Or maybe it was because she'd thrown caution into the wind after she'd lost the last of her support, finally leaving her stranded. She should've run in the end, just like all the other little thieves when they failed his next-to-impossible job.

But Weather still had that strange sense of honor that only worked in her old circles—a trait that she'd foolishly hoped Giovanni would've commended, but naturally exploited.

She jerked her head around as the car stopped, watching one of the men get out and circle the car for her door. The flecks of glittering shards baked into the gray, hexagonal drive winked under the porte cochère's overhead lights, nearly fooling her into believing she was stepping out into a fancy shopping center rather than a casino entry.

When the car pulled away, leaving her and her two new friends behind, her shoulders fell at the sight of the blacked-out glass doors. They escorted her through, where they treaded over red, regal-patterned carpet that stuck to the soles of her boots. She hoped the reason for that was that she'd stepped in something disgusting earlier since the idea of Giovanni throwing a temper tantrum over it brought her a little bit of joy.

Patrons wearing crisp, black suits and pencil skirts lounged near tables with holographic displays and mimosas. Businessmen's cufflinks and watches glinted gold and silver, and one woman's diamond earrings left Weather calculating how many months' rent they could pay for. The thought fell away as she was corralled into an elevator.

She stifled a gag as the strong, smoky scent of cologne played off the floral air freshener, further adding to that sinking feeling in the pit of her stomach. The gold doors slid open to the upper walkway, giving her a prime view of Giovanni's domain through glass-paneled railing. At least it matched the door to his office—and his desk, the sideboard cluttered with alcohol, and nearly everything else inside that room, minus the small safe in the corner.

A petite, mousy-looking woman in a black-and-red casino uniform poured Giovanni a glass of water and scurried out of the room the second one of the goons opened the door. She kept her head down and clutched the pitcher close to her vest. Weather swallowed.

"If it isn't my favorite little thief," Giovanni crooned as he dropped his phone on his desk and leaned back in his chair.

His golden tint—a few shades shy of Weather's own pale—matched the red-and-gold theme of the casino with his loose, blood-red tie. Soft brown hair gave way to flimsy, dull-colored feathers woven into it, covering some of his studs and ear cuffs. His dark eyes had to be the only thing about him that she could connect to his father—Dimitri, the former crime boss whose name used to ripple through a room when he arrived. Even those eyes had one key difference, though: an unyielding hardness that came with making a name for oneself.

"And if it isn't my favorite little tramp," she said, maybe a little *too* confidently.

His smile vanished, and the afterimage of his father sat in his wake.

"Why am I here?" Weather asked, her fingers twitching against her bag.

"Well..." he started, the amused lilt seeping back into his voice. "I have a job for you."

"Giovanni, I think you're forgetting that I got incredibly screwed the last time I took a job from you—"

"And, if I recall, I was generous enough not to turn you over to the authorities for how atrocious that entire situation was handled. So, if you refuse this job, I'll either go ahead and do that now, or I'll be inclined to deal with you however I'd like." A razor-thin blade was flicked from his pocket and carefully set at the edge of the desk.

Holy. Shit.

She tore her eyes away from it, locking back on her opponent. The vicious victory written all over his features made her squirm.

"Well," Weather said cautiously, "I suppose I don't have any other options then..."

"Good. I want The Heart of the King on my desk by the tenth of next month."

Her eyebrows shot up as she re-ran what she'd thought he'd said before laughter bubbled up from her chest. "You're kidding, right? That's the most sure-fire way to get every damn officer in Kingsheart on your ass in a heartbeat."

Giovanni slammed his hand on the desk, and she jumped. Dark, seething anger in his eyes stole away her breath. He was *serious*.

"The tenth, Weather, or I'll deal with you myself."

She slowly started to nod, unable to do much else with how her entire body seized.

"I've even given you a generous opening since you'll be doing this alone." He tossed a faux-paper envelope across his desk. "I've pulled some strings for you to waltz into the New Year's Gala if you'd like. Or you can do it the hard way. Doesn't matter to me since it's not my ass on the line." Then he shrugged.

"I'll take it." The words tumbled out so quickly, she barely realized she'd said them. She shifted from foot to foot, unsure if she should say more, but decided to keep her mouth shut and take the envelope. The damn thing shook in her hands, and she tightened her grip on it to try to make it less obvious.

"Good. Then I'll send you the instructions of where to take that, and I'll leave you to your work." He tapped the hilt of the blade. "And I tend to make good on my promises, should you fail."

Her mouth felt dry. "I'll have it. Don't worry."

Everything after that turned into a blur, of doors and game tables until she was outside again, wandering past building after building until her legs gave out, and she slumped against the smooth stone recess of a Valentian-style apartment building. The shade of the thin, stone balconies overhead didn't do much to cover her, leaving her feeling exposed.

The Heart of the King.

There was no way—was there? Weather stared down at the envelope and blinked back the start of tears.

It's not like you haven't done this sort of crazy shit before, Weather. You want to dig yourself out of Giovanni's debt? Show him you're a jack of all trades.

39
VALENTIA ✦ 2704-12-08

GLACIER

"I wish today was already over," Noa grumbled while she pushed around the fruit in her yogurt.

"I'm guessing you're not looking forward to the ferry ride?" Glacier asked, nudging the handle of his cappuccino.

She narrowed her eyes at him. "What do you think?"

He lifted the mug to his lips as he glanced out the window. Orchards gave way to hilly vineyards and a smattering of stucco mansions. The train cut through a town, cluttered with old, light brick two-stories and crumbling city walls. Farmers markets with red, yellow, and blue-striped awnings were crowded with shoppers, vanishing in an instant like a warm, fleeting memory.

"So..." he started, turning back to her. "Are we meeting your contact tonight? Or tomorrow?"

"Tonight, but you're not going."

He frowned.

"Trust me on this," she said. "You don't want to tag along."

He rolled his eyes, letting it drop as a tablet slid between them and Nyx took a seat next to him with a cup of coffee. Noa shot him a brief, warning look before she cleared her throat and pointed at the tablet. "This for me?"

"No," Nyx said. "I just need to babysit it since it's running a process in the background."

"Is it... anything I can help with?" Glacier asked, drumming his fingertips against his mug.

Nyx shook her head. "I think I'll wait and see what I can come up with on my own first. It's more of a side-project for one of my new resources to keep everything running smoothly."

"A new pet?" Noa asked with a teasing smirk in Glacier's direction. "Sounds like someone's already an outdated model."

"There's a difference between an assistant and an associate," Nyx said.

"Ouch," she hissed. "Downgraded."

He shot her a glare.

"My *assistant* is more valuable," she said, casting Noa a disapproving look, "mainly because we both benefit from what we find. My associates, on the other hand, need to be kept satisfied with a trade of information in order to keep things running. They're certainly not going to work for free. Not to mention that despite most of my tasks being rather easy to pass off, I find I'm thrown a challenging case on occasion with *nothing* to go on." Her words grew a little more stressed and rigid near the end as she kept laser-focused on Noa, who suddenly found the view very interesting.

Glacier's eyes flicked between them, wondering what Noa had asked her to do while he continued nursing his drink. She started to squirm under Nyx's glower, and Glacier's jaw dropped as he saw her begin to crawl out of her seat.

"Not so fast," Nyx said, kicking up a leg to the opposing bench to block her escape.

Noa froze. "What?"

"We should discuss our plans for tomorrow's museum trip. I'd like to have everyone go in and scope out the place since the displays shift around every month for different features and promotions. However, that's heavily dependent on a certain someone's ability to make all of us look presentable. I think that it would probably be best if you and Rune take priority—"

"Actually," Noa cut in, "I was thinking that maybe it would be better if Rune goes with Cecilia to show her the ropes a little more—that, and it would be better to split up the intel crew and the ground team, so I'll just take Glacier instead."

Nyx brows knit together. "But that would leave me with Crow. You know I don't really care for Crow."

"You don't really care for *anyone*."

"I'm fine with Glacier, seeing how he actually has some critical thinking skills and doesn't talk back to me, unlike some people. I'm also a little shocked that you didn't immediately jump on the chance to partner up with me." She eyed her suspiciously. "Am *I* the outdated model now?"

Noa sputtered. "No—But, I mean, since we'll be in public, Glacier needs a capable bodyguard, which leaves me. So don't be so put out." She gave her a flirtatious grin. "At least now I know that my affection hasn't gone unnoticed."

"Shut up." Nyx dropped her leg, freeing her from her temporary prison. "Now beat it before I decide to pair you up with Crow instead."

Noa beamed, cutting Glacier a victorious look the second Nyx checked on her tablet. He sank down into his seat and tried to ignore the gnawing feeling in his stomach that she was planning on using him as a human life vest. She popped up out of her seat and jogged out of the car, abandoning him at the mercy of Nyx right as the rolling hills gave way to the distant coastline.

"How does it feel to be so far away from home?" Nyx asked.

He hesitated, ripping his gaze from the window to his coffee cup. "Strangely... liberating."

"I think that's a healthy way to look at it. Though, I'm not sure how concerned I should be about you two getting along so well." She gestured toward the exit, and he sputtered, choking on his cappuccino.

"I—" he forced out at the tail end of his coughing fit. "I think you mean *tolerating* each other, which is a rather large improvement from where we started."

"Hmm... so what do you have on her?"

"Excuse me?"

"What do you have that's making her warm up to you over the twins?"

"I don't have anything on her," he lied, immediately picturing her terrified face back on the cruise ship. The mere thought of exploiting her like that left him feeling queasy, especially after how Louis had done that to him his entire life.

"Fine," Nyx said. "Then don't tell me."

He sighed. "Look, even if I did have something on her, don't act like you don't have your own secrets to keep."

The way she examined him with her chin raised made something in his core tell him that he'd hit his mark. To her credit, she didn't buckle. She drummed her fingers on the table instead.

"Fair enough," she said, climbing out of the booth. "Just don't think that I haven't noticed you two sneaking off together."

He frowned at the teasing twinkle in her eye before she left. The sadness that gripped him in her wake dragged out a far-off memory of Kat, and when he turned back to the seat across the table, he almost swore he saw her sitting there. His hands curled into loose fists, hating that overwhelming despair that came with the thought she wasn't back in Amarais, waiting for him to come home.

Glacier closed his eyes and dropped his shoulders, meditating until he thought he heard Kat's voice. He shook it away and looked around the car to find it empty, so he crawled out and started after Noa and Nyx.

CECILIA

The ferry glided through the dark water separating north Valentia from south. Cecilia leaned over the boardwalk railing, the sea-sprayed metal slick against her palms. The view of the coastal city they'd stopped in had stolen her breath away with its little off-white stucco façades and brown-red calendrical roof tiles. There was a brightness to it all that made it outshine Amarais's bleak concrete and marble. Maybe it was the laughter and chatter along the sandy beach below or maybe it was the upbeat music pouring out of the open apartment windows.

"If you're not careful," Rune whispered, leaning in next to her. "I'm pretty sure your face will get stuck like that."

She rubbed at her cheeks and tried to suppress her smile before she laughed. "I can't help it! It's all so pretty here. Is this not your first time in Valentia?"

Rune chuckled. "I've visited a couple of times."

"Didn't you want to stay? Imagine waking up to take in the sea air, enjoying fresh food, strolling along the beautiful beaches—"

Crow dipped into view past Rune, bending over the railing and staring down at the people lining the beach below. "Having a million attractive people to choose from..."

"Keep it in your pants," Rune grumbled.

"Just look around—" he continued, grabbing his shoulders and angling him to face the shore again. "See all those hot, half-naked women?"

Rune's eyes nearly rolled back in his head as Crow leaned over the railing again, dropping his voice to a near-mumble. "Some nice-looking dudes too..."

"And how many people do you plan on enjoying yourself with during this trip?"

"As many as I can before we all die horribly." Crow smacked him on the back and brushed past them right as the ferry docked.

Rune grimaced. "I'm going to go ahead and apologize for his behavior."

Passengers began pouring out of the two-tier ship and down the boardwalk. One man jogged ahead with a messenger bag while a family corralled their kids off to the side to apply sunscreen with the boat as a backdrop. It looked like it had been dipped in sunshine with its golden-gleaming lower half and pristinely painted white second floor.

The ferryman whistled and motioned for the queue to start climbing aboard, sending the clusters of people surging ahead, including the rest of their party.

"I just don't understand how you two behave so differently," she said.

"I'm hoping that's a good thing," he said, smirking as they filed into the line.

"Well, I enjoy being around you more than Crow—" She jerked her head away, reddening. *Oops.*

His brows raised for a flickering instant before he dropped his voice into a conspiratorial-like whisper. "And what's that supposed to mean?" It came out velvety and teasing, almost sounding like something his alter-ego might've said back in Corvia.

But they weren't in Corvia. There wasn't a question of who she was talking to here.

Crow waved Rune over as they stepped onto the splotchy topaz linoleum. Instead of dropping it all together to join his brother at one of the open windows, he lingered for another moment until she forced what she hoped was an innocent smile. Rune ducked his head slightly with a breathy chuckle and wove through the benches.

The fluttering sensation finally subsided, but not without taking all her energy with it. Her shoulders fell as she wandered further inside, and her hair whipped around from the whirling fans mounted near the ceiling. She twisted her hand around her bag strap once she spotted Noa and Glacier already on a bench near the middle of the ship.

It looked like they were whispering to each other, but Noa's head was almost between her knees and her fingers were curled around the edge of the seat. Cecilia bit her lip as she drew closer, feeling both concerned if she was okay and worried that maybe she'd caught a glimpse of Cecilia's little slip up with Rune. Sure, he'd said that he and Noa weren't a thing, but did she feel the same?

"Are you okay?" Cecilia asked, taking a seat across from them. "Are you feeling seasick?"

Glacier sheepishly glanced away as Noa's head jerked up. "Um—Yeah. A little. It's um... nothing too bad," she said as Nyx pushed away from the open window and began venturing back toward them.

"At least the water isn't too choppy," Nyx said, taking the seat next to Cecilia and pulling out her tablet.

Glacier shifted, bouncing his knees. "So... Nyx, you said the ferry ride is about twenty minutes, right?"

She nodded without bothering to look up. "Correct. After that, we'll be taking the local line to Casovecchia. I just need to lock in our client once we're settled in."

"Client?" Cecilia asked.

"He's an art patron here who's made some connections after we helped relocate him. He'll be our guy to get us in for a smooth job—Gods, Noa, are you going to throw up?"

"Don't ask me that again or I might," she muttered, swaying a little.

"Well, then..." she said, tucking her tablet back into her bag. "I'll just leave you to that. Maybe I can convince Crow to jump overboard..." Nyx stood and wandered over to the other side of the ship.

Cecilia chewed on the inside of her cheek with the thought that Noa might want to be left alone. "Um, Glacier? How about we go take in the view for a bit? You stayed back earlier before we boarded, so maybe you'd like a better look." She pushed herself up, beaming at him.

Her suggestion was met with a flicker of indecision before he shook his head. "Thanks but go on ahead without me. I'm sure we'll have the chance to enjoy the ocean view on the way back."

"Oh. Okay. Sure," she said, rubbing her hands on her pants as she turned to leave. Her feet dragged a little, and she couldn't help but steal another look over her shoulder as she started toward the others.

Glacier was already talking to Noa again, bringing her a sense of unease. The concern written all over his face was something that'd always been reserved for her or Kat. To see him scoot a little closer to Noa set off every alarm bell in her head until she shook it free from her thoughts.

She was overthinking things. She hoped.

NOA

Noa ran her hands over her knees again as her eyes darted around the open windows of the ferry. The water lapping against the sides of the boat left her head spinning, but she was admittedly relieved that Glacier hadn't left her.

Fortunately—or *unfortunately*, depending on how she looked at it— she stopped picturing the water in favor of replaying the brief yellow flash of the checkpoint kiosk after Nyx had scanned her ID. Glacier had been right. She was modded.

How the hell did I miss that?

Did Nyx feel like she couldn't tell them? Was she worried that they'd judge her for it? If anything, it added further stress to Noa's need to shield both Nyx and Glacier from the Volkov and the psychopaths in Amarais. She knew that needed them, but if she were being honest with herself, she was starting to feel more and more reliant on them. The idea that Nyx was potentially afraid of something that humanized her in Noa's eyes stirred up a torrent of emotions.

"Are you going to say something to her?" Glacier asked.

She shook her head. "It's probably best to leave it alone for now. Until we reach Amarais, it won't be that big of a problem since she's gotten away with it for this long."

"Okay."

Noa decided that would have to be enough for now, hoping that her words wouldn't come back to bite her.

40
VALENTIA ✧ 2704-12-09

CECILIA

Cecilia scooted forward on the pale-yellow couch cushion as Nyx placed each of the fake IDs on the round, faded coffee table with a resounding snap. Six IDs. Six different countries. Six random faces.

Nyx rocked back on her knees against the floor, her silhouette backdropped by the sliding glass door overlooking the suite's view of the tall hills in the distance giving way to dramatic cliffsides. "Now," she said, "the question is whether or not you'll be able to glamour all of us or only a couple."

"I should be able to manage with everyone..." Cecilia answered, lightly touching the corner of the ID with the image of a Rothian woman with short, white hair that almost matched her bleached skin and eyes the color of storm clouds.

"I assume you're only able to manipulate what already exists on us, correct? Like how you managed to work with turning me into Noa back in Southaven?"

Cecilia nodded. "Yeah, it's sort of like... painting on a canvas? I can use my magic like someone would be able to do with really good cosmetics to change up their features, but I couldn't make you taller to match Noa or have Rune match Glacier's height."

"That's fine," Nyx said with a half-shrug. "We can work around that. Decide whatever pairings make sense then."

She bit her lip as she scraped them toward the edge of the table, humming softly to the tune of a gondola they'd passed on their way in—a slow, soothing song that made her forget about the five pairs of eyes pinned on her. Cecilia began shuffling them around, mixing and matching the men and women staring back at her. The bright-eyed Miraltan girl she silently claimed for herself, imagining her opportunity to finally become what she'd lamented to Rune early on in their journey.

She plucked up the Amaraian boy and Bellegardian girl, offering them to Glacier and Noa. "Here, we'll trade places for the day," she said to Glacier before she caught Noa's eyes narrowing on her decided ID.

"Funny," Noa grumbled, swiping the card with a huff.

Cecilia stifled a snicker and collected her eyeliner pen from her pocket. The pop of the cap sounded through the hotel suite. "Ready?"

GLACIER

It took everything in Glacier not to touch his face. The one staring back at him in the local train window had lighter eyes and hair that matched the shade of Cecilia's, neatly styled into place thanks to her careful hand. A single touch would break this spell—the rune on his face. Not that he was entirely convinced it was his. Not with how angular and refined it looked in contrast to his familiar, softer features.

Noa adjusted her grip on the railing at his side, her near-black curls framing a delicate face adorned with illusioned makeup. Her dark-gray eyes never left the window, staring out at the parallel waterway with uncharacteristic fear written into every slight adjustment she made. She acted more like a nervous tourist than the confident, strong-willed Noa he knew.

Should he do something? Nudge her? Ask her if she was okay? Was he staring? He was staring—

"Are..." she whispered, wetting her lips. "Are we *sure* there's not another way in?" She met his eyes, and his heart squeezed.

"There's a moat..." he said quietly. "And most streets are too narrow for there to be a decent walking entrance."

The train began to slow, and he stumbled as she grabbed his arm. The yellow-tinged doors sprung open with a hiss.

"Let's get this over with, I guess," she muttered, stepping out and nearly dragging him after her.

He steadied himself and wrestled free in favor of taking her hand, which surprisingly wasn't met with a complaint. Instead, she death-gripped it. He could feel her pulse reverberating through him with every step past the blur of stray looks that snapped back to their phones and destinations shortly after. The idea of walking alongside Nyx's Rothian glamour would've guaranteed additional whispers with how horribly they'd stand out together.

For once, he missed his own skin. He missed how easy it had been to keep his head down the past few weeks. That was a thought he'd never imagined he'd have.

Noa ripped him from his musings when she skidded to a stop several meters away from the queue for the water taxi, its current vessel loading up the majority of the waiting passengers.

"You okay?" he whispered, nudging her with his elbow.

"Y-yeah. Fine." She took a step forward, and he mirrored the movement, giving her hand a comforting squeeze.

They stopped near the middle of the roped-off queue box, where Noa stood rigid in the face of the gently lapping water as the taxi made its lazy cruise under a bridge decorated with daisies, carnations, and roses woven through the wrought iron railing. Her body relaxed a little, but she remained stock-still like a statue—her breathing so shallow, he was starting to worry she might pass out. It was as if she were somewhere else altogether.

Glacier didn't have time to dwell on it with the next taxi pulling up. Noa recoiled as the pilot tied off the watercraft and started loading passengers, calling out the next destination of the museum. Glacier started forward until he realized that Noa wouldn't budge. He looked back, seeing her shake her head, and let go of her hand to loop his arm around her back.

"I've got you."

His head spun for a second, the words echoing through his head like he'd fallen back into his dream. The surreal, murky feeling of being asleep enveloped him until he stepped into the boat and helped her down after him.

"See?" he said as they took their seats at one of the front benches. "We made it. Nothing bad is going to happen."

The boat's engine sprang to life, and she pressed herself into his side, grabbing onto part of his button-up shirt. So, he sighed and left his arm in the danger zone, wrapped around a trembling psychopath that needed a couple gentle pats on the shoulder as reassurance the boat wouldn't capsize.

"How about let's talk about something to distract you? Like—"

"Do you know how to swim?" she hissed.

"Um, yes?"

"Where the hell did you learn? You don't live near water."

"Well, there are these really amazing things called swimming pools. Incredible that I had access to one in our basement." She punched him in the side, and he winced. "Gods—do *you* not know how to swim? Is that why you're terrified?"

"No—" She shook her head. "I mean—*yes*, I know how to swim, and *no*, that's not why I'm terrified."

"Then did something happen that made you afraid, or—"

"We're not discussing this right now," she growled as the light around them faded away upon the entry to the tunnel.

The other passengers held up their phones as pulsing lights zipped along the curved, overhead displays blending into the brick. Awe and excitement buzzed through every whispered word and sputtering spark that began erupting into tiny fireworks before they drifted back into the light.

The *Galleria Centro-Meridionale.*

Tall, silver-painted archways appeared on their right, adorned with yellow banners and digital sign markers rotating through advertisements of their seasonal displays. The light pouring through stained the water a rippling gold that almost tricked him into thinking they were reemerging outside.

But the boat stopped, anchored alongside one of the arched entrances, and they were ushered off. Everyone's footsteps turned muffled against the red carpet running up the small set of steps past the entrance, and some of their fellow museumgoers stopped to angle their phones to the ceiling. Glacier looked up and gaped at the mural painted around each domed window—a man with a lyre sitting in a meadow of wildflowers, his face obscured by a soft, yellow cloak that spilled outward to encompass all but the dark, starry corners.

Noa sighed, letting go of his hand while they stood in front of several guide kiosks surrounded by visitors. "I don't want to think about leaving," she mumbled. "So, let's take our time while the others start trickling in."

"Yeah," he said, hesitating before he gave a playful nudge and put on a grin to try to lighten the mood. "Let's enjoy some art."

Her eyes narrowed on him. "And keep your hands to yourself." She started forward, strolling into the wide aisles of partitions showcasing glassed-off art in sleek frames.

His shoulders fell as he trudged after her. She slowed and stopped at painting after painting, small sculpture after sculpture lining the maze of fabric-covered walls. The dobbed paint of yellow, orange, and pink suns on landscapes curled outward, consuming the scenes and his attention until the quiet chatter of the museum softened to a muddled pulse.

Glacier frowned, turning to peer through the slim opening with the phantom tug of an invisible rope to guide him. A hand-painted vase—its blue-painted scenes now faded lace, leaves, and rabbits—once used for its practicality. A piece of torn fabric—stitched with tiny runes along its hem that Glacier wished he could read—once used for its protection. A statuette —carved and sanded with precision in the image of a god—once used for its blessing. Now all of these things were held here for their uniqueness. Their irreplaceability. Their craftsmanship. And yet his family had squirreled objects just like this away out of greed over preservation.

That was the thought that surfaced to the forefront of his mind when he stood in front of the next item: a spindly-wired object unmistakably made of platinum with an explosion of citrines set in the center like the noon sun. The Vision of Valentia.

"You can't just run off like that," Noa said through a heavy, panicked breath. "Especially not while you look like—Oh, damn. You must have some keen eyes to notice this thing from back there."

"Yeah..." he said, hesitating as he caught her attention fixed on the glass case. "I guess so." He shifted his footing and glanced around the rest of the partitioned nook. The phantom pull was gone, replaced by uncertainty of how he'd gotten here.

"Easy enough," she said with a chuckle as gave him a pat on the back. "Let's just scope out the rest around here and call it a day."

One of Glacier's hands went to the back of his neck. "Y-yeah, sure."

CECILIA

After Nyx's run-down of what she was finishing working on for museum access and informing Noa that her private tour would be tomorrow, everyone began splintering off. Noa yawned and dismissed herself to her room, Nyx went back to her controls on her computer mat, and Crow slipped out of the hotel without so much as a word.

Cecilia tucked her hands under her thighs and turned her sights toward the window, her heart slowly sinking at the idea that she'd never get to take it all in again. Every short stay left her with the gut-wrenching feeling that this was like some sort of equivalent to her life flashing before her eyes.

"Um..." she started, scooting forward to catch Glacier's attention. "Do you want to take a walk around the city for a bit?"

He hesitated as Nyx cut in. "Not without a chaperone," she said, not bothering to spare either of them a glance.

"I'll take them," Rune said, sending a jolt of surprise through her as her eyes snapped to his chair on the opposite side of the room. "Do you want to go now?"

"I—" Glacier stammered. "I should stay and help Nyx. But you two go have fun." He gave a quick, half-smile before ducking his head again.

Rune stood, taking his afternoon mug of coffee to the kitchen and dumping it down the sink. "Get your bag. Let's go."

The creeping ivy followed them through the small, winding backstreets, leaving Cecilia dizzy when she turned her face to the sky. All the sunshine in the world couldn't put that spring back into her step at the thought of Glacier possibly avoiding her. She caught herself as she slipped on the smooth stones near the canals and laughed it off with an uneasy chuckle when Rune tried to steady her.

"Are you all right?" he asked. "You're awfully quiet."

"Sorry," she said, pushing back a lock of stray hair. "I was just thinking. That's all."

"Do you... want to talk about it?"

"N-no, I wouldn't want to trouble you with any of my stupid thoughts."

"I'm sure your thoughts aren't stupid. You should give yourself a little more credit."

She chewed on her lip as they slowed on a footbridge and ran a hand over the warm railing. "I don't want to add any extra hassle or anything like that. You don't have to babysit me—"

"What? No—I like spending time with you. It's nice to just talk and wander around without thinking about why we're in a place like this to begin with. If...you don't want me here, I can—"

"No- No! I, um... I like having you around." She leaned against the railing and stared down at the stone-speckled concrete. Cecilia didn't know what she wanted then: to tell him all her fears about what might come next as both she and Glacier found who they were without the other, or if she wanted to enjoy each moment for what it was. She cleared her throat. "We should g—"

"Wait, I..."

Their eyes met, and she waited for him to continue. Instead, he leaned in close, his breath tickling her cheek before he changed course.

A kiss.

Brief and new, but somehow familiar.

He pulled away, and her vision glossed over—to the point where she barely registered his alarm, outside of his quick step back. "Cecilia, I-I'm sorry. I didn't mean—I shouldn't have—"

She shook her head and threw her arms around him, burying her face into his chest. "I *really* like you," she said through a gasping breath.

"Then that makes two of us," he said, his arms wrapping around her, holding her tight like she fit there. Like she *belonged* there. A safe, warm embrace that made her forget everything around her in its constant state of change.

Home.

RUNE

Rune took in the scent of fresh-cut flowers as he walked hand-in-hand with Cecilia down a side street littered with greenery shops and carts. For once, he'd been glad that he'd taken a page from Crow's book and thrown caution into the wind. He'd fought with himself over whether or not he should act on his feelings for too long, but Crow's echoing words of enjoying himself before dying rang out louder than the rest of the advice he'd been holding onto.

If this was the end—if this was his final adventure, he didn't want to tiptoe around feelings. Not when he'd wasted so much time in the past pretending he'd been content in the company of others. Neither he nor Cecilia had ever really had the luxury of simply being themselves, which is why he supposed he'd found a familiar spirit in her. Both of them equally lost and afraid of making the wrong move.

He smirked down at her, and she beamed up at him. Her blue eyes danced with excitement that stretched beyond seeing a new place—something he could only equate to seeing a potential new future that neither of them might get to see. He squeezed her hand, and she laughed.

"I don't even know your real name," she said.

He grimaced, embarrassment washing over him. "Well, I... don't know that I would call it my *real* name. That's just a name given to me by my birth parents. The one Corrine gave me I consider to be my true name."

"And what about your surname?"

He sputtered, a laugh escaping him. "What? You want to try it on?"

She blushed. "I-I—um—"

He chuckled, shaking his head. "I think Angelis has a nicer ring to it, don't you?"

Her eyes went wide at the implication, but it felt right to say. *She* felt right. Every other girl he'd ever considered to potentially be his match, he'd found to have a lack of true understanding. But she rivaled him in every sense—pushed him beyond what he thought he should strive for. To be someone he *wanted* to be.

"But it's a Bellegardian name, right?" she asked. "I think Bellegardian names always sound nice, so it can't be *that* bad."

"It's my *father's* name, and it's only there for legal purposes."

She bumped against him, sulking. "Well, then you don't have to tell me now, but... If we're still together when all of this is over, I want you to promise you'll tell me then."

"Okay," he said slowly, considering the agreement. "Then I promise if we somehow manage to stand next to each other by the time this is over, I'll tell you my given name."

She frowned up at him. "And what about your family name?"

Rune leaned down to whisper in her ear. "Monette." When he drew back, he could already see her mentally stringing it onto her name while she bit her lip to suppress a grin. "Don't go repeating that to anyone, got it? Not even Crow."

"I won't tell a soul."

"Good," he said with mock sternness before he broke into a smile again, and she dropped her head against his shoulder as they continued back toward the hotel.

41
VALENTIA ✦ 2704-12-10

GLACIER

Glacier stared up at the ceiling like he was searching for answers in the faint white textured pattern there. Answers regarding Cecilia's cheeriness at dinner and contented sighs when she crawled into bed last night. Answers about the curled-up rugs and stuck doors of his dreams—nightmares—*whatever* he could call them. And answers for why he hadn't managed to hold his ground against Noa. Again.

"So, you're just going to lay on the floor?" Noa peered down at him with a frown.

"I'm... a little distracted. Sorry." He propped himself up on his elbows. "I'm kind of surprised you're not worrying about ripping off your client's arm tonight on your way into the gallery."

She rolled her eyes. "Funny how he told Nyx there's a VIP tunnel entrance after all that. It's primarily for staff since it connects to some of the preservation chambers. I think I would've rather snuck in and stolen it during off-hours after she gained camera access than bother with all this. But at least I won't have to drag you along as collateral." A teasing smirk pulled at her lips.

He bit back a retort that came with the prick of irritation and tried to hook a leg behind one of hers. She hopped to the side, cutting him a smug look. Something told him this had to be normal for her since she never ceased to goad people into retaliation. But she offered him a hand and pulled him to his feet anyway.

"If you need to, you should take some time to rest. Take a walk to clear your head tonight. Being distracted during our sessions is one thing, but it's another entirely when you're working with Nyx."

"I'm supposed to be helping her check everything before tonight, Noa. I don't think we really have the luxury of relaxation time." He began to slide the coffee table over the rug, and she stopped with a sock against the edge of the tabletop.

"Nyx can handle an hour by herself. She's done it before, and she can do it now. Just because she prefers to have an extra set of eyes on things doesn't mean you'll be of much use if you're focused on something else." Her foot fell back to the carpet as her expression shifted to concern. "Are you okay?"

No.

"I'm fine."

Even though she frowned at his answer, she jerked the table the rest of the way into place right as Nyx emerged from her room.

"I'm sending Cecilia and Rune to pick up your dress in a couple of hours," she said without preamble. "Mainly because I don't trust Crow to do it."

"Seriously?" Noa asked with a slight whine to her tone. "Can't I just wear a pantsuit or something? Dresses may *look* nice, but they're impractical."

"That's exactly why you're wearing a dress. It's less threatening."

Noa flopped onto the couch with a groan.

"Look," Nyx said as she fiddled with the coffee maker, "it'll still have all the specially-tailored fail-safes I custom order."

"But it's a *dress*. Not to mention that there won't be anyone around to appreciate it anyway."

"The client will be there," Glacier offered.

"Silvio's gay. He won't be looking for the right reasons."

"Then who would appreciate seeing you in a dress that would suddenly make you willing to wear it?"

Her face went blank for a moment, her eyes focused somewhere past him in thought. "Well, *Rune* certainly likes women in gorgeous dresses."

"What about dresses?" Rune asked groggily from his bedroom doorway, slowly making his way toward the kitchen.

Noa sat up and dug her knees into the cushions, leaning on the back of the couch. "What do you think about me in a dress?" she asked with a seductive smile.

He paused by the couch, looking down at her with bafflement before he gave a half-shrug.

Her smile dropped. "Oh, come *on*—You can't tell me that you didn't enjoy how I looked back in Bellegarde when we attended that stupid gala together."

"It was nice," he said nonchalantly.

"Don't you lie to me. It was better than just *nice*."

"Noa, I think I've made it clear that bad girls aren't my type."

And just as quickly as it left, the grin returned. "So, I'm a bad girl, huh?"

Glacier's hand went to his face, trying not to make any audible noise that would cause her to whip around and send him to the carpet.

Sighing, Rune rubbed at one of his temples. "You just can't help but twist things into what you want to hear, can you?"

She batted her eyelashes at him, which lasted until Cecilia slipped out of her room. Rune's tired moodiness brightened the second he saw her, but it paled in comparison to how she beamed on her way to join him at the kitchen counter.

Glacier pushed down that nagging unease that settled in his core at the mere thought that Cecilia had fallen head-over-heels for a thief. A conman. A *criminal*. But that was him trying to view it as an outsider looking in. He tried to imagine how her parents might worry, despite how Glacier knew Rune's gentle, level-headed character.

Now he had at least one of his answers, but he wasn't so sure what to do with it now. That rift hadn't been nearly as imaginary as what he'd thought, and he feared that he likely had a part in it all in favor of trying to balance his own problems. The only thing in all this that gave him peace was how Rune looked at her—not with the greed he was named for, but with fondness.

Glacier just wished he could shove away that self-pity over Cecilia finding happiness while he tried to poorly cobble himself back together.

"Just in time for my errand," Nyx said, cutting through his thoughts. "I need you two to do me a favor and pick up a dress."

"Let me guess," Rune said, glancing back at Noa. "It's for that one." She wiggled her fingers at him, and he gave her a scolding look. "Stop that."

Noa huffed. "This stupid thing better be exciting to wear, or else I'm going to be pissed."

Rune shook his head as he turned back to Nyx. "Sure, Cecilia and I can pick it up."

"Sure!" Cecilia added with a little *too* much enthusiasm.

Nyx motioned to Cecilia and craned her neck to lock eyes with Noa. "Now why can't you be this agreeable? Everything would be so much easier if the rest of you idiots had her attitude."

Noa made a noise of disgust and dropped her body onto the back of the couch, letting her arms dangle. Glacier circled it, slowing when he noticed her eyes following him. Something in him told him to step away as he passed, so he did—jerking just beyond her reach as she lunged to grab his shirt and *missed*. He slapped her hand away, and her eyes went wide. She scrambled over the seatback, pausing mid-vault as Rune's head whipped around.

"What are you doing? Can't you just leave him alone for five minutes?"

"*Hey*—" Nyx snapped, pointing at Glacier with her sights set on Noa, who continued teetering on the edge. "He's mine. Back the hell off."

Slowly, Noa returned back to her seat, narrowing her eyes at him as everyone returned to their kitchen conversation. He stared her down, trying to hold his ground.

"I think you're out of luck," Glacier whispered, nodding toward Rune. "Your flirting isn't going to work on him anymore."

She blinked, her brows furrowing as she tilted her head in question.

"I'm pretty sure he and Cecilia…"

"Funny," Noa whispered back. "Look, Rune might have a thing for her, but she's out of his league."

"You say that, but I keep seeing them together, and when Cecilia came back from her walk with him yesterday, she was acting super elated about something. I'm pretty sure that they're together now."

Her eyes went wide. "What? I thought Rune was just being friendly in the professional sense, not—well, not being *friendly* with her. He told me he knew he didn't have a chance."

"Rune talked to you about it?"

"*Briefly*. After that, he didn't bring it up again. Did Cecilia say anything about him to *you?*"

"No, but I know her well enough that it's pretty obvious."

"Well, shit. Now who am I going to dress up for?"

"Seriously? That's your priority here?" Glacier hissed.

"Yes, because now he'll only be looking at *Cecilia*," Noa said, dropping her voice to a dejected mumble. "So much for making myself look pretty every once in a while…"

"I don't think that really matt—"

"Shut your mouth. Of course it does. If I'm going to bother with makeup and shit to *steal* something, I want someone to appreciate it."

"There's always Crow."

Noa's eyes narrowed to slits.

"Or… not," Glacier mumbled, glancing away.

"Crow is a grade-A slut, and if you ever suggest that I do anything other than make him extremely uncomfortable again, I'll make you regret it. Now beat it."

NOA

Noa's fingers curled around the box's lid while she stared down at its contents resting on the round dining table. "Nyx!"

"What?" came her half-hearted reply, apparently still busy with all her security monitoring.

"It's *black*."

"I'm quite aware," Nyx mumbled.

"Why? You couldn't have gone for something red? I look incredible in red—"

"Put on the damn dress, Noa."

With a low, irritated growl from the back of her throat, she threw the lid back over the box and shoved it under her arm. "Let me guess, you want me to put on makeup too?"

"That is a requirement..." Nyx said in a near-growl, turning her head to peer at her over her glasses in a standoff until Cecilia chimed in.

"Um—I can help you with your makeup," she offered.

Noa's head turned to where she was seated in the living room chair. Perhaps it was time for a short interrogation... "Come here," Noa finally said, starting toward the bedroom. "Why don't you glamour my makeup instead so we can skip the mess?"

"Oh, sure! That works too," Cecilia said, confidence slipping into her voice as she hopped up and jogged after her.

"Good." Noa shut the door behind them, whirling around to face her. "Are you and Rune together?"

Cecilia's face paled. "I—W-who told you that?"

Instead of throwing Glacier into hot water, she decided to take credit for the discovery. "No one. Since Rune has been outright denying my advances, I've just happened to notice that you two have been acting rather *friendly* with each other recently." Damn, she was good.

"He told me that you two aren't together—"

"We're not," she said, tossing the box on the bed with a sigh. "You're not in trouble, I just wanted the truth."

"O...Oh."

"When?"

"Um... He... Rune kissed me when we were out yesterday," Cecilia said, hugging herself.

Noa rolled her eyes. "Of course he did."

"I'm sorry, I didn't mean to—"

"*No,*" Noa snapped her fingers, and Cecilia jumped. "First off, you should *never* apologize for something that you didn't do. Second off, tell me to back the hell off—say he's *yours.*"

Cecilia's jaw hung slack, stunned.

"Say it," Noa commanded, taking a step forward.

She shrank back, nearly colliding with the edge of the vanity. "H-he's mine?"

Cringing, Noa's hand went to her head as she turned back to the box. "I'll let that pitiful claim slide for now, I guess..." she mumbled.

"Do you like Rune?"

Noa had to fight a chortle before she glanced back at Cecilia, finding her stricken expression.

Shit. She didn't mean to *scare* her. "What? No—no, no!" she said. "I enjoy *teasing* Rune. Trust me when I say that I'm not attracted to him like you are—like... think of our relationship like what you have with Glacier, I think." Whether or not that was anywhere remotely close to true, she wasn't sure, but Cecilia appeared to relax thanks to that comparison.

"Glacier's like a little brother to me. We've talked, but..." She shook her head. "We've never been romantically interested in each other."

"Then just think of Rune and I like that," Noa said with a slight shrug. "I poke fun at him here and there, that's all. If I felt something for him, I would've acted on it by now." She popped the lid back off the box and tossed it across the bright-white, rumpled comforter. Faint padding against the carpet broke through the silence accompanying her pulling the garment up, where it appeared to pour over her hands like ink.

"Is it pretty?" Cecilia asked.

"Pretty *boring* if you ask me," Noa mumbled, laying it out on the bed.

"Oh, wow..." she said, clearing her throat, "that's—uh—pretty short."

"This is short to you? It's only mid-thigh."

"*Only* mid-thigh? My mother would kill me."

Noa scoffed. "You really need to live a little. Now turn around, and I'll slip it on. I mean, unless you want to watch?" She cocked an eyebrow, feeling the corner of her mouth tick up in amusement.

Cecilia spun around and crossed her arms over her chest with a slight huff. "I'm not into women, Noa."

"Yeah, yeah," she muttered, pulling off her shirt, "You're in a happy relationship, blah, blah, blah..." She tossed it past Cecilia, who jolted, and Noa reigned in a snicker.

Noa shimmied into the black fabric tube, feeling surprised about how well it hugged her body. Despite her earlier complaints, she supposed that it'd be worth wearing once after all—even if it was simply for herself. "All right, I'm decent. Do you mind doing me the favor of zipping me up?"

Cecilia hesitated, testing a slight turn before Noa caught the blue of her eyes, and she saw it wasn't a trick. She fumbled with the zipper for a second and pulled it upward. "Is this actually comfortable?"

"I don't think it's all that bad. You might not like it, though." Noa retrieved a small box out from under the bed and plucked out the pair of high heels Nyx had dropped into her lap earlier. "I don't suppose you're able to illusion my hair along with the makeup..."

"No, but I can go get the styling iron."

"You just don't want me to show off to Rune," Noa said with a fake pout.

"N-no—" she said, her voice rising a pitch or two. "Now, stay." Cecilia held out her hand to emphasize her command before she slipped out the door, leaving Noa to clean off the small side table and chairs cluttered with bags and some of Nyx's equipment.

One hit the floor with a rattling thud, and Noa frowned, leaning down to tug open the zipper. A sweatshirt enveloped most of what had to be some sort of compartmented, plastic case. Noa reached inside to uncover it for a better look and ripped her hand free as soon as the door opened. She cleared her throat, smoothing out her dress as she took her seat, but Cecilia didn't appear to notice her snooping since she was too focused on finding an outlet.

"Do you know what you're doing?" Noa asked while Cecilia began running a brush through her hair.

"Seriously? Out of all the girls here, I assumed that you would be the one that wouldn't know how to style your hair."

Noa huffed. "Well, I *can*, but I just choose not to."

"You know...I'm pretty sure you'd have men falling over themselves to get to you if you dressed up a little more."

"Who says I'm into men?"

The brushing stopped. "Oh—I—um, well—I just assumed because of Rune—"

"Relax, Cecilia," she said, chuckling. "I don't have a preference."

"Like Crow?"

"Oh, gods. Don't compare me to him."

"Well, Rune said he dated a girl, but I always find him staring at guys. And I've seen you flirt with both Nyx and Rune, so..."

She clicked her tongue. "Okay, fine," she said. "Yes, we're the same in that regard, but I don't constantly chase people around like him. I prefer getting to know someone first." The complicated case of Shani floated to the forefront of her thoughts, but they had gotten to know each other in the way they'd *wanted* before revealing who they really were.

"So... do you like Nyx, then?"

Noa hesitated, battling with a flicker of indecision of how to define their relationship. "No... not like that. I think we're just different enough that we'd drive each other insane as a couple... But, enough about me." She waved a hand. "I think you're too good for Rune."

"Noa..."

"I'm serious. You're pretty, you have magic, and you may not be street-smart, but you're at least well-educated. Rune's a conman. I'm fairly sure he grew up poor and stole his entire life."

"I'm not high society, Noa," she said, picking up the curling iron. "I may have been raised alongside it, but I was never one of them. I've lived most of my life as Glacier's shadow, having to keep my guard up. I had to lie about who I was—*what* I was. I put on a mask to protect myself and those who depended on me for survival. I couldn't be myself... And Rune understands what it's like to wear a mask like that too—to pretend that you're tougher or better than what you actually are deep down.

"It turns out that magic doesn't matter. I thought that Astor would solve all my problems somehow. I made myself think that our magic would be enough, but we were too different. He grew up thinking that the only way to get what you want was to simply take it, and that was how he survived. Turns out that I'm just not that kind of person."

"Don't feel guilty about him," Noa said, hearing the *click* of the curling iron as a loose, warm curl of hair tickled the back of her neck. "If I had been there when it happened, I would've killed him. I wish the blood was on my hands instead of yours, at least it'd be just another kill for me."

She grabbed onto the edge of Noa's chair, remaining quiet for a moment like she wasn't quite sure what to say next. "It's... actually funny you say that since when we were picking up your dress, Rune told me he would've done it too."

"Then maybe you two are perfect for each other after all."

Cecilia emitted a nervous chuckle. "Because he'd kill for me?"

"Because you're both liars. You're clearly both stupid enough to commit crimes for each other, and you'd both probably get away with it."

"Gee, thanks... Now I really feel like a good person."

"Oh, please. Cecilia, you're probably one of the nicest people out of everyone here. You're willing to sacrifice your happiness in favor of someone else's."

Cecilia sat the iron down with a sigh and motioned to the mirror. "Have a look in the mirror, and maybe- maybe if you say something nice about my work, I'll decide to let you live."

Noa shook her head and stood, heading for the vanity to take in the image of a still plain-faced version of herself that had a softer look about her. The loose curls framing her face, the velvety black dress, the small glimmer of warmth in her eyes staring back at her...

Think of all the people you could've been. Think of all the joy you've been robbed of.

She prayed Cecilia missed the subtle tick of her jaw before she put her hands on her hips and angled herself in the mirror again. "All right. You win. So, are you going to kill me, or do I get to live for now?" She shot her a teasing smirk, burying all traces of insecurity.

Cecilia looked her up and down with contemplation, tapping a finger to her lips. "You can live. For now." She stood a little straighter. "But Rune's mine."

"Now that's more like it."

Cecilia brightened until her eyes went wide and she shoved her hands in her pockets for her eyeliner pen. "And now let's add some fake makeup and set you loose on the world."

Noa barked out a sharp laugh and held still as she felt the soft press of the pen against her cheek, gliding over her skin in a couple fluid strokes. When she opened her eyes, the mirror revealed their new smoky look and deep, red lips pulling into a grin. "Oh, I *really* like you. You definitely made a mistake settling for Rune. You'd be far better with me."

"Very funny," she said, fidgeting with the pen.

"Now to rub it in Nyx's face before I meet Silvio," Noa said, collecting her shoes and tugging them on. Cecilia followed her around the room as she collected the string of keys off the bed and made her way out.

Rune immediately fixed on them as they filed back out, where he stood in the kitchen, looking a little confused. Cecilia walked a little taller as she approached him, but he narrowed his eyes at Noa instead, who blew Cecilia a kiss and shot him a wink. His eyes went wide and protectively wrapped his arms around her the second she was in reach.

So, Noa sashayed over to the coffee table and dumped her keys onto the mat with flourish. Both Nyx and Glacier looked up, earning a once-over from the former and a stunned, slack-jawed stare from the other. Noa cocked an eyebrow. *Interesting.*

"Good," Nyx said flatly, "I'm glad to see that you actually followed instructions." She pulled the keys off the table and set them next to her bag on the floor. "Now go behave for twenty minutes until the car gets here." She waved her away and returned back to her devices.

Glacier, however, *didn't.*

She prowled back around the coffee table as he ducked his head again, and she crouched down next to him. His body went rigid. "If you like what you see," she whispered. "I'd be happy to show you more."

"*Noa*—" Nyx snapped, and Noa shot back up. "Back the hell off my assistant."

Noa frowned and narrowed her eyes, locking into a stare-down until she huffed and walked away. But not without a small smile creeping onto her face. Perhaps she didn't need Rune after all.

42
VALENTIA ✧ 2704-12-10

NOA

Noa turned the Vision of Valentia over in her hands in the privacy of their train cabin, where it and the sunbursts in the yellow carpeting at her feet became the sole reminders of her time there. Well, *that* and the boy sitting across from her, who'd kept her upright for half the trip between the ferries and water taxis.

Glacier's chin rested in his palm while he scrolled through the tablet on his lap, completely oblivious to her staring. He'd declined Cecilia's offer to abandon her on the way there. Held her hand to and from the museum. Guided her through comms when Nyx had looped the cameras for her to steal the key. Looked at her like she was the prettiest thing in the room—even if she'd somewhat manipulated that sort of response from anyone with a pair of eyes.

She was overthinking things.

The key dropped from her hand, falling into its cousins with a chorus of complaints that caused Glacier to look up. Noa cleared her throat and tucked them under her zipped jacket again. "So... Talie, right?" she asked Nyx, stretching.

Nyx pushed up her glasses, peeling her attention away from her phone. "Correct. We'll need to collect the rest of our commissioned fakes after that."

"Wait, you don't have them all?" Glacier asked.

She shook her head. "It was too much to get all at once. The only extras I have are the ones for Mharu and Amarais. Esmedralia, Jinwon, Miralta, and King's were all scheduled for later, in favor of time. The fact that we've made it halfway through them all is a feat in itself..."

"Gods," Noa mumbled. "Don't tell me I have to go back there."

Nyx's eyes narrowed. "Count yourself lucky I don't have the energy to argue about this right now but believe me when I say we'll discuss this later."

"Yeah, yeah..." Noa pushed herself up, starting for the cabin door and half-turned. Sure enough, Glacier was watching her again. Her hand curled around the handle, and she nodded toward it in invitation. "You coming?"

And he followed.

NYX

Nyx rubbed at her eyes, trying to hold sleep at bay—a difficult task with the low droning hum of the train. More work lay ahead of her in the form of a blank login screen, taunting her, waiting for the hours upon hours of painstaking guessing and checking the credentials. And that didn't even include the final decryption key.

She *should* tell Alyvia she was finally in the possession of Juniper's journal but finding it felt like such minor progress when Alyvia was burying the Intelligence Agency's lead. Then again, was it worth risking her losing the motivation to keep going?

Nyx drummed her fingers on the edge of the tablet and paused as a notification popped up.

> I read that you'd like to talk to one of us. I
> honestly can't imagine why, but I'm willing to
> hear you out.

Her brows slowly knit together as she reread it, realizing it likely came straight from Amarais. She suspended her journal login process and dedicated her resources to pinpointing the sender while she decided how to proceed with her communications.

> I want to help.

Short. Sweet. To-the-point.

> Get in line.

She hummed, pushing down that prickling irritation while the three little dots pulsed for a follow-up message.

> The rest of the applicants say the exact same thing.

Fair.

> I understand. However, the difference between me and them is that I can help from the outside. I have access to resources you don't. All I ask is for the chance to build a little trust between us, and I promise that you won't regret it.

> Then tell me what you can bring to the table.

> I can get you information from just about anywhere and set you up with goods from smugglers. Ask, and I'll make it happen.

There wasn't an immediate reply, making her question if she had put too much out there for her sole lifeline into enemy territory. She tapped her thumb against her lips, formulating a new plan just before text appeared on the screen.

> And what's in it for you?

Nyx closed her eyes, thinking of what angle she should use to hit her mark.

> I have quite a few reasons, including potential business that comes with philanthropic practices among them. I understand that Amarais has been cut off from a lot from which its people could benefit greatly with medical technology as well as magic, both of which I am a proponent for.

> You have a funny way of saying you're affiliated with the mod market.

> The phrase tends to leave a bad taste in peoples' mouths, despite the good it can do for those who are just trying to live in the absence of magic.

Another lull in the conversation left her feeling exhausted by this tedious negotiation. She wasn't quite sure what else to give, hoping that the typed reply wasn't one asking for even more details.

> I'm willing to give you a shot. The others don't care for letting outsiders in, but I see the potential benefits. If you can come through for me, then I can make a case for you. How about let's start with names?

> Fake names, of course.

> I go by Nyx.

> Call me V.

She narrowed her eyes at the letter until a small popup notified her that she at least had a location, which was better than nothing if this V person decided this would be the first and last time they'd talk to her.

> Forgive me, but I don't want to misspeak or anything. I use she/her, you?

> Same.

And that gave her a little more to work off of.

I'll be in touch. Talk to you soon, Nyx.

Then she was gone. Nyx flipped over to her tracking program, finding a small radius marked on Amarais's map. At the very least, she'd gotten enough details to potentially figure out the type of people she was up against, and whether or not they would turn on them or welcome their prince back home with open arms.

43
VALENTIA ✧ 2704-12-11

Crow cursed as he stumbled into the hall windows, a dazed grin on his face and the taste of alcohol lingering on his tongue.

He'd been tempted to steal a couple things from the station until he'd noticed a guy watching him over his tablet in the waiting area. *Fuck that guy and his pinstripe suit,* he'd thought on his way back to join the others in their nook. That much-needed stress release had been ruined. His high dashed.

All the stops in their trip had gotten him was another moment in which he'd been forced to sit on his hands and wait. But then he'd run into him at the train's bar, where he made up for it by buying him a drink. And another. And *another.*

He couldn't remember the guy's name, but he learned that he was traveling to Mharu on business. The first stop of the morning. And then he *winked.* Suddenly, Crow's attitude had changed from suspicious to interested. Free drinks and the satisfaction of being ogled? Check and check.

It'd been worth the trade of keeping his sticky fingers to himself, but the longer he carried on, the further he fell into the depths of despair. Who were any of them kidding about collecting all these keys? They were marching toward their inevitable demise. His name would never be whispered among his peers as an infamous thief like Corrine. He'd be erased from history—a nobody and a traitor left to die at the hands of the Volkov. Praying to Lady Geneviève to forgive him for the sins they called themselves wouldn't save him, despite the distant echo of his father's persistent reminder to ask mercy.

Crow fumbled with his ticket at his cabin door, shoving away all his self-pity before he stumbled inside. His crooked smile faded again when it slid shut behind him, and his shadow fell over the two intertwined forms on one of the pull-out beds. The dim entry night light illuminated the familiar features of his brother's face partially buried in Cecilia's hair. His hand cupped the back of her head, keeping her close like she might slip through his grasp like smoke.

Crow swallowed back the lump in his throat and admonished himself for letting his heart ache. He couldn't place if it was because he was jealous that his brother was being ripped from him or if he was jealous because he so very desperately wanted someone with a deeper connection to get tangled up in as well.

He tugged off his boots and curled up on his bench, plummeting from his recent high to a new, gut-wrenching low. Crow closed his eyes and drifted off to the chant of a silent prayer to a goddess he wasn't sure would bother to hear him, begging for forgiveness he didn't deserve. All for the sake of hoping he could mend his loneliness.

CECILIA

Cecilia excused herself once Nyx joined her and Rune's table near the end of breakfast. She'd only caught the faint mention of Nyx wanting to talk to him privately for a few minutes, so she'd taken advantage of the extra time by grabbing a bottle of water and a pill packet on her way back to the cabin.

Sure enough, Crow was still curled up on the bench, his fingers twitching slightly from where his hand peeked out from the edge of his pillow. She crept over, crouched down next to him, and tapped the shade to let in the light, rewarding her with a near-immediate grimace.

"Shit..." he croaked.

"Rough night?"

He squinted, holding up his arm to block the sun. "No more *light*."

"I, um... I got you some medicine. I figured you might be a little worse for wear."

Crow propped himself up, eyeing her suspiciously. "Why?"

"Consider it... a peace offering," she said, staring down at the packet in her hand. "I don't want to fight over which one of us Rune prioritizes. I... feel like I've been doing some of that myself lately, which isn't exactly fair to Glacier either. We all need each other right now, so..." She held it out to him.

He paused before he swung his legs over the edge and took it. "Thank you." He sounded nearly identical to Rune when he'd said it, most of the roughness traded for tired sincerity. "You know..." He chuckled as he pulled the water bottle from her other hand and knocked back the pills. "I thought you and Glacier were together when we first picked you up. Is a prince not good enough for you?"

Cecilia's face heated. "Wh-what? N-no! He's practically my brother. I-I mean, we talked about it once, but..."

"But *what?* You're pretty. I don't get what's going on here."

"I-I, um—Thanks?"

"Did you turn him down, then? Because of age or something? Hey, as long as he's over seventeen, you can legally tap that—"

"*Ew*—no. And *no* I didn't turn him down—"

He guffawed. "He turned *you* down? Holy shit."

"That's not exactly—" She sighed and bit her lip. "It... was a mutual agreement that if we didn't have any other options by the time Glacier was a month away from turning twenty, then we'd get married. We thought that if he took my name that we might be able to give Louis what he wanted, and maybe he'd spare us. So, a platonic marriage. That's all."

Crow tilted his head. "So... Wait... Is he gay?"

"What? No! I—" She shook her head. "Well, I don't think he is, but he's never really shown interest in anyone that I can think of." The fact that Noa sprung to the forefront of her mind left an unsettling sensation in the pit of her stomach.

He hummed, wiping the beads of sweat off his water bottle. "And you're saying he's single..."

Oh no.

"Wh—" She shot upright as the door slid open again, and Rune stepped inside.

"Are you two getting along in here?"

"Yeah, *fantastically,*" Crow said with a devious grin. He capped his bottle and let it roll down the bench until it hit the cabin wall. "Now if you don't mind, I'm going to go win a prince."

"Crow!" Cecilia cried.

"Crow, I'm pretty sure that prince you're going for isn't going to be interested," Rune said as he began pulling his bag out of the overhead compartment.

"Yeah, we'll see about that," he shot over his shoulder on his way out, letting the door snap shut behind him.

Cecilia stood with her mouth hanging open. "I—You—Can't you do something about him?" She motioned toward the door.

"Don't worry," he said, glancing at her with a teasing smirk, "I won't have to do anything with Noa keeping him under constant watch. He'll be back once he gets his ass beat."

GLACIER

Glacier flipped through screen after screen of the Taliean museum blueprints Nyx had given them in preparation of their final key theft before the end of the year. He stifled a yawn as he marked another route with the stylus, silently begging for Noa to return to the booth with some coffee and hot food for their early lunch. The pen clicked against the table when he paused to rub his eyes, catching a glimpse of the fleeting Valentian countryside.

His hands pulled away at the sound of denim scratching against the seat fabric. Crow reclined next to him, an arm thrown over the back of the seat while the fingers of the other tapped against the table.

Glacier frowned, trying to puzzle out the reason for the smug expression on his face. "What are you...?"

They both jumped at the slam of a tray against the table, rattling the plates and sloshing coffee over the sides of the white ceramic mugs. Noa towered over it with eyes narrowed to slits. "Don't think I don't know what you're trying to do."

Crow choked out a nervous laugh. "I-I'm not sure what you're—"

"Get up."

He scrambled up from his seat, and Noa seized him by the collar. "Now," she said with a smile that didn't reach her eyes, "let me make myself abundantly clear. Back. Off. Understood?"

He nodded furiously.

"Good." She let go.

Crow cleared his throat and straightened his jacket, twitching as he started a sideways shuffle out of the car without taking his eyes off her. She waited, staring him down from where she continued to stand at the end of the table until he disappeared, and then took her seat opposite Glacier.

"What... was that about?" Glacier asked, craning to peer over the seatback.

"Oh, nothing," she said, a little extra cheer lacing her voice as she set a plate of bruschetta in front of him. "Any progress on the thing Nyx gave you?"

He shook his head while she wiped off the water glasses and coffee mugs.

"When did you fall asleep last night?"

"Maybe 3:30? I woke up around 6:10 or so, but I couldn't really get myself to drift off again..." Not that he'd tried all that hard after bickering with Kat.

"You could've woken me up, you know," she said, scowling.

"Well, you were exhausted, and I didn't want to bother you."

"Oh, please. I can wake up whenever. If you can't sleep, then we can at least get an early breakfast instead of a weird... brunch thing..." Her face scrunched up as she eyed their vegetable-covered flatbreads. "I don't even think you can consider this brunch."

"It doesn't always have to be a group activity."

"What, you don't like spending time with me all of a sudden?" she asked, putting on a show with a fake pout.

"And here I thought you wanted to get rid of me," he teased.

"I mean," she said, giving a lazy, half-shrug, "I could always just drop you off in Miralta on the way."

"Like you'd survive the boat ride to Talie."

She rolled her eyes, opting to finally take a bite of her meal.

"Hey Noa... have you been to Talie before?"

"No," she said, chewing and reaching for her water. "I've read enough about it. I've certainly seen plenty of news in relation to it. I've just never actually visited because there was usually another sent in my stead."

A different Volkov.

"Speaking of... Is there a reason why we haven't run into them again yet?" It'd been something nagging at the back of his mind each time they'd passed through another country, imagining the Volkov stationed some-where nearby, lying in wait. While something in his gut told him King's Republic, another part of him dismissed it entirely because of how unfazed Noa appeared to be when Nyx had told her they'd be passing through one last time before the end of the year.

"I'm... not sure. It could be that we've simply been moving too much, or maybe they're rethinking how to approach the situation after I dealt with Ezra... I don't think they're in a huge rush to get rid of you since you're technically dead, according to all records right now." She absently drummed her fingers on the table and sighed. "I have to agree that it's rather unsettling since I assumed they'd turn more aggressive because you're with me... But they'll eventually make their way out of their hole again, so I guess we should just be thankful for the reprieve in the meantime while we try to collect the keys."

He nodded absently, despite the unsatisfied feeling washing over him. "I guess... that still leaves us with the question of where the Vault is, assuming we have enough time."

"Yeah... I still have no idea where the hell to start with that. I'll take just about any suggestion at this point."

Glacier sat back, staring out at the last of the fruit trees giving way to smaller hills. "Well... King's Republic or Miralta would probably be the best options, right? After all, King's Republic was literally named for the King of Avaria, and then the Messenger was supposedly Miraltan, right?"

"True... But both of those places aren't exactly *small*. Sure, Miralta's not nearly as big as King's, but that's a lot of distance to cover in a search. Would you hide it in Corris? But then you have to think about *where* in Corris. What about Kingsheart?" She shrugged. "I'm not sure of anything historically important enough that might stand out in either of those places. It'd have to be something that you could place the keys into—like a monument or something, but I don't recall ever reading or seeing anything that would fit the part..."

"Then... what about Tabir? They're fairly similar to Miralta when it comes to magic, right? They have a lot of older, preserved structures and ruins. Not to mention lots of confusing streets to get lost in. I can imagine that there would be plenty of places to hide the Vault there."

"Maybe... Honestly, I don't think this'll do us much good yet, all things considered, but at least we have some ideas. For now, let's just focus on Talie and take it from there."

44
MHARU ✧ 2704-12-12

NYX

V, Juniper, or Kole.

Decisions, decisions...

Nyx drummed her fingers against her thigh and stared at the tablet resting on her lap, half-obscured by sunlight pouring through the cabin window. After the rabbit hole of Amarais information she'd been digging through the past couple days, she'd let it slip to Alyvia that she'd found the journal. Despite her own reservations, Alyvia had been ecstatic, pummeling her with additional questions after her brief check-in until Nyx had to remind her to stick to her end of the deal. At least she was happy. For now.

Then there'd been her brief, private chat with Rune, which she assumed he'd relayed to his brother by now. He'd taken the news that they'd been spotted by their former employer rather well, all things considered, and he'd even asked if there was anything he could do to assist. It'd been the perfect lead-in into asking him to compile as much about Wilton Arrington as possible, which would hopefully give her enough to start sorting through this man's dirty digital laundry.

She thought back to her talk with Daxton and how he was convinced that Arrington was somehow involved in sending the Volkov after him. But then why hadn't he done the same with the twins? There were no signs of that. The only reason she could conjure was the fact that the two of them might be too much of a moving target for the Volkov to handle, but that didn't sit all that well with her. Or perhaps he feared the information they might have, and needed them alive to determine how much damage had been done...

Nyx hummed, noting that Alyvia was dangerously close to striding down Daxton's path. The less she knew from here on out, the better. The girl just needed to keep her head down and sweep a few things under the rug, so long as it didn't get a target on her back. Nyx could keep her mouth shut to stave off that domino effect.

She tapped her tablet to check the status of the journal again, finding it still locked tight before she tabbed back to her notes.

V.

Nyx sighed and stared at the short list under the pseudonym. If she chased this name, it could lead her to information on both Juniper and Kole, so she skimmed it over once more. Her small, snipped screenshot of her pinged radius declared that V had to be somewhere along the southern border of Amarais, which explained why she wasn't opposed to the proposal of using a smuggler. But how likely was it the rest of the rebels were camping out there with her?

She needed a name. She needed *V's* name in order to know who and what she was truly up against. A glance at her old portal notes gave her a bit of a clue as she noted a user tunneling their signal through Synos, tracing back to around the same area V currently resided in. It was a moderator account—one whose posts bled into risky behavior that other forum-goers commented as dangerous and unnecessary.

Nyx flipped back to the pinpointed signal again, checking login patterns. Her glasses slipped down her nose as she ran through the years of encrypted data pouring in and out of that location. Fewer and fewer outbound messages trickled out until she hit a log with none at all. Fourteen years back.

Nyx paused, her fingers hovering over the device with a cocked brow. V didn't integrate with society. V was an outcast. V could very well be used to the lifestyle of a rebel... A *criminal.* She flipped back to the Amarais criminal database, vaguely recalling a few individuals with warrants for their arrest, specifically one out of a pair of siblings who'd been charged with harboring a Miraltan Mage soon after Louis had gained control.

```
Family name: Valeria
Occupation: Royal Assistant Tutor
Current Age: 33
```

V for Valeria. Someone who had been on the run for fourteen years. Someone with a *very* valid reason to enter the resistance with her connection to the late King Cyrus. Someone who harbored Mages in the past— potentially a present-day people smuggler. After all, Glacier's mother had to have come from *somewhere.*

So why'd her brother end up arrested when she somehow escaped? They'd both been housing a Miraltan Mage, which made it reasonable to assume they had a connection to an Amaraian Mage...

Nyx stared at the empty seat across from her. *Wait...*

Was *V* the Amaraian Mage? Her brother was labeled as being imprisoned, which they wouldn't do to a Mage. A Mage would be dead.

Nyx leaned back in her seat and closed her eyes as a new series of questions formed in this ever-connecting web. So, did her brother stay behind to hold Louis at bay when the walls of the palace were closing in on them? Or were they somehow involved in Cyrus's death? Was it possible that V had turned on him and left her brother to take the fall?

"Shit," Nyx mumbled, scrubbing at her face.

The element of danger lingering in the forefront left her grinding her teeth. She needed *more.* If they were going to have Glacier unlock the vault, there had to be zero doubt in her mind that these people didn't have any remaining animosity toward Cyrus or his son.

45

KING'S REPUBLIC ✦ 2704-12-14

GLACIER

Dust lined the shelves, objects and trinkets sat tipped over, and the side tables were scuffed at the corners like they'd been bumped into one too many times with other furniture. Glacier swallowed back that overwhelming feeling of sadness crawling up his throat, threatening to blur his vision through the blue-tinted lens of the room. No orange, crackling hue from the fireplace this time. Instead, he remained seated, waiting for someone who never greeted him.

Empty. Broken. *Lonely.*

He pushed himself up from the sofa and straightened out the rug the best he could. Another glance around the room left him overwhelmed, so he sat on the floor for a few minutes and stared off at nothing.

Kat had probably given up on him. Not that he could blame her. He couldn't fight the feeling that now wasn't the time for soul-searching. He had to press forward. He shouldn't be focusing on himself because the world didn't revolve around him. It only worked against him. It always had. It always will.

Pick yourself up. Stop feeling sorry for yourself. No one else is going to come along and help you.

Glacier grabbed the arm of the nearby chair and pulled himself to his feet. "Kat?" he called out on the room's threshold, letting her name float out into the hallway. No reply.

He rubbed his arms as he passed the wall of windows, avoiding the stillness outside. Each glimpse of himself managed to illuminate every imperfection. He smacked into the office doors and forced out a shuddering sigh before throwing his body into them. Light flooded the hallway, but there was no one inside.

"Kat?" he called again, spinning around to peer down toward the attic entry. No steps.

Glacier chewed on his lip, poking his head into the rooms he passed. All of them left undisturbed. All of them coated in a fine layer of dust.

"If you're hiding, it's not funny. I... I've been thinking about my questions. I might have one." A lie. But that's all he knew how to do now.

When he was asked if he wanted to talk, he lied. When someone pried into his feelings, he lied. When anyone asked if he was okay, he lied.

All he had to do was shut up and help. Stop adding to the burden of those around him—

Who?

He stopped, his boots scuffing against the rug as the world around him tilted. His head spun, and he overcorrected, smacking a hand against the windowpane. The hallway distorted into a wall of windows resembling a train car corridor flying past snowcapped mountains, its emergency alarms blaring in his ears.

Glacier stumbled the other direction like what he imagined being tossed around on a rocky boat felt like, catching sight of his hands coated in blood. A trail of it smeared along the window. The snow evaporated to darkness and the darkness was cut through with fire. His breath caught as he followed the red line to a silhouette blocking his path.

A quiet, raspy chuckle slipped through the intruder's lips as the flames barely penetrated the shadows hiding his face. But Glacier could only stare at the book dangling from his fingertips, convinced it would fall to the floor any second now.

He blinked and it all vanished in an instant, despite how hard his heart still hammered in his chest. The sound of the front door thudding closed and muffled footfalls against the entry carpet sent Glacier jogging down the hall.

Kat.

"You could've left a note—" He stopped short when the entrant came into view: a man dressed in a black peacoat lightly dusted with snow. His blue eyes—the same ocean blue as Glacier's own—stared back at him, crinkling at the corners with that small spark of joy. A spitting image of the photo resting on the desk in the office

"Dad?"

"Hello, Glacier."

He should be happy, but instead, he was confused. "Where's... Kat?"

"She decided to go out for a bit and asked if I would keep you company. She thought that I might be able to help clear your head."

Glacier stared back, unsure what to say. It stung to hear she really had left him, but his dad was standing here, ready to talk.

"How about let's take a walk?" He motioned to the entry closet.

Glacier nodded and shuffled over to retrieve his coat, tugging it on as they filed outside onto the snow-covered path. They took the steps down the slope, making their way around the back of the house into the woods. He inhaled the scent of evergreen and pine—the scent of home. His footsteps slowed, taking his time and enjoying the bite of the cold against his skin.

"I don't know what I'm supposed to do," Glacier finally whispered. "Kat keeps talking like I'm supposed to know something, but..."

"I believe that's because you're still trying to fit yourself into a mold of something you're not, Glacier."

His father came to a stop, and Glacier turned to peer up at him, still feeling just as small as a six-year-old with the few extra centimeters he had on him.

"You're not supposed to be like the kings or queens before you. You're supposed to be *you*."

Glacier scoffed. He certainly was *himself*, but that seemed like something far from desirable. "How am I supposed to be as good as you when Kat is so much bett—"

"You won't be as good as me because you'll be better than I ever was. And it was never Kat's responsibility to take over Amarais."

Glacier released a quiet, bitter laugh. "Just look at me... How am I supposed to guide a country that sees me as the enemy? I don't look the part, let alone *feel* the part, but I don't belong in Miralta either. I don't seem to belong anywhere." He blew out a puff of cold smoke.

"Do you remember when Mrs. Angelis taught you *The Origin of Magic?*"

"What does this have to do with—"

"Just give me a moment, I'll get to that," he replied, brushing the dotting of snowflakes from his blond hair. "Everyone assumes that the Messenger is from what we now know as Miralta, correct?"

Glacier hesitantly nodded, unsure of where this was going.

"Tell me, where is the King from?"

"King's Republic," he automatically answered. "That's where he held his court and everything, right? That's why the Republic is a melting pot of people."

"Then what does your average Republican look like?"

He opened his mouth to speak but closed it again once he realized there wasn't an answer.

"Well?" his father asked with a touch of amusement.

"Well... I guess there's... not really an average Republican 'look,'" he admitted. "They're from all over... Is this supposed to make me feel better or something?"

His father chuckled. "If it did, then that was simply a bonus. My point is that the Republic didn't exist until the King established it, which means that he was from somewhere else. So, let's return to the original question: where was the *King* from?"

Glacier stuffed his hands in his coat pockets and dipped his chin into his collar. If it wasn't Miralta or King's, then that left eleven other countries. Corvia, Mharu, Tabir, Valentia, Esmedralia, Roth, Jinwon, Bellegarde, Astravny, Talie, and finally Amarais. There were some that stood out as more likely candidates than others, but he felt foolish taking a wild guess.

"I... don't know."

His father smirked, placing a hand against his own chest. "The King was from Amarais."

Glacier scowled up at him, shaking his head. "That's not—Why would you think that? Miralta and Amarais have always hated each other. Why would you assume that when the Messenger was Miraltan?"

"That's a fairly compelling argument for what I'm saying, Glacier."

"I don't understand."

He looked up at the dark sky, almost like he could see the history beyond. "There was a point in time where both Miralta and Amarais had no ill-will toward each other," he began, dropping his head again. "After all, there was no magic to spark the current animosity between the two countries. And neither officially existed yet since they were little more than groupings of similar people. Their sole focus was surviving against the creatures that sought to destroy them, regardless of who they were or where they were from. So, all those people stood at each other's sides in solidarity."

He started strolling down the path again, slipping his hands in his pockets with Glacier jogging to catch up to his side. "And, eventually, they won. It was a gradual victory, but they had united with magic as their weapon until it started to gradually fade as well. Unease followed, which brought tension, and later disagreements. Some chose to hold onto the fear of magic falling into the wrong hands, seeing how the desire to acquire it had killed the King in the first place. Why wouldn't Amarais recoil at the pressure from Miralta to aid them in trying to keep it? For the latter, it was a symbol of hope, and soon it became an omen of destruction for the former."

"And you think I'm going to somehow be able to fix it?" Glacier asked. "To undo all those years of hate by just being *me?*"

"I think you're the start of mending what's broken," he said, with a lighthearted chuckle. "There are so many people out there that are just as tired of the fighting as you are—more than you know. It's why Kat wanted you to be a symbol of peace, but I'm asking you to go beyond that. I know it seems like a lot, but you're well on your way. Remember that you're *more* than Amaraian, so you won't ever fit the mold of your predecessors. Embrace that difference. Don't let all of this stand in the way of your place."

He cut in front of Glacier, placing his hands on his shoulders. "You're my son. You were born for this. Don't you ever forget that."

NOA

Noa trudged down the uneven pavement, brushing against Kole's coat every few meters while they endured Ezra's complaints about finding jobs. It'd been the task Myron had given them before leaving to run his own errands. She wasn't even sure what sort of jobs she'd be able to get when she wasn't even ten years old yet, but she guessed that plenty of people were willing to throw a few extra credits her way to run deliveries.

At least, she *hoped*. Seeing the flickering and dying shop signs, the broken and covered-up windows, and the notices of new addresses, she became less and less certain of her potential success. The few well-kept storefronts managed to hold their own in this part of town, though their displays were cloudy and dirty from the snow and salt. She squinted to try to make out if any lights were on through the large windows they passed.

"Just pick a place, Ezra," Kole said with a sigh. "It doesn't matter. It's just credits. I heard that there's a guy in town who's pretty generous with deliveries—"

"It's all a waste of time," Ezra snapped. "Money means nothing when Myron's just going to give us whatever we need."

"I think this is more about responsibility," Kole said. "So, let's just do what he asks and stop complaining."

Noa rolled her eyes and glanced down an alleyway, stopping while they continued forward, absorbed in their bickering. She jogged across the street, her boots scraping against the shifted pavement of the slim offshoot, slowing when the gold-foil name overtop the blacked-out windowpanes caught her eye. The scuffed, looping script read, '*Book Repair &* *Restoration.*'

"It looks abandoned."

She spun around to find Kole staring up at the lettering with a frown, and she turned back to cup her hands around her face against the glass, searching for any signs of life. Noa could only make out dusty floors and tall, metal-caged bookcases with old-fashioned locks. "Maybe it's not…" she mumbled, the puff of her breath obscuring her view. "Wouldn't they have put up a sign?"

She glanced back at him again, where he chewed his lip in contemplation. Ezra remained visible through the alley gap on the other side of the street with his arms folded over his chest and a prominent scowl on his face.

"Come on," Kole finally said with a hint of unease. "We should just go talk to the other guy I mentioned. They'll be easy jobs, I promise. Don't you think that this place is a little creepy anyway?"

"I'm not scared of some book shop, Kole," she replied with a huff. "And I don't want to deliver stuff with Ezra. I'd rather do something else."

He hesitated.

"I'll find something else if this place is closed," she said. "If I *really* can't find anything else, then I'll come find you."

"Fine. Just don't get into trouble. I don't want Myron to be upset." The warning in his tone sounded like a parent talking to a child, but he jogged back across the street. Ezra smirked when Noa didn't follow.

She tried her best to brush it off, giving the door a shove instead. To her surprise, it glided open. Dust motes stirred around her as she stepped inside, her ears perking up at the bell ringing out. Covered shelves were lined up in rows, some grated, others solidly protected, and tools were scattered all over the front desk. She wandered over to one of the caged shelves, hooking her fingers through the metal squares to glimpse the books inside.

Noa could only describe the feeling as wonderment, standing face-to-face with real, paper books. Their contents unedited and uncensored, unlike some of the reading homework she dealt with for online schoolwork.

She'd always attempted to tilt the screen a certain way or try to rub the black bars away in vain.

"Hello there."

She jumped and whirled around, taking in a man behind the counter, wearing a frayed wool sweater over a collared dress shirt. She swallowed, composing her reason for why a nine-year-old was suddenly intruding in his shop. "Do you need help with deliveries or errands?" she blurted.

The man made a noise like he was stifling a laugh. The dim light of the room obscured his features enough that she found it difficult to gauge his reaction, especially after relying on that skill to handle Myron—a habit that bled into every conversation she had now.

"Funnily enough, I was considering putting up a sign for something just like that. I'd just assumed that no one would see it."

Noa brightened, excited at the prospect of working around so many books. He leaned forward, resting his forearms against the desk as she approached. She guessed he was around Myron's age, somewhere in his thirties with short, messy brown hair, but his eyes... His eyes were nearly white and unmoving, even when she swayed to test his sight.

"What's your name?" he asked.

"Noa," she replied, hearing the confusion in her own voice. "You're blind."

He emitted a hearty laugh, and her eyebrows shot up in surprise.

"Oh, that I am, Noa. Which is why I think you'll be rather useful. Though, I wouldn't say I'm completely useless just yet. Call me Lazarus. It's a pleasure to finally meet you."

In an instant, the world lurched forward, propelling Noa through heaps of memories. Her mind snagged on hushed goading between her and Kole as they climbed out one of the mansion's back windows in the middle of the night. Then a sudden, flickering recollection of him having to hold her back from fighting Ezra and tasting blood when she was shoved down into the snow.

She snapped to when she was nearly fourteen, asking Lazarus if he was a Seer shortly after reading books upon books about magic that had been tucked away into the recesses of his shop. It was then that she'd fully understood that even though he hadn't physically seen her the day they met, he was still able to see the entirety of the world around him with his magic.

Time shot forward again like a train tearing toward the next station, remembering how she threw knives at targets over and over again until she had blisters before swapping to the other hand. Then she was back in the shop, letting Lazarus guide her sore fingers in the mending of book pages. She felt more pride in her gentle teacher's approving nods than the same gestures from Myron, so cold in comparison.

Noa stood in front of the final addition to the Volkov, a frail-looking Jinwonese girl with long, inky black hair and dark eyes filled with loss—someone she wanted to shelter and protect. Something that she discovered wasn't necessarily needed in a blur of motion at the dinner table caused by one of Ezra's snide remarks, sending her lunging toward him.

A book was gently shoved into Noa's hands, followed by Lazarus's instruction for her to read it. *The Origin of Magic*. She had stayed up late reading it in her room with a chair shoved under her doorknob just in case she fell asleep with it lying out, worried that Kole would find it—scared that she would lose his trust or hurt him in her conquest for knowledge.

"It's yours," Lazarus had told her when she tried to return it.

So she pried up a floorboard under her bed and hid it there—a secret that she would sleep over. A secret that she was haunted by some nights and comforted by others.

The sensation of drowning washed over her a moment before finding her hands slick with blood, telling herself over and over again that she wouldn't cry as Lazarus shoved the box into her hands. "You were made for so much more than what you've been told. You were born for this."

His final words before the noise of the memories silenced, and she finally jolted awake.

46

KING'S REPUBLIC ✦ 2704-12-14

GLACIER

Glacier opened his eyes to the cabin seatback colored by faint moonlight, transitioning its dull gray to near-white. He shifted a little in his groggy state, tugging at a blanket that wouldn't budge. He twisted around, squinting to make out a silhouette perched on the edge of his bed in the dark.

Oh gods.

A hand clapped over his mouth. "If you scream and wake Nyx, I'll kick your ass."

Noa.

He slapped her arm away, sitting up as she motioned for him to follow her into the hall. The pitch-black outlines of forests and far-off twinkling city lights sent a shiver through him, reminded of something buried in the recesses of his dreams. He shook it away.

"What the hell is wrong with you?" he hissed, rounding on her. "I was sleeping."

"Yeah, well, I *can't.* I'm freaking the hell out. I feel like I'm starting to lose my mind." Noa paced back and forth, throwing her arms over top of her head with clenched fists half-wrapped in her sleeves. "I don't know how the hell I'm going to manage another damn boat ride, let alone the ride back. I don't know where the hell Kole is lurking. I'm having nightmares about Lazarus dying over and over again, and—" Her arms dropped, and she collapsed against the wall. "How the hell am I supposed to manage all of this?"

He hated how relatable that was. "It's okay. Calm down."

Her head thumped against the window. "I'm... I'm just waiting for everything bad to happen at once. I'm not even close to being ready for whatever's coming. I keep getting this horrible feeling that maybe I'm wrong about everything... About the keys, and..."

"We chose to join you, Noa. You're not forcing us to stay."

"But I'm the cause. I'm the one responsible for all of this, and if something goes wrong, it's all on me." Her eyes snapped to his, where he could make out every insecurity and fear weighing on him as well.

Glacier leaned against the wall next to her, rubbing his hands together. "Noa, you were right when you said that everyone here had nothing left to lose. None of us have anywhere else we can go. So, even if this leads us to a dead-end... I'm honestly glad that I agreed to come along. I would've never seen anything outside of Amarais if you hadn't shown up. I would have either died in that ballroom or somewhere else in the palace when the supposed rebels found us. We wouldn't be here. Cecilia and Rune wouldn't have ever met, and I personally can't imagine never meeting any of you. Honestly... it's weird to think that this is the closest I've been to having friends. I'm sure that sounds kind of sad, but..."

She slid down the wall, bumping shoulders with him. They locked eyes again, and her mouth quirked into a slight smile. "I think you need higher standards then, Your Highness."

"Maybe," he said, "Or maybe I'm not quite who I thought I was."

ALYVIA

Alyvia hunched over her desk, speeding past the footage frames of the twins exiting Southaven. Her pulse picked up with it—blood pounding in her ears like an alarm of guilt.

You're exhausted, she told herself. *You missed it because you've been working too late.*

Half-true, but then again, she could have written a script to narrow down her search after she realized just how much work she'd be doing. But her supervisors didn't need to know that, not when Alyvia was on the verge of being rewarded with answers regarding her aunt's disappearance.

It'd begun consuming her thoughts the minute Nyx told her she'd recovered the journal and asked if she would know what the encryption key might be. Alyvia had winced and stared at her contacts, her thumb hovering over her father's name one too many times to ask him if he'd know. She didn't need to bring him into this. Not when what she was doing was potentially treasonous. Instead, she'd have to make an educated guess.

Well, once Nyx got to that point. *If* she got to that point.

But... who was to say that she wasn't stringing Alyvia along?

She stood, her chair scraping against the floor. Her pulse could be felt in her fingertips as she tugged on the hem of her blazer and started into Shane's office.

His head popped up from the mess of synthetic paper scattered over his desk, his eyes brightening. "Did you find something?"

This was her chance to come clean. She could walk away from the idea that assisting criminals would somehow be worth it in the end. Alyvia shut the door behind her, her hand coming away slick. "Shane, I... I have no idea where they went."

Shane's face fell, adding to the mounting frustration with how much she'd been taken for granted the past few weeks.

"Look," she said as calmly as possible, "I'm trying. I really am, and—and honestly, I feel like I'm being punished for doing my job. I found them when no one else did, and now I'm working myself to death trying to find out where they went with one hand tied behind my back because I can't access any additional information to help me determine where they might go, what they might do, or how they act. They could have taken a boat to

Mharu or swung around to Corvia or just went out to sea to take a gods-damned pleasure cruise."

Shane stood, pushing his rolled sleeves back up as he rounded the desk and leaned against it to stand face-to-face with her. "It's okay, Alyvia." The way he said it was much more sympathetic than she'd expected. "I get it. I'm not upset with you. I've been doing what I can to cut through the red tape for you too, trust me."

"Short of sleeping in the office, I'm not sure what else I can do at this point. Not that I've really been sleeping anyway between staying late and getting in early. Even then, I'm not entirely convinced that I'm making any progress." Tears welled up in her eyes, causing him to squirm.

"Jinko and Arrington may not appreciate what you do like I do because they simply don't understand how hard you work. I want you to under-stand that your work isn't going unnoticed, and I'm putting in a good word for you to give you a little more recognition. Just keep doing what you're doing, but don't wear yourself out. There's no use in pushing your-self so hard if you start slipping. Why... why don't you take a half-day? Just go home in an hour and relax."

She blinked. "W-what? No, I still have reports to do, and—"

"I'll give them to someone else. Gods only know that some of these people are only good for doing mindless reports anyway. Your time is far more valuable, and you need to recharge. Take the half-day. We'll be fine for four hours without you."

Hesitantly, she nodded. "O-okay. I'll finish up what I can and follow up before I leave then."

"Good," he said with a warm smile. "Enjoy the rest of the day and get some rest. I'll see what I can do while you're out to help you tomorrow. Don't worry about anything until then."

"Thank you," she replied, awkwardly hovering for a moment before she opened the door and started for her desk, feeling even guiltier than she had before.

47

MIRALTA ✧ 2704-12-15

GLACIER

Glacier stared down at his ID, absently flicking it against his thigh while he and Noa sat side-by-side on the bench near the harbor. Miraltan again, but with a new name and the instruction to keep him and Cecilia separated during boarding to avoid any suspicion.

The biting cold of sea air brought homesickness and dread. But home wasn't what he thought it was anymore. His home was gone—becoming an ever-shifting landscape that left his stomach knotted when he'd glimpsed the coastal snow. He stared down at his boots with one last snap of his ID against his denim pants, where his breath curled out from his lips like in his dreams and their escape from the palace.

Where he would've died.

Noa elbowed his side. "You look stressed."

"I, um... don't really feel comfortable being so close to Amarais."

She leaned in a little closer. "Hey, no one's going to recognize you," she said, giving his upper arm a reassuring squeeze, "They'll just assume you're another Miraltan and move on. Even if they notice your blue eye, the last thing they'll think is that you're *from* Amarais."

Glacier remained silent, unable to make himself say that wasn't what he'd meant. They were going fast—*too fast*, just like he'd told her back on the train, but that also meant they were that much closer to him going back and facing a fate he thought he'd escaped. He preferred the warm, confusing embrace of his dreams over the impending doom of his current reality—stuck between death at the hands of the Volkov and death at the hands of his *people*.

Noa nudged him again. "Nyx is motioning for us to join her in boarding. Let's hurry up and get this over with." She stood, pulling her hands from her jacket pockets as he rose to walk with her.

When they made it inside, they passed through tall archways to the large spiral staircase, trimmed in rose gold. Watered-down seafoam-colored carpeting led them down the hallway like the seashells dotting the edges marked their path. Doors came and went until Nyx stopped in front of one and handed him a key. Then Noa, pointing her to a door across the hall as he vanished inside.

The door shut behind him, and he dropped his bag on the floor. It was a little larger than the suite's tiny cabins, complete with its own private bathroom and a larger closet—not that he would need it. He tugged off his jacket and boots, throwing them near his bag before crawling into bed.

A half-hour ticked by in the midst of their departure while he watched the sun dip past the water, changing the gold reflection an inky black. Sleep refused to take him, despite slowing his breath and closing his eyes. All of his hard work was undone with the faint tapping on his door.

Noa stood in the dim hallway, rubbing her arms. "I don't want to be alone," she whispered—an echo of what had been left unsaid when he confronted her on the last cruise.

So, Glacier stepped aside, inviting her in. He shaded the window and lifted the covers for her, where she climbed in next to him. Her back against his. And then they both fell asleep.

NOA

Snow crunched under Noa's boots and the still air bit at her cheeks. Every step came with uncertainty of where she was going, decked out in her white, tactical gear—a mimicry of Myron striding ahead of her with their hoods down.

Her face had to be turning red by now with the cold, but he kept walking, not bothering to look back and check on her. Not like he ever had anyway. Only Lazarus had ever sat her down in a chair in his cubby of a dining room with burnt-out bulbs she'd slowly replaced with the credits he paid her, along with the open cabinets she organized and padded after his jokes about catching his wrists on the edges. "There's something bothering you," he'd said time and time again, always getting her noncommittal answers about fixing a part of the workshop or its attached apartment. At least he'd asked.

Myron, however, had shaken her awake this morning without a word and shoved her coat in her arms. An unspoken command it was time to go. Just like how she'd woken up to creaking in the hallway when he'd done the same to Ezra, and a year later when she stayed awake into the early hours of the morning until he collected Kole. Not even a whisper of 'happy birthday' before they'd set out, despite the milestone that came with it.

Happy birthday, Noa, she thought to herself. *You made it to twenty. The world is finally yours to take.*

Right after she took this test—whatever it was.

When she followed for Ezra's, Myron had taken him to the edge of the woods and pointed into the dense expanse of trees with the instruction to survive the night. She scoffed from where she'd crouched down in the brush, but Ezra hesitated, shifting his footing like he might ask a question before Myron snapped his fingers and pointed again. She'd supposed his pause was warranted since he hadn't had any survival gear on him.

Ezra had come back wearing a half-burnt coat with a chunk missing thanks to a wolf—or so he'd claimed—which had been enough to send a chill through Noa.

So, she followed Kole the following year, feeling confused when Myron had taken him to a secluded, snowy field. He'd tossed him a dagger, walked several paces away, and declared a duel. Kole's eyes had gone wide, his grip on the weapon awkward, even after the fighting had started. Every step back triggered a growl from Myron—every dodge painted as an insult. But Noa knew that's how Kole fought. Defense over offense, to the bitter end.

When Kole lost, and they returned, Myron shoved him forward, issuing the first hierarchical challenge. That was when Noa had found her motivation to pass whatever test of wills and strengths Myron would throw at her because she wanted to stand at the top. To beat Ezra. To claim her title as the deadliest among them, right under the one man she wanted to challenge more than anything.

That's why she frowned when he stopped at the edge of a lake, frozen over and dusted with snow. "Why... are we here?"

He sighed—the sound carrying that all-too-familiar hint of irritation. "Because Noa, you're going to walk across."

She raised an eyebrow, expecting him to say more. When he didn't, she laughed. Was this a joke? There was barely anything to it—all she had to do was take it slow and watch her footing. This wasn't even a challenge—

"*Noa*," he growled, silencing her.

She hopped down onto the thick edge of the ice, testing her weight with each step forward. Each small moan and pop turned into a thrill, keeping her moving toward the opposing shoreline.

Keep your hands steady.

Ugh. Why don't I leave the page-mending to you while I do the book-binding?

She smirked, almost like Lazarus was whispering in her ear as she crossed the halfway point. The ice groaned, her stomach lurched, and she skidded to a stop. A second shadow loomed alongside hers, towering meters behind.

This is what you get for distracting yourself, she thought, twisting around to find Myron.

"What... are you doing?" she asked. "I'm pretty sure I got this. Get off the ice."

He didn't budge, but her heart stopped when he smirked. "Do you know what your biggest flaw is, Noa?"

Nope. But I'm sure as hell about to find out.

"You believe that you're indestructible."

She would've cackled if it weren't for the fact that she actually feared falling through. Her hands clenched and unclenched like she was about to fist-fight him on the ice, forcing herself not to lock up.

"You believe that you can simply do everything on your own, without the help of anyone else because there's just no possible way that you could get yourself killed from it. And I think I'd like to challenge that."

The smooth, deadly cadence of his voice gave way to a sickening sensation in her gut, feeling like a nightmare version of herself was standing there in his place. The word 'challenge' smacked into her like a dreaded memory —every accumulation of her deliberate stance against him compounding into this single moment to bite her in the ass.

He retrieved a small, cylindrical item from his pocket, complete with a faded red button. A detonator. "Shall we?"

It happened too quick—the button press, the set of rapidly blinking lights at her feet, the shock of cold as she fell under, tumbling through the dark water. Up became down. Down became up. She pushed through muddled senses and sharpened pain, reminding herself not to panic. Panicking resulted in death. Just don't die.

Easy, right? Her lungs disagreed, greedily demanding air as she drew closer to the light. Noa winced when her hands hit the ice, grappling to find where she'd plunged through. More ice. She dragged herself along it, gritting her teeth before glimpsing Myron making his way back to shore. He was leaving her. He was leaving her to *die*.

Too bad she was too stubborn to die. She slammed her fists against the ice, fighting the need to suck in air—fighting the rising panic in her chest that this was the end.

A crack. A pop.

The break spiderwebbed outward and she propelled herself up, her head spinning as she gasped and sputtered between coughs. She fumbled with the edge of the ice until she could pull herself onto it, her teeth chattering on her crawl to the nearest bank, where she collapsed into the snow.

Her body shivered uncontrollably, refusing to move despite how she ordered herself to get up. She was spent. Her body was done. She'd never fight Ezra. She'd never kill Myron. She'd never save Kole.

So, instead, she closed her eyes, and let the world fall into black, save the sound of softly crunching snow.

Noa wondered if being dead sent one's mind on a small journey through their memories, or if she was stuck in some hellish purgatory when she heard the jingle of the familiar store bell. Considering how she couldn't move, she *must* be dead—then again, she felt pain... She chalked it up to being her new normal.

Heat spread along her back, and she slowly opened her eyes. The flickering dance of firelight enveloped the workshop, casting everything in a warm-tinted hue. The open cabinets and locked grates all neatly organized inside, save a few sheets of woven cotton, round brushes, and glue—all items she remembered dumping into containers the last time she'd been around. The crinkling of tissue paper sent her focus to the figure hunched over the desk, where she caught the movement of a brush in hand.

"You're not dead," Lazarus said, still ever-focused on the task in front of him, "just in case you were wondering."

She wobbled, trying to push herself up until a rush of cold air tickled her skin and dropped back to her elbows. "Where are my clothes?" she rasped.

"Drying. And you can forget about me telling you where they are until they're done. I'm not letting you storm back home for you die of hypothermia after bathing yourself in their blood. So, relax for a little while. I'll get you some water once I finish this page. Then we'll talk."

"You knew... Why did you bother with me if you knew I'm a killer?"

He set down his tools and tugged off his gloves. "Always so impatient. You won't even wait for me to fetch you water."

"You're dodging the question, old man."

"You watch your mouth, young lady. And don't move. I'll know if you get up," he said, turning into a scolding parent as he followed his worn trail in the faded, dark-red carpet to the hall—its thorny-edged pattern softened by routine.

"Oh, please. I'm faster than you," she grumbled.

He shook his head, vanishing into the darkened corridor, and she waited for the familiar sound of shuddering pipes. She closed her eyes and listened to the creak of every loose, fabricated board complain on his way back. Each noise intruded her vision, marking exactly where he was from how many times she'd jogged up and down that hall to collect something for him or slip out the back alley with a package.

When she opened her eyes again, a glass of water dangled above her face. She sat up, taking it before he sat cross-legged in front of her. Noa held back a tired chuckle at her effort to hold the blanket up over her chest.

"I don't know why I'm bothering trying to stay decent in front of a blind man," she mumbled, her voice echoing into the glass. "It's not like you didn't undress me already or anything."

He said nothing in return, instead waiting patiently for something she wasn't privy to yet. Frowning, she set down the glass next to him, nearly sloshing the water over the rim. "Oh, just spit it out already. I almost wish that you had just let me die if you're going to do *this*."

"Apologies for not letting you freeze to death, then."

She rolled her eyes, earning a quick tap on the cheek.

"And just because I'm blind doesn't mean that I don't know what you're doing."

"Congratulations. You found me. You saved me. Now what? You want a kiss, prince charming?" She began to comb her hair out of her face with her fingers, cringing at the tingle of lingering cold.

His mouth remained in a thin line. "You asked why I would bother saving you because you're a killer, correct?"

She let go of her hair, letting her hands drop into her lap. Her vision drifted toward the cabinets again, thinking of the time spent pulling everything out while he'd complained that she was ruining his system. He moaned like he was a victim in jest, but she should've realized then that he'd always known more than he let on.

"You're not a killer, Noa. You might label yourself as one, you may have trained to be one, and you may have even actually killed someone—but you're not one."

"I'm pretty sure that killing someone makes you a killer by definition."

"It wasn't of your own volition. You and I both know that this isn't what you wanted. Deep down, you're only doing it to survive because it's your only option."

"I think you have far more faith in me than I do."

"It's only because I've seen what you have the potential to become."

She shook her head with a short, bitter laugh. "Well, it doesn't matter anymore. I'm not going back there. I don't want anything to do with them after this." Not after Myron had left her for dead.

"And where would you go, Noa?"

"I'd stay here. I'd help you run the shop. You've already taught me most of it, so I can pull my own weight."

"And you don't think that he'd figure out where you've gone?"

"No. He doesn't even know if I'm alive. For all that son of a bitch knows, I'm dead and never coming back." A twisted thought of that mansion consumed in fire made her hands curl into fists. She'd wanted to hurt him before—she always had. But now...

"So, when he figures out that you're alive, you don't think that he'll find you here with me?"

Her fists slackened. He was right. It could be a few days, a week, or a month from now, but eventually, he'd know. She'd never be able to wake up in her own bed in the shop apartment and hurry out to unlock the front door for customers bundled up in faux furs from Bellegarde on behalf of their wealthier employers. They'd never be able to enjoy dinner together and gossip about the orders they'd get—something she'd only ever gotten a taste of during their short lunch breaks.

Her vision glossed over as she imagined a life spent here, helping take care of him like he'd taken care of her. One where she would've grown up with scars from too many papercuts and bumping into bookcases, rather than trading blows with her adopted siblings and victims that struggled against her grip while Ezra had dealt the final blow. What had she become?

Don't cry. You're better than this.

But how could she continue on this path, knowing that Myron would rather see her dead than insubordinate? How long would it be until he decided she wasn't worth it anymore?

She reached for her throat, swaying with the phantom sensation of drowning again—of drinking in all that water in the cold, dark depths. Unknown. Unloved. Unable to save herself.

"Noa, you have to go back," Lazarus said, gentle, coaxing words that shattered her.

She began shaking her head until his hands cupped her face.

"Listen to me, Noa," he said softly. "There are different paths we take. All of them have consequences. Some of us are even bound tighter to certain paths than others. You have options, but the best one for you is to go back." She started to speak, but he pulled a hand away, holding up a finger. "Ah—Trust me, Noa. I just need you to trust me."

"Why are you so damn cryptic?" she asked in a near-whisper.

A quiet laugh slipped from him. "I've learned the hard way that there are certain things that you can't run from, despite knowing or not knowing where you'll be taken." He tapped a finger against his head.

"Yeah, well, I'm not a Seer, Lazarus. And if I happen to be one, then I'm pretty sure I'd let whatever higher power decides my fate send me straight into madness because I wouldn't do what I was supposed to."

"There's still a plan for you, even if you're not a Seer or a Mage." He winked like they had some sort of shared secret, despite her bafflement. "Sometimes we need a little more than a nudge to keep us on track. If it weren't for me nearly losing my mind, I would still be straying far from where I needed to go... It can be hard to accept new realities, much like how my learning I was a Seer felt like an excuse for why my vision was deteriorating. I could've ignored it all out of spite, but now I've seen so much of what could happen—of what I know I can and can't fix. I understand my place in the world so I might be able to help it along as a messenger."

Noa lightly punched him in the arm, scowling at the poor joke.

"Now that's not how you treat an 'old man,'" he complained, faking a deep frown.

"So, tell me who your King is, and I'll off him for you," she said wryly.

Her grin faded when he stood, mumbling something in reply she couldn't make out. She reached for his arm, ready to repeat her request before he was out of reach.

48

TALIE ✧ 2704-12-16

NOA

If only you knew.

Lazarus's words skimmed the surface of her mind when she woke, and her hand wrapped around Glacier's wrist. She hated the way her body trembled—the way she'd squeezed his arm a little harder once she understood where they were.

"Where are you going?" she asked, searching the room for any reason why he'd be up.

His fingers grazed hers. "It's okay," he whispered. "I'll be right back."

She let go, and he rubbed his eyes on his way to the closet of a bathroom. A thin stream of light crawled across the carpet in his wake. A shiver ran through her as she shimmied down into the blankets.

Maybe Lazarus had given into his madness before he'd given her the Sword of Astravny. Maybe all of this was a fool's errand that they were all desperately clinging onto for hope. Maybe he'd told the entire truth, and he'd been *her* Messenger, choosing to die in her place so history didn't repeat itself.

The question of whether it was all worth it came next—a question she lingered on in the uneasy embrace of the dark. After all, Glacier had reminded her that they had nothing left to lose. That didn't mean they didn't have anything left to live for.

She swallowed while her fingers played with the corner of the comforter, thinking back to the first time she'd met Nyx—someone she'd originally sought to use until she started waiting for her at train stations and sitting next to her to talk to those who Nyx dubbed their new clients. They'd gone from strangers to partners.

The memory of Rune sliding across from her in a dining car booth cascaded into begrudging allyship in which he played off of her strengths and dampened her weaknesses. He'd manipulated a room so easily, it turned into a dance between them she took to faster than she'd ever imagined. Crow's constant one-ups kept her on her toes too. She'd always be impressed with how quickly he slipped in and out of a job, leaving everything undisturbed like a shadow—a skill she admired and strived for. She hadn't expected to find friends and rivals among them.

When she'd met Cecilia, there'd been that inkling that she might be able to wield her like a weapon, much like the twins. Her magic had left her awestruck, but it'd come with the price of seeing the world through a softer lens—a world filled with hope as one of the last sparks to brighten it.

And then there was Glacier...

The idea of hating him for the luxuries she'd never had rang hollow now. It hadn't been a comfortable one filled with pleasant memories, but one with pain that quieted him. She took solace in knowing he could see right through her, even though she'd always done her best to avoid being stripped down to her core. Every vulnerability and fear he'd seen so far had been handled with more care than she'd ever handled herself—the kind of treatment she never thought she deserved.

The light vanished, and she tensed as the door slid open again. Glacier made a barely visible motion for her to roll over.

"There's no way in hell I'm going closer to the window."

He grumbled and climbed over her, dropping on top of the covers like he planned to stare up at the ceiling for the rest of the night. She pushed her back up against his arm, relaxing at the radiation of warmth there. The soft blue light of the digital clock faded in and out with the minutes until she heard his rhythmic breathing and felt his head lull against her.

It ignited something deep inside her that reminded her of rage, though the taste of blood lingered in its wake. The people she'd surrounded herself with deserved more than she did, despite her selfish actions of pulling them in to save herself.

A silent vow engraved itself on her soul as the numbers changed again. A promise to herself that she'd stand between Myron and the others when the time came. She didn't care if he killed her, so long as they could all walk away. Noa would take the Volkov down with her. She couldn't afford not to. Keys be damned—real or fake—she could at least control this. She'd do it for every person she'd hidden away.

For Lazarus.

For Nyx.

For Glacier.

CECILIA

Cecilia leaned over the ship's railing, trying to peer through the fog. "How much further is it, exactly?" she asked, glancing back at Rune.

"Not too much further, I think," he replied, the corner of his mouth dipping down. "I just think that we might not be able to see it until we're pulling into the port."

"I hate it," Crow grumbled from where he hung onto the bars.

Cecilia sighed and pressed her cheek against the railing. The light sea mist caressed her face and tickled her nose, but it wasn't enough to bring a smile to her face. Rune placed a hand on her back, moving his thumb in a slow circle under her jacket hood.

"Where's Noa?" Rune asked, turning to Crow.

He shrugged. "Probably still in her room. I saw her heading there earlier when I was making my way up top. Didn't bother talking to her because she looked really pissy."

"She gets seasick," Cecilia said absently, her sights still stuck on the foggy horizon.

Crow chortled. "Seriously? Almighty Noa can't handle a couple of waves hitting the boat. That's too good."

"I'd watch yourself," Rune said. "She's already got it out for you after trying to make a move on Glacier."

"Because she doesn't understand that there's a really good opportunity here for me—"

"You mean having sex with royalty?"

"Maybe it's my dying wish, okay?" His voice dropped to a whisper after a brief glance over at the nearest cluster of people. "We're just going to get murdered by Volkov anyway."

Rune scowled.

"Hey," Crow said, swapping to a lighter tone, "look at the bright side— at least we'll all die together!"

"You're not helping."

Cecilia's head popped up at the sound of approaching footfalls right before Nyx stopped next to her, phone in hand. "Good morning, idiots. And Cecilia. I think Noa and Glacier slept the day away yesterday, so now she's extra grouchy this morning. You've been warned."

"What about Glacier?" Cecilia asked. "Is he not feeling well?"

"I think he's fine... but I definitely startled him when I checked on him earlier. He must've still been sleeping because it sounded like I woke him." She hummed, staring past them into the fog. "Shame that we don't have a decent view of the island."

"We were just saying the same thing," Rune said. "Do you think it'll be this bad during the next couple of days?"

She shrugged. "Possibly. It's supposed to be pretty dreary here this time of year. I'm sure it'll stay a little chilly too."

A chime rang out over the intercom system, followed by an announcement for passengers to prepare for their arrival. Nyx shoved her hands into her pockets with a relieved explicative and led the way to the middle of the main deck, striding along the pearlescent white walls. Cecilia glimpsed the back of Glacier and Noa when they merged into the crowd, and she bounced, waving until Glacier saw her and grabbed Noa's arm.

"Are you two feeling better?" Cecilia asked.

"Yeah," he said with a sheepish smile. "I think I just need some rest." He glanced over at Noa, whose face was half-tucked into her zipped-up jacket collar.

Crow smirked, eyeing her. "Seasickness, huh?"

Her eyes narrowed on him, and his amusement fell away.

Rune cleared his throat. "I believe what my brother meant to say was that he hopes you feel better once we're on land."

"Tell him to kiss my ass."

"Noa," Nyx interjected, motioning for her to follow. "A word."

Noa grumbled and cut between Rune and Crow, shoving the latter hard enough he stumbled. "What the hel—"

"Don't act like you didn't start that," Rune said.

Cecilia hugged herself, biting her lip while she turned back to Glacier. The distant look in his eyes and the ever-so-slight frown tugging at the corner of his mouth gave her pause. She followed his line of sight like running her hand along a thread until it smacked straight into Noa. Her stomach dropped before her head whipped back around and caught a glimpse of lights cutting through the fog.

"Glacier, look!" She grabbed his elbow and spun him around, trying to suppress her unease with the view. It took everything in her not to accidentally dig her fingertips into his jacket sleeve. Out of all the people to show interest in—*Noa?*

Noa, a killer. Noa, the woman that was using him to get to the Soul of Amarais.

Cecilia's eyes skimmed over the winding city streets illuminated by streetlamps and the clashing clusters of shops giving way to townhouses and squat, brick apartment buildings along the cobbled walkways trailing the rocky cliffside. Private boats wobbled in the confines of the docks below, where workers started back up the winding stone-slab steps.

"Funny," Rune said quietly. "It sort of reminds me of the outer rings of Kingsheart, aside from this city looking more cohesive."

"Really?" she asked. "It looks a bit jumbled to me..."

"Well, when you have twelve types of people with their own styles of architecture, it turns into a bit of a mess. It's a beautiful mess, though."

"Hopefully we'll get to see it," Glacier said under his breath.

Cecilia rocked against him, looping her arm through his. "Let's try to enjoy our first New Year's celebration outside of Amarais," she whispered. "Let's make the best of it and see where we go from there."

NOA

Noa jogged across the crosswalk lines painted into the brick, liking the feel of solid ground under her boots. Tiny lights alternated colors around overhead fabric banners, all inked with lyrics or musical notes to the Taliean New Year's tune hummed at nearly every street corner. The melody pried its way in, threatening to force Nyx's earlier discussion from her mind.

She kept close to Nyx's side, chewing on the inside of her cheek.

"I can try to handle it on my own if you don't want to go—" Nyx whispered.

"No," Noa said. "No, if you're nervous about trading information with this guy, then I'm going."

"Like I said, it's probably nothing, but he's been acting a little strange during our recent communications. I'm wondering if something spooked him..."

"It doesn't happen to be anything vital to helping us with this job, does it?" Noa asked, slowing with her as they got in line to board a dull-blue trolley covered in rotating ads with scannable codes on the windows.

"No, he's more of a... tracker, sort of."

"You looking for someone?" Her brows knit together, and Nyx held up a finger before climbing on board. She trailed behind to where she'd claimed one of the middle, open rows of seats, and slid in next to her.

"I'm actually looking for a few people now, specifically former colleagues and connections of Daxton. He mentioned he hadn't been able to get a hold of them recently, and they're just... gone."

"You're sure it's not—" Noa glanced up at a passenger walking by and cleared her throat, drawing a small V on her chest.

"If it were *them*, then we'd be dealing with death certificates," she mumbled. "The rest are simply *missing*—some flagged, some not. It's a little bizarre to see so many of them completely overlooked though... I'm not sure what the Republic's regulations are on activity like that, but I'm assuming that someone needs to report it before it's flagged instead of an automated activity timer."

"That seems... sort of weird."

"What's weird?" Glacier asked, dropping into a seat behind them and leaning forward.

"Maybe we should talk about this later," Noa said, hating how he deflated and fell back into his seat right as Cecilia took the spot next to him. Glacier's one- or two-word answers to Cecilia's questions and chattering left Noa drumming her fingers against her knees. Each start and stop of the bus sent her paranoia into overdrive, reimagining every person hopping off or jumping on as a sickeningly familiar face.

Finally, Nyx made a move to stand, and Noa led the way onto the sidewalk again.

"Are you going to show me their profiles?" Noa asked under her breath.

"After we get information from this guy. I think it might help tie everything together, and I certainly don't want to jump to any wild conclusions before then. Rather not waste our time, especially when I've been busy with certain side projects..."

Noa bit down on her tongue as they took a diagonal turn down an alley, darkened by the overhangs. Small storage hubs rotated through box rental deals from mounted wall displays within. Nyx ducked inside one of them, claiming she needed to pick up keys for their apartment before they continued down a few more side streets.

The metal stairs reverberated through the narrow passage on their way up to the second floor, dumping them in front of a door with chipped, forest-green paint. Noa frowned while Nyx unlocked it and made her way inside.

Smooth, stone columns and rounded archways separated the main living space, kitchen, and entryway from the hallways that Noa assumed led toward the bedrooms and bathrooms. A large, woven tapestry with an old-fashioned lighthouse hung over the TV and fireplace, mounted near the top of the lofted ceiling. The furniture was cube-like and simplistic, yet still managing to look plush and comfortable. Whites and greens, along with sandalwood accents gave the place a cozy feel, despite the minimalism.

"Could be worse, I guess," Crow said as they wandered into the open foyer.

"You realize that this is an entire floor of a building, right?" Rune asked. "Our apartment back in King's was the size of the damn living room, and you want to complain about *this?*"

Crow made himself at home anyway, falling into the white, modular sofa and kicking up his feet onto the blocky coffee table. Nyx quickly shoved the table out from under his boots with her own.

"Hey!"

"Beat it, whore," she said. "I need the space."

He glowered up at her before he grabbed his bag and slunk down the hallway after Rune and Cecilia.

"So, here's what we're going to do," Nyx began, sliding the computer mat canister from her bag. "Since the party is tomorrow night, Glacier and I will need to get in and look around now while we can. After that, you and I can meet my informant while Rune and Cecilia go pick up half of the party clothes. The rest will be delivered here in about an hour while we're working."

Noa cringed when she didn't mention Crow. Leaving him here alone with Glacier wasn't an option after his sudden, obvious advances.

"You're meeting an informant?" Glacier asked. "I thought you said that you didn't have contacts in Talie?"

"An informant just feeds information. They don't actually have any connections like a general contact does. They just gather and report. Contacts get us in the door certain places, which is why I've had to go through the painstaking process of hacking in our party-goers for this event with well-researched new money connections that no one will know here anyway."

"You'll be joining us to meet the informant," Noa said.

"Tonight?" he asked.

"After this setup, yes," Nyx said. "So take a seat and let's get to work."

49
TALIE ✧ 2704-12-16

GLACIER

Cold curled around Glacier the moment they stepped back outside. He tried to tell himself the chills spilling down his neck were from the misty air slicking his skin, but he tugged up his hood anyway, sticking close to Noa. He flinched at every ad that flashed in the windows they passed and ducked at each looming shadow. Every face blurred down the narrow streets like smeared paint.

Calm. Down.

"Just stick close and keep quiet," Noa whispered when they slowed near a couple buildings with water stains running past the protruding brick and windowsills. "You'll be fine."

Nyx turned down the alley, stumbling once and cursing at the loose pavers. The doors they walked by were sealed off, and steel construction signs were crammed into caged windows. It opened up into a squared-off courtyard with browning plants under drooping trees in the corners and a murky fountain clogged with leaves in the center.

"*Oy.* You are?" A man pushed off a wall opposite them, his accent jarringly different from the Taliean ones he'd encountered since their arrival. Instead, his light lilt sounded rougher around the edges—distinctly Astravnian.

Two more men rose from a bench off to the side, decked out like the first in brown and black pleather jackets with scratched-off logos and scuffed jeans.

Seemingly unfazed, Nyx stopped a couple meters short of him, leaving a small gap between her and Noa's immediate range. "Nyx. I take it you're Adam."

Noa rolled her shoulders, nodding in Adam's direction with a grin before launching into a string of Astravnian. Glacier guessed his expression wasn't all that far off from Adam's wide-eyed surprise, but he appeared to relax once she was through. When she swapped back to international, her voice captured that light accent to match his. "It's been a while since I've had someone else to talk with."

Glacier's eyes slid between them, noting their dull-brown hair—though his was a shade or two darker—brown eyes, and pale skin. He'd never stopped to consider that as her birthplace before with it being an island, despite how she didn't seem too inconvenienced by the cold in Amarais. For some reason, he'd imagined her as a mixed citizen of the Republic, able to wear any identity she could and make herself another face in the crowd.

Adam smirked, replying in Astravnian before setting his sights on Nyx again with a motion to Glacier and Noa. "Who are these two?"

"My assistant and my bodyguard." Nyx jerked her head in the direction of where Noa stood behind her, and she wiggled her fingers at him. "I'm going to assume that's not a problem?"

"Not at all. Sorry for the lack of notice, but I also brought a couple of friends of my own." He nodded toward the other two, hovering a little closer to Noa than Glacier felt comfortable with.

"Fair enough. You have my information?"

Adam paused mid-nod, locking eyes with Glacier. His breath caught, and his head started to spin. The phantom scent of smoke filled his nose. He could've sworn he'd seen a red ring around Adam's irises as he started speaking in Astravnian again.

Noa's hands fell from her pockets, curling into fists, and Glacier tensed.

A shadow moved from the corner of his eye, and he jerked forward, feeling a brush of air flit past him. One of the *bodyguards* lunged for Nyx, and she bolted toward Adam right as Noa intercepted. She rammed her shoulder into his torso, sending him stumbling back, like the wind had been knocked out of him.

Glacier's body locked up in terror. Blood pounded in his ears. And he gasped as he flailed backward, choking on the collar of his jacket.

Don't panic.

He threw his elbow back as hard as he could, hearing a curse, followed by a hard *thud* in Glacier's stumble forward. His head whipped around to find Noa standing over the second attacker right before the thumping of boots on pavers hurtled toward them. Glacier nearly tumbled backward into the stagnant fountain as Noa brought the heel of her hand to the first attacker's head, sending him sprawling.

Glacier's ears perked up at a clattering sound on the other side of the courtyard. When he found Nyx staring back at them, hovering over Adam's prone form, Glacier's body might as well have turned to jelly.

"All right, What the actual fuck just happened?" Nyx demanded.

Noa pointed straight at Adam. "That dumbass said something to his goons about how we brought a Mage with us and told them to 'grab the Miraltan.'"

Glacier's sputtered, vehemently shaking his head. "But I'm not a Mage—"

"Well, *we* know that, but *he* clearly thought that for whatever reason."

Nyx half-growled, dropping to her knees and sifting through Adam's pockets before holding up a memory card. "Got it. Let's go. We'll discuss this shit on the way back."

"What about all *this?*" Glacier motioned to the bodies, panic rising in his voice. "Are they dead?"

"No, but that can be arranged," Noa said. "Especially if they jump up and try to grab you again." She spun him around, pushing him behind Nyx as she hurried past.

They turned the corner, walking a couple of blocks before Noa spoke again, "Maybe they assumed that Glacier's a Mage *because* he's Miraltan?"

Nyx stared at her like she'd hit her head. "Now, why the hell would they think that? That's like saying that someone's Tabirian or Taliean or Valentian—so, hey! Maybe they're a Mage because they come from a place that's perfectly fine with magic. Wow! It's like the whole damn island is suddenly populated with Mages out of nowhere. *Incredible—*"

"I'm not a Mage—" he repeated, bringing them all to a halt.

"Yes, we get that," Noa said firmly. "There's no need to get defensive, we're just trying to make sense of why he'd think that."

Nyx forced out a frustrated breath, starting to regain her cool. "Let's just hurry up and look at what kind of data he had. It could be a trap, so I want to pick up a device to burn on our way back to be safe."

Glacier rubbed his arms, unable to fight off the chills spreading through him. Every few meters, he glanced over his shoulder and then jogged to catch up with Noa and Nyx again. The good news: the faces of the people they passed weren't blurred this time. The bad news: he searched for red rings in each of their eyes.

He didn't even register the box shoved into his hands, let alone when Nyx had popped into a store on the walk back. He only realized his arms were wrapped around something once they were inside the apartment.

"Took Crow with us to get the party attire," Noa read off her phone. "Smiley face... Thanks, Cecilia. That's one less problem to worry about while we figure out what the hell's on that memory card. I seriously hope it was worth it because I'm beginning to wonder if I made a mistake in letting those assholes live."

Glacier dumped the box onto the kitchen counter, pausing at the quiet *tip, tip, tip.* His brows knit together while he stared down the sink. Nothing.

"If we had killed them," Nyx said, "it could've set off a chain reaction of even more problems that I don't think any of us would care to deal with right now."

"Is there a leak?"

"What?" Noa asked, frowning at him.

He held a finger to his lips in the midst of strange looks, but it sounded so close—almost like it was right next to him. He took a step back from the counter, catching a cluster of blue, iridescent droplets on the floor between him and Nyx.

Nyx stepped away too.

Tip.

Her face paled. *"Fuck—Shit—Damnit!"* She grabbed her right arm, twisting it around where Glacier discovered her black sleeve darkened with the blue liquid. Noa stepped toward her, but Nyx reeled back. "No, no— you stop right there—"

And she did, but not without locking eyes with Glacier.

"Nyx, we—" he started.

"Stop," she growled through gritted teeth, taking another retreating step. She grappled with her sleeve, smearing the soft, flesh-colored casing with blue. When she had it bunched up at her elbow, she let go, and it began its downward crawl. The arm didn't bend or move in reflex like he'd expected, and his heart sank the second she mumbled another curse.

Glacier shot forward as she tried peeling back her glove by rubbing her working hand against her pants. He curled up her sleeve, and she stilled.

"It's okay," he said, flipping it up again and again, building the roll back up to her elbow. "I already sort of guessed you were modded."

She hesitated, but he could feel her eyes stuck on him. "You... you don't find it a little fucked up that someone sporting mods is out here trying to save magic?"

Glacier chuckled. "One could argue the same about me, right?"

"At least you've never been told you've blackened a part of your soul with a machine."

"True. But whoever told you that likely never gave you the chance to show them how great you are. It's their loss. You're stronger than they'll ever be."

For a second, he could've sworn he saw tears form in Nyx's eyes as he held his hands between them, stained blue.

"Um... is this toxic?"

She snorted. "Only if you lick it."

Noa cleared her throat. "I'll go find a towel."

Glacier helped her with her gloves, his thumbs running over the soft lining now sticky in one. A black-sewn logo gleamed under the recessed lighting. Tailor-made, just like he'd thought.

Noa dropped to her knees next to him and began wiping down Nyx's arm. "There's a slit here..."

"Figures," Nyx mumbled. "That fucker had a knife, but I thought he missed."

"You sure you don't want me to go back and kill him now?" Noa asked with a raised eyebrow.

"I have half a mind to do it myself."

"Well, I'm assuming that he nicked something important, right?"

"I won't really know for sure until I open it up and take a look. Unfortunately, I usually need someone to help me since it's a little difficult to fix things with one hand." She grimaced, holding her arm to her side as she moved into the living area.

"Where are you going?" Glacier asked, flicking excess water from his hands at the sink.

"To get my bag for my repair shit—"

"I'll grab it. You sit down." He wiped his hands on his pants as he jogged past her. The door to her and Noa's room sat propped open, one bag tossed on the bed and the other sitting neatly on the floor. He scooped up the latter and hurried back to where Nyx stared down at her mat on the coffee table.

"Roll this up for now. I'll need the space."

So, he dropped the bag while Noa sat down with a couple extra towels and began rifling through it. "This it?" she asked, pulling out a flat, square bin with dividers.

Nyx nodded and took a seat on the floor—a cue that both he and Noa followed to huddle around the table. She laid her arm against it, her eyes narrowing as she struggled with her modded wrist. Glacier rolled it flat, and she sighed.

"Thank you," she mumbled, and pressed in the sides, triggering a *click*. "I'm going to warn you that this part can be a little disturbing for some people... There's no plate or anything under this layer of synthetic skin— just a frame, unlike the shield plate in my hand. All these moving parts are starting to hurt like a bitch since it's all hooked up to nerve endings and there's no fluid left to keep everything functioning. So, if you're too squeamish or you don't think you have steady enough hands, then do us both a favor and let Noa do it."

"Whoa, hey—" Noa said, holding her hands up. "Just because I kill people doesn't mean I have a steady hand like a surgeon. I'm allowed to be sloppy."

"Lovely," Nyx grumbled.

"Look, I'm just saying—"

"It's okay," Glacier said. "I can do it."

Nyx pressed her finger against her arm until it split at an invisible seam and slid it open down the length of her forearm. When she peeled it back, a thin mesh cage rolled back with it, giving way to tubes in place of veins and metal contraptions in place of muscles. She pointed at a box at her wrist.

"There's a switch on your side. You see it?"

He angled himself for a better look past the silicone flesh. "Yeah, I see it."

"Okay. Wait until I tell you to toggle it. It'll shut everything off, so it's going to be a little painful, especially on empty." She pointed to the gauge, where a small, red exclamation point blinked inside a triangle.

"Just tell me when."

She took a deep breath. "Now." She tensed up the second he flipped it and hissed, causing Noa to lean away.

"I feel like you're going to take a swing at me..." Noa mumbled, flinching at Nyx's brief glare.

She sighed, returning to Glacier. "Okay, now to find the leak." Her fingers ran over one of the tubes near where the cut had been. "Well, that was easy..." She lifted it with a finger, bending it enough to show off a small slice.

Noa popped open the case while Nyx rattled off all the parts she needed during the remainder of her inspection. "Fortunately, I think that's it. I don't think he got anything else. It could've been much worse, seeing how there's a lack of mod scrap shops around here—Talie being a magic-preserving country and all..."

"So, you'll be able to have two functioning arms by tomorrow?" Noa asked, snapping the case shut.

"Assuming he didn't destroy anything vital I'm not seeing." She pointed to the end of the tube that ended at the wrist contraption. "Now, I need you to pull this out. I'll press the buttons to release it, just don't tug on it too hard or else it might tear and gunk everything up with tubing plastic. Then I'll *really* be pissed. If it's stuck, say so. More than likely I just didn't push the buttons down completely, so it didn't release."

He nodded, waiting for her to signal to pull it free. They repeated the process with the opposite node, and then she handed it over to Noa for her to measure and cut a new one. Once replaced, Noa passed her an iridescent bottle of blue fluid and a funnel that Nyx walked Glacier through replenishing.

"And now," Nyx said, seeming less than thrilled, "I get the enjoyment of nearly biting my tongue off while you flip the switch again. Just get it over with."

He turned it on, and it hummed back to life. Blue shot through the tubes, and her fingers began wiggling.

"Honestly, I'm a little surprised that you aren't absolutely disgusted," she said, folding the skin back into place.

"It's not like it's your fault. I just assumed that you were referring to a missing arm instead of some sort of chronic illness when I noticed that you favored your left arm a little more than your right. Getting flagged by a few mod-weary places might've helped narrow that down for me too."

"Huh..." she said, her mouth tipping up at the corner. "Boy, do I know how to pick assistants." She glanced over at Noa. "Did you figure it out too?"

"Glacier told me, but I didn't really believe him until we left Tabir."

"Wait, Tabir? When did you figure it out, exactly?"

"Um, well..." He chewed on the inside of his cheek in thought. "After we talked back in Corvia... the left hand, the tailored gloves... You came from money, so there was a likeliness that you would have enough money for a medical modification, so..."

"Gods, you figured it out after a whole *day* of knowing me. Damn, did I make the right choice."

He sat up straighter with a bit of pride, and Nyx chortled—a short-lived moment of amusement that fell away with the opening and closing of her fist. "Does... anyone else know?"

"No," Noa said. "As far as we can tell, the others don't know. I don't think that they'll honestly care though, Nyx. You don't have to keep secrets like that. It doesn't matter to us."

"Yeah," Glacier said, "and if you're worried about Cecilia, I can already tell you that she won't care. She's been taking care of a half-Miraltan her whole life. She's pretty understanding of people's circumstances. Though, I understand why you're using the gloves since the skin doesn't look quite right."

She nodded, holding her arm up. "Yeah, unfortunately, it's hard to mimic the right creases and everything without a really good artist. The downside is that it can still get messed up if you're not careful, so I decided not to fool with it. Gloves were easier, and I didn't really mind it." She dropped it back into her lap. "I guess I'm a little confused about why you told Noa instead of Cecilia in the first place."

Noa shifted, pulling her sleeves over her hands. "Well, I caught him acting weird, so I cornered him."

"And I wasn't planning on telling anyone because I wasn't completely certain..."

"Nyx," Noa started, leaning against the coffee table, "if you don't want us to tell, we won't. But I think you should. I can't imagine anyone here judging you for this, but I understand if you're not ready to share that."

Nyx stared down at her arm. "It's... complicated. I think I need some time. I've honestly never been all that comfortable with it."

"That's okay," Glacier said. "I get it."

She swiped at her eyes and cleared her throat. "Let's—um... Let's take a look at this data I got a hole in my arm for," she said, pushing herself up. "And then I'll try to siphon funds from his bank account."

50

TALIE ✧ 2704-12-16

NOA

"Are they all related to magic?" Glacier asked, his eyes roaming over the profiles tiled across the mat screen.

Nyx hummed, tapping a finger against her lips. "It certainly seems that way... Daxton does have a connection to magic studies."

"You mentioned that he was working on a device a while back, right?" Noa asked. "Something he was tinkering with in his spare time to potentially mimic what a Reader might be able to do. Do you think this is related?"

"Wait, a Reader?" Glacier asked, glancing between them.

"They're... like cousins to Seers," Nyx said, tilting her hand back and forth.

"They can see auras," Noa clarified. "Seers are sort of a weird grab-bag of senses, but Readers can pick people out of a crowd with their magic. They can trace it since everyone with magic has a unique signature, or at least, that's what older academic studies claim."

"The last one recorded died over maybe a couple decades ago," Nyx said.

"There aren't any more left. It's partially why Daxton began working on this in the first place, though I believe he's still trying to fine-tune the second stage. Right now, he said that it can only detect magic. It can't narrow things down to a unique finger-print-like level yet. Though, if he was reaching out to all of these people with his research in mind, I can see it being very possible..." She retrieved her phone, tapped something out, and dropped it next to the mat. "Now we wait for him to answer while we take a closer look." She leaned forward, nudging around the profile card until Glacier joined in.

"There are two Mages here," Glacier said, adding a label to the top of his set—a man and a woman.

"A student and professor here..." Nyx mumbled, labeling her own as 'Academic.' "And then there are three former alumni, all from universities with an emphasis on magical studies."

Glacier frowned, tilting his head. Whatever was running through his mind didn't matter to Noa then since she was stuck on his eyes. Her fingers dug into her sleeves to stop her nails from biting into her palms. If she'd been any slower back there, Glacier could've been hurt. The thought of that happening cycled through her mind since the walk back.

Nyx's phone buzzed, breaking her concentration.

"You're right, Noa. He was a little hesitant to mention it, but they were all chipping in to work on it at some point."

Noa chewed on her lip. "So, who would want seven people to vanish like that? Would it really be over this tool?"

"Maybe a business competitor?" Glacier said. "There could be someone with a similar item that wants to sell to a private market or something, right? Maybe seven people would raise too much of a red flag if they all turned up dead, so they hired the Volkov to make them all disappear instead?"

"Maybe... but something about that theory feels... *off*... When did each of them stop communicating with Daxton?"

Nyx picked up one of the tablets. "It looks like it started at the beginning of the summer. About five months ago, give or take."

"How often?"

"It's a bit scattered. Two were separated by a couple of days, and the rest vary anywhere from one to four weeks."

"And when did the last one vanish?" Noa asked, closing her eyes and recalling the timeframe for the beginning of the disappearances. It wasn't possible for the Volkov to be involved with the distinct lack of activity around then. It'd given Myron enough free time to poke around into Noa's personal life and Lazarus.

"It was one of the Mages—the guy—he stopped responding as of the thirteenth."

"Of this month?" Glacier asked, his eyes darting to the mat's clock. "That's three days ago."

She nodded and set the tablet down to share her findings. "Yeah, the girl disappeared a couple of months ago. As far as I can tell, the two of them didn't know each other either. Their only common connection appears to be Daxton."

"That and magic," Noa mumbled, resting her chin against the heel of her hand.

Glacier stood, swaying slightly. Noa shot up, adrenaline shooting through her at the sight of his hand on his head.

"Are you okay?" she asked.

"Yeah." He grimaced and shook his head. "Yeah, I'm fine. Just got a little dizzy for a second."

"Please tell me you actually slept back on the boat," Nyx said. "I don't want to imagine you staying awake all night and just staring up at the ceiling."

"I slept. I promise. I'm probably a little dehydrated or something..." he muttered on his way to the kitchen.

Noa watched him go, slowly dipping back into her seat when the tap turned on. She ran her hands over her legs. "So... is the other data from that asshole Adam decrypted yet?" she asked, her mouth twitching.

"Maybe in another minute or two." Nyx tilted the cheap tablet's display. "It's close. I'm just hoping that it's not garbage."

"If it is, I'll go finish him."

A notification popped up on the screen, and Nyx scooped it up. "Well,

well…" Her thumb ran over the edge of the screen, each swipe knitting her brows together. "What the hell…?"

"What?" Noa asked, briefly catching Glacier returning to his seat with a glass of water.

"Take a look for yourself."

She took the tablet and started reading through the lines of text. Her grip tightened against the plastic case, ignoring its complaints under the pulse of her fingertips. "Why would someone have this? This is—"

"Fucking dangerous to keep a list of, let alone pass around?" Nyx finished. "Yeah, I know."

"What? What is it?" Glacier asked.

"A damn list of Mages living in Kingsheart," Noa said, handing it off to him.

"I… don't understand. Why is this dangerous to have? We're talking about King's Republic, not Amarais…"

"Because," Nyx said, "there are people out there who do stupid shit and mess with things they shouldn't. And if that list fell into the hands of someone that was close enough to Kingsheart and either hated Mages or—gods forbid—had a fucking grimoire—"

"That's enough." Noa jumped up. "I think that's enough of this for now." Staring into Glacier's eyes now left her feeling sick. "You don't think that Adam has anything to do with these seven people disappearing, do you?"

"No," Nyx said, tugging the device from his hands. "I've been tracking his movements for a bit before we got here since he was passing me less sensitive information—completely unrelated to this. From what I can tell, he's been keeping to Talie most of the time. He doesn't travel to Kingsheart, let alone anywhere near the Republic."

"Then that brings me back to why the hell he'd panic, single out Glacier as a Mage—when he clearly *isn't*—and turn on us? He assumed something, and then he decided it was worth turning on us to grab a non-Mage. Why?"

"What, exactly does a grimoire do?" Glacier asked, his complexion looking a little pale.

Noa fought back her horror. He was thinking of Adam—about his suspicion of Glacier being a Mage. Her stomach churned, and she turned to Nyx, who refused to make eye contact with her.

You bitch.

"You don't want to know," Noa said.

"But—"

"Trust me on this, Glacier." The sharpness of her words sent him shrinking back, spreading guilt through her. She found it hard to swallow as she stared down at the mat, memorizing the features of each person staring up at the ceiling. "You... you don't suppose that someone was hunting down Mages and happened to run into the rest of these people along the way, do you?"

Nyx hesitated, unease slipping into her tone. "It's possible... or someone could've discovered Daxton's device and decided they didn't like the idea of someone potentially being able to track them if... well..."

"Motherfucker," she hissed, covering her mouth.

"Considering where we are right now, and what we're here to do, I think this situation fits a little too well, don't you?" she asked, leaning back in her chair. "A Seer claiming that your Seraphine's little champion, meant to unlock this supposed Vault."

"If you don't shut your damn mouth, I will beat your ass." Noa pointed a finger at her.

"Do it, bitch," Nyx said, leaning forward. "You saw what I did to Adam with a metal-plated fist."

"That's enough—" Glacier stood. "I may not understand exactly what a grimoire does, but I get that it's something to do with Mages and it's *bad*. What I don't understand is how this is connected to us finding the Vault."

Nyx motioned to the table. "It means that this can be prevented from happening again should this key-hunting expedition turn out not to be a complete hoax. Noa, as the supposed one tasked with opening the Vault, would be able to stop it."

Noa shifted uncomfortably, feeling a horrible weight settling on her chest.

"And... if we're all wrong?" he asked, his hands falling to his sides.

"Then things are going to get much, much worse," Noa said under her breath. "Especially for Mages."

"And we start the countdown to the end," Nyx added.

"The end of... what?"

"Of everything." Nyx's eyes settled on him, dark and as void of hope as her words. "I'm sure you recall the beginning of the story. We'll be... *resetting*. We'll have to fend for ourselves—no more magic. Just us... and whatever's lurking in the dark."

Noa forced out a nervous laugh, sounding frayed at the edges. "But this is nothing by speculation! We don't know if they're disappearing for that reason, or if it's something completely unrelated—"

"Then I guess we'll have to find out, won't we? And I really do hope that we're wrong."

Noa stole another glance at Glacier as those blue and green eyes stared down at the mat in stunned, uneasy silence. Her vision slipped downward, tripping on each letter of the missing peoples' names—meaningless when set apart from the rest of the words. Meaningless like how she'd deemed her existence for so long.

Seraphine's. Little. Champion.

Her stomach lurched like she might heave. Every doubt she had regarding this fool's errand cracked, her shields gone from the reality she was facing. The idea that Lazarus had descended into madness now a work of fiction she'd concocted to make this pill easier to swallow.

He'd given her the first key.

He'd told her the truth.

He'd been her Seer—*her Messenger.*

And he'd died. He'd died to give her enough of a reason to throw herself straight into this nightmare for *revenge*—that had been her drive.

What the hell kind of champion does that? A simple answer, really: one doomed to fail.

ADAM

Adam woke to the rattling of his phone against the side table, the screen piercing through the dark room. He grimaced as he smacked his hand over it, pain shooting through him to tell him it wasn't his morning alarm. The memory of being peeled off the pavers made his arms scream.

Godsdamn. Nyx hits hard.

By the time he'd caught his reflection in the apartment's living room mirror, the whole side of his face had started to blossom into a sickly, yellowish hue. At least the couch made sense now after how badly his head had spun. But he should've splashed some water around his eyes and walked it off.

Groaning, he sat up and fought back the wary chill spreading through him. The phone fell from his grip, tumbling into his lap.

"Shit—"

The name on the screen taunted him with each subsequent ring.

Just... don't pick up. Take a walk. Leave your phone. Find—

He sighed and put the phone to his ear. "You in Kingsheart yet?" he asked, rubbing his forehead.

"No, not yet. Decided to check in first since it's been a few days. I'm in Bellegarde now."

"I... haven't really been able to do much more, if that's what you're checking on, but..."

"But?"

"I... I ran into a Seer. A strong one."

The wait for a reply took an eternity, half-expecting a snide remark.

"And you lost them?"

"Yes, but if I catch them again before the boats shut down, then—"

"Don't make a godsdamn scene, understood? We can manage without a Seer, and an unwilling one can be a *lot* of trouble."

Adam held the phone away from his ear, wincing. "Okay," he mumbled.

"Just stick with the plan. Keep me updated." A short beep followed, indicating the conversation was over.

He tossed it against the arm of the couch and leaned back into the parting cushions, exhaustion consuming him. When his eyes closed, the city spanned out around him, each small spark a candle, save the smoldering fire on the edge of his reach.

Adam opened his eyes again, landing on where his grimoire rested—its velvety cover and inky-black pages singing a quiet, coaxing song only he could hear. Past it, three silvery pairs of dots followed his every micro-movement, all jittering with anticipation and energy he didn't have.

Instead, he thought of a different set of eyes he'd overlooked, mistaking the waves of raw magic crashing into him for his companions. Eyes belonging to the most powerful Seer he'd ever imagined encountering in his lifetime.

Green and blue.

TO BE CONTINUED

MORE BY CARA NOX

For an up-to-date list of all of Cara Nox's books visit their website:

caranox.com/books

ACKNOWLEDGMENTS

First and foremost, I have to thank my dear sister for yelling at me whenever I was incredibly hard on myself. My cheerleaders, Amanda and Phil, who supported my queer little dreams. My precious critique partners, Melissa and Cybil, who also endured my ugly crying and helped me as much as I've hopefully helped them in our writing journeys. My accidental alpha and interested beta readers, Anna, Chloe, and Dominique—bless your patience with me. Ryan, for your editing wisdom and guidance when I over-thought so many rules and under-thought others. Additionally, thank you to all the wonderful writers I swapped initial chapters with and mentors I submitted to, who shot me my very first set of feedback that led me to revamping my introduction to this series into the heist-gone-sideways I originally pitched it as and didn't quite hit the mark for. I'm grateful to everyone who has helped shape this book into the little chaos monster it was meant to be.

And finally, thank you, the reader of this book. I appreciate your support, and I hope you're looking forward to the continuation of Noa and Glacier's adventure as much as I am, as well as the many wild stories I've been working to unleash in the future.

ABOUT THE AUTHOR

Cara Nox is an urban and science fantasy writer, combining their love of magically-inclined chaotic idiots and modern/futuristic tech. They also love mysteries, thrillers, and anything that draws inspiration from stars. Cara works as a web developer by day, holds BA in Japanese Language and Literature they occasionally use to read video game announcements, and resides in Ohio with their younger sister and two black cats.

For more information on all of their books, visit **caranox.com**.

To find some of their newest works-in-progress, bonus content, serialized stories, where they're at on social media, how to get deals on their current and upcoming works, and where to preview the first few chapters of their other books, visit **caranox.com/links**.